D0096866

HAVE MERCY

sw

Dear Reader:

It is a pleasure to have the honor of publishing Earl Sewell; a long-time friend and an established peer. Earl has written or contributed to more than a dozen titles and has a way with words that have made him a National Bestseller time and time again. He is not only smart, but his humility makes him stand out as a man of integrity and a force to be reckoned with.

In *Have Mercy*, Mr. Sewell raises the bar on his own writing by penning a fast-moving, engaging, unforgettable story of romance, intrigue and suspense. Marshall Turner has the type of life that most men crave. He is married to a woman that he adores, he has a beautiful daughter, and he is an overall happy person…until a man with absolutely nothing going for him takes it all away. Years later, and after much pain and reflection, Marshall has moved on from his failed marriage—stemming from the death of his daughter. Just when life becomes bearable once again, Marshall is given the opportunity to take revenge on Luther Parker, the murderer of his child who has escaped capture for way too long. Anyone with a heart will be compelled by this story as we witness a man deal with a decision that most of us could never comprehend.

Thank you for supporting Mr. Sewell's efforts and thank you for supporting one of the dozens of authors published under my imprint, Strebor Books. I try my best to bring you cutting-edge works of literature that will keep your attention and make you think long after you turn the last page.

Now sit back in your favorite chair or, better yet, chill in the bed, and be prepared to be tantalized by yet another great read.

Peace and Many Blessings,

Zane

Zane
Publisher
Strebor Books International
www.simonandschuster.com/streborbooks

ZANE PRESENTS

HAVE MERCY

EARL SEWELL

SBI

STREBOR BOOKS

NEW YORK LONDON TORONTO SYDNEY

SBI

Strebor Books
P.O. Box 6505
Largo, MD 20792
http://www.streborbooks.com

ISBN 978-1-59309-265-8
LCCN 2009924323

First Strebor Books trade paperback edition June 2009

Cover design: www.mariondesigns.com
Cover photograph: © Keith Saunders/Marion Designs

10 9 8 7 6 5 4 3 2 1

Manufactured in the United States of America

For information regarding special discounts for bulk purchases, please contact Simon & Schuster Special Sales at 1-866-506-1949 or business@simonandschuster.com

The Simon & Schuster Speakers Bureau can bring authors to your live event. For more information or to book an event, contact the Simon & Schuster Speakers Bureau at 1-866-248-3049 or visit our website at www.simonspeakers.com.

"It's not the load that breaks you down,
it's the way you carry it."
—LENA HORNE

ACKNOWLEDGMENTS

I can hardly believe that *Have Mercy* is my tenth novel. It seems like only yesterday I was struggling to finish my first book. Although this novel is a milestone, I feel as if I have yet to hit my full stride. For my loyal readers, this means I still have plenty of stories to tell. The rhythm and flow of this novel is unlike any I've written in the past. The characters came forward from somewhere deep within my creative soul with one hell of a story to tell. At times, during the creation process, I was so immersed in the story that I became each of these characters. I felt their love, their pain, their regrets, and their sorrow. Part of the storytelling process, at least in my mind, is the author allowing himself to get wrapped up in the passion of the story being created. As the writer, if I don't feel what my characters are going through, then I know my readers will have a challenging time as well.

Many of you know that I hail from a very large family. My father is one of eighteen children and my mother is one of eight children. With both sides of my family having Southern roots, there were always pearls of wisdom filled with life lessons floating around at any given time. Phrases like "*A hard head makes for a soft behind,*" or "*every day above ground is a good day. If you don't believe me, try missing one."* One of the most popular words my Southern great-aunts and uncles were fond of using at the end of their sentences was *"mercy."* If they were having a good day, they'd say, "Mr. Charlie didn't work me too hard today, mercy." The reason the word meant so much is because during the time they came of age, life wasn't particularly fair or kind, whether it was navigating complicated employment issues, matters of the heart, or life in general. If a little mercy came your way, that was reason enough to be thankful. That simple pearl of wisdom was the creative seed I planted and nurtured, until it became *Have Mercy*.

There are many people I need to thank, but, first and foremost, I have to give praise and glory to God for giving me such a wonderful gift.

To Illinois State Trooper Darrin Rice, thank you so much for answering all of my questions.

To Mary Griffin, Sandy Cook, Lindell Slaughter, Jackie McKean, Susan Boler and Marie Walton, thank you so much for reading this book and providing me with excellent feedback and comments. Without your help, this book might never have gotten finished.

To Zane, words cannot express how proud I am of you and your accomplishments. You are a pioneer and a visionary who has done something very extraordinary and unique. Nine years ago we met through an online writer's group at a time when we were both self-published authors. We began a friendship that has lasted for nearly a decade. Years ago, you opened a door for me, which gave me an opportunity that might have otherwise been delayed. Now we've arrived at a new juncture where you're once again opening a door of opportunity for me. I am forever grateful for your continued support and belief in my abilities, as well as your unwavering willingness to help others.

To my agent, Sara Camilli, thank you for all of your work with helping me move this book forward. I truly appreciate all of your time and effort.

In case I forgot anyone, which I often do, here's your opportunity to be recognized.

I would like to thank _____ for _____ because without your help I'd be _____. You're the biggest reason for my success because_____.

Feel free to drop me a line at earl@earlsewell.com. Please put the title of my book in the subject line so that I know your message to me is not spam. Make sure you check out www.earlsewell.com and www.myspace.com/earlsewell

Finally, be sure to visit Earl Sewell's Travel Network at www.earlsewelltravelnetwork.com. Sign up for my free deals and steals travel newsletter as well as finalize all of your travel plans. Whether you're going on a cruise, taking a vacation to the Caribbean, or going to visit friends and family, let Earl Sewell's Travel Network take you there.

All My Best,

Earl Sewell

September 26, 2008
Written while in Baltimore, MD
4:35 p.m.

∼1∼
CARMEN

Carmen swiveled her wrist to glance at her wristwatch as she shuffled up the steps of Nikki's apartment building. It was 6:00 a.m. on Saturday and the Chicago air was already heavy with sweaty humidity.

"I hate this sticky and clammy weather," Carmen complained as she wiped perspiration from her forehead and the base of her neck. "Nikki had better have her behind out of bed," Carmen muttered as she noticed a peculiar, scruffy-looking man exiting the brick building. The man was wearing a green T-shirt and cutoff blue jean shorts with black grime stains on the thighs. The grungy man had a face that only a mother could love and reminded Carmen of the scrawny rock and roll icon Mick Jagger. As she approached the entrance, he held the door open for her.

"Thank you," she whispered as she eased by him and walked over and pressed a silver button on the wall to call for the elevator. She stared mindlessly at the orange elevator light, paused on the eighth floor. She sighed impatiently, then turned around to look out a nearby window while she mulled over her thoughts. Carmen was disillusioned with the fact that Nikki wasn't doing anything useful with her life. Her baby sister had a day job at an adult bookstore as a peep show girl and an evening job as a stripper at a seedy gentlemen's club. Carmen was sure their parents had to be turning over in their graves, knowing that Nikki was making a living exposing her body to men old enough to be her grandfather. That wasn't the way either of them were raised. *Yeah*, Carmen whispered to herself as she continued to glance out the window. *Nikki's life is dreadful, in my opinion.*

Carmen shouldered much of the blame for Nikki's appalling lifestyle, and the guilt she toted around was a heavy burden on her heart. Carmen continually attempted to clear the unspoken tension between her and her sister, but reconciling with Nikki was turning out to be a monumental task.

Their mother had passed away years ago from a combination of cancer and being a perpetual worrywart. Two years later, their father, Anthony, died. At the time of his death, Carmen was twenty-one years old and became guardian of her then fifteen-year-old sister, Nikki. The untimely loss of their father was the root of the tension between them. Nikki blamed Carmen for the death of their father and she knew it, although Nikki hadn't verbalized it as much lately. Blame and guilt were parasites eating away at Carmen's soul and she was tired of toting around her baggage of unhappy feelings. Carmen exhaled, hoping the shift in her breathing pattern would rid her mind of the unwanted and haunting thoughts. She turned back around to check the progress of the elevator and noticed that the scrawny man who had held the door for her was still hovering around the door-way, glaring at her. He licked his lips, flicked his tongue at her a few times, sounding like a dog slurping up water, and brushed his fingers across the stubble on his chin. Carmen translated the glint in his lustful eyes and realized he was having a sexual fantasy about her in his mind.

"Go to hell," Carmen snarled at him as she flipped up her middle finger. "Damn weirdo." The man didn't seem to mind

Carmen's harsh words because he continued to glare at her. "Nikki has to stop moving into these apartment buildings filled with freaks and crackpots," she muttered as the bell on the elevator chimed.

Carmen stepped inside the elevator and pressed the third-floor button. When she got off the elevator, she noticed that the hallway carpet was wet. She wrinkled her nose because the musty and moldy odor was overpowering. She moved quickly down the enclosed corridor toward Nikki's apartment. Curling her fingers into a fist, Carmen drummed on the door with her knuckles. A short moment later, Frieda, Nikki's roommate, answered the door.

"Hey, Frieda," Carmen greeted politely as Frieda allowed her access to their small, cluttered, two-bedroom apartment. The place was littered with piles of laundry that needed to be either cleaned or folded but Carmen couldn't tell which.

"Is Nikki out of bed yet?" Carmen asked, crinkling her nose while comparing the untidiness of the apartment to Nikki and Frieda's chaotic and messy lifestyle.

"Why are you asking a question that you already know the answer to?" Frieda scraped her fingernails up and down her belly before releasing a loud yawn that assaulted the already stale air with the rotting smell of her morning breath.

"You know damn well Nikki and I are vampires and function only after the sun goes down." Carmen tried to inconspicuously cover her nose with the palm of her hand. Frieda's breath literally smelled like spoiled food and its foul odor was making her dizzy.

"Well, she's the one who told me to be here this early. I've got to drop my car off at the repair shop, and she promised me that she'd drive over there with me, so that I wouldn't have to sit there and wait while a mechanic worked on my car."

"Yeah, yeah, yeah," Frieda answered as she scratched the side of her neck. "She told me all about it. I think that she would have left work earlier but this older dude walked into the tavern and started paying her some attention. And you know how Nikki has a soft spot for older men."

"I know," Carmen answered. She wasn't giving her full attention to what Frieda said because she didn't want their conversation to last longer than necessary. The only thing she wanted her to do was to stop talking. Carmen sauntered into the kitchen area and inspected a banana sitting on the countertop. After checking it thoroughly for bruising, she decided that it appeared safe enough to eat.

"He was a nice-looking man," Frieda continued, to Carmen's annoyance. "He looked like he used to play football or something. You know the type that probably has a large stash of money hidden somewhere."

"Humm," Carmen coyly answered, hoping that Frieda picked up that she didn't want to continue their conversation. Carmen noticed a chair that wasn't cluttered with clothes positioned in a corner of the room. She decided to sit down and wait for her sister.

"You don't seem like you're in a talkative mood. But then again, you never are. I'm going to go back to my room. Besides, Francisco came over early this morning and gave me some grown-man loving. My body trembles just thinking about having my ass in the air while he sucks on my sweet, juicy Spanish pussy." Carmen could not have cared less about Frieda's sex life; and if her pussy was as funky as her breath, Francisco had to be one nasty motherfucker to put his face anywhere near her smelly ass.

"Yeah, whatever. You're telling me way too much information," Carmen said and began to leave. She was glad Frieda was taking her body funk back into the bedroom.

"There is no need to be jealous, honey."

Oh, Lord, here we go, thought Carmen. *Now she thinks that I'm being insulting.*

"You and your stuck-up attitude will get a man to fuck you right one of these days. Hopefully he'll be able to mellow you out some. How long has it been now since that no-good professor dumped you? What, nine years? Or is it ten?" Freda snickered. "He had your head all messed up when he cancelled the wedding on you after you'd spent all of your money planning this elaborate event, which you specifically told me I wasn't invited to. I still haven't forgotten that evil shit. I'm glad he cracked your prissy little face and left you all broken up. You needed to be taught a lesson." Frieda used threatening hand gestures to emphasize her point.

"Frieda, it's too damn early in the morning to dig up old shit and start a fight with me. I didn't come over here for that." Carmen was more than willing to bare her claws and stir up an ugly argument if Frieda didn't back down. "Trust me; you do not want to toy with me this morning."

Frieda chuckled. "You don't scare me, honey. Not one bit." Frieda said her peace and then made her way down a narrow corridor to the bedrooms. She banged hard on Nikki's bedroom door.

"Your snooty-ass sister is here," Frieda said, loud enough for Carmen to hear her. The animosity between Frieda and Carmen was like a knife in her back that she couldn't reach. In fact, as Carmen saw it, Frieda was a part of the reason that her relationship with Nikki was so sour at times.

After the death of their parents, Nikki and Carmen moved into an apartment in the Ravenswood community on Chicago's North Side. Carmen, who had always been more mature than her years, worked as an audiovisual supervisor at a branch of the Chicago Public Library and attended Truman Community College in the evening. Carmen was responsible, levelheaded, and ambitious. Nikki, on the other hand, was an impressionable and rebellious high school sophomore who didn't respect her older sister as her guardian. Nikki was an untamed free spirit who was fascinated and seduced by Chicago's nightlife and the freedom it represented. She would often sneak out of the house on school nights and hang out with her friends at the beach, someone else's apartment, or a neighborhood park where she and her friends would loiter and be loud as well as rude. One night, after waking up and discovering that Nikki had once again snuck out of the house, after she'd specifically told her not to, Carmen decided she'd had enough of Nikki's disobedience. She went searching for Nikki to confront her and perhaps physically fight her, if that's what it took to make Nikki abide by her rules.

"Nikki! I am not going to allow you to hang out on street corners all night with your friends and come home whenever you feel like it!" Carmen shouted at Nikki after she'd located her and forced her to come home against her will. Carmen had spent an hour combing neighborhood streets, and her temper had reached its boiling point.

"Are you listening to me?" Carmen barked at her sister as they reentered their small apartment. Nikki's ears were completely closed to Carmen's ranting. She stood defiantly in the center of the living room with her arms folded across her chest and her eyes fixed on a wooden support beam in the ceiling.

"What are you trying to do? Get pregnant and drop out of high school?" Carmen continued her ranting, not worrying about whether or not her neighbors would make a phone call to the police and report a domestic disturbance.

"For your information, I am not trying to do anything, especially get pregnant. It's boring around here and I'm just having fun." Nikki had no respect for her older and wiser sister.

"No, not yet, but if you stay on the path that you're on, you will end up being another teenage mother, or even worse, some young girl locked up."

"Please! I'm not even going out like that. Your comment proves how little you know me," Nikki answered defiantly.

"Then who are you? Tell me; I want to know. Tell me what you're about, Nikki. What do you want to do with yourself? Help me understand." Carmen genuinely wanted answers but wasn't sure if Nikki even had a clear idea of who she was or what she wanted to do with life, outside of aggravating the hell out of her.

Nikki responded by working her neck and allowing her body language to speak as loudly as her words.

"There isn't anything for you to understand except that I've got my own life. And I control what I do, when I do it, and how I do it. So get off of my damn back and leave me the hell alone!" Nikki said her peace and felt as if she'd finally put Carmen in her proper place. Nikki was about to step away, but Carmen blocked her path.

"You may have your own life, but you don't have a pot to piss in or a window to throw it out of. I pay the bills here, Nikki. I am the one who is making sacrifices so that you can complete school. I'd like to go out and party, too, but I can't because I have to set an example for you. Don't you understand what I'm trying to do? Don't you care about the sacrifices I'm making for you?"

"Carmen, you're trying to be someone that you're not! You're not my mama and you're not my daddy. And if you keep trying to control me, I'm going to make you regret the day you were born." Before Carmen could stop herself, she hauled off and whacked Nikki with the palm of her hand as hard as she could. "I'm tired of your damn mouth and attitude, Nikki. If you don't get your shit together, you and I are going to do something we'll both end up regretting!" Carmen howled at her baby sister.

Nikki's chest began heaving with anger and resentment. She lowered her eyes to slits as she allowed her rage to consume her.

"Oh, you've done it now!" Nikki hollered out as she allowed her fists to fly and fight Carmen back. The two of them fought and flung each other around the apartment, knocking over furniture, until they finally wrestled to the floor. They pulled each other's hair and clawed at each other's skin. They shouted angry words as they tried to gain an advantage over each other. After struggling on the floor for a long moment, they both stopped once they'd reached exhaustion. Although Carmen had gotten the best of Nikki, she wasn't willing to concede her loss. When Nikki finally had enough, she asked Carmen to let her go. Carmen stopped pressing her elbow against Nikki's neck and allowed her to stand. Once she was on her feet, Nikki went directly to the bathroom. Carmen lightly touched her stinging face, then looked at her fingertips that were spotted with blood.

"She's scratched me all up," Carmen uttered as she took a glance around their modest apartment, which now looked like a train wreck.

After their confrontation, Carmen went into her bedroom,

picked up the phone, and called her girlfriend Millie. Millie was special and unique; she was an Irish girl who was raised by a black family. Millie was twenty-six and five years older than Carmen. Millie was Carmen's confidante as well as a close friend.

"I don't know what I am going to do with Nikki," Carmen explained to Millie. "We actually had an all-out brawl tonight. I'm surprised no one called the damn cops. I pushed her so hard against the wall that there is a big body imprint in it now. After I did that, I thought she'd had enough, so I turned my back to her. She snatched a lamp off of the end table and smashed it against my back and shoulder," Carmen said, still fuming with anger.

"Do you think it's safe for you to stay there?" Millie asked.

"Yes, it's safe. I'm not afraid of Nikki. After she smashed the lamp against my back, I lost it. I was on her like flies on shit and I damn near choked her to death. I am not going to allow Nikki to run me out of this house."

"Have you guys ever considered going to a therapist? You know, to get some professional help?"

"Trust me, there will be no need for professional help if she tries to fight me again. I will put her six feet under and that's no joke." Carmen was filled with anger and vengeance.

"You don't really mean that. She's your sister and siblings fight sometimes. Although you guys really take it to the extreme."

"Millie, I tell you, I'm doing everything that I can to get her through high school. I'm tired of being nice; I'm putting my own happiness on hold to make sure she has a fighting chance and she doesn't appreciate any of it. She's a selfish and trifling little girl who thinks she knows everything. I can't tell her anything. She will not listen and it's frustrating. I think she's bipolar."

"She's not bipolar. A little high-strung, but not bipolar." Millie wasn't about to support Carmen's rationale. "Maybe it's the crowd she's hanging around with. Maybe she's under a lot of peer pressure; that's always difficult to deal with. Who was Nikki with when you found her tonight?"

"Her tack-headed friend named Frieda. The daughter of the devil, in my opinion. Frieda is a rough-looking girl who has been in and out of juvie countless times. She's standoffish, has a nasty attitude, and is quick to jump to her own conclusions."

"She sounds like a real piece of work." Millie cleared her throat. "This Frieda girl might be the cause of the tension between you and Nikki, if you think about it. When you and your sister first stepped out into the world on your own, everything was going smoothly. Then, when she transferred to her new school and hooked up with this Frieda chick, everything seemed to spiral out of control."

"You could have a point there, now that I think about it. I remember Nikki telling me that she had a hard time making new friends and how everyone at the school seemed to have it in for her. It could be that she's behaving like this to prove that she's tough enough to hang out with this Frieda girl and her clique."

"Maybe you should consider moving. Getting Nikki into a different environment might help."

"Millie, I'm not Rockefeller. I don't have the resources right now to make a move. Besides, I don't want to go through the hassle of breaking the lease. Even if I did move, I wouldn't be able to go far. I need to stay close to my job and school. But Nikki and I are going to have to work out our problems before we kill each other." Carmen paused and then rotated her neck to release some of the tension that was trying to provide her with a massive headache. "Look, I don't want to talk about Nikki any more. Let's talk about something else. How are things with you and Chuck, now that you guys are shacking up?"

"Things are going good, although he's still talking about moving back to Kansas City so that he can be closer to his family."

"Well, what are you going to do if he does?" Carmen asked as she moved over to the mirror and inspected her wounds. Her face was rather red and she could clearly see where Nikki had scratched her. *I should kill that girl*, she thought to herself as she reached for a towel.

"I'm not going anywhere until I finish school. I only have two semesters left at Truman Junior College and then it's on to a four-year university. After that, I plan to go to graduate school," Millie said with absolute certainty.

"So what's up with you and the English professor? Why did he want to see you after class the other night?"

"To ask me out on a date." Carmen laughed nervously.

"You're kidding me. Why didn't you say something to me?" Millie was upset that Carmen had failed to mention this.

"I'm frustrated and at my wit's end with Nikki. It slipped my mind. I meant to tell you about it."

"Look, girl, Nikki is going to be Nikki. When that girl turns eighteen, she is not going to be worried with you, especially if she continues to defy you as she's been doing lately. I know that you want the best for her and all, but you have got to think of yourself as well."

"It's hard for me to let go. I feel such a sense of responsibility for her. Especially now since both Mom and Dad are gone." Carmen paused as she briefly thought about her parents. She missed them deeply and longed for the chance to talk to either of them one more time. She stopped thinking about her parents and answered Millie.

"Anyway, Professor Green is a nice man but—"

"I had a feeling that the professor had a thing for you," Millie interrupted. "He is a handsome-looking man and you're a beautiful woman. If you guys hit it off, you're going to be a hot couple. If I were you, I wouldn't let him get away."

"Can I tell you something, Millie? Something personal?" Carmen asked.

"You know I'm your girl. I know that we haven't known each other all that long but I truly feel as if I've known you for much longer. So ask as many questions as you'd like; I'm all ears."

"I like Professor Green a lot, but I'm afraid of dating him. He is thirty years old and more experienced."

"What does his age have to do with anything? You're twenty-one and he's thirty. So what?"

"I see with you, I have to come right out and explain it."

"Come right out with what?" Millie asked, utterly puzzled.

"He's experienced and I'm not. He's probably been with other women and I've never been with a man. I'm afraid that I will not know what to do or he may not like my body. Do you catch my drift now?" Carmen asked.

"You're still a virgin?" Millie chuckled. "That explains a lot."

"What's that supposed to mean?" Carmen had taken offense to the comment.

"It means that I can tell that you haven't been getting it; that's all. You're all wound up. But there is nothing wrong with being a virgin. If I could turn back the hands of time, I'd be a virgin, too. I wouldn't have given in to peer pressure."

"I've been with boys before, so I'm not at a total loss. I've never gone all the way. I've come close a few times, but I changed my mind." Carmen sighed. "So, what was your first time like?"

"I'm not going to lie to you. My first time was supposed to be perfect, but it wasn't—the first time happened when I was seventeen and going into my senior year at Proviso West High School. I gave up my virginity to a college boy named LeMar. We were at his house in his bedroom one afternoon while his parents were at work. I got caught up in a Luther Vandross song called 'Superstar.' Luther's voice was sweet and clear and LeMar was positioned on top of me, nibbling on my ear and telling me how much he loved me. I remember feeling his hands gently gliding over my nakedness and getting goose bumps while I spread my legs open a little wider for him. LeMar had a mighty chest, strong shoulders, and an ass that had dimples in it. I caressed his ass and thought that his strokes were going to feel so strong and powerful. LeMar was an excellent kisser and when he held my face in his hands and kissed me tenderly, my body responded immediately. I raised my legs in the air, wrapped them around his body, and locked my legs at the ankles. He positioned himself just right and began to enter me. I thought, '*Oh my God. This is it. I'm actually going to do it.*' The first moments of penetration made me cringe."

"So, what did you do? I mean, when it was hurting," Carmen asked.

"LeMar wasn't a rough guy who jumped up and down on my stomach. When I said that it hurt, he stopped. He was very patient with me. It took a few more tries before he actually penetrated me. I'm not going to lie and tell you that my first time made me see stars. I think I was so wound up and nervous at the time. When we tried again later, I'd learned how to relax and it felt better."

"So what ever happened to LeMar?"

"Unfortunately, our romance was a summer thing. We spent a lot of time together during the summer, but then he went back to school in the fall. He completed his bachelor's degree in Texas. We kept in touch with each other for a little while. We talked on the phone and wrote love letters. Then his parents divorced and he ended up living in Fort Lauderdale with his mother."

"Did you love him?" Carmen asked.

"I have loved every man I've ever laid down with. That's not to say that I have a bunch of skeletons in my closet, but I believe in love and I believe that there is someone for everybody. LeMar was special, though. Although he wasn't my best lover, he was my first, and you never forget the first person you made love to." Millie paused and there was a brief moment of silence. "So, do you think that you're going to give Professor Green that opportunity?"

Carmen laughed nervously. "I believe I will let him take me out on a date. Lord knows that I haven't been on one in ages and I'm way too young to be sitting around the house like some old woman. And as much as I hate to admit it, Nikki is probably getting more action than I've ever gotten." Millie and Carmen chuckled.

"Thank you for listening to my madness, Millie," Carmen said, truly appreciating Millie's attention.

"You don't have to thank me for that. As much as you've listened to me ramble on about all of my issues, it's welcoming to hear someone else's drama for a change."

Carmen could hear the smile in Millie's voice, and the image of Millie's smile blanketed her and made her feel warm and at ease.

Carmen's train of thought was interrupted by Nikki, who came out into the living room wearing blue sweat pants, a "TLC" sweatshirt that said "Ain't too Proud to Beg," a baseball cap, and dark black sunglasses. Nikki had not matured much since she'd been on her own. She still liked marching in the opposite direction of what was normal.

"Nikki, it's humid, hot, and sticky outside. You're going to sweat like a pig in those clothes."

"It's okay. I got the air conditioner in my hoopty-mobile fixed. One of my neighbors, who looks like Mick Jagger, fixed it. I can turn it on if I get too hot, but you know me. I'm always cold so it's unlikely that I'll get hot."

"That guy doesn't look like the mechanical type." Carmen gave her sister a sarcastic glance.

"And what's that supposed to mean?" Nikki instantly picked up on her sister's sarcasm. "Why are you always judging people?"

"Never mind," Carmen uttered. She was not in the mood for an argument. "Let's go, so we can drop off my car and get it repaired."

"Yeah, let's go before you piss me off." Nikki moved past her sister and walked out of the apartment.

Carmen pulled her blue Dodge Daytona into the parking lot of the Magic Muffler and Brake Shop on Stony Island Boulevard. It was a quarter to seven and there were already five people standing in line at the door because service was given on a first-come, first-served basis. Carmen parked her car and then stood in line and waited with the other patrons. A few moments later, she saw Nikki creeping into the parking lot in her rusted-out Nissan Sentra with one red door and one white door. Carmen noticed that all of Nikki's car windows were rolled down. It was a clear indication to her that her air conditioning wasn't working at all.

The shop owner finally opened the door and began attending to customers in the proper order. While the owner was out inspecting the car of another customer, Carmen noticed one of the mechanics arriving. Carmen stared at the brawny man wearing a blue mechanic's suit that zipped up the front. His skin was the color of gingerbread, and he had sizable arms, a wide chest, and broad shoulders. He didn't appear to be the type that worked out at the gym; his burly build seemed to be more genetic. The brawny man went to the back of the garage where the supplies were stored and then reappeared a few moments later behind the front counter.

"Who's next?" he asked, with a forceful tone in his voice.

"I am," Carmen answered.

"What kind of car do you have?" he asked without looking up, as he rested his fingers on the computer keyboard, eager to input her information.

"Dodge Daytona," Carmen answered and watched the man's thick brown fingers slowly peck the information into the computer. Carmen didn't understand why she imagined his thick fingers toying with her womanhood. She had to quickly ease the thought from her mind.

"What's your address?" he asked.

"1642 East Fifty-sixth Street."

"Oh, you stay over in Hyde Park. That's Obama's neighborhood," he commented. "How long have you lived over there?" He took his eyes off of the computer screen and met her gaze. She noticed that his skin had become slightly glossy with sweat from the humidity. His face was unyielding and his expression was uncompromising. She suddenly felt as if she were being interrogated rather than flirted with.

"I've lived there a little over a year now. I teach first grade at

Bret Harte Elementary School." She didn't want to tell him that, but for some reason, she couldn't make herself shut up. Maybe it was because of his strict glare. It had somehow overpowered her and caused her to say more than she wanted to. She offered a Pollyannaish smile in an attempt to break the intensity of his glare. That didn't help. He kept his blazing eyes on her. Carmen suddenly wondered what had gone wrong in his life.

"What kind of problems are you having?" He broke eye contact abruptly and continued to peck at the keyboard.

"When I press the brakes, I hear a scrubbing sound," Carmen answered, with a soft voice.

"It is a scrubbing or squeaking sound?"

"No, it's definitely a scrubbing sound. And the brakes almost touch the floor before the car begins to stop." Carmen noticed the monogrammed lettering on his overalls. His name was stitched in yellow letters. Luther was his name. He typed in some more information and then asked for her car keys.

"I need to test drive it before I pull it in and get it in the air."

"Okay," Carmen said as she handed over her car keys. Luther walked out to her car, got in, and drove off. A few minutes later, he returned and pulled her car into the far stall. Carmen observed from a distance through a glass window in the lobby as he pressed the air drill to the wheel lugs and removed the tires one by one. Carmen then felt a light tap on her shoulder.

"Do they have a soda machine in here?" It was Nikki. She picked up a muffler brochure from the countertop and began fanning herself as if she were sitting in church trying to keep cool.

"No, I don't think that they do. There is an Amoco gas station across the street. I think that they sell cold drinks," Carmen said.

"Do you have any idea of how much longer it's going to take to get an estimate?"

"It shouldn't be too much longer. He has my car in the air right now."

"Well, I'm going to run over to the gas station and get me something to drink. It's hotter than hell out here."

"I told you that your ass was going to burn up."

"Whatever," Nikki answered. "I'll be right back." Nikki turned and left without saying another word. Carmen turned her attention back to her car and saw Luther was waving his hand, signaling for her to come and take a look at what he'd found. Carmen walked through the garage toward Luther.

"You're going to have to get the front brake pads replaced. The rotors need replacing as well." He pointed to the silver disk that the pads rubbed against in order to bring the car to a stop. "The scrubbing sound that you were hearing was the sound of metal rubbing against metal."

"Shit!" Carmen hissed, because it was starting to sound as if the repairs were going to set her back financially.

"How long has the brake light on the dashboard been on?" Luther asked as he continued his inspection.

"I don't know—three, maybe four weeks." Carmen shrugged her shoulders.

"If you had brought the car in sooner, you wouldn't have this problem." Luther didn't mean to be cold with his answer; he was only telling her the truth. Carmen's mood changed in that instant.

"How much is this going to cost me?"

"I don't know. I'll have to look at the cost of the parts." Luther was now inspecting the rear brakes.

"I don't want to spend a small fortune on repairs; I'm letting you know that right now." Carmen became standoffish. She hoped her attitude would indicate that she'd done some kind of research on brake repair jobs and wasn't going to pay one cent over what she considered to be a fair price.

"Your rear brakes will last a little longer, but not too much longer. You'll probably need to replace them by this winter." Luther continued his inspection. He was now focusing on the muffler system.

"Do you see this?" He pointed to a brown rust spot in the muffler pipeline. That's the beginning of a hole. By the time the winter sets in, you're going to have to replace this pipe or your car will sound like a tank coming down the street." Luther did one more check to make sure that everything was tightly secure. Carmen stood with her arms crisscrossed. Her irritation level was rising with each second that ticked by. She simply wanted to know the cost of fixing the brakes; she could not have cared less about the muffler. Her main concern was that her car came to a stop when she pressed the brake pedal.

"Okay, let's go back up front and I'll give you an estimate."

Luther stepped back behind the counter, began looking up the cost of the parts, and calculated the cost of the labor involved. He leaned toward her, resting his arm on the countertop and began explaining the itemized list he'd placed before her.

"The brake pads are seventy-nine dollars and ninety-nine cents. The new rotors are one hundred dollars each; you need two of those. The labor will cost you seventy-five dollars. There is a two-dollar disposal fee, plus tax, brings your total to this right here." Luther circled the number.

"Three hundred eighty-seven dollars and ninety-nine cents!" Carmen blurted out the words before she had a chance to adjust her tone. "Don't you have some kind of discount or sale going on?"

"No." Luther was sharp and abrupt with his answer.

"Well, I think that you're robbing me and charging me way too much!" Carmen got loud with Luther. There was no way she was about to let him take advantage of her like this. She wanted him to look at the estimate again and give her some type of discount, especially if she was about to spend damn near four hundred dollars.

"Look, lady!" Luther barked. He had an evil glare and viciousness in his voice. "I wasn't the one who was driving around in the damn car for a fucking month with the motherfucking brake light on. I don't set the goddamn prices; the factory does!" Carmen flinched with fear. She thought for sure the mechanic had lost it. She was not expecting to get an explosive reaction from him. At that moment, the shop owner walked back in with a customer. He'd overheard Luther and quickly pulled him into the garage area for a private conversation.

"What the fuck is wrong with you, man!" Carmen overheard the owner rip into Luther as the door to the garage area slowly shut. "You don't talk to my customers like that!"

Luther glanced at Carmen and his eyes were blazing with resentment. Carmen wanted to leave, but she couldn't because her car was still in the air. The owner cupped his hand and placed it at the back of Luther's neck so that he could hold his gaze.

"She can kiss my ass, man!" Luther howled out loud enough for Carmen to hear.

"That's it. Get out of here!" the owner shouted back.

"Fuck you, man. I didn't need this shitty-ass job anyway!"

Carmen watched as Luther gathered his belongings and left. A moment later the owner came back and spoke with Carmen.

"Look, ma'am, I'm so sorry that he yelled at you like that. I'm only going to charge you a flat three hundred dollars for the repairs to your car. Is that fair enough?"

"Okay, but where is Luther going?"

"Ma'am, he had two strikes against him already." The owner paused.

"But I was the one who provoked him. I don't want the man to lose his job because of me." Carmen felt horrible.

"Miss, we get upset customers all the time. It's part of the business and he knows that. He should not have used that threatening tone with you. I've spoken with him about his tone of voice on several occasions and warned him about it. He had a final warning yesterday. I'm a small business owner and how my customers are treated is very important for my referral and repeat customers. I don't want my customers to have a bad experience when they come here. Do you understand where I'm coming from?"

"But…" Carmen's voice trailed off.

"Ma'am, do you want your car repaired or not? I can get another mechanic started on it right away."

"Yes," Carmen answered as she watched Luther chase down a Stony Island bus that was heading north.

-2-
LUTHER

Luther located an empty seat at the rear of the bus. Once he got himself situated, he slid open a window so that a breeze would cool off his hot and sticky skin. He crumpled his front pants pockets, listening carefully for the sound of crinkling plastic. He reached into his right pocket and pulled out a wrinkled pack of cigarettes and a lighter. He removed a cigarette, pinched it between his lips, and spun the wheel of his lighter. Luther slumped down in his seat and allowed the nicotine to relax him. He was about to close his eyes and free his mind of all his problems and issues. When his eyes connected with the disapproving gaze of an elderly woman sitting in front of him, he paused. She'd twisted herself around in her seat to find the source of the repulsive scent of smoke. The upset elderly woman pointed to the posted "no smoking" sign, but Luther didn't give a damn.

"Go on; say something! I dare you to," Luther snarled at the older woman who was clearly frightened by his aggressiveness. To avoid any additional altercation with him, she got up and moved to another seat.

Luther took a long drag and blew the smoke out of the open window. "I can't believe my day has gotten fucked up," he uttered to himself. He noticed that it was almost his stop, so he reached ip and pulled the cord, which alerted the driver. When the driver stopped, Luther bolted out of the rear door and flashed across the street to make his connection with the Sixty-third Street bus. He rode the bus down to King Drive, which was filled with the usual crowd of vagrants, drunkards, addicts, and young drug pushers cruising about in luxury cars. Luther lived nearby in a rundown apartment building on Prairie Street where rent was cheap. His shabby dwelling consisted of three musty rooms, all of which had soiled green shag carpet with matching wall paint. The paint on the walls had chipped and left jagged designs. White pipes from other apartments snaked across the ceiling of his unit like a complicated spider web. The pipes hissed constantly and sprung leaks wherever they saw fit.

Luther entered the vestibule of the building and saw his electric bill on the floor with a shoe print on it; it had been opened. *One of the crackhead squatters no doubt had opened it thinking that it was some kind of check*, he thought to himself as he pushed his basement apartment door open. Luther walked down a few creaky steps and flipped on his lights. A polluted odor of cooking gas attacked his nose and he thought the stovepipe had cracked. He went to the kitchen and opened the small window above the stove to allow some fresh air to come in. He noticed a cluster of cigarette butts, matchsticks, and booze bottles on the ground outside of his kitchen window. *Damn vagrants have been loitering outside of my window drinking and smoking again*! Luther hissed to himself. He began pulling the stove away from the wall but stopped when he noticed the sink had backed up and the basin was filled with brown water.

"Damn," he said to himself.

He stooped down, opened the cabinet doors under the sink,

and grabbed the plunger. He plugged the sink ferociously until the brown murky water retreated down the drain. He went into the living room to sit and think. He'd attend to the issue of the stovepipe once he got his thoughts in order. The only furniture he had was his bed, a folding chair, and a small color television, which sat on the floor. He flipped on the television and watched a mindless program about cops who patrolled beaches. A short while later, there was a thundering knock on his door.

"Who is it?" he asked, with a hostile voice.

"Mr. Packard is outside and he wants to see you." It was a strange woman and her voice was filled with nervousness.

"Shit!" Luther cupped his hands and buried his face in them. Nervous adrenaline shot through him like a river and he could feel his anxiety rising. Packard was the last person he wanted to see.

"Okay. Tell him I'll be out there in a minute," responded Luther.

"Come on, man! He promised me a little something if I got you right away." The woman pounded the door again. At that moment, Luther realized that Packard had put some junkie up to this for the promise of drugs. Packard was foul and evil like that.

"Hurry up, man!" The woman was now desperate. Luther attempted to organize his thoughts. *Why does Packard want to see me?* he wondered. The woman began kicking the door with her foot. The thudding sound echoed throughout the basement apartment.

"Come on, brother! Where are you at, in the bathroom or something?!" the woman shouted. Finally, Luther opened the door and saw a boney woman with large almond eyes. Her hair was uncombed and matted, a clear indication that her addiction meant more to her than her appearance. The two of them stepped out of the building and the woman rushed over to Packard's black Chevy Blazer.

"See, I got him for you, baby. I got him; he's right there." She impolitely pointed at Luther while laughing nervously. Packard had one of the men in the back seat hand her what she'd worked for. The woman snatched the narcotic out of the man's hand and rushed off down the block.

Packard was a former cop who'd turned into drug dealer and a gangster who was not to be toyed with on any level. He was an unyielding barracuda of a man who was old enough to be Luther's father. His facial features were strong and imposing, like he'd seen more tragedies than most would see in their lifetime. His eyes appeared to be sun beaten but were as sharp as a hawk's. Packard was a former amateur bodybuilder and his physique was well-maintained. He didn't look his age because he still spent a fair amount of time at the gym. He had been abusing and terrorizing Luther with fear and intimidation since he was a small boy. Today was not the day Packard planned on putting an end to the seeds of fear he'd planted in Luther years ago.

Packard signaled for Luther to move closer. Luther attempted to place a smile on his face to give the illusion of being happy to see him.

"How old are you now, Luther?" Packard's eyes were red with anger.

"Twenty-nine," he answered, feeling his shoulders tense up. He could tell Packard was in an evil mood.

"Who hooked you up with the mechanic's job?" Packard asked.

"You did." Luther was jittery and spoke softly like a child. He hated himself for being so weak. "Packard, let me explain."

"Did I ask you to explain?" Packard cut him off. Luther stood silently like an obedient pet.

"Whose apartment building are you living in for practically nothing?" Packard asked.

"Yours," Luther responded.

"And what were you doing before my divine intervention blessed you with a job and a roof over your head?"

"I was working at a car wash for peanuts."

"And what else?" Packard pressed the issue.

"I also begged people for money," Luther answered, ashamed of his inability to be more of a man.

"And who was the one who got the attempted robbery incident erased from your record?"

"You," Luther answered again.

"That's right, Luther, me. And look at how you repay me for my kindness. I put my solid reputation on the line for you and you make me look like a damn fool. I'm the one who called in a favor so that you could get the job at Magic Muffler. Do I look like a fool to you, Luther?" Packard's voice was much more vicious than ever.

"No." Luther suddenly felt the urge to pee.

"No! Is that what you said?"

"Yes."

"No, Luther. I must look like a fool to you because you're trying to play me for one. And you know I can't let that happen. You know that I can't let these people on the street think that I'm soft."

"I'm sorry." Luther quickly offered his apology as he backed away from the car door. He feared that Packard would shoot him down where he stood.

"Sorry! That's right, Luther. You are about the sorriest son-of-a-bitch I've ever known. How long were you working at that job?"

"Seven months."

"Seven months," Packard repeated in disgust. "Your big, dumb, sorry ass could only keep a job for seven months."

"It wasn't my fault," Luther tried to explain once again.

"It wasn't your fault?" Packard glared at Luther. "It's always your fault, Luther. It's always your fault because I say it is and don't you ever forget that. You hear me, boy?!"

"Yes," Luther answered, staring at the ground. He didn't like being belittled. In the back of his mind, he told himself that one day he'd get his revenge and make Packard respect him; one way or another.

"The only reason I stuck my neck out for your sorry ass is because I feel somewhat responsible for how useless you are. But you know what? I'm done with giving charity to your pitiful soul."

Luther gritted his teeth and clenched his fist. He was contemplating whether or not he should hit Packard with a solid right hook to the jaw and deal with the consequences later. *After all*, he thought, *I don't have shit to lose.*

"What? You want to do something? I see that look in your eyes, boy! Come on, take your best shot." Packard held up his gun to show Luther that he meant business. "I'll put a bullet in your ass and stuff your body down a damn sewer," Packard barked at him. Luther could see that Packard was determining whether or not to end Luther's life.

"I'm sorry." Luther once again offered up an apology.

"Good. For a minute there I thought I was going to have to commit homicide this afternoon," Packard said as he put his firearm away. "But I am going to evict you."

"Don't put me out on the street, man. I don't have any place to go," Luther pleaded. Packard released a wicked laugh.

"You've got exactly two weeks to pack up your shit and get

the hell out of my place. Oh, and, Luther, if I were you, I'd make sure that I didn't stay the full two weeks. Strange things happen to old buildings like the one you're living in. Sometimes buildings like that one mysteriously burn to the ground." Without sharing any additional information, Packard sped off down Prairie Street.

Luther loathed himself for not having enough courage to stand up to Packard. Luther ground down hard on his teeth as he held back the sensation of shouting out in anger and frustration at the complications of his miserable life. He walked back inside his shabby apartment and lay down on his bed. He curled up into a fetal position and hugged himself for comfort. He focused his eyes on the feet of the silver radiator in the corner and began to think about his mother, Sugar, and the event that had altered the course of his life.

On his tenth birthday, Sugar had promised to take him shopping for fresh workout clothes and a football so that he'd be ready when football tryouts were held at a local neighborhood community center. Luther, knowing how short-tempered and forgetful Sugar could be, wanted to be on his best behavior so she'd keep the promise she'd made to him. On the morning of his birthday, he got up extra early and assembled the best breakfast their bare cupboards had to offer. He made two scrambled eggs, toasted the last slice of bread and covered it with strawberry jam. He made sure everything looked perfect on the white paper plate before he walked toward her bedroom. The moment he opened her bedroom door, he wrinkled his nose, not wanting to inhale the musty odor wafting in the air. As he approached his mother, who was resting on her back, Luther noticed a syringe dangling from the joint of her left arm. He knew right away that Sugar had been shooting up again. Still not wanting to give up hope of having a good birthday, he swallowed down his edgy emotions and called to her.

"Mama?" he whispered softly. He set the plate of food down on the bed next to her hip, then gently rocked her bony shoulder. Sugar's eyes flipped open suddenly and startled Luther. Her eyes were filled with hell's fire and Luther quickly realized that he'd made an awful mistake.

"What in the hell do you want, boy?" Sugar snapped at him, causing him to bow his head down and project his voice toward the floor in shame.

"I…" Luther had trouble getting his words out. "Nothing. I mean…I didn't want anything. I mean—"

"Speak up. I can't hear your dumb ass!" Sugar berated her son.

"I was wondering if you're ready to go to the store. And I made you some breakfast." Luther pointed to the food near her hip.

"That football and some new clothes are the only things you care about, isn't it?" Sugar continued to scold her son for putting unwanted pressure on her.

"No, Mama. I just…" Luther paused to get his thoughts together. "You promised you would—"

"I don't remember making you any promise." Sugar began coughing violently.

"But you did. You said we could go shopping today."

"You want that stuff really bad, don't you?" Sugar stopped coughing and glared at him with contempt.

"I'll work for it," Luther answered, attempting to strike a new deal. "I'll clean up; I'll do the laundry; and I'll be quiet when you have company over. I can wait outside, or something, when Packard is here. I won't make a sound, I promise."

"Let me think about it," Sugar said and turned her back to him. "Leave the food. I'll eat it in a minute. And shut my door on your way out," she told him as she removed the syringe from her arm and began scratching uncontrollably.

Later, Sugar and Luther walked four miles to a local sporting goods store. Luther followed Sugar toward the back of the store where all of the sports equipment was stocked. He picked out the brown-and-white leather football he wanted and watched Sugar as she stuffed the ball inside of a large bag she'd brought with them. Sugar marched over to the sporting apparel aisle, located Luther's size, and quickly shoved some items into the bag.

"Carry this and come on." She gave Luther the items she'd gotten for him, then snatched his hand and raced toward the front door. Neither Luther nor Sugar noticed that a security guard had been watching their every move. When the guard yelled for them to stop, Sugar dropped Luther's hand and took off running. Before Luther could react and run out of the door, the guard nabbed him. Sugar rushed out the door, disappeared into the crowd of pedestrians, and never looked back. When it became clear that Sugar wasn't going to return, the police were called. Later, a squad car and two officers took Luther back to his home address. When the police gained entrance to the apartment, what few possessions Luther and Sugar had were gone. The only thing left was a plastic bag filled with his clothes in the center of the floor. It was clear to both Luther and the police officers that Sugar had left in a hurry and had no intentions of ever returning to see about Luther's well-being.

—3—
MARSHALL

Marshall was very excited as he and his wife, Stacy, entered the cab of the Skyride and watched as a male, theme park employee closed the door and locked it from the outside.

"Make sure you keep your safety belts fastened. The Skyride is about five minutes long. The guy on the other side will let you out," the employee informed them.

Once Marshall and Stacy were situated, the employee gave the ride operator the thumbs-up signal and the Skyride began to move forward. Marshall and Stacy were pulled along and gently hoisted high above the crowded park filled with meandering patrons who were in no hurry to get to any particular destination. They both glanced out of the window as the ride took them higher above the crowd.

"This is so wild, Marshall," Stacy said, as she swept her hand up and down his chocolate thighs. Marshall was wearing a pair of tan Dockers with a matching short-sleeved shirt. His legs were sexy and muscular and Stacy loved stroking them, especially when she was on her knees circling her tongue around the head of his pride. "You're a state trooper and you're supposed to uphold the law, not break it."

"This is the exception to that rule," Marshall replied as he placed her cheeks in his hands and kissed her before she could respond.

"After all these years, your kisses are still so sweet." Stacy looked at him as if she wanted to devour him. "How did you even come up with this crazy idea?" Stacy wanted to hear his explanation once again for what they were about to do.

"It came to me one day, while I was at work. I was thinking about you—actually I was daydreaming about you—and this fantasy came to me. Sometimes really freaky and kinky shit exposes itself in my mind." Marshall smiled at her.

"You think I'm not going to do it, don't you?" Stacy asked, sensing that Marshall believed she wasn't as bold and as adventurous as he hoped she'd be.

"I didn't say that, but if you're not comfortable, I understand. I'll admit that this particular sexual desire of mine is rather wild and racy," Marshall said, unashamedly.

"I've taken my panties off already and I want you to give me everything that I've got coming to me." Stacy spread her legs open and unlatched her safety belt. "Get on your knees, baby, and do your thing." Stacy wasn't about to deny the man she loved so much this particular sexual fantasy.

Marshall unbuckled his safety belt, repositioned himself, and got down on his knees before her. He guided her legs up on his shoulders and raised her white-and-yellow sundress higher so that he could get to her paradise.

"This is so wild, Marshall. If we get caught—" Stacy stopped talking the moment Marshall began placing sweet and delicious kisses on her thighs. "Oh, you are so wrong. You're not playing fair. Why are you doing this to me, baby?" she whispered. "You know how weak I get when you start kissing on me like this."

"Close your eyes and go with the moment. We don't have very long," Marshall uttered as he began sweeping his tongue around the border of her shine of love.

Stacy obeyed her husband. She closed her eyes, surrendered to the moment, and spread her legs a little wider as the Skyride moved along. Marshall treasured her scent, her flavor and the way her body came alive when he touched her. He swept his tongue up and down the length of her goddess until her back arched with pleasure.

"Damn, you're making me too wet and lusty." She cradled his head so that she could guide him to her most sensitive spot. Marshall moved his tongue counterclockwise around her love bead at a rhythmic pace, a signature move that he was confident would bring the prize of her sweet nectar.

"Ooo, that's my spot, baby. Damn." Stacy became more vocal as she thrust forward. Marshall gently penetrated her with a finger. He'd found a sensitive wall inside of her and brushed against it.

"I love your long fingers, baby." Stacy's legs began to tremble as some of her essence began to spill over. Marshall swallowed her spirit as he continued working toward bringing forth an orgasm.

"Oh, shit!" Stacy cried out. "You're going to make me cum, baby."

"Umm-hmm," Marshall muttered as Stacy's back arched and her thighs clapped against his cheeks.

"Oh, shit!" she hollered out repeatedly as Marshall feasted on the sweetness of her honey pot.

"Okay, stop," Stacy begged Marshall but he refused to move. "You win, baby. Damn, you know my body so damn well." She locked her legs at her ankles and tightened her thighs against Marshall's face. "If you don't stop, I will suffocate you," she warned him.

"I might like that," Marshall said the moment he came up for air.

"I don't believe that you have me with my ass all exposed in a damn Skyride in one of your freaky-ass fantasies." Marshall smiled at her while taking a seat next to her.

"Now we're part of the Skyride club," Marshall joked as he listened to the screams of thrill seekers being spun around on a nearby rollercoaster ride.

"I know that you don't think this shit is over. You're not about to get my ass all wet and not give me some dick," Stacy said.

"We don't have to, babe. I just wanted to eat your pussy." Marshall chuckled.

"That's not enough for me. You need to finish the damn job. I want to feel you inside of me right now. I want you to feel how warm and succulent my pussy is." Stacy unbuckled Marshall's belt, unzipped his shorts and removed his pride.

"That's what I'm talking about. A big, thick-ass chocolate dick that's standing at attention," Stacy said as she stroked Marshall's manhood. She raised her dress above her hips, no longer caring if anyone in the cab in front or behind them saw what she was doing. She positioned herself above Marshall and turned her back to him. She lowered herself down and guided his shaft inside of her moist pussy.

"Ooo," she cooed with sweet pain as she attempted to take all of him.

Marshall placed his hands beneath Stacy's ass and spread her cheeks a little wide so it was easier for him to get inside of her. He slapped her ass a few times. "Handle me. Ride it." Stacy began riding his dick and the sight of his glistening dick bathing in the wetness of her pussy ignited his passion.

"I can feel you opening up for me," he said as he flexed his ass muscles to extend himself and go deep inside of her. Can you feel me? Can you feel me hitting your walls?"

"Yes, baby," Stacy cried out with sweet pleasure. Marshall smacked her ass a few more times.

"Ooo, I like it when you slap my ass!" Stacy said and began to ride him with more authority.

"That's it, baby. Pound me," Marshall said, encouraging her to ride him even harder.

"Oh shit!" Stacy dug her fingernails deep into Marshall's thighs.

"Come on, I feel you. Give me my nut. Bust a nut for me, baby." Marshall held onto her ass until he felt her thick honey oozing down on the head of his manhood. The orgasm consumed Stacy and made her tremble uncontrollably.

"That's what I'm talking about," Marshall said as he took his focus off of her ass and placed it on their surroundings.

"Oh shit." Marshall laughed. "The ride is almost over." Stacy bounced a few more times on his dick before she got up and straightened out her clothing.

"This is far from over," she said as Marshall hurriedly attempted to calm his pride down while fastening up his shorts.

"It's over for now," Marshall continued to joke.

"You've gotten me all hot and didn't finish up. You just wait. I'm going to make your ass pay for this shit," Stacy said.

"Now, don't write a check your ass can't cash because we can get in line again and take the ride back to the other side of the park," Marshall said as one of the employees opened the door to let them out of the cab. Stacy and Marshall stepped outside.

"That sounds like a plan to me," said Stacy. Marshall could tell that she was all energized and on fire. "Come on, with your bad ass. Don't get scared now." Marshall insisted that they take the ride once again.

"You know that Quentin, Dawn, Lena, and Kenny are waiting for us to get off this ride. Look, there they are over there waving at us," Stacy pointed out. "Don't worry. I've got something for you later on." Marshall and Stacy caught up with their other family members who were also at the theme park.

Marshall and Stacy's daughter, Lena, along with Marshall's brother, Quentin, his wife, Dawn, and their son, Kenny, were standing next to a musical double-decker carousel filled with children screaming out with laughter and joy.

"How was the ride?" Quentin asked.

"It was the best ride in the world," Marshall boasted. Stacy playfully punched him for saying too much.

"It was a fun ride," said Stacy.

"Good. We're trying to decide where we should eat," Quentin said.

"Any place is fine with me. But, before we go, I'm going to run over there to the restroom," Stacy said.

Marshall quickly trailed behind Stacy. "I need to do the same thing."

When Marshall and Stacy returned, the discussion among the group had changed from where they should eat to what thrill ride they should visit next. Neither Marshall nor Stacy made any attempt to resolve the issue. Marshall indiscreetly slipped his arm around Stacy's waist and pulled her close to him. The moment he pushed up against her warm body, his manhood began to come alive. He craned his neck down and inhaled the sweet scent of her perfume. He loved his wife and daughter. He loved their marriage and the life they'd built together. He and Stacy were married when they were both twenty-three. Now, fifteen years later, Marshall was just as openly affectionate and protective over her as he was when they first met.

"I can feel you," Stacy whispered. "Would you calm down before you pop out of your shorts?" Stacy teased him.

"Okay, I'll stop being so bad," Marshall said. He was about to release his embrace, but Stacy reached behind her and gave his manhood a good squeeze when no one was looking.

"I'll kill that later on," she whispered to him before squeezing him one last time.

Marshall leaned closer to her and spoke purposely in her ear. "Baby, I can't wait that long." Marshall's warm breath gave her goose bumps.

"I've told you to stop playing around," Stacy scolded him.

"I think I should let you guys go ahead to ride the bumper cars and roller coasters," Dawn said. "I don't want to stand in a long line for hours to get on a ride that's going to upset my stomach."

"Now wait a minute," Quentin openly disagreed with his wife. "We all came here together and we should all stick together. It doesn't make any sense for you to walk around by yourself."

"Quentin, you and Kenny are going to want to hit the water rides and all of the other big rides, and I'm not getting on any of them. You know how roller coasters scare the hell out of me," Dawn countered.

"That's the point, Dawn. That's why people ride them." Quentin was clearly irritated with her.

"Why don't we vote on it?" Marshall stepped in and presented a solution to a problem, hoping to avoid watching Quentin and Dawn get into an argument that would spoil the spirits of everyone.

"Everyone who wants to stick together from this point on, raise your hand." Everyone, with the exception of Dawn, raised a hand.

"It's settled then; we all stick together," said Quentin as he readjusted his blue Chicago Cubs baseball cap.

Dawn huffed and Marshall noticed how Quentin shot warning daggers at her with his eyes. It was clear to Marshall that Quentin was in no mood to deal with Dawn or her attitude.

"Then where are we going to start?" Dawn asked, giving in to the will of the group.

"The bumper cars, Mom. Let's hit the bumper cars first. They are up there and to the left," said Kenny, who was eager to drive.

"That's a great place to start," said Quentin. "Let's go."

They all began walking in the direction of the fun ride. All but Dawn rode and enjoyed the rides at the theme park. The Iron Wolf, American Eagle, and Batman the Ride were clearly the favorites of the guys. The Old Time Cars and small rollercoaster rides were most enjoyed by Stacy and Lena. By five-thirty in the afternoon, the blazing sun and heat were unbearable.

"Whew, the sun is cooking my behind today," Quentin complained as he wiped his forehead with a napkin. They had arrived at a concession stand near the Tunnel of Love water ride.

"Do you guys want to stop and get something to eat now? I need to sit down," Dawn said.

"I wanted to hit the water ride real quick," said Stacy. "Tell you what. Why don't you guys get something to eat while Marshall and I hit the Tunnel of Love. We'll come over here as soon as we get off."

"That's cool with me. You guys go and have a good time. You've been behaving like two lovesick teenagers ever since you got here," said Quentin.

"It's like that for us." Marshall didn't like the attitude in his brother's voice.

"Yeah, whatever. Go on and have a good time. We'll be sitting over there. Come and find us when you get done," said Quentin.

"Okay, we'll see you guys back here in a little while," said Marshall as he and Stacy hurried off.

Marshall stood in line behind Stacy, whispering and nibbling on her earlobe. "You know you look good in that sundress."

"Is that a fact, Big Daddy?" Stacy responded with feistiness, acting as if she were Regina from the *Steve Harvey Show*. Marshall got a big thrill whenever she put on the sassy-and-sexy Regina act.

"Don't you start talking to me like that out here." Marshall was feeling twinges of sexual electricity pulse through him.

"What's the matter, honey? Am I too much woman for you? Because you know that we have a whole lot of unfinished business," Stacy said as Marshall placed his hands on her hips and pressed himself against her rump.

"Ooo, what's that? A pistol?" Stacy continued to behave naughtily. "You need to come up and see me sometime, Big Daddy, so you can unload that weapon of mass seduction." Marshall and Stacy got a charge out of their little foreplay sex game. Hollywood was the name of the foreplay sex game they were playing now. They'd pick a memorable character from the silver screen or television and become that person. They would play and tease each other throughout the day, which would build anticipation for what would come later that evening. Since Stacy had picked Regina, one of Marshall's favorites, he thought that he would spice up their game a little. He decided that he'd role play as Al Pacino's character, Tony Montana, from the movie *Scarface*.

"That's okay," Marshall began mimicking the character. "When you see me tonight, I'll introduce you to my little friend," he whispered in her ear so that his voice wouldn't carry.

"Oh, Big Daddy, if a little friend is all you've got, you'd better call for reinforcements," Stacy fired back over her shoulder.

"I don't need 'reinforcements,' baby. My little friend is as long as a Cadillac."

"Hmm, it sounds like your friend might have exactly what a big girl like me needs. A large motor."

Marshall split open laughing, causing him to step out of character. He hugged her tightly and whispered, "I love you," in her ear.

When Marshall and Stacy returned, they were both full of merriment. However, it was obvious that Quentin and Dawn weren't as happy with each other's company. They both had disagreeable expressions on their faces. They were sitting at a picnic table like two bookends with the kids in the center.

"They don't look happy," Stacy commented before they reached the table.

"Yeah, you noticed that, too, huh?" Marshall answered.

"I'll talk to Dawn," Stacy said. "Maybe I can get her to at least look like she's having a good time."

Lena looked up from her plate of food and noticed Marshall and Stacy approaching. She sprang up from her seat and rushed toward her parents. She smashed her body against Marshall's and locked her arms around his waist. They gave each other a strong hug.

"Daddy, I want you to win me one of those giant stuffed animals. I want a big brown tiger," Lena said, trying to persuade her father. "It would look so cool sitting in my room."

"All right, Lena, I'll try to win one for you," Marshall said without putting up much of a fight.

"Have I ever told you two how happy you make me? Have I ever told you how much I love both of you?" Stacy asked.

"We make you happy?" Lena repeated her mother's words.

"Yes, you do, and I love the both of you with all of my heart," Stacy added.

"I'm so lucky," said Lena. "So many of my friends have parents that hate each other, but you guys still like each other and I think that is so cool. But don't act all starry-eyed when you're around my friends. Just act normal, okay?" Lena pleaded with them.

"Now you've done it. We're going to be openly affectionate as soon as we get around your friends." Marshall laughed jokingly. Lena was serious about it, but he wasn't about to stop showing his affection for his family simply because his daughter didn't think it would look cool in front of her friends.

❦

By seven o' clock that evening, their day of fun was at its end. Marshall had won a big brown tiger for Lena by making three baskets in a row at a carnival-style game. He'd actually paid twenty-five dollars for it by the time he'd made the shots, but he didn't mind. Stacy had gotten Dawn to loosen up a bit and at least give the appearance she was having fun, which made the afternoon more bearable. It was now time to begin the journey home, so they all piled into Marshall and Stacy's minivan.

"Marshall, would you mind stopping at Wal-Mart while we're out here?" asked Dawn, who was more jovial than she had been all day.

"No, not at all," he answered.

"Girl, that's a damned good idea. I need to pick up some things for the house and I'd rather do it now than later," Stacy admitted.

"What do you need to pick up at Wal-Mart, Dawn?" Quentin questioned his wife.

"Well, we need to replace several blown light bulbs, which I've asked you time and again to replace, but you haven't. We're out of soap because you like to leave the bar at the bottom of the tub where it melts away. And I need to pick up something to unclog the drain that you were supposed to do weeks ago." Dawn was very critical of Quentin.

"Damn, man. She's on your case," Marshall commented.

"Okay, I'm sorry I asked. I meant to get to all of that stuff, but it slipped my mind," Quentin said, wanting to end her negative comments about him.

"I'll bet Marshall doesn't take as long as you do to fix simple problems." Dawn was now being spiteful.

"Honey, laziness is a trait that all men have. They don't allow stuff like that to aggravate them. They weren't trained to think about others. They'll leave toe-nail clippings scattered around the house and eat food that you specifically got for yourself and not them. I mean, honestly, why do men eat stuff that they know they didn't purchase?" asked Stacy.

"My bad, baby. I said I was sorry about that," Marshall offered, apologizing again to Stacy for eating her cake earlier during the week.

"All right, all right. I get the point." Quentin tossed up his hands, not wanting to hear any more man-bashing. Marshall pulled up to the front of Wal-Mart and let Stacy, Dawn, Kenny, and Lena out while he parked the van in a parking spot near the entrance. He put the car in park, but left the engine running so that the air conditioner would keep the cab of the van cool. Quentin opened Marshall's glove compartment and found some CDs.

"Oh, my Lord. What in the world are you doing with a 'Best of Bobby Blue Bland' CD? This music is so old. Granddaddy used to listen to this stuff," Quentin said, laughing, as he flipped it over and read the song list on the back. "Aw, man, I haven't heard these songs in ages. Bobby was one of Granddaddy's favorite singers."

"Do you remember the summers we spent with him and how he'd come home from working at the steel mill and play his music?" Marshall asked.

"How could I forget?" Quentin said. "He'd come into the house with his paycheck in one hand and a bottle of alcohol in the other. Once he got comfortable in his seat, he'd say, 'Come on over here, boys. I want each one of you to grab a foot and pull off my work boots.' We'd damn near pass out from the funk that rose up out of those boots." Both Marshall and Quentin chuckled.

"His feet smelled like rotten eggs," Marshall recalled.

"After we took his boots off, he'd say, 'Go over to the record player and put on Bobby Blue Bland," Quentin added.

"Wait a minute," said Marshall. "Remember how he'd always say, 'mercy,' whenever something was bothering him or if he wanted to add more meaning to what he was trying to say?"

"Oh yeah," Quentin replied. "That was just the time period he grew up in. Migrating from Mississippi to the North and listening to blues music is what people of his generation did."

"'The blues is about life, boys.'" Both men said in unison as they continued to mimic their grandfather. "You're going to have some blues in your lifetime and you'd better hope life has a little 'mercy' for you.'" Both men were bellyaching from laughing so hard at their grandfather's words of wisdom.

"I picked up the CD at a garage sale a few weeks back," Marshall said. "Stacy looked at me as if I were crazy when I purchased it. Lena says that Bobby can't sing worth a lick. But she's a part of the hip-hop generation, so she wouldn't understand."

"There was so much truth in their music," Quentin said, as he put the CD back.

"There certainly was," Marshall agreed, then paused for a moment. "Look, man…" Marshall hesitated and then quickly looked around outside to see if Stacy and Dawn were on their way back. "I don't mean to get in your business, but how are you and Dawn doing?"

"You are dipping in my business," Quentin responded abruptly. "We're all right."

Marshall had struck a sensitive nerve that he hadn't intended to. He only wanted to offer a willing ear if his brother needed it.

"What about you? How is that nutty-ass father-in-law of yours doing? Does he still think Stacy married the wrong man? Does he still think she could have done better than you?" Quentin asked.

"Theodore and I will never get along. We're two different types of people. He has his views and I have mine. He has a lot of hang-ups and twisted viewpoints. But, shit, he lives in Florida now, so he's not a problem any more. I don't have to see him so much."

"Well, good for you," Quentin said, clearly irritated.

"Look, I was only trying to help. I didn't mean anything by it."

"I don't need your help. Dawn and I are doing fine."

"Hey, then, I won't say anything else about it," Marshall said and dropped any further conversation.

—4—
CARMEN

Carmen's doorbell buzzed while she was trying to pull down a box of shoes from the top shelf in her closet. She hustled out of her bedroom and over to the front door. She spoke into the intercom.

"Who is it?" Carmen asked.

"It's me and Frieda; buzz us in," Nikki said. Carmen pressed the button, which triggered the door buzzer downstairs. Carmen unbolted her door for them. She went back to the bedroom closet and stood in front of it, once again looking at the box on the top shelf. She jumped up a few times until she snatched the shoebox she was trying to reach. They were all going out to the Wild Hare, a reggae-style nightclub, to celebrate Carmen's birthday.

"Hello, are you in here, Carmen?" Frieda spoke aloud as she entered Carmen's condo.

"Yeah, I'm in here, in the bedroom. I'll be out in a minute!" Carmen hollered.

"Girlfriend, you shouldn't leave your door all open like that. I know this girl who got messed up doing that. Her maniac neighbor saw her open door and came in and beat the hell out of her. It was on the news a few weeks ago. I think Oprah even did a show about how not to become a victim," Frieda said, matter-of-factly.

Carmen was a bit snobbish and prided herself on living in a nice condominium, which didn't have the caliber of people Frieda was speaking of, so she didn't put much stock into the warning she'd issued. Carmen walked out of the bedroom and into the living room where her guests were waiting. She paused and looked at them with a critical and disapproving eye as she evaluated their outfits. Frieda had on a hot-red spandex dress that pinched every fat bulge on her body. The dress had a neck clasp and a V neckline that amplified the stretch marks on her D-cup-sized breasts. Frieda's hot pink shoes didn't match her dress and her chubby legs lacked any type of muscular curvature. Nikki, didn't look any better. She was wearing the identical dress, only in black. Nikki was also wearing an oversized wig from the Chaka Khan and Diana Ross collection. Everything about their appearance made them look like cheap prostitutes as opposed to classy ladies going out for a fun evening.

"I don't have maniac neighbors, Frieda. Everyone in this building has a respectable job."

"And what's that supposed to mean? Are you trying to say that none of these high-class idiots will ever snap out, go crazy, and shoot up the place?

"That is highly unlikely in this neighborhood," Carmen said. She hoped her words sliced Frieda's feelings in some fashion. As much as Carmen hated to acknowledge how she truly felt, Frieda was like spoiled food that made her stomach turn sour every time she was around her.

"Wait-a-minute. Stop it right there." Nikki jumped right in the middle of their conversation. "I'm not going to put up with you two bickering with each other tonight. Both of you are going to play nice and we're all going to have a good time. We are going to go out to the club, strut our stuff, and perhaps pick up some men who'll want to buy us drinks all night."

"Nikki, you know her ass is tripping since she's another year older. She doesn't have a man, hasn't had a decent man in years, and doesn't have a clue how to get a man. Hell, she probably doesn't even know what a good, solid dick really looks like. She's probably used to seeing hard dicks in textbooks and shit. You see, Carmen," Frieda was now speaking directly to Carmen, "a really good dick looks like it hits parts of your pussy that will make you see stars. A good-looking and hard dick will make you want to drop to your knees, put that shit in your mouth, and suck on it until you drain it."

"I really don't need a sex education class from you, Frieda," Carmen snapped.

"Oh shit, maybe you don't. Maybe your prim and proper ass is in the closet. Damn, I never even thought about that shit. Are you gay, girlfriend?" Frieda asked, laughing out loud.

"Excuse me! I'm not in anyone's closet and I'm not gay!" Carmen gave Frieda a nasty glare; she didn't see the humor in her accusation.

"Lighten up, girl." Frieda continued to laugh; she'd gotten under Carmen's skin. "You know what. You should let me hook you up with somebody," Frieda said, still toying with Carmen.

"Oh really, someone like who?" Carmen asked in order to humor Frieda. However, before Frieda could even answer, Carmen turned her back on her and headed toward the bathroom to finish getting dressed. There was no way she was going anywhere with any of Frieda's filthy and shady associates.

"Francisco has plenty of buddies." Frieda spoke louder as Carmen walked away. "He might have one who can put up with your ass. You know, one who doesn't speak English." Frieda and Nikki began laughing.

"Whatever," Carmen snapped.

"Wait a minute, Carmen." Nikki stopped her sister before she entered the bathroom. "What are you going to wear tonight? Something sexy and provocative, right?" Carmen met her sister's gaze.

"I'm putting on something very sexy and tasteful. When I come out, I'll show you what I mean. You guys could learn a thing or two from me on how to be more alluring to attract a better class of men," Carmen said, with supreme confidence.

"The day I start taking fashion lessons from you, honey, is the day that I'll be flat on my back inside a coffin." Frieda laughed at Carmen who then entered her bathroom and slammed the door shut.

"Ooo, I can't stand that girl!" Carmen growled as she removed her outfit from a hook hanging on the back of the bathroom door. She'd been starving herself for the past two weeks in order to look right in it. She was thankful that her stomach wasn't bloated, which generally happened around this time of the month right before her cycle. She turned her attention to the mirror on the medicine cabinet and, for a moment, she could see the strong resemblance she had to her mother, Lola. Carmen had her mother's smooth skin, the color of gingerbread. She had inherited her mother's brown, catty eyes and full, luscious lips. She also had her mother's smile and finer grade of hair. She missed her mother and wished that she was still around to help her celebrate her birthday. Carmen exhaled before she began to put on red lipstick. She puckered her lips and blew her reflection a kiss; like she'd seen the actress Sallie Richardson do in a movie once. In her mind ,she knew that when a man would approach her, his eyes would focus on her succulent lips, alluring figure, and seductive smile.

It had been eight months since she'd broken up with her last boyfriend, Bernard. He was thirty-six years old, had a sexy, bald head, and was an amateur bodybuilder. Brawny men with broad shoulders, a mighty chest, and strong arms were the type of men Carmen was generally attracted to. Bernard started off being very attentive to her. He'd compliment her, talk to her all of the time, and was generally a good guy. When they first made love, Carmen was eager to see what Bernard was working with. She'd hoped that he had a nice-sized dick that was proportionate with the rest of his body. When she got her chance to see his package, she was disappointed to find that his balls were bigger than his dick. She thought that once he was erect, the full package would be more appealing. Once his banana-shaped dick got hard, she could glare at it.

"I know. My shit is huge, isn't it?" Bernard proudly boasted. Carmen didn't want to hurt his ego or pride and lied.

"Yes," she answered. When she surrendered herself to him, he wasn't long enough or thick enough to make her body respond in any meaningful way. As he selfishly fucked her, she hoped he'd be quick about it so that she could finish the job with one of her toys. Carmen's relationship with Bernard had come to its conclusion when she realized he was a very jealous and insecure man who didn't trust women. Carmen believed that this was because his mother had had multiple affairs and paid Bernard cash to keep it a secret from his father. Carmen grew tired of continually being accused of seeing other men and having to reassure him through constant ego stroking. Once she broke off the relationship, Bernard turned into a stalker who refused to allow her to live in peace. He showed up at her apartment unannounced one evening and tried to force his way inside.

After that incident, she had to get the police involved and immediately filed a restraining order against him. Bernard despised her for it and, a few weeks later, he decided to take out his anger by breaking into her condo and destroying it. Carmen was so happy that she'd purchased a home security system. When the police arrived, Bernard was arrested, charged, and was now serving five years for burglary.

"Boy, I certainly know how to pick them," Carmen whispered as she tried to clear her head of the unwanted memory. Just as she'd gotten thoughts of that incident out of her head, another unwanted and very painful memory surfaced without her permission. Her mind began taking her someplace she didn't want to go.

"God, why couldn't I have been stronger on the night my father was murdered?" she asked her reflection. Carmen wished she had gone downstairs to see about her father on the night a burglar broke into their home.

"He'd still be alive if I had. And perhaps I would have seen who the killer was and sent the son of a bitch to prison for what he'd done." Carmen closed her eyes. She tried to convince herself that she needed to forgive herself and get rid of that piece of emotional baggage. Carmen concentrated and shoved her unwelcome memories back into a bolted chamber of her mind. There was no way she was going to let her demons run free and ruin her birthday.

Once her mind was clear, she picked up a red scarf and tied it around her neck. She took a deep breath, looked in the mirror once more, and opened the door.

"Well, guys, how do I look?" Carmen asked as she struck a pose.

"You look like you," said Nikki.

"You look like you're headed to a job interview," said Frieda. "Honey, you look like that nutty white chick, Elaine, from *Seinfeld*. You've got to get daring and start showing off some of your assets like me." Frieda stood up, adjusted her breasts, and struck a pose.

"I will never lower myself to that level, Frieda. You will not be able to turn me out the way you've turned out Nikki." Carmen didn't mean to sound so harsh and blunt, but she couldn't help it. She had to say exactly what was on her mind.

"I didn't make Nikki do anything that she didn't want to do. She was a freak long before she met me. You just didn't know it," Frieda snapped back.

"Will you guys stop it?!" Nikki once again jumped in. "Damn, I'm tired of you two fighting over me. I swear, you guys sound like you're in competition to see who will have the most control over me. I am my own person and do what I want to do. I'm twenty-five years old now, and I believe I've earned the right to dress and behave anyway I see fit."

"Nikki, you could be—"

Nikki cut her sister off. "Carmen. Just stop. Tonight is about you, not me."

Carmen conceded and held on to the rest of her thoughts for the moment.

"Good, now that all of that is settled, can we get a move on? I'm ready to shake my ass and attract a drunken fool who wants to spend all of his money on me," Frieda said eagerly.

"Yeah. Let's go," Nikki said, and began walking toward the door.

When they arrived at the reggae club, Carmen quickly spotted an available booth beside the stage. She suggested they claim it before anyone else did. Once they did, Frieda and Nikki decided to head toward the washroom to make adjustments to their revealing outfits. Carmen agreed to stay and watch their seats. A few middle-aged men approached her and asked for a dance. Carmen quickly turned them down; she wasn't ready. She ordered herself a Strawberry Mojito, and it took no time for the waitress to have the bartender make it and present her with it. She enjoyed the taste of her drink while she listened to the sensual sounds of island music. A few couples were on the dance floor seductively snaking their hips to the rhythm of the music. A short while later, Carmen spotted Nikki and Frieda returning from the bathroom, laughing.

"What are you two laughing so hard about?" Carmen asked, wanting to get in on the merriment.

"Girl, this damn fool with a lazy eye came up to me and started talking smack," said Nikki, barely able to contain her laughter.

"He was as ugly as Lil' Wayne and came up with the goofiest line." Frieda continued, "He said, 'My name is Al and I'd like to be your pal.' He tried to make his voice sound all deep and shit."

"Wait, wait, wait." Nikki was nearly in tears now. "So I told him if he was looking for a pal, he needed to take his ass to the anti-cruelty society and adopt a dog." Nikki burst out laughing again.

"Then his boy," Frieda continued on, "who was watching him make his moves, yelled out, 'Dammmnnnn! Your ass got served!'" At that point, Carmen began laughing with them. Carmen turned her attention back to the dance floor, which was packed with gyrating people dancing with seductive and sensual abandon.

"Come on; let's go dance," Nikki said as she grabbed her sister by the arm and jerked her out of her seat. Once they found a tiny slice of real estate to dance on, Nikki began shouting out and singing along with the music. It didn't take long for men with heat, hunger, and lust in their eyes to notice Nikki's stripper-like dance moves. A tall, bony man approached Nikki from behind, put his hands on her hips and began to mirror her moves. Another short man, with very bad skin, approached Carmen, grinding his hips and smiling, hoping he'd get an opportunity to ride her ass the way the other man was riding Nikki's.

"Let's go back over there," Nikki whispered to her sister. "Near the stage, where that man is taking pictures. I want to get my picture taken tonight before I get all sweaty."

"Okay, after this song is over," Carmen said, and continued to dance.

"What's the matter, baby?" asked the hip-grinding man who'd approached her.

"Nothing," Carmen said and continued to dance with the man, but at a distance.

Carmen danced a few songs with the man and later danced with several other more attractive men. Nikki and Frieda surprised Carmen with a special birthday cake and got all of the patrons in the club to sing "Happy Birthday" to her. This made her feel very special.

At 3:15 a.m., the three women called it a night and left the club. They piled into Carmen's car, loaded with alcohol and laughter. Carmen had drunk a cup of strong coffee before they'd left the club to help her stay alert during their drive home.

"Damn, my feet are killing me." Carmen glanced at Nikki, who was in the passenger seat kicking off her shoes. "Oh shit, that feels so much better."

"Honey, I hear you," Frieda chimed in as she also kicked off her shoes, and slumped down in the back seat. Carmen turned the ignition key, but the engine sputtered and wouldn't start.

"Girl, don't tell me your car won't start." Carmen looked over at Nikki, who had a concerned look on her face. "Didn't you just get this car fixed?"

"Yeah, but I had brake work done, not engine work." Carmen tapped the gas pedal a few times, turned the key again, but the car refused to start.

"Come on, baby. Don't do this to me. Not tonight," Carmen pleaded with her car. She paused for a long moment and then turned the ignition key again. The engine whined and sputtered before reluctantly catching a full engine crank and starting up.

"Get my ass home so I can get in the bed," said Frieda drowsily. Carmen noticed the red, "check engine" light blinking. *Damn*, she thought to herself before she sped off into the night, praying she would get the car home before it completely conked out. An hour later, Carmen pulled up in front of Nikki and Frieda's apartment building on Seventy-first and Prairie.

"When you guys get upstairs, come to the window and wave so I know you've made it in safely."

"All right," answered Nikki.

"I hope you had a nice birthday, Carmen," said Frieda. Carmen appreciated her being nice to her for the entire night. "But you know this doesn't change shit between us. I'm going to be in your ass whenever I see fit."

"Yeah, yeah, yeah," Carmen said, impatiently, "now get out of here and get on upstairs." A few moments passed before she saw Nikki come to the window and wave. Carmen pushed the gas pedal. Her car hesitated, then crept along slowly, bucked like an untamed stallion, then picked up speed. She rushed down Prairie Street barely stopping for stop signs. Right before she reached Fifty-fifth Street, the engine shut completely off and her car began coasting along like a ghost floating through the night. Carmen pulled the car over to the curb under a lamp post that had a blown bulb. She tried to restart her car, but it only sputtered and whined. "Come on now, baby, please start," she pleaded with the car as she pumped the gas pedal and continued turning the ignition key. However, it was no use; her car had conked out.

"Shit!" Carmen howled. She was stranded in a seedy section of the city. Out of her passenger window, she glared at the open space of a vacant lot where a building of some kind once stood. Through the dark, at a distance, she could see the rusted pillars of the elevated El train tracks. Out of her driver's window, there was a lone, three-flat building, surrounded by more vacant land, which gave her a creepy feeling. She glared out of her front window and noticed that all of the street lamps were out.

"Damn!" she bitched. She was now closer to her Hyde Park condo than she was to Nikki and Frieda's apartment.

"Okay, Carmen, don't panic." She began searching for her cell phone but remembered that she hadn't brought it since the purse she was carrying was so small.

"Goddamit!" she said, as she flung her purse into the passenger seat.

Come on, girl. Get it together. What are you going to do? It's very late and your car has stopped in a neighborhood where crime is a way of life. Carmen got her thoughts in order and decided that the best thing to do was to leave the car, get up to Garfield Boulevard where she would be able to find a pay phone, or better yet, catch a cab or the Fifty-fifth Street bus back home. She got out of the car and walked down the middle of the street instead of on the sidewalk. Not wanting to hang around on the empty street longer than necessary, she walked briskly. She made it through the dark and dangerous street and onto Garfield Boulevard. She walked east about a half a block and stood in front of the bus stop sign. Although she was still in a rough area, she felt slightly safer since it was well lit. Some traffic was moving along Fifty-fifth Street and there was a collection of harmless derelicts drinking alcohol and arguing about whether Barack Obama was going to be the first black president. Twenty minutes later, a bus finally came along and Carmen quickly got on, paid her fare, and sat directly behind the bus driver. There weren't many people on the bus, but those who were, had their eyes fixed on her. Once she got back home safely, she kicked off her shoes, crashed on her bed, and fell asleep with her clothes on.

Carmen opened her eyes the next afternoon and focused her attention on her alarm clock. She saw it flip from 1:59 p.m. to 2 p.m. and wanted to roll back over and get some more sleep. Her stomach refused to allow her to rest any longer; it began doing flips. She rolled onto her back, ran her fingers through her hair, and took a long stretch to bring her body fully to life. She got out of bed and walked into the kitchen. She picked up the phone on the countertop and dialed Nikki. The phone rang for a long time before an answering machine finally picked up.

"They must not be there," Carmen uttered before hanging

up without leaving a message. She massaged her temples in an effort to fight off a headache that was trying to complicate her day.

"I have to go and see about my damn car," Carmen complained. She took a few deep breaths and then got ready to head back to the spot where her car had stalled.

—5—
LUTHER

It was 3:00 p.m. when Luther emerged from his basement apartment and stepped out in the muggy summer air. He squinted for a few moments to give his eyes a chance to adjust to the brightness of the day. Luther had made the decision to spend the day loitering in front of a liquor store, getting high. Normally, he would have waited until he got off work before he drank. But since he was out of a job due to that crazy woman barking at him, it gave him the perfect excuse to drink his misery away. As he was about to light a smoke and puff on some nicotine, he became distracted by a woman across the street shouting obscenities at her car.

"Goddamn piece of shit!" she yelled as she tried to get the car to start.

Luther recognized the woman immediately. It was the woman who'd gotten him fired and sent his life into a tailspin.

"You've got to be fucking shitting me," Luther said as he put away his cigarette.

He watched her as she popped the hood of the car and looked under it for something. *She has no idea what to do*, he thought and chuckled to himself as he watched her frustration mount. Luther was getting a twisted kind of joy as he observed her.

"I've spent a damn arm and a leg on getting your brakes fixed and this is how you repay me!" Luther continued to listen with amusement as she squawked at her car as if it were a lover who'd betrayed her. "That's it. I'm trading your no-good ass in the first chance I get." Carmen kicked the car.

Luther got tired of watching her and decided to head to the liquor store. He had no intentions of helping Carmen, until a devilish thought entered his mind.

"I can probably turn this situation into some quick cash," he said to himself. He looked at Carmen once again and it was clear that she was very upset and in need of help.

"Let me take a look at it," Luther hollered as he walked across the street toward her. As he approached the passenger side of the car, he noticed her car had stopped directly in front of a red fire hydrant. Luther immediately noticed how quickly Carmen's expression changed when she saw him.

"You weren't expecting to ever see me again, were you?" Luther asked.

"Umm…No, I wasn't," replied Carmen.

"I can take a look at it for you," Luther offered. "I shouldn't help you out at all, but I'm not low-down like that."

"I am really sorry you lost your job. After you left, I tried to tell the owner it wasn't your fault, but he didn't seem to care about hearing my side of the story as much as he cared about letting you go."

"Shit happens," Luther said as he tucked his head under the hood and began inspecting the car. "Tell me, what was your car doing before it stopped?" Luther asked as he checked the connections on the battery posts.

Carmen exhaled away some of her frustration and discomfort, shut her eyes for a moment, and began explaining how her car had conked out.

"When was the last time you had a tune-up on the car?"

"Tune up," Carmen uttered as if his words were foreign to her. "Never. I put gas in it and go. I inherited the car and it has run fine for years. I've always taken it in for oil changes; isn't that enough?"

Luther laughed at her response as he lifted one of the black wires off of a spark plug. He touched the plug with his index finger and discovered that it was wet. "Hold on a moment," he said and rushed back inside of his apartment for some tools. He came back in a flash and removed the spark plug with a socket wrench. The tip of the one spark plug he removed was completely charred.

"This is your problem, right here. Your spark plugs are shot and need to be replaced."

"Oh, God, that's going to cost me a ton of money, isn't it? Damn!" Carmen couldn't deal with another large repair bill right now.

"Well..." Luther smiled and thought to himself. *Maybe my day will turn out to be worth something after all.* "For a car like this, a service shop would probably charge you around one hundred and sixty dollars to put it on the diagnostic machine to tell you what's wrong with it. But since I already know what the problem is, I'll fix it for one hundred dollars."

"One hundred dollars!" Carmen growled with aggravation.

"Hold on now, that includes parts and labor. Honey, that's a deal you can't beat." "I don't know about this."

Luther was right but she truly hated being in such an awkward position.

"Look at it like this. If you call a tow truck it's going to cost you no less than fifty dollars to get it towed to a tune-up shop; then one hundred and sixty dollars for them to tell you what's wrong. On top of that, they're going to charge you an arm and a leg to fix it. You could easily be out of three or four hundred dollars. Think about that," Luther said, raising his voice and then lowering it again.

"Okay, I see your point," Carmen conceded. "Can you take care of it today? I don't want my car to stay here another night."

"Yeah, I can probably handle it today for you. We can hop on a bus, and head down to the auto parts store to pick up what I need."

"Luther is your name, right?" Carmen decided that it would be wise to be friendlier toward him.

"Yup," he said as he looked at her and bit his bottom lip.

"How long is this going to take?" Carmen asked.

"Not long. I can do a tune-up in about thirty minutes."

"Well, I guess your plan is the best thing going." Carmen let down the hood of the car and locked it up. "Come on then. Let's go on down to the auto parts place."

The two of them walked a few blocks west and stood at a bus stop at the corner of State and Fifty-fifth Streets.

"It looks like it's going to take a minute before the bus arrives. I'm going to go into Kentucky Fried Chicken and use the bathroom. I'll only be a minute, okay?" Carmen said to Luther as she rushed off.

"That's cool," Luther said as he took a seat on the bus bench.

The thumping bass sound of an SUV with a high-powered amp pulled into the Kentucky Fried Chicken parking lot. The boom from the bass was so strong it rattled the windows of the fast-food restaurant. Luther turned around to see who was driving the truck making all the noise. His heart began racing when he saw Packard roll down the window and turn his system down.

"Luther!" Packard hollered to him, "Get over here." Luther tried to exhale away his anxiety, but it only made him more tense.

"What's up, Packard?" Luther said, with disappointment in his voice.

"Are you out of my building yet, boy?"

"No, not yet, but I wanted to talk to you real quick about the apartment." Luther's speech was fast and hurried. "I don't have a job right now, man, and I was wondering if you could give me a break on the rent for a minute until I get back on my feet."

"A break!" Packard opened the door and stepped out of the car. He placed his hand on Luther's shoulder, right behind his neck so that he could control his movements. Packard's hands were abrasive, and callused. He began squeezing Luther's neck harder than necessary. "Yeah, I'll give you a break, Luther. I'm going to give you the best break in the world. I'm going to free you up." Packard paused in thought. "You know, I'm the closest thing you have to a father. And a good father must make certain his son grows up to be a man who knows how to take care of himself. So, in that regard, Luther, I'm going to help you out. I'm going to help you be an independent man who knows how to stand on his own feet. Don't worry about the rent. As far as I'm concerned, you will never have to worry about paying rent at that place ever again, okay?" Packard said as he slapped him hard on his back before getting back in his Blazer.

"Wow…" Luther smiled. "Thank you, Packard. I'll never forget this." Luther followed Packard and stood next to the car door. "I'm going to do real good this time. I'm going to get it together and make sure that I don't ever get into a situation like this ever again." Luther felt relieved that Packard was showing some compassion.

"I know that you are, Luther." Packard smiled, then started his truck up and took off.

As soon as Carmen came out of the restaurant, the bus came along and both Carmen and Luther boarded it. Since the air on the bus was stale, Carmen sat next to an open window hoping to catch a fresh breeze as the bus moved along. Luther sat next to her and began mumbling.

"What did you say?" Carmen didn't quite understand what Luther was rambling about.

"Nothing," Luther replied, "I was talking to myself a little. So, what do you like to do for fun?" Luther wanted to get to know her a little.

"What do you mean?" Carmen asked.

"You know, what do you do for fun? Do you like to party, go to the movies, that sort of stuff?" Carmen really wasn't in the mood for casual conversation. She was mentally recalculating her budget.

"Nothing, really. I'm a homebody. I only go out every now and then."

"Really? Me too," Luther answered, pleased that they had something in common. Luther began to study her flawless skin and finer grade of hair.

"You're mixed with something, aren't you? You got Indian or something in your family?"

"Hispanic," Carmen answered. "My mother was African American and my father was Latino."

"Yeah, I've heard Blacks and Latinos mix nicely and make pretty babies." Luther smiled and allowed his thoughts to consider what it would be like to make love to a beautiful woman like Carmen. "So do you speak Spanish, too?"

"Luther, does it really matter?" Carmen was annoyed more at her situation than she was at him.

"Hey, I'm only trying to make conversation to get your mind off of your situation. I don't mean any harm."

Carmen unpredictably felt ashamed for being curt with him. All Luther had been trying to do since he met her was to help. Now, he was letting her know that he had the presence of mind to be concerned with her feelings. She focused on Luther for a moment and saw nothing about his appearance that appealed to her. However, she found herself looking beyond what was on the surface. *Perhaps I'm judging a book by its cover rather than its contents*, she thought.

"You're right, Luther. I'm sorry. I didn't mean to be short with you. To answer your question, my Spanish is not very good."

"I see." Luther paused. "Can I ask you a personal question?"

"It depends on how personal the question is," Carmen said.

"Do you have a man or boyfriend?" Luther asked flat out.

"Can't you tell that I don't? If I did, he would've been taking care of my car." Carmen's words came off kind of harsh, so she rephrased her response. "I don't have anyone right now, nor am I looking."

"Men are too much drama, huh?"

"What about you? Do you have anyone special in your life?" Luther was surprised that Carmen asked him the same question.

"Me? No, not at all." He chuckled and Carmen sensed the pain floating beneath his words. .

"Do you have any children?" she asked.

"No, I don't have any. My situation isn't quite right to bring a kid into it. Once I get my act together, maybe I'll be able to find the right woman. I need a good-natured woman who knows how to raise a family as well as take care of her man. I need a woman who'll be around when the rubber hits the road and times get hard."

"You sound like a lot of women I know who say the same things about finding Mr. Right," Carmen said.

"Well, it isn't easy, you know. Like me, for example. I figure a guy like me would never have a chance with a woman like you. I don't have a college degree or wear a suit and tie or have a big office in a high-rise downtown. But I don't mind working and I do everything possible to keep a job, but sometimes, the shit hits the fan." Luther paused. "If it weren't for bad luck, I wouldn't have any at all. I may not have a degree, but if you put me on a job working with my hands, I learn very quickly. Show me how to do something one time and I got it." Luther showed Carmen his hands.

"Luther, you make me and other women like me sound as if we're superficial. Just because a guy has a degree and works downtown doesn't make him the perfect choice for someone like me. I think that's part of the problem between men and women. Some women look at a man and fall in love with his success or material things that he can buy for them. They're not interested in who he is as a person. Then some men only see women as bitches or whores who are to be used for their personal satisfaction and nothing more. I think if people would stop looking at the surface and focus on what's really on the inside of a person, we'd all be better for it."

"Is that what you do? Do you look at what's on the inside of a person?" Luther's question was filled with the hope that Carmen would see his torn heart and help him fix it.

"Yes, I do," Carmen said, matter-of-factly. "I think that a man like you has potential. You're willing to admit you have some shortcomings; you know what they are, and you're willing to do something about it. Some men are unwilling to admit they have issues that need to be addressed. Even the brothers in corporate America."

"So, what do you do for a living?"

"I'm a school teacher."

"That's nice. I hear that teachers are always in demand and hardly ever out of work." There was silence between them for a moment; then Luther spoke again. "Look, I'm going to come clean with you. You seem like a person who listens to people. I really want to do something with my life, you know. I'm tired of running the streets, but it's so hard to do anything when you're a guy like me. I barely made it out of high school and don't know much about anything. But you know something? I'm going to be like Obama and make change. I'm tired of merely existing. I want a better life for myself and I'm willing to work hard to get it. Come Monday morning, I'm going to get a fresh start. I'm going to stop sitting on my ass and hanging around in front of the liquor store drinking."

"Good for you, Luther. That's the way you have to be when you want to make a change in your life. You've got to make some plans and follow through with them." Luther liked Carmen's positive words of encouragement. All his life he had longed for someone to truly care about him and be encouraging.

"Do you really think that I can make it? I always feel like I have limited options. Shit, with me it's purely about survival," Luther spoke honestly.

"Luther, I've been a teacher for a long time and I always tell my kids that if you believe in yourself and do whatever it takes to reach your goals, anything is possible. You have your health, your strength, and it seems as if you're not afraid to take on new challenges." Carmen continued to be encouraging.

"You don't know how good it feels to hear somebody say that to me." Luther bowed his head and chuckled again. "I know that we've just met, but it really feels good to know that you think I can make it." Luther smiled at Carmen and, for the first time, she saw something different and more fragile in his eyes.

"Of course, you can. That's the way life works. Things don't always go like you plan, but you've got to deal with the pitfalls and do what a man has got to do," Carmen said.

"I know that's right. Lord knows, nothing has ever gone right for me.

Ever since I was a kid, somebody has always done something to hurt me. Even my own mother."

Carmen noticed Luther's voice became cheerless as he spoke of his mother. His voice took on a sadder quality.

"She would always tell me she never wanted me and hated the day that I was born. One time she bought me a pair of shoes that were too small since they were cheap. When I started walking on the heel of the shoes, she beat my ass for tearing them up. That's messed up, isn't it?" Luther asked.

"That's horrible," Carmen said, saddened to hear that particular story.

"I'm over it now. It's no big deal." Luther swallowed his pain.

"What a horrible thing for your mother to say and do." Carmen sympathized with him.

"Deep down inside, I don't think she knew what she was doing. She was on drugs most of the time I lived with her. One thing led to another and I ended up in a foster home, which, in my opinion, was no better than living with my mother."

"I know. I've had some emotionally abused foster children in my class before. I'm very familiar with how problematic some situations can be. I'm so sorry things weren't the way they were supposed to be for you, Luther." Carmen really felt bad for causing him to lose his job.

"Come on; our stop is next," Luther said as he reached up to pull the stop cord. The two of them got off the bus and went into the auto parts store. Luther got the parts he needed and Carmen paid the clerk. As luck would have it, they were able to catch a bus heading back right away. They quickly got back to Fifty-Fifth Street and headed east toward Prairie Street. When they turned onto Luther's block, the police had the street shut off to traffic.

"What in the world is going on?" Luther wondered. The scent of smoke, wafting through the air, caught his attention. Luther glanced down the street and saw his apartment building on fire.

"Oh no!" Luther shouted out as he raced down the street. Carmen was about to run with him, but she noticed that a City of Chicago tow truck had hitched up her car and was towing it away. It was then she remembered that her car had stopped in front of the fire hydrant. She quickly ran out in the street and attempted to stop the tow truck driver, but it was too late. She would have to pick up her car from the city pound and that was going to cost her more money that she didn't have.

-6-
MARSHALL

Marshall stood at the door and flipped the light switch to the *on* position in Lena's bedroom. Lena's bedroom was a mess and Marshall wasn't happy about it. Her floor was cluttered with clothes, mostly outfits she'd pulled out to try on and then never replaced. Books, magazines, and stuffed animals were also strewn across the floor, making it difficult for anyone to enter the room without stepping on something. Her dresser drawers were sitting wide open with clothes drooling over the edges. Marshall looked around the room with a critical and disapproving eye. He noticed that Lena had fallen asleep with her purple bed linen completely covering her head.

"Lena!" his voice boomed, indicating how dissatisfied he was with her lack of neatness.

"Yeah?" Lena awoke from her slumber.

"What's going on with this bedroom? Why is it such a mess? Have you lost your mind or something?" Marshall asked her a series of questions before she could even remove her head from beneath the covers.

"I'm going to get to it," Lena said as she became more aware and alert.

"How did this room get so junky?" Marshall wanted answers.

"Mommy told me to go through all of my clothes and pull out all of the stuff that was too small, so that we could give it to Goodwill. I'm still working on doing that project." Lena sat upright, yawned, and removed her iPod earphones.

"You shouldn't sleep with those things in your ears. You'll go deaf before you reach your twenty-fifth birthday." Marshall picked up a T-shirt that was on the floor in front of him and placed it in a nearby laundry basket. "I want this pigpen taken care of today. And I want the rest of your household chores completed before your uncle arrives." Marshall continued to give her grief about the untidiness of her room.

"Okay. I'll take care of it this morning. Are we still going out for our bike ride later on?" Lena stood up and raised her arms high in the air, stretched, and yawned once more. "Can I get a piggyback ride to the bathroom?"

"Why? Is there something wrong with your legs?" Marshall was still bent out of shape about the room and he wanted Lena to understand that it was unacceptable to be so lazy.

"No, I just want a ride." Lena pouted as she looked into his eyes.

"You've gotten too big for that, Lena." Marshall twisted his torso and popped his back.

"Please, Daddy. I know that I'm a little big for that sort of thing but I really want a piggyback ride. It's only a few steps." Lena smiled at him and batted her eyes, as if her blinking would cast a magic spell on him. Lena wanted to make sure that she could still get her way with her father, even when he was mad at her.

"Okay." Marshall gave in to her request. "But I want this room spotless. Do you hear me?!" Marshall exclaimed.

"I hear you." Lena smiled at her father.

"Good." Marshall went to the side of her bed, turned his back to her, and squatted down so she could hop on his back. He tucked his arms behind her knees, stood up, and began walking out of the room.

"Giddy up," Lena commanded as she locked her arms around his neck. Marshall played along with her and behaved like a horse. He took her down the hall and dropped her off at the bathroom door, feeling proud that he still had the strength to honor his teenaged daughter's childish request.

"It's a good thing that I have a strong back." Marshall contracted the muscles in his shoulders. "You're ready for this bike ride, right? We're going to ride between fifteen and twenty miles today," Marshall reminded Lena once again.

"I'm ready. We did twenty-five miles last weekend and I wasn't even tired." Lena flexed her calf muscles. "See, Daddy? I'm already starting to get some muscle definition. I can't wait to start high school in the fall. My legs are going to be cut and when I try out for the basketball team, I'm going to be dunking on the upperclassmen," Lena proclaimed with supreme confidence.

"You know, you're a bit much this morning. One minute you want a piggyback ride like you're a five-year-old girl, and the next minute you want to tell me how you're going to kick butt and take names."

"That's a woman for you, Daddy," Lena said, toying with him. She smiled innocently at him and then blew him a kiss before she shut the bathroom door.

"When did she grow up on me?" Marshall mumbled as he stepped away from the door and moved down the hallway. "It seems just like yesterday I was driving her home from the hospital being extra careful. I wanted to make sure I got her there safely." Marshall thought about that moment so many years ago. He had kept looking in his rearview, smiling at Stacy, who kept fondling Lena's little feet and fingers. He was so proud to be her husband and her lover. He was also swollen with pride over becoming a father for the first time.

"Marshall." Stacy called out his name. She was speaking through the intercom system piped throughout the house. He answered her, using the intercom that was near the staircase.

"Yeah, baby," he answered, as he pulled the white response switch downward.

"Are you and Lena eating this morning? I'm making some pancakes and eggs," Stacy informed him.

"I'm hungry!" Lena shouted through the closed bathroom door.

"Yeah, baby, hook us up," Marshall answered.

Marshall walked down the groaning staircase toward the front door. He pulled open the door and stepped out to retrieve the morning newspaper. *It's a perfect day,* Marshall thought as the warmth of the sun was kissing his skin. He walked down the front porch steps and out to the center of his lawn, where he picked up his newspaper. One of the top headlines read: "Southside Apartment Building Fire May Have Been Caused By A Faulty Gas Line." Marshall began reading the story about a dilapidated, three-story apartment building that had caught fire. After reading the sketchy details of the story, he thought about whether or not he had enough insurance on the rental property he and Stacy owned on Eighty-seventh and Blackstone.

Marshall had inherited the three-story building from his father.

He went back inside and entered the kitchen where Stacy was standing at the island counter pouring three glasses of cranberry juice. The scent of buttermilk pancakes wafting throughout the kitchen made his stomach growl. He noticed Stacy, dressed in a navy Donna Karan business skirt suit with matching pumps that gave just the right amount of flex to her calf muscle. Marshall approached her from behind, slid his arms around her tummy, and kissed the side of her neck.

"You taste good, baby," Marshall whispered as he palmed her fanny. "You feel good, too."

"Marshall, stop."

"You didn't say stop when we were on the Skyride," Marshall reminded her. "You couldn't get enough of me then."

"Ha, ha, very funny," Stacy said, moving away from the center island. She sat down at the kitchen table that was under a chandelier, next to a window, and near the back door. "So today is the big day for you, right?" Marshall queried his wife once again.

"Yes, and I can't wait to close on the property. The commission I'll make off this deal will most certainly put some fat in our banking account. Plus, these clients have referred two of their friends who are looking to purchase homes in the same price range. I was thinking that with the money that's going to come in, we should remodel the basement and then put the house on the market." Stacy floated her idea out to Marshall.

"Put the house on the market? What for, Stacy? I love this house." Marshall didn't like Stacy's idea.

"I know you do, but I saw this beautiful home that is about to go on the market in Highland Park. It's a stately-looking home. It's gated and has a driveway made of red cobblestones with a heated, three-car garage, five bedrooms, three-and-a-half bathrooms, and a beautifully finished basement. It has a family room with a fireplace and the property is sitting on a one-third acre of land. Marshall, the place is absolutely breathtaking." Stacy continued to give the property rave reviews.

"Okay, what's the real deal, Stacy?" Marshall suspected that Stacy had already mapped out a plan that she hadn't told him about yet.

"Wait a minute, there is more."

Marshall could tell that Stacy was making her case.

"The first floor has an office with a full bath and, baby, the master suite is absolutely gorgeous. It has a fireplace, a whirl-pool, a luxury bathroom, and huge, walk-in closets. There is no way we'd ever have a fight over closet space again. Not to mention that the home has beautiful, vaulted ceilings with sky-lights and a spiral staircase. Oh, and there is a small, square-shaped swimming pool in the back yard along with an enclosed patio deck." Stacy moved over toward Marshall and sat on his lap. She began kissing him repeatedly on his lips and then nibbled on his neck. "Now, doesn't that sound like the house of our dreams, baby? We could do all kinds of freaky and kinky shit in a house that size." Stacy purposely spoke in his ear.

"You are so bad. I knew you were setting me up," Marshall answered, feeling his manhood starting to throb with desire. Stacy continued to shower him with her sweet, juicy, and suc-culent kisses. Marshall surrendered to his emotions and slipped into a euphoric love coma as she presented him numerous reasons for why he loved and cherished her. Marshall was so proud of his wife and her success. He had supported her when she wanted to quit her job as the vice president of sales and promotions at a large book distributor to pursue a career as a real estate agent. She'd made a commitment to work tirelessly and become the best possible agent she could be. Stacy was gifted when it came to selling products or ideas. She could sell heat to the sunshine, wet to water, and hard to a dick. Marshall loved his wife and the life they'd built and shared. She completed him. They'd learned how not to disrespect each other or harbor resentment when things didn't work out as they'd planned. He and Stacy had superb communication and made it their personal mission to resolve all of their disputes. Marshall had the family he'd always wanted, the life he'd always wanted, and a supreme love that filled his heart with overflowing joy.

"Baby, the house sounds like it's really nice. How long have you been looking at it?" Marshall knew Stacy better than she knew herself.

"I've been inside of it twice and I've fallen in love with it. I already know how I want to redecorate it," Stacy said meekly.

"How much does the home cost, Stacy? You've got very expensive taste. Sometimes your taste can get a little too expensive for my blood." Marshall looked at her with his chin tilted.

"Well, you're right. It is on the expensive side but you get what you pay for." She immediately began to argue her point. "We'd be able to swing the mortgage comfortably if you sold the property on Eighty-seventh and Blackstone." Stacy winced; Marshall would not sell the building without a damned good reason. The property was an excellent source of supplemental income and Marshall wasn't the type of man who'd overextend himself financially.

"How much does the house cost, Stacy?" Marshall asked once again.

"The asking price for the house is four hundred and fifty thousand. But I can work with the owners and see if I can get them to lower the price a little. Plus, Lena would be in one of the best school districts in the state." Stacy continued her campaign of trying to win Marshall over.

"Stacy, Stacy, Stacy," Marshall repeated her name. "We will have to talk about this one. That is on the high end of our budget, don't you agree?"

"I know it is, but it's well worth it. Marshall, I guarantee you that every night you will feel like the man of your house."

Marshall began laughing dryly.

"I'm the man of my own house right now." Marshall smiled coyly.

"Good"—Stacy ran her fingers though his hair and cupped her hand over his ear—"I plan to make sure that you graduate from being man of the house to the king of your fucking castle," she whispered seductively, then ran the tip of her tongue around the rim of his ear.

"Oh, you're good," Marshall muttered as he tried not to surrender to the passion of the moment.

"Can we seriously talk about it tonight, baby? Hmmm? We can talk about it while your dick is in my mouth." Stacy once again spoke purposely in his ear.

"You're not playing fair, Stacy," Marshall said as he smacked her ass.

"Slap my ass again," Stacy ordered and he complied. "Good, it's settled. We'll talk more about how we can manage this later on tonight. We'll also discuss a time when we can drive out to the property so you can see it. I know you're going to fall in love with it." Stacy stood up and removed herself from his lap.

"You've got this all figured out, don't you?" Marshall glanced down at his erect manhood, then squeezed it a few times for a little personal pleasure before he focused on calming his sexual beast down.

"Marshall, baby, I know this is going to work out. I can feel it. I know once you see this house, you're going to feel the same way. There's no way you're not going to like this home. Plus, we can get real freaky in the pool during the hot summer nights."

"Oh, gross! I do not want any little brother or sister to babysit," Lena blurted as she walked into the kitchen. She'd overheard what Stacy had said to Marshall.

"Watch your mouth, young lady; you are not grown," Stacy warned. She didn't like Lena's tone of voice.

"Mom, just don't get pregnant, okay? That would be so embarrassing. My friends would not want to hang out with me anymore if they knew that my parents are still doing it." Lena moved over to the cupboard and removed a glass.

"I don't give a rat's fat ass about what your friends think." Stacy immediately became irritated by Lena's comment.

"Mom, lighten up. I was only kidding," Lena said as she sat down at the kitchen table. "It's cool, you guys love each other so much. My friends say that their parents are nowhere near as affectionate as you guys are. I tell them that my parents act lovey-dovey all the time."

"And what do you know about acting lovey-dovey?" Marshall inquired of his daughter.

"Come on, Dad, get with it. I'm about to go to high school. Besides, I think it's nice that you guys hardly ever argue and you're always happy to see each other. When I get married, my husband is going to be super rich, worship the ground I walk on, and romance me until the day I die," Lena said with absolute certainty.

"Well, allow me to enlighten you on a few things, Miss Know-It-All." Stacy placed Lena's food in front of her. "Marriage takes a lot of hard work, patience, and sacrifice. And a man is much more than someone who gives you money and romances you.

Secondly, I don't even want you thinking about marriage, babies or a family of your own until you are out of college." Stacy had insisted time and again that Lena remained focused on getting a college education and not think about the rosy world of romance—at least not at her young age.

"Yeah, I hear you," Lena muttered softly.

"Besides, you shouldn't rush to get old. You should enjoy being a little girl," Stacy continued.

"Mom! I'm not a 'little girl.'" Lena hated it when her mother called her a "little girl."

"Okay, you're a young lady. But you're still too young to be concerned with romance," Stacy said, with absolute resolve.

"Yes, Mom," Lena answered her mockingly.

"Lena, I'm not trying to be mean-spirited. You're a bright, intelligent young lady with a good head on your shoulders. And I love you. But there is only one queen in this house."

"That's right," Marshall chimed in, "and there is only one princess in this house as well." Lena smiled at her father, who seemed to understand her a little better than her mother did.

"That means stay away from those boys. Especially senior boys," Stacy added as an afterthought.

"Boys? What boys?" Marshall didn't like the idea of his daughter dating.

"Don't worry about it, Marshall. Lena and I have had several mother-daughter conversations during her piano lessons," Stacy clued Marshall in.

Stacy set Marshall's plate in front of him, then grabbed her own and sat down.

"Lena, would you please say grace?" asked Stacy as the three of them held hands.

"Thank you, God, for our food that we're about to receive

and for our health. Thank you, God, for blessing me with a wonderful father and mother who love me, protect me, and guide me. Amen." Lena smiled at both of her parents.

"That's my baby." Stacy squeezed her daughter's hand, letting her know she was very proud of her. "Where are you guys riding to today?" Stacy asked.

"I'm going to put the bikes on the rack and drive to the lake front. We'll start up north on Fullerton Street, ride back south to Forty-ninth Street, and then swing around and come back."

"Marshall, that's a long distance. Don't have my baby out there stranded," Stacy cautioned.

"Mom, don't worry. It will be a piece of cake. I'm a much stronger rider now. Daddy has been training me so that I'll be able to do a fifty-mile ride. Eventually, I'll be able to do a one hundred-mile ride just like him." Lena reached over and placed her hand atop her father's.

"You guys be careful. I don't want you riding your bikes out in the street. People drive crazy nowadays. Especially young folks. They drive with the seat reclined and music turned up loud enough to wake the dead."

"I'm teaching her everything she needs to know, babes. How to keep a pace, how to hold her position in a line, and how to listen to what her body tells her. She's doing great and, as she continues to improve, I think we'll be able to do an organized ride before this summer is over."

"I don't understand what your-all's fascination is with riding a bike long distance. When I was a little girl, riding around the neighborhood was good enough for me. Doesn't your behind start hurting, Lena?" Stacy asked.

"It used to, but it doesn't anymore. I've gotten used to it," Lena said as she placed a spoonful of food in her mouth.

"Well, make sure you don't fall and scrape up your fingers; you've got piano practice on Monday," Stacy said.

"Mom, I don't fall anymore. I'm almost a professional."

"Well, professional or not, don't fall. Oh, and when you get home, take down your hair so I can wash it and style it."

"Can we talk about that?" Lena asked. "I mean, I'm fourteen years old now and the pigtails are a bit much for a girl my age."

"What do you mean? I like the way your mother does your hair," Marshall asked.

"She wants to get a perm and her hair cut like Rihanna, Marshall. Remember?"

"Oh, yeah, I forgot about that," Marshall mumbled.

"Well, can I get a perm, Daddy?" Lena asked.

"That's between you and your mother," Marshall said, backing out of the conversation.

"No it isn't," argued Stacy. "If she gets a perm, it means one of us is going to have to pay to keep her hair maintained."

"And?" Marshall said.

"It can get a little on the pricey side, Marshall. She'll have beauty shop visits at least twice a month. And every four to six weeks she's going to need a touchup, and that's going to cost more."

"Do you think it's worth it?" Marshall asked Stacy.

"It's not a question of whether I think it's worth it or not. It's about maintaining it."

"Daddy, please let me get a perm so that I don't look like a runaway slave after all workouts."

"Lena, your hair is beautiful the way it is." Marshall reached out to stroke her hair.

"Geeze!" Lena slumped down in her seat and began pouting.

"Give me some time to think about it, okay?" Marshall said.

"Stop pouting, Lena; he didn't say no. But I'll make sure he does say no if you don't straighten yourself out in that seat." Lena immediately sat up in her seat. She glanced at her father, who winked at her. She smiled back; she was going to get her way.

The three of them finished eating breakfast and Lena automatically began doing the dishes without having to be told. After that, she went about the business of doing her chores. Marshall went out to the garage and pulled the bikes down from the roof rack. A short time later, Stacy came out to her car, parked in the driveway.

"Okay, I'm off," she said to Marshall, who was checking the tire pressure on the bikes.

"Okay, baby, good luck." Marshall kissed her good-bye.

"Oh, and, Marshall, have that dick standing at attention for me tonight. I'm going to want a good ride myself." She blew him a kiss, then got in her car.

"You are so nasty, but I like it." Marshall laughed.

"Don't overdo it today." She smiled, then pulled off.

— 7 —
LUTHER

Luther meandered toward his fire-damaged apartment building on Prairie Street, which looked more gruesome than ever. The brown brick was charred with black blemishes from the fire that prior Saturday. It was the first time Luther had been back since the fire, and the site of his destroyed home caused a swell of untamed emotions to fill his heart. He slowly shuffled up the steps and was greeted by the stench of charred wood, seared metal, and scorched brick. The unpleasant order of stagnant water, which floated through the air, was almost overpowering. He cuffed his hand and covered his nose, not wanting to inhale toxic fumes too deeply.

There was a flimsy barrier of yellow police tape that crisscrossed the doorway that Luther yanked down. He stepped inside the building hallway crunching on broken glass with each step before reaching the door of his basement apartment. The moment he turned the doorknob, the door fell off its hinges, tumbled violently down the steps of his apartment, and splashed in some standing water. Luther then realized the building was probably a structural hazard and extremely dangerous for him to be in. However, at that moment, he didn't care. He was determined to see if any of his belongings had survived the blaze. He nervously crept down the steps into the bowels of his pitch-black apartment.

With each step he took, the wooden step hissed and split, threatening to detach from the wall and leave him stranded in the dark, hollow belly of the building. It was pure black inside his apartment so he turned on a flashlight he'd borrowed from a local merchant. Luther truthfully thought he'd be able to salvage something, but from the looks of things, nothing was worth keeping. He waded through the puddles of water and went from one end of his apartment to the other, looking at gaping holes that allowed him to walk through the walls in order to enter another room. There were colossal craters in the ceiling that allowed him to look straight up to the third floor of the building. Water was still streaming down through one of the holes. He made his way toward the kitchen and sitting on the window sill was his toolbox. He picked it up and moved toward a sliver of sunlight, splintering in from above. Luther stood silently for a moment, holding onto his only possession as he brooded over his situation. He was unemployed, homeless, and penniless.

"Damn!" he howled with disgust. At that moment, he heard one of the wooden planks on the steps split. Someone was coming, *but who*? he wondered. *Who would come into a burned-out building?* Luther stepped back through a wall and into the front room where the steps were to see who had come in.

"Who in the hell are you?" a thunderous voice demanded to know. Luther flinched; the voice startled the hell out of him. He squinted his eyes since the person was shining a flashlight beam into his eyes.

"I'm going to ask you one more time. Who in the hell are you?" The man's voice was more forceful and stern.

"My name is Luther. I used to live here. Who in the fuck are you?" Luther snarled.

"My name is Quentin. I'm a police officer with the bomb and

arson unit. I'm here investigating the cause of this fire." Quentin coughed a few times.

"Would you please take the light off of my eyes, man." Luther had grown tired of squinting.

"You do realize it's not safe to be in here, don't you?" Quentin asked, questioning Luther's mental state.

"Yeah, I know. I was trying to see if I had anything left worth keeping." Quentin lowered the light from Luther's eyes. He then flashed the beam toward the ceiling and glared at the black stains from the damage.

"Where were you when the fire broke out?" Quentin asked as he continued to survey the damage.

"I was at the auto parts store," Luther answered as he made his way toward Quentin.

"Did you leave the stove or anything on?" Quentin continued to question Luther.

"No, the damn thing was ancient and didn't work well. I had to constantly fiddle with the gas pipe." Luther was now directly before Quentin.

"Why, was it leaking gas?" Quentin asked.

"This building was always leaking some type of odor. When I came in from work one day, my apartment smelled like gas. Other times, it smelled like raw sewage. So you tell me, was it the stove or the sewer gas that sparked the fire?"

"Do you smoke cigarettes, Luther?" Quentin purposely ignored Luther's question.

"What's up with all of the questions? I didn't set this place on fire." Luther was suddenly edgy and suspicious of Quentin.

"I didn't say you did. But, from the looks of things, the fire started in your unit." Quentin went over to the seared stove. "How long do you think the stove had been malfunctioning?"

"Shit, man, I don't know. The place came with the stove. For all I know, the damn thing has been that way for years," Luther answered with agitation.

"Did you report the faulty stove to the landlord?" Quentin asked, unafraid of Luther's jumpiness.

"No." Luther knew Packard wouldn't have given a rat's ass about the faulty stove.

"My hunch is that vagrants loitering outside of your window inadvertently caused this fire. There is a graveyard of cigarette butts and matchsticks on the other side of this window."

"Well, that wouldn't surprise me. The window faces a vacant lot of land. People stand there to drink, smoke, and do whatever, out of the direct eyesight of the police. You know what I mean?" Luther was hoping that Quentin would catch his drift.

"Yeah, I get the picture. Who owns the building?" Quentin turned his attention back to Luther.

"Packard, a dude named Packard," Luther answered as he made a move to exit.

"Does he have a last name?"

"I'm not sure," Luther said, as he took a step.

"Then how did you pay your rent?" Quentin was curious.

"I pay in cash."

"How long have you lived here?"

"Not long." Luther was getting short with Quentin. He wasn't about to tell him anything about Packard.

"Where can I find Packard?"

"The hell if I know, man." Luther was clearly aggravated. If Quentin wasn't a cop, he would have left a long time ago.

"Does he know his property has been damaged?"

"I said, I don't know, man," Luther barked. "This building may be in his name or someone else's. I'm not sure."

Luther took his toolbox and headed back up the stairs and outside. Quentin trailed closely behind him.

"Here, take my card. If you run across this Packard fellow, let him know that I would like to speak with him," Quentin said.

"Okay."

The two of them walked down the sidewalk toward Quentin's unmarked police car.

"Remember, if you see Packard, tell him that I need to speak with him."

"No problem," Luther said as he put Quentin's card in his pocket and watched as he pulled off. No sooner had Quentin turned the corner, than Packard pulled up.

"Luther!" Packard acted as if he were happy to see him.

"How does it feel to be a man standing on his own two feet?" Packard taunted him. Luther couldn't say a word; he was trying to contain his fury. All he could do was glare at Packard with contempt.

"Are you trying to eyeball me, fool?" Packard's tone was a threatening one. Luther forced his eyes to break contact and looked toward the ground.

"No, Packard," Luther mumbled.

"Good. I would hate to think you were trying to buck up on me." At that moment, another car pulled up and a white gentleman wearing a gray business suit and carrying a briefcase got out of the car.

"Finally, this fool has showed up. This lazy son-of-bitch insurance man was supposed to be here a week ago to handle my claim. That's what I get for fucking around with some no-name insurance company." Packard got out of his car and spit on the ground. "Luther, meet Mr. Charlie, my insurance adjuster."

"Hello," Luther greeted the man.

"Nice to meet you," the man said and then he and Packard headed for the burned-out building. Luther was suspicious of Packard so he decided to do some quick snooping. He went over to Packard's SUV and peeped in the window. He saw matchbooks littering the front seat and suspected Packard of purposely aiding the gas-line fire for the insurance money. *That's why Packard said that I would never have to worry about paying rent there again.* Luther began walking away from the Blazer, feeling rage swelling up inside of him. Luther also felt as if he'd arrived at the end of his rope. However, his mind did begin to put together a likely scenario about the fire. *That's why Packard was so damn concerned with getting me out of the building.* Luther had an epiphany. *Packard had been planning to torch the building all along.*

"That son of a bitch purposely did this shit to me." The thrust for revenge quickly penetrated Luther's mind and heart. At that moment, a voice from deep within him told him to steal Packard's Blazer.

"Taking something from Packard is a bold and daring move," Luther said aloud. "But I'd damn sure feel good about it. This is my chance to get even with that fool, for once and for all." Luther looked over at Packard's truck. He was thankful that he hadn't brought any of his goons with him. Luther had no plan as to where he'd go with the vehicle or what he'd do with it once he had it. He wanted to hurt Packard in some way. Luther took a hammer out of his toolbox, approached Packard's ride and smashed out the driver's side window. He was thankful that Packard didn't have an auto alarm. He snatched some wires from under the dashboard, reconfigured them, and stuck a long screwdriver in the ignition. Once he got the car to start, he quickly put it into gear and sped off.

—8—
MARSHALL

Marshall was beginning to sweat as he secured both his and Lena's expensive road bikes atop the roof rack of their blue minivan. As he made his final adjustments, ensuring that the bikes were safe and sound, he heard his cellular phone ring. He pulled out his phone and glanced down at the caller ID.

"Quentin, where are you, man?" Marshall spoke aloud before he answered the phone. He didn't want his brother to hear the frustration in his voice.

"Q, where are you? Lena and I are getting ready to pull off and you're not here. You're still coming on this bike ride with us, right?" Marshall frowned because he sensed that his brother would not be joining them.

"Yo. What's up, man?" Quentin greeted.

"You. Where are you?"

"Well, it looks like I'm not going to make it this time around. I hate having to cancel on you like this, but I've got this suspicious apartment fire that I'm investigating. I have a pushy insurance adjuster and the building's owner on their way to see me. He was also bitching about his car being stolen and is finishing up a missing vehicle report with an officer on the scene," Quentin explained.

"Tell them to wait until Monday morning. What's the big rush for the police paperwork?" Marshall asked. He really wanted his brother to join him on this outing. Marshall had been looking forward to the quality family time the three of them would spend together.

"I would, but the captain is on my back to bring this one to a close. Why? I don't know but those are the orders that I'm under," Quentin continued, to explain the bind that he was in.

"Is this that fire that happened last week that I read about in the paper?" Marshall asked, vaguely recalling the suspicious apartment building fire.

"Yeah, was over on Prairie Street. I drove over there earlier today."

"That's dangerous. Be careful."

"Marshall, this is what I do for a living, remember? I came back to the station and was all set to leave and head your way." Quentin sighed. "Then the captain called me and told me that he wanted me to close this one sooner rather than later."

"I understand. Do what you've got to do. You can catch Lena and me when we go out on a ride next weekend," Marshall said, despite the raging disappointment in his heart.

"Cool. I'll give you a call tonight to find out how things went. Give Lena my love," Quentin said before saying his final goodbye to Marshall. Marshall and Quentin were very close and the bond they shared was unbreakable. With both men choosing careers in law enforcement, they'd been pushed to their psychological limits and had seen a fair amount of disturbing situations that caused them to lean on each other for support and comfort. Having seen so many tragic situations in their lives caused both men to truly treasure the quality time with each other and family.

"How do I look, Daddy?" Lena asked, as she approached him. Marshall smiled at his daughter, who seemed to have grown up overnight. Lena was a tall and lean young lady with mahogany-colored skin. She had an oval-shaped face and thick black hair that was neatly braided in cornrows. She had on a blue and gold cycling outfit that matched the colors on her bike.

"You look like you're ready to go out and win the Tour de France," Marshall complimented his daughter.

"You never know. I may do that one day," Lena said as she entered the garage.

"You're right. You probably could win, with your competitive spirit." Marshall loved that Lena was into fitness and sports. By being active, it would help her to build self-confidence.

"Are you about set?" he asked Lena as he tossed a duffle bag filled with cycling gear into the minivan.

"Yeah. I'll be ready in a moment. I have to run back inside the house real quick, to see if my cycling gloves are in my room. I could have sworn that I left them out here in the garage." Lena exited the garage and trotted through the back yard toward the house.

She returned a short time later with the gloves. Marshall then secured the house before driving off toward the bike path that ran along Chicago's lake front. The day was perfect for the ride he had planned. The sky was blue and crisp and there wasn't a cloud in the sky. When Marshall and Lena arrived at their starting point, Marshall was thankful that he was able to locate a parking space immediately. Once the minivan was parked, both Marshall and Lena began the process of removing their road bikes and gathering up their gear. Marshall made some last-minute adjustments to both of their road bikes and then locked the minivan.

"Are you ready, Daddy?" Lena had one foot already locked in place on her pedal.

"You first. I'll be right behind you!" Marshall exclaimed as he placed his car keys in the rear pouch of his cycling jersey. The two rode along at a leisurely pace, maneuvering their way around joggers, dog walkers, rollerbladers, and people out for a stroll. Marshall allowed Lena to lead, so he would ride at her pace and not inadvertently leave her behind. He also wanted to keep a close eye on her, to look for signs of fatigue, in case she bit off more than she could chew with riding a longer distance. Before long, they reached Oak Street Beach, packed with sunbathers and street vendors selling cold drinks.

"Can we stop and get something to drink from the concession stand?" Lena asked as she coasted along, looking over her shoulder at Marshall.

"Yeah, that's a good idea," Marshall agreed, wanting to make sure she stayed well-hydrated. "How are you feeling so far?"

"I feel great. I'm not tired or sore in the least." Lena dismounted her bike.

"What about your legs?" Marshall wanted to be absolutely sure that she wasn't fatigued.

"Daddy, really, I'm okay. I can handle this ride. My legs feel strong. They're not stinging or anything. I told you. I'm ready for a nice long ride like this. I wish Uncle Quentin could've made it, though. He makes me laugh all of the time," Lena said as she approached the small concession stand. Marshall purchased two bottles of Gatorade from the vendor and they drank them before continuing along. It felt wonderful to be out with Lena. Marshall enjoyed their casual conversation about how excited she was to be entering high school and about how she couldn't wait for basketball tryouts.

"I'm going to see if I'm good enough to play on the varsity team," Lena said excitedly.

"Slow down, Lena, and take one step at a time."

"But I'm good enough to play with the older kids. You and I both know it."

"You're good. I'll give you that, but you have to take baby steps before you can run."

"We can skip the baby steps and go for it all," Lena said jokingly. In what seemed like no time at all, they approached Navy Pier, a large tourist attraction filled with shops, entertainment, and souvenirs. They rode past the pier and headed toward Grant Park. Grant Park was overcrowded with people because of the annual "Taste of Chicago" food festival.

"Daddy, we should go over there," Lena suggested. It was clear to Marshall that she wanted to be in the middle of everything.

"Not today. We don't have any locks for the bikes. And pushing a bike through a crowd that enormous would be a real hassle. Maybe you, your mother, and I will come down tomorrow and walk around."

They continued on toward Hyde Park and Lena was cycling masterfully—much better than Marshall had anticipated. Lena was a becoming a strong rider and Marshall loved that she listened to his instructions as they coasted along. *She's such a good girl*, he thought. Before long, they made it to Fifty-first Street and crossed over Lake Shore Drive via the overhead walkway. For doing so well on the ride, Marshall wanted to treat her to ice cream from Baskin-Robbins, which was just ahead of them. Even if she ran into a little fatigue on the way back, he was proud of her.

Once there, they decided to get out of the blazing heat and sit inside the air-conditioned ice cream parlor. Lena ordered a scoop of Rainbow Sherbet, her favorite flavor. Marshall ordered himself a scoop of Black Walnut ice cream, then located a table where the two of them sat.

"Whatever happened to Dana, your girlfriend who went out with us for ice cream a few months ago?" Marshall asked with interest.

"It's a long story," Lena said as she enjoyed her treat.

"Long story? What happened?" Marshall pressed his daughter for more details.

"She's not my friend anymore. I told Mom about what happened just before eighth-grade graduation," Lena explained.

"And?" Marshall wanted Lena to continue.

"Daddy. It was just…okay." Lena paused and then huffed. "You promise you won't get mad if I tell you what happened."

"I promise. I will not get mad." Marshall wiped the corners of his mouth with a napkin.

"I'm serious. I don't want you getting all mad." Lena was very cautious.

"Sweetie, you can tell me anything. I've told you that a thousand times. You can always talk to me. I don't want you to ever be afraid to talk to me."

"Okay. I'm not friends with Dana anymore because of something she did."

"What did she do?" Marshall asked casually.

"She was really liking this boy named Derek, who was on the eighth-grade basketball team. Derek didn't even know she existed because he had a girlfriend," Lena explained. "So one day, Dana told me that she was going to make Derek her boyfriend. When I asked how she was going to do that, she told me that she didn't know yet, but Derek was going to be her boyfriend, one way or another. Then, just before graduation, Dana sent me a text message asking me to meet her after school behind the building."

"But you've been told to walk home every day directly after school," Marshall reminded her.

"I know, but this one time I didn't. Dana said that it was very important that I meet her after school, so I said, okay, but only for a minute. So when the dismissal bell rang, I went to my locker, got my stuff, and went around to the back of the building. When I got there, Derek and a few of the boys from the basketball team were with Dana. When I asked what was going on, Dana says to me, 'I told you I was going to make him my boyfriend.' The next thing I knew, all of the boys on the team formed a big circle around Derek and Dana so that they could make out. From what I could see, his dirty little hands were all over her. She let him touch her breasts and her butt. I was like, 'Ya'll are nasty!' and I was about to turn and leave. Then all of the boys formed a circle around me and wouldn't let me leave."

"They did what?!" Marshall tried not to sound angry, but he couldn't help it. As a loving and caring father, he wanted to always be around to protect his baby.

"You promised not to get mad, Daddy," Lena reminded him. Marshall took a deep breath and allowed Lena to continue.

"So one of the boys said to me, 'Why don't you get with the program and get down with us like Dana is' and I was like, 'Ya'll are trippin'.' So I tried to push my way through the closed circle, but they wouldn't let me out. One of the boys tried to touch me and I backed away. I told them, 'If anyone touches me, there will be hell to pay.' Well, I guess they didn't believe me. One boy touched my shoulder and I dropkicked him so hard in his Johnson that I swear I saw his eyeballs pop out. He fell to his knees and I ran all the way home."

"Why didn't you say something to me about this?" Marshall demanded.

"Daddy, there was really nothing for you to do. Besides, I handled myself very well."

"They were holding you against your will, honey. I could've at least talked to the principal about it and we could've identified the young men and had a very serious conversation with them." Marshall made sure that he spoke in a very calm manner even though, on the inside, he was riled up.

"Well, Mom told me to tell you, but it slipped my mind. I was focused on doing well on my final exams. Then Mom and I got caught up shopping for a graduation dress, getting my hair styled, and all of that stuff. It really wasn't as bad as it sounds."

"So what happened to Dana?" Marshall wanted to know the rest of the story.

"She actually called me later that day and asked me if I thought she was a whore. I was like, 'Yeah, you are a whore.' After that, we stopped talking. I don't want to be around some chick who tries to set me up to be groped on by a gang of boys."

"I think you've done the right thing by putting some distance between you and her. But I'm still concerned that Dana is headed down that particular path. Her actions scream 'low self-esteem.'"

"Dana does have a self-esteem problem. She's always kissing butt and trying to get people to like her. Sometimes she acts so phony when she's around the popular kids."

"If she's not careful, she's going to be a teenage mother," Marshall said as he finished off his treat.

"Dana's mother had her when she was very young. That's why her grandparents are raising her. I think her mom is way out there. I'm not sure if Dana's mom is on drugs or if she's just crazy. Dana never likes to talk about her mother." Lena bit into her ice cream cone.

"What about her father?" Marshall asked.

"He's in jail, I think."

"Wow," Marshall said as he sat and thought about Dana. In his mind he wanted to do more to help young people through their teen years. As he looked at Lena, he began to think about her as a toddler. He thought about all of the hopes and dreams he had for her. He thought about his personal pledge to make sure that she was always safe, never wanted for anything, and had plenty of opportunities to succeed. After hearing what Lena had gone through, he immediately recognized the need for more men of honor and integrity to step up and take ownership of kids who might be on their own.

"Are you ready to head on back?" Marshall asked.

"I'm ready," Lena said, rising to her feet. Marshall tossed out their trash and then stepped back out into the blazing sun.

"Come here, Lena," Marshall said. Lena turned and stepped closer to him. Marshall then embraced her tightly and kissed her on the forehead.

"I'll always be here for you, if you need me," he whispered to her.

"I know, Daddy," Lena whispered back. "I love you."

"I love you, too," Marshall said as his heart swelled with love and pride.

Both Marshall and Lena mounted their road bikes. Lena waited for a moment to get instructions from Marshall about their route.

"Do you want to take a different route back?" he asked.

"It doesn't matter. I'm cool with whichever way we go."

Marshall briefly thought about taking a side street instead of the bike path along the lake front but then quickly changed his mind for safety concerns. "Let's ride down the sidewalk back toward the bike path."

"Cool." Lena began heading in the direction of the bike path.

The path was adjacent to Lake Shore Drive. Marshall briefly glanced over at the moving traffic and noticed a motorist in a high-performance car who appeared to be traveling faster than necessary. After the car disappeared down the road, he then turned his attention back to Lena and they continued to ride side by side laughing and talking. Lena was filling Marshall in on all of the juicy gossip on celebrities that she'd been reading about in her magazines. Marshall listened attentively as she talked about singer Ne-Yo.

"He is going to be my husband someday," Lena proclaimed. "Just the thought of being his wife is exciting."

"Wait, what about the other little rapper you used to like when you were younger? What's his name?" Marshall paused in thought. "Little Puppy Chow?"

"No, Daddy. His name isn't Puppy Chow; it's Bow Wow," Lena corrected him.

"Same difference." Marshall laughed.

"I love Bow Wow, too," Lena admitted.

"You're only fourteen years old. Give yourself some time to really fall in love. Right now you're just infatuated," Marshall lovingly teased his daughter.

"Dad, I'm just joking around. I really don't want to marry either one of them. It's a fantasy. I've got so much that I want to do before I settle down. I have to finish high school, as valedictorian, of course. Then I have to decide on which historically black college I want to attend. After I graduate, I'm going to head off to graduate school and get my Ph.D. in psychology. Then I'm going to start my practice and help people deal with their emotional and psychological troubles. After that, I'm going to write a book about how to succeed in life. Once those things are done, I might have time to slow down enough to find a husband and settle down."

"That's my baby! Keep your head on straight and your eyes on the prize. They'll be plenty of time for boys when you are forty-five years old."

"Forty-five! I'm not waiting that long, Daddy." Lena glanced over at him as if he'd lost his mind. Marshall laughed out loud.

"I'll let you in on a little secret. Daddies don't like the idea of having to give away their daughters at any age." Marshall continued to laugh.

"Well, you're going to have to get over that one." They approached a water fountain on the path and Marshall began to slow down.

"I'm going to pull over and get some water. Keep going and I'll catch up with you," he instructed Lena.

"Okay," Lena said and continued on. Once Marshall satisfied his thirst, he mounted his road bike once again and zoomed off to catch up with Lena. She'd gotten a good one hundred meters ahead of him. As Marshall willed himself to pedal faster and reel Lena in, his focus was taken off of her and shifted to the traffic moving along Lake Shore Drive. Several motorists were blowing their horns at another vehicle that was driving erratically. The erratic SUV suddenly picked up speed, veered off Lake Shore Drive and zoomed across the landscape. Marshall immediately thought the driver was suicidal, planned to cut across the bike path, and drive directly into Lake Michigan and drown himself. As he followed the angle of the out-of-control vehicle, he noticed that it was on a direct collision course with Lena.

"Lena!" He screamed her name at the top of his lungs. His heart began racing as a bolt of panicky adrenaline shot through him. Lena heard him, pulled over onto the grass and stopped directly in the path of the Blazer. She didn't see the vehicle coming and had no time to react. The sound of the impact was hauntingly loud and eerily silent at the same time. Marshall pumped his pedals as fast as he could and got to Lena in a flash. She'd been knocked off of the bike and tossed in the air about twenty-five yards away from the impact.

"It's not that bad, it's not that bad, it's not that bad—" he kept repeating to himself as he tossed the bike to the ground and dropped to his knees next to her. Lena's body was going into shock and shaking uncontrollably.

"Lena, baby, I'm here!" Marshall took a quick survey of her body. Her left leg was crushed completely, and there was a deep gash in her abdomen that was bleeding heavily. Her hair and face were streaming with blood since her helmet had gotten knocked off. Her body continued to twitch violently as she began slipping away from him.

"It's okay, baby. It's not that bad. You're going to be just fine." Marshall smeared away the blood that was on her face and looked into her eyes, which were wide open and fixed on his.

"Somebody help me! Call nine-one-one! Please!" Marshall screamed. He panicked. He couldn't locate his cell phone and feared that he may have inadvertently left it inside of the mini-van. Lena's breathing became fast and frantic. Lena managed to raise her arm up and Marshall immediately took hold of her hand. It was clear that she was having trouble getting oxygen. Her almond eyes began floating upward.

"Lena! You hang on! Daddy's getting help!" Marshall was afraid to move, afraid to do anything accept remain with her.

Lena squeezed Marshall's hand as tightly as she could before her eyes gently rolled upward and disappeared.

"Lena!" Marshall cried out her name just as her hand went limp. She was gone.

"Lena!" Marshall shrieked. "Lena! Come on, baby." Marshall repositioned himself and embraced her body. At that moment, grief began to choke the life out of Marshall. It was as if some-one had poured a pail of bitterly cold ice water down his back. He bucked his spine, arched his head back, and tearfully gazed up at the sky. His mouth dropped open wide and he attempted to howl out mournfully but no sound would pass through his lips. His chest only ballooned with suffering pain until he could only inhale short wisps of air. Finally, when his body could no longer inhale air, it stopped moving as if every part of his being had become unexplainably lifeless and frozen in an instant. Then his body yielded and allowed him to exhale, forcing Marshall to scream out in grief-stricken anguish.

—9—
CARMEN

Saturday evening, Carmen was walking down her block heading home from Blockbuster Video. She was all set to enjoy a calm evening sitting at home and watching the movie *Hitch*, starring Will Smith. She hoped that the romantic comedy would help her get through being depressed about her car conking out. It had cost one hundred and fifty dollars to have her car towed back home from the police impound and an additional fifty dollars parking violation fee for parking in front of a fire hydrant.

"I'm broke as hell," Carmen muttered to herself as she approached her building. She let herself inside the building and then in her condo. She walked into the kitchen, opened up the refrigerator, and pulled out the pint container of Ben & Jerry's chocolate ice cream along with a two-liter bottle of Pepsi. With a glass of soda and ice cream in hand, she headed to her bedroom. She popped in the DVD and moved back to her bed, where she sat Indian-style. She grabbed the television remote and then her ice cream. She turned on the television just in time to catch a segment of the evening news.

"Today, on the city's South Side, there was a fatal hit-and-run accident. What was supposed to be a fun summer outing for a father and his daughter quickly turned tragic when the driver of an out-of-control vehicle veered off Lake Shore Drive, striking and killing a fourteen-year-old girl. The driver of the vehicle then fled the scene, even though witnesses tried to restrain him until police arrived. An eyewitness saw the entire tragic event." Carmen was thunderstruck as she listened to a man wearing a Chicago White Sox T-shirt describing what had happened.

"It was the most horrible thing I've ever seen," said the man. "I was jogging along the path when I saw the SUV come speeding across the grass and onto the path. When the father saw the out-of-control vehicle, he called out his daughter's name. As she stopped to see what he wanted, the vehicle slammed into her. It was horrible. I'm still shaking from what I saw. It was horrific." Carmen gasped at the eyewitness account. The newscaster continued with the rest of the details.

"Chicago area detectives are now searching for that vehicle, which fled the scene, and the person who was driving it. If you have any information—." Carmen clicked the DVD remote and her movie started. Listening to the story about the little girl was depressing her even more than she already was. She loved children; that was the reason that she'd become a teacher. She couldn't wait to become a mother herself. More often than not, she found herself stopping by the baby department whenever she went shopping. She enjoyed looking at the different styles of baby cribs, blankets, and outfits. The tiny bibs, socks, and undershirts warmed her heart. She would often daydream and think that if she had a little girl, she'd have her dressed up in beautiful little dresses with matching shoes, along with matching hair ribbons. If she had a little boy, she'd dress him up in little blue jean outfits that snapped apart, making it easy to change his diaper. Now that she'd turned thirty, the yearning for a child increased. On several occasions, she had thought about going to the fertility clinic and picking out some sperm. But she didn't have the guts.

Just as Carmen's movie was getting interesting, someone buzzed her doorbell. Not expecting any company, she had a half-mind not to answer. She paused her movie and headed over to the intercom system on the wall next to the front door.

"Who is it?" she asked.

"It's me, Nikki. Open up the door." Carmen buzzed her sister into the building. Nikki walked in the door wearing a low-cut blouse that revealed more cleavage than necessary. She also had on tight shorts that clung to her behind so snugly that Carmen could see Nikki's ass cheeks plopping out from beneath the fabric as she walked past her.

"What's wrong with the people in your high-priced-ass condo?" Nikki scoffed. "Your snobby neighbor was acting as if I was a prostitute or something."

"I thought you were into that sort of thing. I thought you liked men ogling at you," Carmen commented as she shut the door and locked it. She followed Nikki through a corridor past the dining room where her cherry wood dinette table was perfectly set. Nikki went into the kitchen and sat down at Carmen's small kitchen table.

"So, what were you in here doing?" Nikki queried as she surveyed Carmen's spotless kitchen wondering to herself if the countertops had ever been used for cooking.

"I was watching a movie and eating ice cream," Carmen replied.

"What are you all upset about?" Nikki asked, knowing her sister's habits all too well.

"What are you talking about?" Carmen answered, not wanting to disclose anything to Nikki.

"I know you. Whenever something is bothering you, the first

thing you do is start eating ice cream. Let me guess, chocolate, right?"

"No!" Carmen lied with a smile.

"Daddy always made you feel better with food whenever you were upset. He catered to your every mood." Nikki had a slight tone of bitterness in her voice.

"What's that supposed to mean?" Carmen answered sharply, sensing an unwanted argument on the horizon. They locked their gazes upon each other as silence hung in the air threatening to erupt if the course of the conversation didn't change.

"Do you have anything to drink?" Nikki asked. Carmen exhaled as she opened up the cabinet above her sink. She pulled down a small glass and then opened up the refrigerator.

"Will papaya juice work for you?" Carmen asked.

"Do you have any gin?"

"No, I don't have any gin." Nikki hadn't been there a solid ten minutes and she was already annoying Carmen. Carmen contained her attitude as best as she could. The last thing she wanted was to get into a bitter argument with her sister. They'd come a very long way since Nikki's high school days and Carmen was so encouraged that she and Nikki were on speaking terms again. Carmen was actually glad that Nikki had dropped by. She wanted to talk to her about a program she'd found at a community college for people who needed to go back to school and get their GED. Carmen knew Papa had to be turning over in his grave, knowing that one of his daughters was working as a peep show girl, exposing her body to strange men for small change. It was obvious Nikki didn't like doing it by the way she complained about the man ogling her when she came into the building. But Nikki would never admit she didn't like what she was doing. She was stubborn like that, but Carmen knew Nikki better than she thought she did. Carmen wasn't going to give up on her sister; she loved her so much and wanted Nikki to see and trust in her own potential.

"Let me see that photo that's stuck on the refrigerator door," Nikki said as she eyed the photo from afar. Carmen handed her the old family photo.

"I remember this day," Nikki said with a smile. "We were having a backyard barbecue." Nikki studied the photo of her, Carmen, and their parents. "We all looked so happy back then. Daddy loved me. He loved us and always wanted the best for the family," Nikki whispered as she glared at the photo. Carmen noticed tears beginning to fill Nikki's eyes.

"Take it, if you want it." Carmen viewed Nikki's sudden emotional state as a breakthrough. She was happy to see that Nikki was recalling some of the lessons their father had tried to instill in them.

"I need to go to the bathroom," Nikki said as she abruptly got up and dashed away. Carmen deduced that it was overpowering to see a photo of herself before she had taken the wrong path. Carmen sighed and then began to think about the past as she waited for Nikki to return.

＊＊＊

The night before their father's death, the three of them were sitting at the dining room table. Anthony, their father, had light-caramel skin and beautiful curly, black hair. He was a tall man with deep-set eyes, thick eyebrows, and a charming smile. Anthony was sitting at the dinner table, helping Nikki study for a big science exam. Carmen entered the room with a calculator to add up the family bills.

"Papa, the phone bill is high this month. In fact it has doubled since last month. It's up to one hundred and twenty dollars." Carmen had become the budget manager of the house shortly after her mother passed away.

"What! How did it get that high?" Anthony was not pleased to hear about the bill.

"I don't know. I haven't been using the phone. Have you made any long distance calls?" Carmen asked.

"No. Check the phone log and see where one hundred and twenty dollars' worth of calls were made to."

Carmen knew the extra expense of the phone bill agitated him. The family was accustomed to living off of two incomes, but when her mother passed on, the loss of income had placed a financial strain on them. While Carmen reviewed the bill, Anthony continued quizzing Nikki for her exam.

"You are so astute. I get the feeling that you are going to be a scientist when you grow up." Nikki was the type of young lady that always needed additional encouragement since she struggled as a student. Anthony understood that Nikki needed extra attention and gave her bundles of love and support.

"Really, Papa? Do you think I can be a scientist?" Nikki asked, not truly believing in herself or Anthony's assessment of her intelligence.

"Of course I do, Nikki. When you apply yourself, that brilliant mind of yours shines through. What I think is that you're so smart that you intimidate the other kids in your eighth-grade class, which is why they pick on you sometimes and try to make you feel less intelligent than you are." Anthony paused and smiled at Nikki. "You have to stop allowing other people to sell you bad energy. You have to be your own person. You have to be confident and strong." Anthony continued to plant seeds of knowledge so that Nikki could grow mentally and emotionally stronger.

"Hmmm. It seems as if a majority of the phone calls were made past ten-thirty at night and were made to this number." Carmen pointed out the number to her father.

"Wait a minute. No one but me is allowed to be on the phone after nine o'clock, and I haven't been on the phone." Anthony took the bill and reviewed it more closely.

"Well, it wasn't me," Carmen quickly responded. "I know we're on a tight budget. I'll bet Nikki has been slipping around calling that boy from Indiana," Carmen accused her sister.

"You need to get out of my business and get some of your own!" Nikki barked at Carmen for ratting her out.

"You're not old enough to have any business!" Carmen matched Nikki's anger and resentment.

"Hey! Both of you shut your mouths right now!" Their father's heavy commanding voice boomed over theirs. "Carmen, you're older and should have more self-control over your outbursts. Nikki…" Anthony turned his focus back to her.

Nikki folded her arms across her chest and stared up at a corner in the ceiling, dreading the lecture she was about to get.

"Look at me when I'm talking to you," her father snapped. Nikki challenged him by not complying with his order. "You've got three seconds to roll your eyes down from your head before I twist your neck off." Nikki reluctantly met his gaze. Anthony leaned in close to her, meeting her gaze and refusing to let it go.

"You know the rules of this house. We do not lie to each other. We respect each other and we do not sneak around! Understood?" Anthony thumped his index finger against the table several times.

"I haven't been sneaking around, Papa," Nikki lied. "I would never sneak around behind your back."

"Yeah, right!" Carmen knew that Nikki was trying to stick to her lie, even though she was clearly busted.

"Carmen!" Anthony gave Carmen a warning. "If you sneak around on the phone, you will sneak around out in the street. And no daughter of mine is going to be sneaking around behind my back." Anthony was very firm with Nikki. "That is not an option! My job as your father is to educate you, love you, and provide a good home for you. I'm not raising some young lady who can't take care of herself and has to resort to dancing on a pole at a strip club." Anthony's intense gaze upon Nikki made her feel horrible and her tears began to flow.

"But I'm not doing anything like that," Nikki fired back as her tears continued to run like a waterfall.

"And I never want you to. I don't want you to be the woman that my mother was. I don't want you dancing around naked in front of lustful men who only want to use you for their personal pleasures. I don't want you sneaking around with some young man whose only desire is to get between your thighs." Anthony didn't tone down his words. He was very direct and very clear. "Nikki, I'm very disappointed with you. After your mother died, the three of us sat down and discussed what we'd have to make in order to live on just my income. We are on a budget and you've caused us to go over it. So, in order for us to get back on track, you are going to have to find a way for us to save one hundred dollars. When the Sunday paper arrives, it will be your responsibility to clip coupons."

"Papa, I don't want to clip coupons! I hate when we go to the store and hold up the line with stacks of coupons. It's embarrassing. I feel as if we're on welfare or something."

"I don't care if you're embarrassed!" Anthony was angry at her response. "I'm doing the best that I can, Nikki, and I'm not going to let you or anyone else make me feel bad because things are a little tight." Anthony's jaws were tight. It was a clear indication to Nikki that he meant every word he said.

"Fine," Nikki answered defiantly.

"Good; now you're grounded for two weeks. No television and no phone privileges for you. You and I are also going to continue our conversation about boys as soon as I'm finished writing the monthly checks."

"My life sucks," Nikki grumbled. "Can I go to my room?"

"Yes."

Nikki got up and left the room, stomping her feet in protest before allowing herself to burst into tears.

"This place feels like a prison!" she shouted as she hustled up the stairs to her bedroom.

"I don't know what I'm going to do with her," Anthony griped. "She is becoming very defiant, and I don't understand why."

"Hormones, Dad," Carmen suggested.

"What?" Anthony didn't fully understand.

"It's her hormones. I don't think you'll ever be able to fully understand what a woman goes through," Carmen tried to explain.

"Well, you're older. Help me understand?" Anthony truly wanted to know her point of view.

"I'll talk to her, Dad. Maybe she'll listen to me," Carmen offered, hoping to ease some of her father's burden.

"No need for that, Carmen." Anthony wasn't about to shift his burdens onto Carmen. "Nikki is being difficult for a reason that I'm going to find out. Being hardheaded is no way to go through life. Nikki has a tendency to lie to me and I don't like it. I will not have my daughter sneaking around behind my back like some wayward hound." Anthony raised his voice in anger. "My daughter will not be the type of young lady that has a gang

EARL SEWELL

of boys trailing behind her trying to sniff her ass. My mother was that type of woman. As one man entered in the front door, another one was running out the back door." Anthony paused and sighed. "Let me see all of the bills," he said and then began the process of writing checks.

— —

Nikki returned from the bathroom and guzzled down her papaya juice. Carmen waited, searching for the perfect moment to present Nikki with her proposal about going back to school and obtaining a GED.

"I need one hundred dollars from you," Nikki said as she slammed down her glass.

"What?" Carmen asked, not expecting her sister to ask for money.

"You heard me the first time. Why do I have to repeat it?" Nikki's words were demanding and forceful.

"Nikki, I don't have one hundred dollars to give you, especially right now, with my car in need of repairs," Carmen added with a sigh.

"Yes, you do, Carmen. You always have money. Don't you want to help me?" Nikki attempted to make her sister feel guilty.

"Help with what, Nikki?" Carmen asked.

"I'm in a jam with one of my bills. When I get paid, I'll get it back to you."

"Get paid? Did you get yourself a regular job?" Carmen asked with a bit of hope.

"No, but I've met this dude with some big connections. His name is Packard. He's about to make some moves and open up this gentlemen's club called Big Daddy's where I can dance. He said with my sexy looks and hot body, I can pull in big money— as much as one thousand dollars a night."

"A gentlemen's club, Nikki?" Carmen was totally disappointed.

"I'll be doing the exact same thing I'm doing now, Miss Judgmental. The only thing that will change is I'll be making twice as much money, and I don't see a problem with that."

"I'm afraid for you, Nikki," Carmen said, taking Nikki's empty glass and placing it in the sink to be washed later.

"Afraid? Why? It's safer than being a peep show girl at the adult bookstore. I am tired of exposing myself for chump change. I'm ready to make some big money. Packard even talked about taking me to Las Vegas. He knows some high-rollers out there who are always looking for girls like me."

"You see, that's what I mean." Carmen had found an opportunity to question if Nikki was really happy with what she was doing. "You don't sound as if you're very happy with your life. I found a GED program you can take. You can go back to school, get your diploma, and take a decent job. In fact, I am sure I could pull a few strings with the principal at my school and get you a clerical job in the school office while you go through the program." Carmen sat back down at the table with Nikki and noticed how she had tilted the chair up on its hind legs and allowed the back of the chair to land against the wall.

"You could move back in with me, Nikki. As long as you continued working toward getting your diploma, I wouldn't ask you for anything." Carmen paused in thought for a brief moment, then stood up and went into her bedroom to retrieve the paperwork for the program.

"So, what do you think?" Carmen asked upon her return.

"Let me ask you something. Every two weeks you get a paycheck, right?" Nikki asked.

"Yeah, so—"

"Schoolteachers make what? About forty-one or forty-two thousand dollars a year. When you break that down, it comes out to about one thousand dollars a week. If ten dudes come in Big Daddy's and spend one hundred dollars, I've made your salary in one night. If more men come in, then I'll make above and beyond your salary. We're talking cash money here, Carmen. I don't have to worry about taxes or anything. Being an exotic dancer is simple. It's all about catering to men and their egos. It's about giving them the illusion that they're God's gift to women. Now, for that same amount of money, you have to deal with some snotty-nosed kids who are barely able to write their names. You have to deal with the government taking your hard-earned money and deal with the IRS at tax time."

"Teaching is a respectable job, Nikki!" Nikki's hardheadedness was exasperating Carmen. "I don't want you to have to strip for a living because you dropped out of high school. You're so smart, Nikki. All you have to do is apply yourself."

"Oh, boy. Here we go. Now you're sounding like Daddy, trying to make everything in the world be about hard work and respect. He worked his ass off twenty-four-seven and barely had enough money left over to put food on the table. I'm not going to be like that. I'm going to get paid. And if showing my ass to the world puts cash in my pocket, then that's what I am going to do."

"Think about the future, Nikki. You are not going to have your looks forever. What then? What happens if you get sick or need medical attention? How are you going to cover the bills? What about a retirement plan for when you grow old?"

"Shit, I'll be like everyone else and go to Cook County Hospital if I get sick. They don't charge. As far as getting old goes, I haven't figured that one out yet."

"Nikki, you're missing my point." Carmen was growing tired of battling wits with Nikki.

"What point? Since you have some rinky-dink job as a school-teacher, you feel like you're better than me?"

"Nikki, this isn't about me. It's about you. I worry about you. You can do so much more with your life."

"Well, that's why it's my life and not yours. I can do what I want, when I want, and how I want. I am a grown woman now and I don't have to listen to your lectures."

"Nikki, I am not trying to lecture you." Carmen tried to ease the tension in the air. Carmen then tried to take a different approach.

"Nikki, you are right. You are a grown woman and I am not in the business of trying to raise grown folks. All I want you to do is consider what I have said, okay?"

"You know what?!" Nikki got offended. "I don't need your judgmental ass talking to me like I'm some kind of idiot."

"Nikki, let's not fight. I don't want to fight with you. I only want to see you do better for yourself; that's all."

"No, Carmen, you want me to be just like you. And I'll never be like you and I don't want to be. Shit, I didn't have to ask this hard for money from Daddy. It was easy to get it from him. In fact, had you been woman enough to call for help on the night he died, he would still be here and we wouldn't be having this conversation, now would we?" Nikki's words were filled with animosity and ill will.

"You didn't have to say that, Nikki. That was a low blow," Carmen fired back, not willing to take Nikki's insults or criticism.

"Well, the truth hurts now, doesn't it!" Nikki's heart was filled with disgust.

"Is that what you came over here for, Nikki?" Carmen was now upset and it was apparent by the uneven inflections in her voice. "To make me feel like shit, about what happened? I can't change the past. I wish could, but I can't!" Nikki and Carmen glared at each other—neither willing to back down.

"So, are you going to loan me the money or what?" Nikki asked without shame or embarrassment.

"Tell you what. I'll loan you the money if you will agree to at least go down to the place and register for school."

Nikki rolled her eyes a bit before she answered, "Yeah, okay, I'll do it."

"I am serious, Nikki. I'll even go there with you."

"Damn! I said I would," Nikki fired back, annoyed. "What more do you want?" Nikki had grown tired of hearing Carmen's terms.

"Good. Give me a moment to get dressed and we'll walk down to a cash station," Carmen said as she headed toward her bedroom.

—10—
MARSHALL

By the following evening, word had spread throughout the family about the tragic loss. Stacy's parents were on their way from their home in Miami. Neighbors were over offering their help with house cleaning, funeral arrangements, and other small and large tasks that came with the grieving process. There was a gathering of friends from the law enforcement community, both in and out of uniform, who stopped by to offer their support. They also assured Marshall that everything possible would be done to catch the hit-and-run driver and bring him to justice.

"We're going to keep this case in the media and ask the public for as much help as we can," said Taylor, the detective from the Area Two Crime Unit. He was speaking to Marshall and Stacy about the investigation process.

"I can't believe my baby is gone." Stacy wasn't in the right frame of mind to deal with someone speaking to her about the investigation. Marshall held onto her tightly and allowed her to bury her face on his shoulder and cry at will. He, on the other hand, had begun pushing his grief deep down inside so that he could control the powerful and unpredictable emotion.

"Let me assure you, Marshall, that I've got my men on this one. We are not going to let this dirt bag get away," Taylor continued.

"Has anyone located the SUV yet?" Marshall questioned with flames of revenge blazing in his voice and eyes. It was much easier for him to allow the emotions of rage and retribution to come forth rather than his anguish.

"Not yet, but trust me, I will not rest until it is recovered. You have my word on it," Taylor said.

"Has my mother made it here yet?" Stacy mumbled in Marshall's ear. "I want to see my mother."

"She hasn't made it here yet, baby." It tore Marshall apart to see his wife in so much pain. "She's on her way, though." Marshall continued to comfort his wife as best he could.

"Marshall, I feel bad about having to ask more questions at a time like this, but do you remember the license plate number on the truck? None of the eyewitnesses saw the plate number," asked Taylor.

"The only thing I recall are the letters 'CDF.' I would have gotten the full plate but I didn't want to leave my baby," Marshall explained. He got a little choked up but once again clenched his jaws and held his breath in anger so that grief would not consume him.

"Well, as you know, every little bit of information will help," said Taylor, trying to be as reassuring as possible.

"Help!" someone blurted out. "That's what I'm here for." The loud, raspy voice of Stacy's father entered the room before he did. Captain Theodore J. Colman was an ex-military man who had served the country during the Korean War. He loved to boast about how he had served under General Douglas MacArthur during the amphibious landing at Inch'on, and how his unit had fought its way into Seoul, South Korea, and recaptured the capital. After the war, Theodore came home and began working in real estate. Years later, he started his own company, and, over time, became an independently wealthy man. Money was no object to Theodore. In his mind, money could solve anything. Theodore finally invaded the room and stood in the center of the floor where everyone could see him.

"Daddy." Stacy sounded like a frightened adolescent rather than her normal self.

"Don't worry, sweet pea. Daddy is going to catch and punish the heathen responsible for this!" Theodore made eye contact with everyone in the room. He was a tall man who was well into his seventies sporting a military-style crew cut the color of snow. His eyelids sagged downward around the outer edges of the sockets, but his eyes were as sharp as a hawk's. June, Stacy's mother, walked into the room and sat down on the other side of Stacy. She hugged her daughter tightly, causing Stacy to erupt and begin sobbing uncontrollably once again.

"June, take Sweet Pea in the other room. I'll be there in a moment." Theodore cast his gaze upon Marshall. His eyes were full of judgment and disenchantment. Marshall suddenly felt as if he were half the man Theodore was.

"Soldier, give me a status report." Another thing about Theodore that didn't sit well with Marshall was that whenever they had a disagreement about anything, Theodore had a habit of calling him "Soldier." In a matter of two minutes, Theodore had gotten on Marshall's nerves. Theodore had bullied his way into an emotional situation and made it worse.

"The police are doing all they can to locate the car and the person who was driving it." Marshall spoke directly to Theodore.

"It appears to me like there isn't enough being done to find this heathen." Theodore's voice started trailing off like an old lion who'd lost his ability to roar.

"Sir," Taylor, the detective, spoke, "my men are on it. They're out there now searching the entire city for this vehicle. We're even using the media to help get the word out to the public. We're confident someone will call in with a tip."

"Hogwash!" Theodore blurted in a raspy voice. "People aren't going to call in for free. You've got to give them some incentive. I'm going to offer a twenty-five thousand-dollar reward for anyone who can provide information on the heathen responsible for running down my granddaughter! You go and get that out to the media. Let them know money is available. That should get things moving much quicker."

"All right," Taylor said in a calm tone, not allowing Theodore to rattle his cage. "I'll make sure the media gets the information."

"Good man. We're going to hunt this heathen down and smoke him out." Theodore began coughing and couldn't bring himself to speak further. He eventually had to excuse himself and headed into the other room where Stacy and June were. Marshall sat on the nearby sofa, head down between his shoulders.

Quentin kneeled next to Marshall and spoke. "Marshall, don't you let that old man break you down. You need to be strong. Do you hear me?"

"I've fucked up, Quentin. I've fucked up big time, man, and I don't know how to fix this." Marshall blamed himself for everything.

"Marshall, we're going to do all we can. The minute I hear anything, I'll give you a call," Taylor said, then lightly placed his hand on Marshall's shoulder as a gesture of compassion and loyalty.

On Monday morning, Quentin, Marshall, Stacy, June, and Theodore went about the business of making home-going arrangements for Lena. When all arrangements were finalized, Lena's services were scheduled to take place on a Thursday morning.

By Thursday evening, Lena had been put to rest in grand fashion with plenty of flowers and kind words by friends and family. The repast at Marshall and Stacy's house was filled with people who shared fond memories of Lena. By eleven o'clock in the evening, all of the guests had left with the exception of Stacy's parents, who were staying for a little while longer to offer additional support and comfort.

Marshall couldn't sleep at all. He was too wound up and too tense to think about resting. He didn't want to grieve. He wanted to get revenge and vowed to get it one way or another. He went into the basement and unlocked his gun cabinet. He planned to use a special weapon to blow off the head of the man who'd ruined his life. As he was removing one of the revolvers, Theodore approached him from behind.

"What you doing?" Theodore asked.

"Getting ready," Marshall answered as he set several more weapons down on a nearby countertop.

"Getting ready for what?"

"What do you think?" Marshall wasn't in the mood for conversation.

"Marshall—"

"Don't you say a damn word to me right now! I don't want to hear it. Just shut up and leave me alone!" Marshall picked up his weapon and headed back upstairs. He exited the house and went out to his police cruiser. He fired up the squad car, turned on the police radio, and listened. He was hoping that someone would say that they'd found the missing SUV and the fool who was driving it. If and when they did, he planned to issue his own brand of justice.

"Marshall." It was June, Stacy's mother. She'd walked out of the house and caught Marshall before he pulled off.

"What?" Marshall shot daggers at her with his eyes.

"It's Stacy. She really needs you. Can you come in for a moment? Please." It was difficult for Marshall to say no to June who had been like a mother to him as well. Marshall sat in the car for a long moment before killing the motor and heading back into the house.

—11—
LUTHER

When Luther impulsively stole Packard's SUV, he felt an incredible sense of power. He felt as if he'd finally done something to take command over his out-of-control life. As he recklessly sped away in Packard's car, he had no idea of where he was headed or what he wanted to do. He was only living in the moment and celebrating a personal triumph over the man who'd been his oppressor for so long. When Luther drove to a nearby forest preserve, he'd located a secluded parking spot where he'd planned to leave the car until the police or Packard found it. As he was about to step away from the vehicle, he noticed a black duffle bag sitting on the floor behind the driver's seat. Curious as to what was inside, Luther grabbed the bag and unzipped it. Inside, Luther found stacks of paper-wrapped money.

"Oh, shit!" Luther said aloud as he picked up a stack of money. "There is nothing but one hundred-dollar bills here. This must be some kind of payoff money."

He got back into the SUV and locked himself inside. At first, he was feeling very uneasy and unsettled; Packard would be pissed off. But then something happened to him. He told himself, "I deserve this money. Packard burned me out and has pretty much left me homeless. I could use this money to get the fresh start that I've been talking about." Luther felt panicky and overjoyed at the same time.

"I need a little something to calm my nerves and help me think clearly," he said to himself. He drove to a nearby liquor store and picked up a bottle of Hennessy and a bottle of Hypnotiq. Luther drove back to the forest preserve and mixed the two, creating a cocktail called The Incredible Hulk.

"It's time to celebrate!" Luther said out loud as he mixed his drinks and indulged. After guzzling down his liquor, Luther decided that he wanted to spend the night at a luxury hotel in downtown Chicago. He fired up the SUV and sped off toward downtown.

As he drove along, he rummaged through Packard's music collection and found a CD by a rapper named The Game.

"Yeah, this is the shit here!" Luther proclaimed as he placed the CD into the player. He was feeling grand as he drove along with the music blasting loudly. Luther glanced down at the ashtray and noticed several paper-wrapped sticks of marijuana.

"Oh, it keeps getting better and better," he said as he picked up a joint and fired it up. Luther reclined in the seat so that he could relax completely. He turned onto Lake Shore Drive, which offered him a straight shot to all of the downtown Chicago hotels. As he sped along Lake Shore Drive with his music blaring and his joint perched between his fingers, he glanced over at Lake Michigan and tried to appreciate the beauty of the water and Chicago's skyline. He felt incredibly mellow, at ease, and relaxed. His eyes began to get heavy with weariness.

"Oh, it's time for a nap, player," he whispered aloud to himself. Forgetting that he was still driving a vehicle, Luther allowed his intoxication to seduce him into sleep.

"Get out of the car!" Luther was jolted awake by a chorus of screaming voices.

"What?" Luther felt someone tugging on him and instinctively fought them off. "Leave me the fuck alone!" Luther shouted out as he sat upright. He quickly took in his surroundings and realized that something horrible had happened. The SUV had crashed into one of the gigantic shoreline boulders. The motor of the SUV was whining loudly because his foot was still on the gas pedal. Luther lifted his foot and glanced out of the rearview mirror. It was then that he saw a man down on his knees wailing out loud. The wail was a mournful one. Luther adjusted the mirror once again and saw that the man was kneeling next to a body.

"Get out of the car, man!" Someone reached inside of the car and tried to remove the car keys from the ignition." Luther pushed the man to the ground and began to panic as he saw a mob of people moving swiftly toward him.

"You've run over someone!" he heard someone from the mob cry out.

"Oh, God!" Luther panicked and quickly put the SUV in reverse. He backed up and sped away as quickly as he could. He drove recklessly across the landscape and back toward Lake Shore Drive. He blew his horn continuously and almost ran over several joggers in his attempt to flee from the scene.

"I don't want to go to jail." Luther was scared out of his mind. "It was an accident," Luther said out loud as he began to hyperventilate. He drove back onto Lake Shore Drive and sideswiped a concrete barrier. The sound of shattering glass and buckling metal intensified Luther's desperate escape attempt.

"I've got to dump this truck!" he said with fright. "No one saw me. No one saw my face," he tried to convince himself. Luther exited Lake Shore at Thirty-first Street and zoomed west, away from the lake front. He ran a red light and nearly collided with a Chicago Transit Authority Bus. Once he reached Federal Street, where some of the city's public housing projects were located, he drove into the parking lot and parked the Blazer next to a green dumpster. As casually and quickly as possible, Luther grabbed the duffle bag of money and fled.

⸺•⸺

Over the past few days, Luther had worked hard to push the memory of the accident out of his mind. He repeatedly told himself that he never stole Packard's car and wasn't in any way involved in a hit-and-run accident. Luther repeated these thoughts to himself every second of the day until in his mind it became the undisputable and absolute truth.

He took the money he'd found in Packard's Blazer and rented himself a partially furnished studio apartment on Fifty-second Street at the corner of Woodlawn Avenue. The place came with a white stove, a refrigerator, and a small wooden desk that had deep scratches in it. There was also a metal chair and a small color television. There was a Murphy bed that could be raised up and placed in a closet if guests came over. The white tile in the bathroom shower had been recently replaced along with the tile on the kitchen floor. It was perfect for Luther and much better than Packard's dump. Rent was five hundred and fifty dollars a month and Luther paid six months of it in advance. This left him with ample money to buy new clothes, bed linen, dishes, a better television, and a stereo.

A week after the accident, Luther was taking an evening stroll down Fifty-third Street to the local Osco Pharmacy. He picked up paper towels, toothpaste, a toothbrush, soap, deodorant, and a telephone. On the way back to his new apartment, he stopped at a pay phone and contacted the phone company so they could come out and connect the phone line for him. He then popped into a local restaurant and ordered himself a catfish dinner complete with coleslaw and French fries. Once he returned to his apartment, he ate his food slowly, savoring every bite and feeling like, for once in his life, things were looking up for him. Although at times he was lonely since he didn't have friends or family, he was making the best of it. Once he finished dinner, he turned on the television. The sound came on first before the picture did. He could hear a reporter talking about the hit-and-run accident he was involved in a week ago.

"Police are asking anyone with information to contact Area Two police headquarters," said the newscaster as the picture finally came into view. Luther was now looking at a detective standing in front of a clump of microphones. There were several people behind him who appeared to be the parents and grand-parents of the hit-and-run victim. They all appeared grief-stricken. Luther felt their pain and the blood in his veins began to pulse with trepidation as he listened carefully.

"The family is offering a twenty-five thousand-dollar reward for anyone who has information leading to the arrest and con-viction of the person responsible for the tragedy. If you have any information, please contact Area Two headquarters." Luther clicked the television off. He couldn't endure listening to the report any longer. He felt horrible and smeared away his own tears of sorrow for what he'd done. *I wasn't involved with that*, he reminded himself again and again. *You are not in trouble*, he thought. *They don't have anything. Besides, you were nowhere near the accident. You were downtown at the Taste of Chicago food festi-*

val. Luther willed himself to believe that his words were true.

Saturday morning, Luther was awakened by the sound of garbage dumpsters banging against one another. The sanitation workers were making an enormous ruckus as they hauled away the trash. He brought himself fully awake by taking a deep yawn and stretching his body all the way out. *From now on I am going to work on being positive and getting my act together,* he thought. Luther freshened up and then left his apartment to take care of some errands. He went to a nearby mall and purchased some clothes. Then he stopped to pick up a newspaper and began the process of searching for a job.

The phone company activated his phone service a few days later. As soon as the phone technician left, Luther began phoning potential employers and setting up job interviews. To Luther's surprise, he was able to set up two interviews that same week. One was for a mall security guard; another was for a doorman at a luxury condo north of the city on the Gold Coast. Not willing to stop there, Luther decided to travel to Cook County Hospital and fill out a job application. He'd overheard, on many occasions, that the facility was constantly searching for janitorial staff.

Feeling good about himself and what he'd accomplished throughout the day, Luther decided he'd treat himself to dinner at a neighborhood restaurant on Fifty-third Street called Mellow Yellow.

Hyde Park was a friendly community that had a mixture of Black, White, Spanish, and Asian cultures. The Fifty-third Street strip was the nucleus of the neighborhood. It was lined with restaurants, grocery stores, and a movie theater. Walking was the best way to get around this neighborhood. He walked into Mellow Yellow and was given a seat at the window where he could watch foot traffic.

"Your server will be with you in a moment, sir," remarked the hostess as she placed a menu in front of him.

"Thank you," Luther responded. Luther looked over the menu and decided he'd have the T-bone steak with mashed potatoes and a beer to wash it all down. He closed the menu and rested his elbows on the table. He began to question his ability to handle the pressure of being independent. *What if he ran out of money, and had to live on the streets? What if none of the job interviews panned out, then what?* Fear and insecurity were two of Luther's most daunting demons. He always felt as if he were born with an irreversible curse. He'd been told by his mother, Sugar, on countless occasions, that he was worthless and useless. Sugar blamed him for everything that went wrong in her life. Although Luther was almost in his thirties, he was still battling with the emotional scars of being abandoned by Sugar. He closed his eyes and tried to push his unwanted thoughts into a deep chamber of his mind. When the unwanted thoughts were gone, he opened his eyes and gazed out the window. He saw Carmen approaching wearing a Barack Obama T-shirt with blue shorts and white gym shoes. She was listening to an iPod and appeared to be taking an evening walk. Luther quickly sprang to his feet, knocked on the glass hard with his knuckles, and began waving to get her attention.

"How are you doing?" he yelled from behind the glass, oblivious that other customers had turned in their seats to see why he was talking so loudly. Carmen smiled and waved hello to him. Luther was filled with excited energy as he smiled back at her.

"Did you get your car fixed?" Luther continued to loud talk from behind the glass.

"What?" Carmen stopped walking. She didn't understand a word he had said.

"Your car." Luther made a gesture with his hands simulating a person driving a car. "Did you get your car fixed?"

"Oh…" Carmen finally understood what he was saying through his hand gestures. She shook her head no. Luther waved his hand frantically, asking her to come inside and sit with him. Carmen shook her head back and forth, declining his invitation.

"Please." Luther put his hands in a praying position and looked as sad as he could. Carmen suddenly realized Luther still had her parts to fix her car and maybe his offer was still open, so she decided to go in.

"Hey," Carmen said as she stood in front of an empty chair at his table.

"Have a seat." Luther motioned for her to sit down. "Are you hungry?"

"I'm okay. I've got food waiting for me at home."

"Did you cook?"

"No, I still have to cook."

"There will be no cooking for you on this warm summer night. Dinner is on me." Before Carmen could decline his offer, the busboy came over and set a glass of water in front of her along with a breadbasket and some butter. The smell of the warm bread cinched it for her.

"Did that fire destroy your entire apartment?" asked Carmen.

"Yeah, it pretty much destroyed the building."

"I am so sorry to hear that. It seems as if ever since you met me, you've had nothing but misfortune."

"No, none of what happened had anything to do with you. Shit just happens sometimes."

"You seem awful up-tempo about things," Carmen said as the hostess handed her a menu. Carmen began glancing at her options.

"It's the new me. I'm working on being much more positive

about life in general. I'm rolling with the punches these days and I refuse to allow anything to get me down."

"Are you guys ready to order yet? Or do you need some more time?" The young female waitress came up to the table with her pen in position to write down their orders on her pad.

"I'll have the T-bone steak with mashed potatoes and a beer," said Luther.

"And how would you like that cooked, sir?"

"Well done, please," Luther answered. "Order up, Carmen; it's on me."

"I'll have the chicken Caesar salad with ranch dressing."

"Okay," replied the waitress and took their menus. "I'll put your orders in right away."

"I was about to say that, in this world, you've got to work hard at things, you know," Luther continued. "Up until now, I haven't been doing the things I need to do to make it."

"Tell me, Luther. What did you do before you were a mechanic?" Carmen's interest was sparked by Luther's sudden openness.

"Nothing. You see, when I was a kid, I became a ward of the state and had to live in a foster home. I was lucky, I suppose. The people the state placed me with were in it for the money. They didn't put their hands on me, but they did make me feel insignificant to a certain degree. They made me feel like I was dumb as hell because I wasn't smart enough to do my school-work on my own. I struggled in school. I was the kid who got teased since my clothes weren't always clean. I was the kid who no one cared about, sitting in the back of the classroom. By the time I reached high school, I was labeled 'learning disabled' and was placed in remedial classes. I developed an 'I don't give a damn attitude' and the teachers did the same."

Luther took a sip of the water the waitress had set in front of him. Carmen didn't say a word; she waited patiently for him to continue.

"Anyway, the only reason I didn't drop out was because of auto mechanic's class. When it came to cars and engines, I knew what I was doing. I enjoyed reading about what makes them work and how to fix them. I was the smartest kid in the class when it came to cars, and my instructor told me I should consider a career in auto mechanics or engineering. He told me I should be designing engines and building cars for Ford or Dodge. He even said I could be one of the mechanics working on cars at the Indianapolis 500, making tall dollars."

"So did you go to college and pursue that?" Carmen asked, genuinely interested.

"Like I said, I was only good at working on cars. When it came to my other subjects, I had major trouble. Things didn't click for me like they did for other kids. I took the ACT and scored like a two on it. I couldn't get into college with a score like that. I even took the test a second time and got the same score. It didn't matter though. Even if I had passed it with flying colors, the foster parents I was with were on my back to leave. Once I turned eighteen and graduated, they would no longer receive money from the state for me. That meant they wanted my ass out of their house."

"Luther, that was a horrible thing for them to do." Carmen was once again feeling very sympathetic to Luther's plight.

"I'm cursed, I suppose. The dice never roll my way."

"So, what happened when you turned eighteen?" Carmen picked a slice of bread from the breadbasket and set it on the plate before her.

"I had to get a job. I took on handyman work around the neighborhood and made a few dollars, but the pressure was on me to leave. Even though I offered to pay for my upkeep, the couple was already looking into taking in a five-year-old and my room was where they wanted him to go. I eventually landed two jobs. One at a car wash on the West Side near the United Center and the other job was as a security guard for a clothing store on Madison Street. I left my foster parents and found an elderly lady who lived on Adams Street. She rented me a room in her home, which supplemented her income."

"Well, good for you. It sounds as if the people you were staying with were bad news. Malcolm X Junior College is near Adams Street. Did you ever consider going to night school?" At that moment, the waitress returned with their dinners.

"Can I get you guys anything else?" she asked.

"No, thank you," they replied in unison and she quickly left to attend to another table.

"No. I was too busy worrying about keeping a roof over my head. Rent for the room was seventy-five dollars a week, which wasn't bad for me. I stayed with the elderly woman for nearly ten years and she never once went up on the rent. She was as sweet as they came."

"Well, what happened to her?" Carmen asked.

"Her health began to fail and she needed twenty-four-hour medical care. Her family ended up placing her in a nursing home and then turned around and sold her home. So I had to leave."

"How did you end up with the job as a mechanic at the muffler shop?"

"Well, one day while I was working at the car wash, a man who used to date my mother came through. We made small talk and I mentioned to him about my situation. You see, after the elderly woman's house was sold, I ended up living at a nearby YMCA. Anyway, I told the guy that I was good underneath the hood of a car. He told me a buddy of his owned a car repair shop and owed him a big favor. He had sympathy for me and told me he could hook me up with a job. He also said he owned a three-flat building and the basement apartment was vacant. The rest, as they say, is history."

Carmen was silent for a moment, taking in and analyzing Luther's story. She pitied him for having to survive on his own at such a young age and admired him for finding a way to make it. He didn't give up hope and she thought that was commendable. She thought that all Luther really needed was someone stable in his life who'd give him the loving home he never had. But Carmen was curious as to why he didn't mention any girlfriends or relationships. Even when the situation seems hopeless, women are notorious for helping a man along.

"You mentioned on the bus that you didn't have any children."

"Who, me? Hell no! I'm not into kids. I don't want any! They're too much trouble, and cost way too much. Besides, I'm not the fatherly type."

"Okay." Carmen's reply was dry. She was not exactly sure what to make of his response. In the back of her mind, she wondered if there was room for him to change his fixed attitude.

"So do you have a special someone in your life?" Carmen was curious as hell.

"No, I don't have anyone. The last serious relationship I had didn't work out."

"Was it a bitter breakup?" Carmen continued to pry.

"Something like that. My girl was cheating on me with a guy I considered to be a friend at the time."

"Oh, I'm sorry to hear that. What about your biological mother? Where is she?" Carmen continued to probe into Luther's background.

"Let's not talk about her. She means nothing to me," Luther said rather abruptly. Carmen realized that she'd struck a tender nerve.

"Look, I'm sorry. I didn't mean to snap at you." Luther paused and then continued. "The fire was a good thing. It has helped me to make some decisions. I have a few job interviews next week, plus, because of the fire, I've run into a little extra cash. I've got a studio apartment over on Woodlawn now."

"Well, that's wonderful, Luther. I'm glad to hear things are working out for you." Carmen smiled at him. *Luther isn't a bad-looking guy*, she thought. *A little rough around the edges but that can be fixed.*

"What about you? Have you gotten your car up and running yet?"

"No, it's sitting on my street." Carmen sighed.

"I lost my tools in the fire," Luther lied. He'd actually left them in Packard's Blazer. "But I can get what I need and drop by one day this week and take care of it for you."

"Really? Luther, that would help me out a great deal." Carmen perked up at the thought of finally getting her car up and running.

"I love to help out when I can." Luther smiled as if she were the only woman in the world. "Thanks for having dinner with me. Talking with you has helped."

"Well, thank you for inviting me to have dinner, Luther. This is very nice of you," Carmen said as she picked up her fork and began to eat her salad.

—12—
CARMEN

The following morning, Carmen was busy with house-keeping chores. She had to get her bedroom in order, clean up her bathroom, and gather up items that needed to be dropped off at the cleaners. She reflected on her dinner yesterday with Luther and came to the conclusion that she really enjoyed the conversation they'd had. Carmen was relieved that Luther didn't allow the fire and his job loss to stop him from moving forward and doing what was necessary to survive. That was a commendable quality about him and, in her mind, that was an indication of someone who was tenacious and persistent. After spending the enlightening evening getting to know him better, her observations of Luther caused her to analyze whether or not she'd ever consider having a romantic relationship with him. Carmen understood that Luther was rough around the edges and needed to gain more confidence in himself as well as build better social skills. The fact he didn't have any children was a huge plus; she wouldn't have to deal with any baby mama drama. Her last semi-serious relationship, prior to the psycho, Bernard, was with a man named Frank who was recently divorced and the father of two kids. Frank was always short on cash and constantly complained about his ex-wife and all of the drama she was creating for him.

"I still can't get over the fact that he took me out for dinner at a pizza parlor and used coupons to cover the meal," Carmen muttered to herself as she picked up several articles of clothing that were on the floor next to her bed. "Then when Frank and I got back to the car he asked if he could borrow three hundred dollars." Carmen griped at the memory of that moment. After she'd ended all communication with Frank, Carmen added a new rule to her dating guide: Don't date recently divorced men. She placed that rule right next to the one about men with multiple children by different women.

Carmen walked into her living room, placed her iPod on the docking station, and turned it on. She listened as Jill Scott's voice filled the room and popped her fingers to the groove of the music.

"Overall, I think that Luther is genuinely a decent person," she said to herself as she walked over to a window and drew back the curtains to allow sunlight to shine through. "All he truly needs is a strong, loving, and nurturing woman like me in his life."

Listening to Jill Scott gave Carmen a burst of energy and she decided to wash the loads of laundry she'd been neglecting. She went about the task of sorting all the clothes. When she was done, she realized that all of her efforts were in vain; the stackable washer and dryer in her condo was malfunctioning.

"Shit," she hissed as she surveyed the piles of clothes on the floor. "I should take the shit up to the Laundromat," she said, although she truly hated the idea of lugging the clothes that far. "Well, one thing is for sure, I'll be able to finish reading my novel by Angie Daniels," she told herself. Carmen walked into her kitchen to grab some large bags from the cupboard. She suddenly remembered that her car still hadn't been repaired.

"Damn it!" Carmen's burst of energy was giving way to total frustration. At that moment, something came to her.

"Nikki. I'll call Nikki and have her take me," she spoke aloud. She located her cell phone and called Nikki, but received a message that her number was temporarily disconnected. Carmen then dialed Frieda to see if she could put Nikki on the phone for her.

"Hello," a groggy voice answered.

"Frieda? Is that you?" Carmen asked, unable to clearly distinguish her voice.

"No, bitch, it's Jennifer fucking Lopez." *Yup*, Carmen thought, *that's ignorant-ass Frieda.*

"Where's Nikki?" she asked.

"In her goddamn skin!" Frieda began snorting on the phone. She was attempting to extract a thick clump of mucus from her sinuses.

"Ha, ha, very funny. I need to speak to her." Carmen was persistent.

"About what?" Frieda continued to snort. She sounded like a pig grunting with glee at the sight of a fresh mud pen.

"None of your business." Carmen got snippy with her.

"Hey, chick! You're calling my damn house. This is my damn cell phone, not hers. Her credit is so bad that she can't get a phone in her name. Her ass needs to hurry up and put some more minutes on her prepaid phone." Frieda had finally gotten that annoying wad of glob out.

"Hold on a minute," Frieda said, sounding as if she had a mouthful of water. "Okay, I'm back," she returned, sounding a bit better.

"Just tell Nikki to call me when she gets a moment, okay?"

"I'm not her damn secretary. Call her ass back later on when she gets up. You know damn well she's shaking her ass all night. You should try coming down to the spot and shake your ass... Never mind, I forgot. You don't have a lot of ass." Frieda began laughing at her own joke.

"I have enough ass to do what needs to be done." Carmen wasn't about to take any of Frieda's bullshit.

"Well, you need to shake that money-maker a little harder, girl. But, then again, that really isn't your thing," Frieda joked.

"You don't know what my 'thing' is. For all you know, I could be living a secret life. I could be a madam. As a matter of fact, I could use a workhorse like you in my stable. Come work for me so that I can put that hot ass of yours on foot patrol. Come on. I know you'd be a good money-maker." Carmen let Frieda know that she could get rude when the occasion called for such harsh means of communication.

"Oh shit! Where did that come from? You went all pimp on me." Frieda laughed. "So it's true what they say about girls who look all conservative. You bitches are really undercover freaks!"

"I'm willing to bet that I'm freakier than you'll ever be." Carmen was now filled with fire and feistiness.

"Well, listen here, Freak Nasty. Nikki's new man, Packard, opened up his club called Big Daddy's and he's throwing a Freak of the Week party. Why don't you flip yourself inside out and let the freaky bitch you've been keeping under lock and key come out and play. The party is taking place Friday. They'll have vendors selling sex toys, all kinds of other shit."

Carmen felt bold and daring. "I might check that out."

"Bring it on, bitch. I'd love to see your narrow ass get turned out, the way I turned out Nikki."

"Frieda, you don't have the right equipment to turn me out."

"You don't know what I've got. Besides, there's more than one way to turn a bitch out."

"Whatever, Frieda." Carmen dismissed Frieda's bold comment.

"Hey, if you're too scared to come out for a night of erotic fun, I understand," Frieda taunted.

"You know what. I might surprise your ass. Give me the address of the place." Frieda's challenge emboldened Carmen.

"All right, Freak Nasty, you have a pen?" Frieda asked.

"Yeah." Frieda gave Carmen the address and all needed details. "Now can I speak to Nikki?" Carmen asked.

"Nikki isn't here," Frieda answered truthfully.

"Where is she?" Carmen asked once again. "And please don't say that she's in her skin."

"She's probably with Packard somewhere, riding his dick. That motherfucker is putting down some serious pipe because Nikki will do anything for him," Frieda said.

"What's he like?"

"Packard. He's a real pistol," Frieda said with respect and envy.

"What's that supposed to mean?"

"You don't cross men like Packard. If he says bark like a dog, you'd better start barking. Packard has money, influence, and power. He's a shady son of a bitch but he's also well-connected," Frieda said, clearing her throat.

"If he's all that, then why is he with Nikki?"

"Shit. She's young and has a hot pussy, but you wouldn't know anything about a hot pussy. Your shit stays iced down." Frieda laughed at her own wisecrack.

"Fuck you, Frieda," Carmen snapped.

"No. Fuck you, bitch." Frieda annoyed Carmen to no end; she was so unpredictable and catty. Before Carmen could respond to Frieda's last insult, Frieda had hung up. Carmen called back right away but the phone rang without being answered.

"No, that trifling bitch didn't hang up on me!" Carmen didn't want to believe Frieda had actually done that. "Argh!" Carmen grumbled with irritation.

Carmen decided to call a cab to take her to the Laundromat on Fifty-third Street. Once she arrived, she dragged her heavy sacks of clothes inside and found a few available washers. She stuffed her clothes in them and then walked next door to the grocery store where she purchased some detergent. She came back, broke a twenty-dollar bill in the change machine, and started her loads. An hour later, she was folding her clothes on a table. After she was done, she placed all of her belongings back in bags and located her cell phone to call a cab to take her home. No sooner had the phone begun to ring, than Carmen spotted Luther strolling along the sidewalk. Carmen waved to him and Luther approached her to have a quick and casual conversation.

"Hey, Carmen. What's up with you today?" Luther asked as he stepped inside with a smile on his face.

"Well, right now I need to see about getting these bags of clothes back home. A sister could use a lift. Do you have a car?"

"Damn. I don't have a ride or I'd be more than happy to give you a lift." Carmen could tell that Luther was embarrassed that he didn't own a car. "I tell you what. I'll carry the bags back home for you."

"No, Luther, it's okay. The bags are way too heavy to carry all the way back to Fifty-eighth Street. Where are you headed?"

"I was actually on my way to the hardware store to pick up some tools."

"I promise you that, later today, your car will be up and running." Luther smiled warmly at Carmen.

"Okay." Carmen gave in. "Get what you need and I'll call a cab so that you can ride back to my side of the neighborhood. My car is parked on the street." Carmen smiled back at Luther, who went to a nearby auto parts store and picked up everything he needed to repair Carmen's car. He even set aside some extra cash so that he could return the money she'd already spent. He wanted Carmen to understand that he was doing the work free of charge.

Carmen's block was lined with tall green trees whose leaves provided just the right amount of shade on a sunny day. The scent of freshly cut grass and flowers wafted in the air along with the sounds of wild parakeets, sparrows, and cardinals chirping.

"Is this an apartment building?" Luther asked as they exited the cab.

"No, it's a condo," Carmen said as she paid the cab driver while Luther removed her bags from the trunk.

"Damn, girl, you're living large." Luther was impressed with the stateliness of the building. He thought he was living pretty well in his section of Hyde Park, but now he realized he was in the low-rent district.

"I live on the first floor. I can get the bags up the landing on my own. I just need you to carry them over to the door." Carmen picked up a smaller bag and began heading toward her door.

"I would invite you up for something to drink, but my house is a mess. I was in the middle of cleaning when I decided to do all of this laundry," Carmen said as she opened the door, which gave them access to the vestibule of the building.

"That's okay." Luther wiped the beads of sweat from his forehead with the back of his hand. Carmen suddenly felt bad because he was sweating.

"Tell you what. I'll go get you a cool towel and a cold drink. How does that sound?" Carmen asked.

"Do you have a beer?" Luther asked, hoping she'd say yes.

"No, I'm afraid I don't. But I do have wine coolers. Will that work?" Carmen hoped her alternative was satisfactory.

"That's even better." Carmen dragged her belongings inside her condo. Once inside, she grabbed one of her face towels and soaked it with warm water. She wrung out the excess water, then pulled the wine cooler out of the refrigerator before heading back outside to reunite with Luther.

"This is a really nice area over here," Luther said once again. "It's quiet and vagrants aren't hanging out on the corner with nothing to do. Shit, I wouldn't mind living like this."

"You never know what could happen. You're getting things together and anything is possible when you focus on your goals." Carmen truly wanted to be encouraging to Luther. She thought that by providing him with those few extra words, she was in some small way helping to rescue him from an unfavorable situation.

"Yeah, you're right," Luther replied, thinking about how much he'd love to move in with her. She could have the responsibility of the mortgage and he'd help out wherever he could. *Perhaps I could pay the light bill or the phone bill*, Luther thought.

"So where is your car?" Luther asked, feeling a strong desire to be her man, especially now that he knew where she lived.

"It's over there, parked near the corner." The two of them walked over to Carmen's car.

"Pop the hood for me," Luther requested as he stood in front of the car. Carmen pulled the hood release and then got out of the car to watch what he was doing. Luther opened up the socket wrench set he'd purchased and leaned over the motor searching for something.

"What are you looking for?" Carmen was nervous about him working on her car, suddenly remembering that he wasn't a certified mechanic. She now had concerns that he'd do more damage that would end up costing her more money.

"I'm looking at how many screws I have to take loose in order to get to the plugs." Luther pointed. "Do you see this metal plate right here? The old spark plugs are under there. I have to take it off."

"Is it hard to change the plugs?"

"It depends on the car, but for the most part, no. It's a matter of removing them one at a time and setting the new spark plug with a gap tool."

"Okay, you've lost me. What in the world is a gap tool?"

Luther laughed as he thought of a way to explain it to her.

"Well, let's see." Luther reached into his pants pocket and pulled out his keys, which had a gap tool on the key ring. "This right here is a gap tool." Luther showed her a round metal object about the size of a half-dollar that had writing on it.

"These numbers tell you how far the spacing is on the plug." Luther could see he was losing her, yet again. "Think of it like this. Have you ever seen a person with a large gap in their upper front teeth?"

"Yes, I see it with my students a lot."

"Well, the gap tool allows me to adjust the space between these two points on the plug. Just like spreading or closing the gap between a person's teeth." Luther showed Carmen the small metal hook at the top of the plug and the round circular nipple below it.

"Oh, okay, I see."

"When your car comes off the assembly line, your plugs have to be set a certain way in order for your car to perform right. If the gap is off, it does things like hesitate, stall out, etcetera—"

"Okay," Carmen replied, understanding what he was saying to her. "So, how do you know what the correct setting is for my car?"

"Good question. When I was at the auto store buying the spark plugs I looked up the settings in an auto book." Luther winked at Carmen. "Don't worry. I got this." He laughed out loud.

Once he replaced the plugs, he had Carmen start the car, which cranked up without a problem. "Voila, Miss Carmen," Luther said with pride as he slammed her hood shut. "Let's take it for a spin to make sure that it's responding the way it should."

"Yes, yes, yes!" Carmen shouted with glee. She was happy her car was running. Luther gathered up the tools he'd purchased, and got in on the passenger side.

"Can a brother get a lift back home?" Luther asked playfully.

"You most certainly can," Carmen said with a joyful voice. Carmen drove Luther back to his apartment and pulled over in front of his building.

"Well, thank you very much, Luther. You don't know how much you've helped a sister out." Carmen was truly grateful.

"You're very welcome." Luther paused as he shifted in his seat to look at her more closely. He studied her caramel skin, her full lips, and her light-brown eyes. He felt his heart flutter slightly. He liked Carmen and he wanted to see her again, but he wasn't sure how to express it. Then, an idea hit him.

"Say, maybe sometime you and I could hang out at the lake front and chill. You know, just to chitchat." Luther offered what he thought was a casual date that Carmen would agree to.

"I'd like that, Luther. Maybe next weekend we can hook up. Then you could tell me how your job interviews went."

"Yeah, let's do that. I've got a feeling my life is about to change in a very good way." Luther couldn't help smiling at her. It was the way she was making him feel that had him dancing with joy on the inside.

"I'll give you a call next Saturday, okay?" she said as Luther got out of the car.

"You take care now," Luther said as he stepped away.

"See you later, Luther," Carmen said, as she pulled off. "He may have more potential than I originally thought," Carmen said out loud as she drove back home.

~13~
MARSHALL

Nearly two weeks had passed since the accident and the police still had no clues and no suspect. True to his word, Detective Taylor had called in a few favors and gotten the media to agree to air a public plea from the family. Cameramen had set up their equipment on the front lawn and hooked it into their satellite feeds on their media vans. Neighbors had set up a makeshift memorial on their front porches as a show of both sympathy and support. Among the flowers and candles, the media would tape the family's plea for help. Once microphones were arranged in a neat cluster and the cameras were ready, the family emerged from their home to make their statement.

"Twelve days ago," Stacy began, her voice shaky but controlled. Marshall was clenching his teeth both in anger and frustration; he had not been able to capture the criminal. "A driver in a black Chevy Blazer recklessly ran down and killed my baby girl, Lena," Stacy continued, holding up an enlarged photograph of Lena. "The coward then fled the scene. There is a reward of twenty-five thousand dollars for anyone who has information leading to the capture and arrest of the individual responsible. Please help us bring this hideous person to justice before he harms anyone else." After Stacy offered her plea for help, Marshall stood in front of the microphones.

"I know that there is someone out there who knows something. You may have heard someone talking about it or maybe you have an idea of who this reckless person is. Please. Don't think that you're doing them a favor by protecting them. And please don't be afraid to talk to the police about any information you might have. It is vitally important that we get this person off our streets." Marshall then turned the microphone over to Detective Taylor, who took questions from the media about the ongoing investigation.

Over the next several days, a flood of phone calls came into police headquarters. Citizens claimed they knew the driver but wanted the reward money before they provided any information. Despite a few promising leads and checking them out, police were unable to make a connection to the crime. By the fourth week, the trail was still cold.

Although Marshall was an Illinois state trooper, his branch of law enforcement had no jurisdiction over the case. The Chicago Police Department had its own vehicular homicide unit with a well-trained law enforcement staff. Marshall wanted to help with the investigation, but Detective Taylor didn't want Marshall involved in that capacity. It would be too risky if Marshall took out his anger on an innocent person whom Taylor brought in for questioning.

Marshall couldn't sit idle. Waiting for something to happen wasn't his style. He worked below the radar with Quentin, who had pulled some strings and gotten an old friend to toss him and Marshall a few leads that had come in. Not wanting to leave any stone unturned, Marshall and Quentin followed up.

Marshall was now following up on one of three leads. He had just pulled into a low-rise housing project to speak with a man who claimed he had seen the entire incident and had a description of the man driving the truck. Marshall parked his squad car in front of the address the woman had given. There was a group of young men standing around watching his every move, waiting to see which house he was going into. He walked up to the door with the number "367" above it. He knocked hard and waited a moment. An elderly man with kinky salt-and-pepper hair, wearing overalls, came to the door. He was hunched over and balancing himself on a cane.

"Come on in," he said with a voice that was deeply Southern but had a hint of urban influence. He turned away from the door without even looking up at him. His apartment was full of cats, one of which rubbed against Marshall's leg. The smell of a litter box assaulted his nose, along with the irritating sound of meows from multiple cats. The man sat down in his recliner and exhaled as if the act of walking to open the door had sucked the life out of his body.

"What do you want?" he asked, finally craning his head up to look directly at Marshall. "Oh, you're the police." The elderly man was surprised. Marshall took a seat on the well-worn sofa. He had to scoot to the edge so that he wouldn't sink down.

"My name is Marshall and I'm with the Illinois State Police. I'm helping the Chicago Police Department follow up on a phone call you made regarding an accident involving a little girl you claim to have seen about four weeks ago."

"Accident? Man, I ain't seen no accident." The man began rubbing the palm of his hand around the bow of his cane. His twitching seemed to stem from his age and deteriorating condition. "I want you people to do something about them young hoodlum boys who hang around my house. They're selling that crap to everyone. I call the police every day and they don't do nothing!"

"Sir." Marshall looked at his notes for his name. "Mr. Boler, you can't call the police for one crime expecting to get help on another."

"Why not? That's what you do, isn't it? You catch criminals? For all you know, one of those boys standing out there could have run that little girl down. All of them drive crazy. They speed down through here all of the time like bats outta hell! It's a miracle that none of them have run down any of us old folks. Check them out, I say. All of them can be put in jail for something. I guarantee you that! I'm old, but I am not crazy. Most of them boys out there have mothers strung out on drugs. Their fathers are in jail and the social workers are letting the streets raise them. It's a vicious cycle, I tell you, set up by" — Mr. Boler paused and swiveled his head around to make sure no one was listening—"the government. That's who's really behind all of this. They're trying to kill all of the poor people."

Marshall sighed. He realized this lead was another dead end and a waste of his time.

"Look, Mr. Boler, I'll let the area crime unit assigned to your neighborhood know of your concerns about the young men loitering." Marshall stood up and excused himself.

"They won't do anything. I call them all the time!" Mr. Boler shouted.

"I'll have an officer come by and take your complaint." Marshall now had the door open. He glanced at the old man one last time and then left.

Marshall's next stop was the home of a park district employee by the name of Tee who was working the day of the accident. She lived at an apartment complex on Sixty-third and Cottage Grove Streets. When he walked up to her building door, there were doorbells, but none of them had names assigned to them.

He rang them all, but no one answered. He stepped back and looked up at the windows hoping to see a sign of someone peeping out trying to see who was ringing his doorbell. He had no such luck. He had given up on the lead and turned to leave, but bumped into an overweight, middle-aged woman carrying in her groceries.

"Excuse me. I'm so sorry about that." Marshall immediately offered his apology.

"That's okay, baby. No harm done," she replied with a jolly smile.

"Maybe you can help me. I'm looking for a woman by the name of Tee Jones. Do you know where I can find her?"

"Yeah, that's my granddaughter. I know where you can find her, but I doubt that she'll be of much help to you."

"Why do you say that?" The woman set her bags down on the stoop and wiggled her swollen fingers.

"It hurts my heart to say it, but my granddaughter is a thief, a liar, and a drug addict. I tried to raise her right, but these streets are full of evil. I don't have the time to deal with her stealing from me to support her drug habit."

Marshall exhaled with a frustrating sigh since he had run into yet another dead end.

"What did she tell you, anyway? Why are you here?" asked the woman, as she picked up her bags.

"She claims she witnessed an accident involving a young girl a few weeks ago. I came here to ask her what she saw," Marshall explained.

"Baby, I'm sorry, but she lied to you. She's been in a rehab program for the past month. I put her in there myself and that's where she's at now. She must have gotten to a phone somehow and contacted you. There must be a big reward or something out there for her to have gone this far. She'll do or say anything for money to get high. That crack cocaine has really messed her up."

"Yeah, I understand. There is a reward for my daughter who was killed by a hit-and-run driver and I'm trying to find the person responsible." Marshall divulged more than he wanted or needed to.

"I'm so sorry. I heard about that on the news. I don't know what to say."

"There is nothing to say. Thanks for your help," Marshall said, and walked away. He was exhausted and upset that, for their own selfish reasons, individuals were toying with his emotions at a time like this.

Marshall came through the back yard from the garage and entered the house through the kitchen. When he walked in, June, Stacy's mother, was sitting at the kitchen table drinking a cup of coffee. June was a heavyset woman with long, silver hair and rich, cinnamon-brown skin. Her eyelids were noticeably puffy and the whites of her eyes were slightly red. She glanced up at Marshall long enough to make eye contact and acknowledge his presence. She attempted to place a cordial smile on her face, but the smile quickly faded. She placed her gaze back inside the coffee cup.

"Where is Stacy?" Marshall asked, not allowing June to tune him out.

"She's resting. You shouldn't wake her; she needs her rest." Marshall set his binder, filled with notes about the case, on the countertop.

"Is there any more coffee left?" he asked, as he moved toward the coffeemaker.

"Yes. I made a fresh pot." June was silent for a moment. "I can't get it in my head that Lena is gone." June sniffled and quickly grabbed a paper towel off of the spool in front of her. Marshall took a seat and scooted next to her, placing his arm around her.

"Mother June." Marshall paused trying to find his words. "I should have had Lena wait with me at the water fountain. I should have been more responsible. I—"

"Marshall. Shhhhh. Stop beating yourself up over it. It was an accident. It was a horrible, horrible accident." June's voice trailed off into silence. She gazed back down inside of her coffee cup and didn't say another word. Marshall walked out of the kitchen and into the dining room. He kicked off his shoes and lay down on the sofa. He tried to get some rest since he hadn't been able to for days. As he tried to relax, he began to feel guilty. He felt as if he should be out looking for the criminal who had taken away his pride and joy. He stared up at the white ceiling and replayed the video of what had happened over and over and over again. Then, before he realized it, tears began to flow from his eyes. Marshall willed himself to pull it together. Once he had his emotions in check, his body shut down and he was able to rest.

Marshall awoke from his sleep in the middle of night and went upstairs to his bedroom. He was surprised to see Stacy was awake, sitting and gazing out the bedroom window.

"I didn't realize you were awake," Marshall said as he walked over to her and knelt down beside her. He placed his hand on her thigh and bowed his head. He felt like a failure as a father and a police officer.

"Tell me how you feel." Marshall mumbled.

"I don't know what I feel," Stacy answered. "There are no words for what I feel. If there were, I would tell you. Right now, I just want to know why? Why did this happen? Can you tell me that?" The painful question silenced Marshall because it was one that he could not answer.

"I'm sorry, Stacy. I am so sorry." Marshall clenched his hand into a tight fist. He squeezed as tight as he could.

"You should not have ridden so far, Marshall. I told you before I left that I thought it wasn't a good idea. Why didn't you listen to me? Can you tell me that?" Stacy's voice was edgy and her questions were stabbing him with the precision of a swordsman.

"I don't know, Stacy. I just..." Marshall's voice trailed off because he didn't have a good answer to her question.

"None of this would have happened had you listened to me and ridden a shorter distance." There it was. The blame. Stacy had been distant with him since she blamed everything on him. She didn't say it directly, but didn't have to. Marshall suddenly felt lightheaded and disoriented. He gathered himself as best he could and sat on the edge of the bed. Stacy didn't bother to move from her position. She sat silently and continued to glare out of the bedroom window.

"I feel cheated. I wanted to see Lena blossom into a beautiful woman. I wanted to see her have children and a family of her own. I wasn't supposed to outlive her. What terrible sin have we committed to warrant this type of punishment? Can you tell me that? What did we do wrong to be punished like this?" Stacy said with a voice that constantly trembled.

"Don't you think that I wanted to see those same things? I'm not on some joy kick here, Stacy. And if you want to blame me for what happened, then come out and say it. Come on. Say what you really think. Go ahead. I can take it. But what I will not put up with is you bad mouthing me behind my back." Marshall was on edge and ready and willing to take the emotional pain Stacy wanted to put on him.

"I don't want to blame you, Marshall." Stacy began crying. "I only want my daughter back."

"So do I." Marshall rose to his feet and exhaled deeply several times. His emotions were not going to be contained this time around.

"I want you to promise me something. I want you to promise me you'll find the person who did this and make sure that son of a bitch suffers!" Stacy said.

Marshall knew that she, too, was moving toward the anger stage of grief. She wanted just as much retribution as he did.

"An eye for an eye and a tooth for a tooth. I promise. I will not rest until the person who did this is dead." Marshall's mind had just cracked. He had no intention of going through the criminal justice system once he located the person responsible. At that moment, the splinter of revenge ran deep and he knew, with absolute certainty, that he would murder the culprit.

"I need to know something from you," Marshall continued. "I want to know if you still believe in me. I want to know that you still love me." There was a long and eerie pause before Stacy answered. They both realized they'd arrived at a very pivotal point in their relationship.

"Yes," Stacy muttered, but Marshall didn't believe her. In his mind, her answer wasn't genuine.

Marshall and Stacy were having a difficult time adjusting to a different life that didn't include their daughter. They both went back to work, but this time, they buried themselves in it. They allowed their work to consume them so that they wouldn't have to deal with the pain they were both experiencing. Both of them wanted to talk to each other but neither one was ready to open up his heart. Their emotional wounds were too raw. When Marshall arrived home from work, he spent all of his free time following up on leads involving his daughter's case. Stacy spent all of her free time with her parents.

Marshall was following up on yet another lead given to him by a friend of Quentin's. Marshall ran the risk of tainting the investigation, but he couldn't stop searching. He simply couldn't. This time he headed to Mellow Yellow restaurant in Hyde Park to see an employee named Shawn Bigford. He claimed he wanted to share what he had seen. When Marshall arrived, he asked the hostess if he could have a few words with Shawn.

"Yeah, he's in the back," answered the young, college-aged hostess. She picked up the phone and pressed the intercom button. "Shawn, to the front, please," the hostess paged. A few minutes later, a young man with gingerbread-colored skin and a bald head appeared. He was wearing a white shirt and a black tie along with a white apron wrapped around his waist.

"Yeah, what do you need?" he asked the hostess.

"This officer is here to see you." The hostess casually pointed to Marshall.

"Oh yeah, how you doing?" Shawn wiped his hands on his apron, then extended one out to Marshall for a handshake. "Come on back here into the break room and I'll tell you what I saw. Hopefully it will help you out with the investigation."

"Lead the way," Marshall said, hopeful this lead would turn up something useful.

"Would you like something to drink?" Shawn offered.

"No, I'm fine. Thanks for asking, though."

"I'm sorry that I couldn't meet you earlier, but my schedule changed at the last minute," Shawn apologized.

"It's okay," Marshall replied as he opened up his notebook to take Shawn's statement. "Can you tell me what you saw?"

"Wait a minute. You're him. You're the man with the little girl." Shawn was glaring at Marshall, studying his features carefully. In one breath, Marshall was happy Shawn recognized him from the scene, but in another, it filled his heart with pain.

"Yes, I'm her father. I'm also an officer." Marshall clicked the button on his pen and placed it on the pad. "Why don't you start from the beginning?"

"Look, I don't want the money or anything. I've got a kid too. I have a little boy and I just want to help out," Shawn said.

"I understand, Shawn. But please, if you have information, tell me," Marshall pleaded with the young man.

"Well, I had just gotten off from work and was riding my bike back home along the lake front. I rode up to you when you were getting a drink of water...I was the guy on the yellow bike."

"Yes. I remember you," Marshall said excitedly. He knew, for a fact, that Shawn had been there.

"I saw the entire thing." Shawn paused. "I still can't get those images out of my mind."

"Were you able to see the driver? Would you be able to give a description of him?" Marshall asked, praying that the young man would be able to provide him with the information that he needed.

"No. I can't give you a description of him, but I do know for sure he was a guy. When I saw him taking off from the scene, I chased him and got close enough to get a license plate number."

"You did?" Marshall could barely speak. Marshall was only able to get a partial plate number: "CFD."

"The license plate number on the car was 'CFD 1865.'"

"Are you positive that was the number?" Marshall was scribbling down the information frantically.

"Yeah. I'm positive. I made myself remember it by saying that

CFD—Chicago Fire Department and 1865 was the year that the Civil War ended. So, yeah, that's the number."

"Why didn't you tell the police this?"

"I hung around for as long as I could to give a statement, but the police were asking everyone else questions. I had to leave because I had to get home to my son. If I didn't get home on time, my wife would've been late for work. I thought for sure that, by now, the guy would've been caught. But when I saw the news conference, I thought I'd better call to share what I know."

"Shawn, you're a godsend. Thank you. Thank you so much." Marshall quickly stood.

"Hey, I'm glad that I could help." Shawn extended his hand for a good-bye shake, but Marshall gave him a brotherly embrace instead, before leaving abruptly. Marshall wasn't in his squad car so he didn't have access to the computer to look up the license plate. He searched for his cell phone but he didn't have it on him. He saw a pay phone on the corner so he gathered up some change to call in for a Department of Motor Vehicles report on the plate number. When he got to the post, the phone company had removed it.

"Shit." Marshall hissed. His mind was racing a mile a minute. He ran back to his car and sped toward home.

When he arrived, he pulled up directly behind his squad car. His intention was to punch in the vehicle plate number immediately. But he was interrupted by Theodore who was standing in the yard smoking a cigar.

"Soldier, we need to talk. Pronto," he said, demanding Marshall to stop whatever he was about to do.

"Not right now, Theodore, I've got something I need to do." Marshall ignored the old man's request for attention.

"When I say that we need to talk, I mean right now. Stop what you're doing; talk to me."

"No," Marshall replied defiantly as he searched for the keys to the squad car. At that moment, Theodore walked toward Marshall and made him stop searching.

"You're going to listen to me and you're going to do it now!" Theodore barked.

"Fine, Theodore, let's do it your way." The two men stepped into the back yard.

"I'm disappointed in you, Marshall."

"What?" Marshall really didn't have time to hash this out with him.

"When you married my daughter, I wasn't happy about it. You were not of her caliber. You didn't have much money and you were too damn dark, in my opinion." Theodore was purging a lot of old bullshit he'd wanted to say for years.

"What in the hell are you saying, old man? I'm not good enough for her because I'm 'too dark'?" Marshall thought the old man had gone mad.

"Yeah, that's what I'm saying. There were plenty of decent-looking gentlemen she could have chosen, but she picked you." Theodore had a sour frown on his face.

"Why you old, cynical, color-struck motherfucker!" Marshall was pissed off.

"Watch your language!" Theodore demanded. "When you married my daughter, you promised you wouldn't break her heart. You gave me your word that you'd be a good man to her. But you lied to me. It doesn't surprise me, though. Most of you, if not all of you darker ones, lie anyway. Now I've got to come in here and fix things so that my daughter is happy again. And it's your entire fault, you know. You're the one who caused all of this.

You're the one who is responsible for all of this pain and misery. You need to burn in hell for what you've caused to happen."

"You know what?! Pack your shit and get the fuck out of my house." Marshall was now completely irate. *He's picked the wrong fucking time to push my buttons.*

"What? You can't throw me out. My daughter lives here and I'm welcome to stay as long as I like. No one throws me out of anyplace." Marshall's fury was blazing like an out-of-control wildfire. He was under an enormous amount of pressure and stress. The last thing he wanted to hear was criticism and old Southern views about light- and dark-skinned people. Marshall couldn't believe that Theodore had picked a time like this to come out of a bag on him.

"I said, pack your shit, motherfucker, and get the hell out of my house!" Marshall shouted at the top of his voice.

"You know what!"—now Theodore's blood was boiling as well—"No one around here has the courage to tell you like it is, except for me. You're a bad father, Marshall. You put my granddaughter in harm's way and now you want everyone in the world to agree with your bad judgment call. Well, I'm telling you right now, mister. You will not get any sympathy from me. No, sir, I'm holding you fully accountable for this." Theodore had the nerve to point his finger at Marshall, which caused Marshall to snap. Marshall stormed back inside the house with fury and determination. Stacy was coming toward him to find out what all of the yelling was about, but Marshall marched directly into the basement and retrieved his revolver: the Glock with scope and laser beam. He loaded the weapon and put a bullet in the chamber. He took off the safety lock and went back upstairs.

"Marshall, what's going on? Where are you going with that

gun?" Marshall didn't say a word. His mind had cracked once again and he aimed to set Theodore straight once and for all.

"Marshall!" Stacy shouted.

"What's going on?" June asked as she exited the bathroom.

Marshall marched down the hallway past June, whom he almost knocked down. He turned the corner in the living room, stormed past the sofa and piano, then ran up the staircase. He went into the guest bedroom where Stacy's parents had been sleeping and snatched their partially unpacked suitcase from the corner. He took it back down the stairs and out to the yard where Stacy and June were talking to Theodore, who was just as angry. Marshall tossed the suitcase at Theodore. He then pointed his revolver at Theodore and placed the red laser beam directly between his eyes.

"Theodore! You're not welcome here! Leave!" Everyone looked on in utter shock at the extreme measures that Marshall had taken.

"Mother June, I don't know how you do it, but you must be an awfully strong woman to have put up with this fool for so many years." Marshall's voice was thorny and ablaze with rage. He was on the verge of something unimaginable.

"Marshall! You are not kicking my parents out of my house." Stacy tried to get Marshall to lower his gun, but he held her back and kept his eyes locked on Theodore.

"Your father has the fucking nerve to come into my house and say to me I was never good enough for you because I'm 'too dark.' He called me a liar and told me I was a 'bad father.' Motherfucker, fuck you!" Marshall raised his weapon in the air and discharged it. "The next one is going directly between your eyes!"

"Theodore! How could you say things like that?!" June turned to Theodore and shouted at him.

"Well, it's the truth. My granddaughter would still be here if it wasn't for him. He's the one everyone should be angry with, not me. I loved my granddaughter and now she's gone." Theodore began sobbing.

"I don't think you really loved her, old fool. How could you? She had my blood running through her veins. Besides, she may have been 'too dark' for you to love!" Marshall's words were meant to cut deeply into Theodore's conscience. Theodore bucked up and made a threatening move toward Marshall.

"Go ahead. Do something."

"You need to leave now!" Marshall's jaws were tight. "I am not playing with you, Theodore. I will shoot you down like a wild animal."

"Marshall." June stepped in front of his aim to protect her husband. The laser beam was now aimed at June's throat.

"Marshall, baby, please put the gun down!" Stacy pleaded with her husband. Marshall didn't listen so Stacy got in front of her mother to protect her. The laser beam was now aimed at Stacy's heart.

"I'm sorry he said those mean things to you." Stacy put her hand on his wrist and began to lower his arm so that his gun wasn't pointed at anyone. "You don't want to hurt anyone. Put the gun away, baby." Marshall kept his glare on Theodore, who finally realized that Marshall was serious and meant what he'd said. "Please put the gun away," Stacy pleaded. Marshall allowed his shoulders to relax, and allowed his arm to come completely down.

"Theodore doesn't think sometimes when he speaks. That's just the way he is. He's hurt just like you, but he doesn't know how to deal with it. So he's lashing out at everyone who is close to him. I'm sorry for what he said to you. I truly am," June said in defense of her husband.

"Marshall," June spoke softly, "let us stay here for the night. Okay? I promise you that, in the morning, Theodore and I will get a hotel room." Once June got Marshall to agree, she went and took Theodore by the hand and led him away from Marshall and the house.

"Stacy," Marshall turned his attention to her, "I'm sorry. I cannot allow him to disrespect me in my own home. You know that."

"He's my father, Marshall," Stacy said.

"What? You don't think I was justified? You think I was wrong? You're my wife; you're supposed to be on my side," Marshall barked.

"What if I say something that you don't like, Marshall? Are you going to pull a gun on me, too?" Stacy asked.

"Stacy. You're taking this all wrong," Marshall tried to explain.

"No, Marshall, just leave me alone. You had that damn gun aimed at me, too. I saw the rage in your eyes, Marshall. You were going to kill my father," she said as she turned and walked away.

"So what does that mean, Stacy?" Marshall asked, but Stacy didn't say a word. She exited the yard and rushed down the block to catch up with her parents.

—14—
LUTHER

A number of Luther's job interviews didn't pan out. He had one left at the Cook County Hospital that would take place in a week. In an effort to keep moving forward and not put all of his eggs in one basket, Luther filled out applications wherever he could. He went to places like the *Chicago Tribune*, the *Chicago Sun*, hotels, and local hospitals. Luther didn't care what type of work he did as long as he was working. He was now sitting in the center of his living room floor, searching through the employment section of a newspaper.

"Computer programmer? Nope, don't know anything about computers." Luther was talking out loud to himself. "Handyman needed." Luther perked up as he read the listing: "*Carpentry, plumbing, and electrical work. Must have experience. Call Mr. Jones.*" Luther didn't know a damn thing about plumbing or carpentry, but he was willing to learn, if it landed him a job. He circled it and dialed the phone number. He got an answering machine so he left his name and his number. As soon as he placed the earpiece back on its cradle, the phone rang.

"Hello," Luther answered quickly, thinking maybe some employer wanted to set up an interview.

"Hey, Luther, this is Carmen. How are things going? Any luck with locating a new job?"

Luther smiled at the sound of her voice.

"No, nothing has come through for me yet," Luther answered honestly.

"Do you want me to help you land a job?"

"Help me, how? Are you going to go and do the interview for me?" he teased.

"No, but sometimes it helps if you practice some standard answers for some of the questions they will ask you."

"I'm not applying for the CEO of some major corporation. I'm just applying for entry-level positions," Luther explained.

"Luther, that's all the more reason you need to practice answering questions. What about your resume? How's it looking?" Carmen inquired.

"Resume? I just go and fill out an application. It's got all of the same information." Luther had never once thought about typing a resume.

"Luther, honey, it doesn't matter. You need to have a resume because it shows you're serious about finding a job. I don't care if you're applying for a street sweeper position or a garbage man position. You should always have a resume ready to go." Carmen had decided that she was going to put a little effort into Luther.

"Carmen, to be honest, I don't have that much to put on a resume. It's not like I've had a ton of job experience." Luther was all set to shoot down the idea of creating a resume that didn't have much meat in it.

"Luther, neither does a kid straight out of college. We all have to start somewhere. At some point, all of our resumes didn't have much meat on it."

"I'm not that good at putting those types of things together."

"Luther, I will help you. All you have to do is ask."

Luther smiled through the phone. He was overjoyed that a woman like Carmen had taken an interest in seeing him succeed. No one had done that since he was in high school.

"Carmen, will you please help me put together a resume?" Luther formally asked.

"Cheez, I thought you'd never ask. I tell you what. Meet me at Bret Harte Elementary School at three-thirty today and we'll go from there," Carmen suggested.

"You've got a deal." They exchanged a few more pleasantries and then ended their conversation.

As Luther made his way toward Bret Harte school, he spotted Carmen standing at a green door that opened to the playground. Luther picked up his pace the moment he saw her.

"Would you get in here?" Carmen harassed him. "School doesn't start until next week so we can use the school equipment to do what we need."

Luther stepped inside of the hallway. *All schools look alike*, he thought to himself as he scanned his surroundings.

"This way." Carmen walked up a small flight of stairs in front of them. Luther noticed how she gathered up her ankle-length skirt in one hand and held onto the railing with the other hand. He lustfully watched her ass and hips as they swung from right to left with every step she took. *Damn, I want to get all up in that*, he thought.

Carmen's black wavy hair was pulled back off of her face and rolled into a perfectly shaped circle at the back of her head. She had a hairpin that looked more like a tiny sword keeping it in place. Everything about Carmen said "schoolteacher" and "super freak" all at the same time. They walked down to her classroom, room 306. All of the desks were small and lined up in rows. The top rim of the blackboard had the letters of the alphabet both in capital and small letters. On the left side of the room was a coat closet for students. Near the front of the room was a reading rack filled with children's books.

"Over here, Luther."

"Oh, I'm sorry. It's been a while since I've been on the inside of a classroom like this. Everything is so small. When I was a kid, everything looked so big."

"I know. A lot of the parents say the same thing when they come inside the classroom." Carmen walked over toward the right side of the room, where there was a row of computers sitting on a table that ran the length of the room.

"Have a seat," Carmen said, as she sat down in front of a keyboard. Luther sat down in one of the small chairs and leaned in to watch what Carmen was doing.

"I've gone ahead and created the shell for your resume. All I need you to do is tell me where you worked and what you did. I'll phrase it right so it sounds like every duty you had was an important one." Carmen gazed at Luther, noticing his gingerbread skin and his soft brown eyes.

"Why are you doing this?" Luther asked.

"What do you mean?" Carmen replied, as she placed her fingers on the keyboard.

"Helping me out like this? You barely know me, but you're willing to go out of your way to help me." Carmen placed her hands down on her lap and spoke softly to Luther.

"You said something to me the other night when we had dinner that opened my eyes and I want to see you succeed. I want to see you make it. I want to see you live up to your potential."

"Man." Luther exhaled. "This sort of thing never happens for me. Everyone around me always expected me to get into some kind of trouble. I don't know how I stayed out of mess with the law, but I did. I'm not saying I'm perfect, but I don't consider myself a criminal, either. I've never been arrested; I don't have a record; and I don't do drugs. Well, not the hard stuff, anyway. From time to time, I'll smoke a joint, but that's it. I live one day at a time and whatever happens just happens." Carmen smiled at Luther.

"At least you're honest with yourself, Luther. That's a worthy quality to have." Carmen felt good about encouraging Luther.

"I try to live my life that way. I try to make an honest living. I want to get a steady job, a decent place to live, and a woman who understands me. A woman like you."

"My, aren't we bold?" Carmen laughed. "You come right on out and say what you want."

"Hey, that's my style. Why beat around the bush when you can simply go for it?" Luther was starting to really feel good about being with Carmen.

"I guess you have a point there," Carmen agreed.

"So, you're saying there is a chance for me, right? If you give me a chance, I promise, you will not regret it. I'll treat you like a queen, never do you wrong. I won't mess up. I promise you that." Luther was sharing his affections for her the best way he knew how.

"Hold on a minute," Carmen began laughing, "we're supposed to be working on your resume."

"I know, but if you tell me I have a chance with you, trust me, I'm going to work hard to find a job to take care of you." Luther wasn't going to take another step until he knew if he had a shot at being her man.

"Oh, so now you want to take care of me?" Carmen smiled.

Luther was serious about the way he was feeling. "I will be the type of guy who will never leave you. I'll bring my check home every week and give it to you."

Carmen focused on his sincere eyes. "Well, let's work on getting you a job first, all right?"

"Can I take you on a date?" Luther asked, completely ignoring what Carmen had said.

"Luther," Carmen paused to choose the right words, "you need to take one step at a time. Okay? Once you get on your feet, then we can consider going out on a date."

"That's all I wanted to know." Luther was bouncing up and down with jubilation on the inside. He'd met a stable woman, one with a good job who was willing to help him and that's all he truly ever wanted.

Luther had arrived for his interview at the Cook County Hospital thirty minutes early. He was applying for a janitorial job. He walked up to a side entrance and the automatic sliding door that didn't open. He glanced up and noticed that the laser sensor was dangling as if it had been struck by an object. He stepped to the side, opened the side door, and entered into the prescription pick-up area where patients were sitting and listening for their names to be called. The patients were a bizarre mixture of the elderly, foreigners, and the homeless. Luther paused for a moment to read the posted signs to see which direction he needed to go. The sound of heavy, violent coughing was constant and distracted him for a moment. An elderly woman, who appeared to have one foot in her grave and the other one planted on earth, couldn't control her coughing attack. Luther decided to head down the corridor to the main lobby where he could ask for directions. He stopped at the visitors' station and asked an attendant to direct him to the human resources department.

"It's down the hall," she said. "It's on this floor but on the Winchester Street side."

"Thanks," Luther replied and stepped away. Since it was still very early, Luther decided to take a seat in the waiting area to kill time. He glanced around his surroundings and noticed all of the signs: *"All hospital employees must display their ID at all times"* and *"Twenty-four-hour interpreter service."* The hospital also had its own police department run by the Cook County Sheriff's Office.

Finally, Luther went down the hall to the human resources department ten minutes ahead of time. When he got to the receptionist, he signed himself in and was given some employment forms to fill out.

"I have a resume," Luther announced with an overwhelming amount of pride. He'd never felt this confident before and realized it was because of Carmen. They had spent several afternoons going over some possible interview questions and what his reply should be. He felt as if he were a contestant on a game show who knew all of the answers. Carmen had also insisted he buy a suit for the interview.

"Okay, sir, just give it to me when you bring back the forms," said the woman, who then picked up a phone that had been ringing. Luther sat down at a table near the rear of the room and began filling out the forms. A few minutes later, he was all done and handed the forms back to the receptionist.

"Okay, Luther, have a seat and Mr. Waters will be right with you." Luther took a seat and picked up a copy of the *Chicago*

Tribune that was on a small coffee table near him. He found the horoscope section and read his, which said that his financial situation was going to be improving.

"Luther," a voice called out his name. Luther looked up. "I'm William Waters." Mr. Waters wasn't what Luther expected. He was a thin, puny, black man who appeared to be borderline anorexic. He was approaching Luther with his hand extended.

"Sorry to keep you waiting."

Luther stood up and shook the man's hand.

"Nice to meet you," Luther replied.

"Same here. Come on into my office." Mr. Waters stood aside and directed Luther into his office located behind the receptionist. They both sat at a small round table. Mr. Waters began looking over Luther's resume while he sat anxiously awaiting the first round of questions.

⸺

Later that evening, once he got back home, he called Carmen to tell her about the interview.

"I smoked the interview, girl." Luther was very excited because it had gone well. "I did just like you said. I stayed calm, I listened to the questions, and I thought about my answers before I said anything."

"Good for you, Luther. I'm happy to hear it went well."

"And dude was impressed by the fact I had such a nice resume typed up for the job. I was doing so well that the guy started telling me what I'd be doing and even started showing me around."

"Well, Luther, it sounds as if you got the job. The fact that you were shown around is a very positive sign."

"I know that I got it. I can feel it." Luther was overjoyed.

"Did he say when he'd call you back?" Carmen asked.

"He said I should hear something back within a day or two."

"They need to do a background check; that's why they have to wait," Carmen explained.

"I don't care. I'm ready to go to work and make some money." Luther's enthusiasm rang out in his voice. "And it's all because of you, Carmen. I've got another chance to get it right because of you."

"Luther, you did it all by yourself. All you needed was a little confidence booster."

"Man, I feel so good," he said.

"Luther," Carmen said, "it's only six o' clock, and I usually take a walk in the evening. Would you like to walk with me along the lake front?"

"Carmen, are you asking me out on a date?"

"No, Luther, I'm asking you if you'd like to take a walk along the lake front; that's all."

"Well, it sounds like a date to me." Luther laughed. "Where should I meet you?"

"Meet me at the Fifty-fifth Street underpass in about thirty minutes. I usually walk down to Forty-seventh Street and back."

"I'll be there," Luther said and hung up the phone.

–15–
CARMEN

The crowd outside of Big Daddy's Exotic Dance Club snaked around the building. There was a mixture of both men and women, young and old, that couldn't wait to get inside the place. As Carmen approached one of the bouncers, she could hear the sound of music emanating from inside.

"Excuse me," she said to a tall and imposing-looking man who looked as if he could crush a human skull with his bare hands.

"What do you want, shawty?" The bouncer glanced in her direction.

"I'm on the VIP list," Carmen said, feeling a little tipsy from the three glasses of wine she'd drunk in order to get up the nerve to actually show up. She'd caught up with Nikki earlier that day and told her that she'd be coming to the Freak of the Week party. Nikki was excited about Carmen coming and made sure that her name got on the V.I.P. list. The bouncer studied Carmen for a long moment.

"So how freaky do you get, shawty?" the bouncer asked as he pulled a sheet of paper from the inside pocket of his suit.

"Why are you asking me a question like that?" Carmen asked.

"Only the serious freaks make the V.I.P. list and I don't ever recall seeing you here. I want to make sure that I'm not missing out on something," he said as he unfolded the sheet of paper.

"I'm a friend of Nikki and Frieda. Do you know them?"

"Oh shit. Hell, yeah. I know them, especially Frieda. Woo, she's got a serious freak bone. What's your name, shawty?"

"Carmen."

"Oh yeah, your name is on the list with a star next to it." The bouncer unlatched the red velvet rope that separated them. "Go on in, shawty, and get your freak on. The male strippers are on the first floor and the female strippers are on the second floor. My name is Big Bounce. If you need anything, give me a holla."

"Okay, Big Bounce." Carmen touched Big Bounce's massive chest as she moved past him. "Ooo, you feel good." She flirted with him a little, to see what type of reaction she'd get from him.

"Hey, I feel good all over. Why are you stopping with my chest when there is so much more to check out?" Big Bounce wasn't shy about sharing himself with the ladies.

"Maybe next time, baby," Carmen teased. Being able to get Big Bounce riled up gave her more confidence in her ability to attract a man. Big Daddy's was a Las Vegas-style exotic dance club that catered to the erotic desires and fantasies of both men and women. It was a place where the bold and uninhibited could come and indulge themselves in a world of lust, sex, and desire. The décor of Big Daddy's was upscale and chic, a welcome surprise to Carmen because she didn't anticipate the place being so clean. Carmen located a seat in the VIP section situated near the stage. She was positioned perfectly to get a great view of the male strippers who'd be performing. Once she was situated, a waitress came over and took her drink order.

"I'll have an Apple Martini," Carmen said to the young waitress who scribbled down her request.

"Will anyone be joining you?" asked the waitress.

"No," Carmen answered. Carmen glanced around the room,

which had quickly begun to fill up with ladies eager to see the male performers. On the right side of the room were vendors selling their products. Just as she was about to go check things out, Frieda showed up.

"I can't fucking believe it. The wicked bitch of the west has come out of her ice castle to play with fire," Frieda said, as she sat down.

"Nice to see you, too, Frieda," Carmen greeted her. At that moment, the waitress returned with Carmen's drink.

"So what do you think of the place?" Frieda asked.

"It's different," Carmen answered as she took a sip of her Apple Martini.

"Have you ever seen a male stripper, Carmen?"

"Sure I have," Carmen lied.

"I'll bet you have." Frieda didn't believe Carmen.

"Where's Nikki?" Carmen asked.

"She's back in the office with Packard handling some business with his top clients. She'll be out soon enough."

"So when does the show start?"

"In a few minutes. I'm the emcee tonight." Frieda grinned at Carmen with a devilish smile.

"What's that look for?"

"Nothing, girl. I'm just shocked you're actually here."

"Well, the world is full of surprises." Carmen once again glanced over at the vendors. A parade of women were browsing the goods and Carmen wanted to go check out the tables.

"Go check it out," Frieda encouraged. "Your seat will not be taken. I'll have the waitress bring me a 'reserved' sign."

Carmen wandered over to the vendors who were selling everything from lingerie to sex toys. There was an assortment of vibrators, rabbit ears, and even chocolates shaped like penises.

She didn't make a purchase because she didn't see anything that caught her eye at the moment.

"Okay, ladies. Let's get this party started!" Carmen turned and looked at Frieda, who was up on the stage with the microphone. There was a chorus of cheers that billowed upward from a room packed with anxious and lustful women.

"Ladies, now we all like a good piece of dick. We all like a dick that stays hard and brushes against the walls of our pussy just right," Frieda said to a chorus of laughter and cheers from the audience. "Yes, ladies, there is nothing like a good dick that makes you shiver just thinking about it. A dick that makes you want to drop to your knees, open your mouth and suck on that beautiful motherfucker until that hot liquid shoots out and splashes all over your skin."

"Ooo, yes, girl!" a woman cried out. Carmen finished off her Apple Martini and then ordered another as she continued to listen to Frieda warm up the crowd.

"Ladies, I'm talking about a dick that can get all up in your pussy. I'm talking about a man with an ass so tight you can't wait to dig your fingernails into it. I'm talking about a back so strong that the power of its thrust is enough to make you howl out and sink your teeth into the side of his neck like you're a blood-thirsty vampire."

"Ooo, shit girl! Tell the motherfucker with that dick to come over here and see me!" another woman shouted. A loud roar of laughter erupted.

"Ladies, let me bring out a man with a bronze dick that will surely have your mouth watering. Man of Steel. Come do your thing, baby." The stage lights went down for a moment and a smoke machine began blowing white mist onto the stage. Soft red lights came up and then an Adonis of a man emerged from the thick mist while the sound of Usher singing his hit song "Make Love in this Club" played in the background. Carmen got swept up in the energy of the crowd as the stripper danced sensually, removing his clothing to expose his chiseled abs, thunderous thighs, and powerful chest.

"Over here, baby! Over here." A woman sitting at the table next to Carmen called for the stripper, who came over to her, sat on her lap, and began rotating his hips.

"Oh, my God," Carmen said aloud. "That shit looks so good." Carmen felt herself coming alive. Butterflies were dancing around her tummy and her pussy was suddenly asking for all kinds of attention.

"Waitress." Carmen stopped her waitress and ordered another Apple Martini.

"Okay, ladies, did you like the Man of Steel?" Frieda was now back onstage.

"Now, ladies—oh, you're in for a real treat now. How many of you have ever wanted to fuck a male gymnast?" The eruption of laughter and cheers grew to earsplitting levels.

"I do!" Carmen shouted above the noise. She was now just as excited and filled with as much yearning as the other women. Carmen was starting to feel very relaxed and at ease.

"Ladies, this next man will definitely spread your legs open wide and give your pussy mouth-to-mouth resuscitation." Frieda glanced at Carmen and winked at her. "Ladies, brace yourselves because a Cowboy named Shotgun is about to enter the Pussy Pound!" The stage lights once again went out. The fog machine began blowing white smoke, red and blue lights began swirling around, and the sound of a police siren wailing filled the room. Then, from the smoke emerged a man so sexy that Carmen stopped breathing for a moment when she saw him step onto the stage. The women loved him. They cheered him on as he stood at the center of the stage. With extreme and precise muscle control, he began to wind his hips, showcasing his sexual prowess and defining exactly how to penetrate a woman. The move was so sexy that women began taking photos of the man with their digital cameras and cell phones. Shotgun then jumped down from the stage, walked out into the audience, and approached Carmen, who was screaming out for him. Shotgun allowed Carmen to put her hand right down the front of his pants.

"Let's see what you're working with," said Carmen as women all around her were screaming.

"I'm going to be working with you in a minute," Shotgun said with a sexy smile. The wine and the martinis Carmen had been drinking had made her hot. She wanted to feel Shotgun's dick but what she ended up feeling was a pair of handcuffs.

"What in the world is this?" Carmen asked as she pulled out the silver handcuffs for everyone to see. The ladies screamed with excitement.

"Those are for you, girl," said Shotgun as he locked his hands on Carmen's hips and hoisted her up onto the stage before she could stop him.

"No, no!" Carmen said as she tried to get down, but it was too late. Shotgun had jumped back up onto the stage and ripped off his pants. His only clothing was a hot-red G-string. He slowly approached Carmen, who was backing away from him.

"Girl, what the hell are you backing away from all that man for? Damn, Shotgun, you picked the wrong bitch!" screamed a woman who was clearly upset that Carmen didn't want to play along.

"He didn't pick the wrong one!" Carmen shouted back at the woman and then stopped so that Shotgun could reach her. She swallowed hard, took a deep breath, and stood her ground like a grown woman, unafraid and confident that she could handle anything that Shotgun dished out.

"Give me the handcuffs." Shotgun extended his long, muscular arms. Carmen gave him the handcuffs which he then locked around her wrists. Shotgun stepped close to her and lifted her locked wrists up in the air before bringing them down behind his neck. Shotgun then lifted Carmen up so that she had no choice but to wrap her thighs around his waist. He began simulating the act of fucking her while standing up. Carmen could feel Shotgun's erect Pride slapping the bottom of her ass.

"Oh, my God!" Carmen cried out because she couldn't believe she was actually doing what she was doing.

"Come on. Grind those hips, girl!" Shotgun told her what to do. Carmen didn't back down from his challenge and began moving her hips as if she were fucking the shit out of him. Carmen was on fire. This was bold and unfamiliar territory to her. It was both frightening and exciting at the same time because the seductress within her was being born.

"Get him, girl! Break his ass down!" Carmen heard someone from the crowd shout. Shotgun gently placed Carmen on her back and then rose up to a full standing position. He did a few sensual moves that excited the women and then straddled Carmen.

"Come on with it!" Carmen was on fire and ready to be taken to whatever level of pleasure Shotgun could offer. Shotgun began to split. He slowly spread his legs apart and then gently rested himself on top of Carmen. He began simulating the act as Carmen tossed her handcuffed wrists over his head so that she could grab his ass.

"Oh yes!" Carmen screamed out as she dug her fingernails into his ass while enjoying the feel of his cock pushing against her hips. Carmen got so caught up in the ecstasy of the moment that she felt a small orgasm erupt.

"Ooo, shit!" she cried out with embarrassment. Shotgun then stood up and helped Carmen get to her feet. He held her close to him so that she couldn't see what was going on behind her. Shotgun continued to grind up against Carmen as the Man of Steel approached her from behind. The two men then sandwiched Carmen between them. The sight of the onstage threesome caused the audience to scream with wild abandon. By the time the men were done grinding against her, Carmen needed to go freshen up; her panties were wet and sticky.

When Carmen arrived back home after her night of erotic fun, she was on fire and in need of attention. Her pussy was throbbing, her nipples were sensitive, and she wanted to be touched. She took a shower, hoping it could quell her thirst for penetration. However, the shower only heightened her senses and made her body yearn even harder for satisfaction.

"Damn," Carmen hissed as she dried her wet body with one of her favorite towels. "I can't wait to play with myself," she said as she stood before her bathroom mirror and applied a strawberry-scented lubricant to her skin. Once she was done, she entered her bedroom and opened up her top dresser drawer. She pushed her panties to the side and removed her toy that she'd named Morris Chestnut.

"Morris, I hope you're up to the challenge tonight," she said as she checked to make sure the batteries were still strong. Carmen got positioned comfortably on her bed and placed Morris at her side. She then closed her eyes and imagined a faceless lover who knew all of her magic spots. Her lover would take his time. He'd whisper in her ear and tell her how much he desired her. He'd tell her how much he'd been thinking about her and how hard his dick got when he did. Her lover would nibble on her earlobe, and kiss her neck while sweeping his long, soft finger up and down the lips of her paradise. She'd spread open her legs for him and enjoy the feel of his body weight on top of her.

"Oh damn," Carmen cried out as she reached for Morris. She allowed Morris to buzz around her clit which caused her to immediately grind her hips. She allowed Morris to slip inside of her. Carmen's pussy gabbed and squeezed her toy with out-of-control desire. Carmen slid Morris in and out of her but Morris suddenly died out.

"Morris, damn you!" Carmen shouted. She tried to turn Morris back on, but the batteries were dead. "Shit, shit, shit, shit," Carmen repeated. She tossed Morris to the side and placed one of her pillows between her thighs.

"I need some real dick," Carmen admitted to herself as she felt her womanhood contract and release.

"Damn, this is driving me crazy!" Carmen said as she tried to satisfy her hunger for a man. Then it hit her. Carmen knew exactly where she could order up some dick at such a late hour.

"Luther." She spoke his name as she glanced at her alarm clock situated on the nightstand. It was three o' clock in the morning.

"If I call him at this hour, he is certainly going to know that I'm making a straight-up booty call," Carmen said to herself as she weighed the pros and cons of calling Luther for an intimate time. After giving it some serious debate, she concluded that she wanted to simply fuck Luther. She wanted him to come over and put her flame out. Carmen picked up her phone and called him.

"Hello," Luther answered. She could tell that he had been asleep.

"Hey you," Carmen greeted.

"Carmen?" Luther was shocked to be getting a call from her at this hour.

"Yeah, it's me. What are you doing right now?" Carmen wanted to get directly to the reason behind her call.

"I was sleeping, but I'm up now. What's going on?"

"I need some company. Can you come and keep me company for a little while?" Carmen asked as she sighed.

"Yeah. I can do that. I'll get up right now and get dressed."

"Okay. I'll be waiting for you. Oh, and Luther, just so that we're clear. I hope you're rested up because I need a hard dick tonight," Carmen said and then hung up the phone before Luther could respond.

Carmen rushed around the house to prepare her room. She went into the kitchen and pulled some candles down from the cupboard. She turned on her iPod and selected her love song collection that had a mixture of old school and current artists from Teddy Pendergrass to Kem. She then rushed back to the kitchen, placed some grapes and sliced pineapples in a bowl, and brought it into the bedroom along with some wine coolers. She made sure her bathroom was spotless and then put on a sexy, red silk camisole that she hoped he'd notice and appreciate. As Carmen relaxed on her bed and listened to a song called "Differences" by Ginuwine, she closed her eyes and imagined how good Luther would feel inside of her. She imagined how succulent his lips would taste and the sweet things he'd say to her. She hoped that Luther would take her soaring to new pleasurable heights. She hoped that he could bring out the freak in her that she didn't even know existed. Just as Carmen's fantasy was getting good, she heard her buzzer.

"It's about time you got here," she said as she walked over to the door and buzzed him into the building. She opened up her front door and watched as Luther came up the stairs.

"I'm right here on the first floor," Carmen said as she stepped back inside her condo.

"Hey," Luther greeted her. He was smiling very hard.

"Glad you could make it."

"Oh, I don't believe this. Me being here with you like this. I never would've thought something like this could've ever happened." Luther kicked off his shoes.

"I told you before. Life is full of surprises." Carmen didn't feel like having a lot of conversation. She wanted to keep up the momentum, so she escorted Luther into her bedroom.

"Oh, sweet," Luther said, popping his fingers to the music.

"Not as sweet as my love is going to be," Carmen said as she stepped into his embrace. Luther held onto her tightly as he glanced into her eyes.

"You want this, don't you?" Luther said.

"Yes." Carmen surrendered to him. Luther dropped his mouth open and leaned in to kiss her. His kiss was way too wet and sloppy. His tongue invaded her mouth and flicked rapidly from left to right like a fish flopping out of water. Carmen pulled back from him and wanted to immediately go get a towel to wipe her face off.

"Get up on that bed," Luther said as he began undressing.

"Okay," Carmen said. She had hoped that his kissing skills would've been better. Carmen opened up the drawer on her nightstand and handed Luther a condom.

"Oh, I can't feel the real thing?"

"You either put that condom on or get nothing at all."

Luther situated himself on top of Carmen and kissed her again. That kiss was even worse than earlier. Carmen broke away from the kiss by turning her head. Luther took it as a sign that she wanted him to stick his drooling wet tongue in her ear. His heavy breathing and slurping sounds made her cringe.

"Yeah, baby, I'm going to give it to you good," Luther said as Carmen tried to direct him away from her ear. When he finally picked up the hint and began kissing her neck, she felt his saliva dripping out of her ear. *Oh God,* she thought.

"Let me at them nipples, girl." Luther raised her camisole and began twisting her nipples.

"Luther, slow down. My nipples aren't wrenches."

Luther paid little attention to her words. He was too caught up in the excitement of being with Carmen.

"You ready." Luther opened up the condom package and put it on.

"Hang on," Carmen said as she turned on a nearby lamp so that she could make sure that Luther put the condom on. She watched him, noticing that his pubic hair needed to be trimmed down and shaped up. It looked as if he had a mini Afro between his legs and that was not appealing to her. Carmen was most certainly having her regrets.

Carmen cringed when he penetrated her.

"Oh yeah, this shit feels good to me," Luther said as he began thrusting violently. "Oh, this is so good," he repeated. Luther's rough thrusting quickly turned into all-out rough pounding.

"Isn't this dick good to you?" Luther asked as he pounded harder.

"Luther…" Carmen was trying to tell him to slow down but he was in his own world.

"Oh goddamn, Carmen," Luther cried out as he allowed the full weight of his body to rest on her. Carmen shifted her body beneath him so that she could breathe.

"Luther—"

"Yes, baby, I know. This shit is good to you!" Luther pounded her harder. Carmen quickly realized that giving Luther this opportunity wasn't such a good idea. She was ready for their encounter to end. She locked her legs at the ankle and squeezed her vaginal muscle, which would make Luther have an orgasm.

"Oh yes, baby, I feel you squeezing my shit," Luther said as his body locked up, then remained still for a moment before finally releasing his essence. Carmen felt his hot liquid oozing out into her vagina.

"Shit, Luther, get off of me. I think the condom broke!" Carmen forced Luther to get off of her and as she feared, the condom had broken because of Luther's roughness.

"Shit!" Carmen rushed into the bathroom.

~16~
MARSHALL

Marshall finally received the phone call from Detective Taylor that he'd been waiting for. Marshall was anxious and ready to ride with police to arrest the registered owner of the vehicle and bring him to justice for vehicular homicide.

"Have you assembled a team to go pick up this dirt bag?" Marshall asked Taylor as he prepared to join the police.

"Marshall, we've run the plate number that you've given to us and it does match the description of the car that witnesses gave to us. However, the car was reported stolen on the day of Lena's accident."

"What? You're kidding me, right?" Marshall couldn't believe what he was hearing.

"No, I'm afraid not. The car was reported stolen around eleven o' clock in the morning. I even pulled a copy of the police report and spoke to the officer who took the report who confirms that the registered owner, a man named Packard Bell, made the report."

"Goddamn it!" Marshall griped.

"And since your accident didn't happen until late that afternoon, the person driving the car at the time was probably the reckless car thief."

"I know, Taylor; you don't have to explain the loophole to me." Marshall paused. "Aren't you going to at least bring the guy in for questioning? Can we verify where he was at the time of the accident? Perhaps he recovered his car and was—"

"Marshall," Detective Taylor said, interrupting him. "Calm down for a moment. We're going to bring him in for questioning but, at this time, he is not a suspect."

"Well, can I come and watch the questioning?" Marshall asked. There was a long moment of silence before Taylor answered. "I'm okay. I can handle it," Marshall reassured Taylor, who was trying to get a sense of his mental state.

"Marshall, there is one more thing you should know," Taylor said.

"What's that?"

"We've recovered the vehicle. It had been dumped in the parking lot of a nearby public housing complex. The car had been stripped down. The only thing that was in the car was a toolbox with various tools and the initials 'L.P.' carved into several wrenches and a hammer. I had the car towed over to the crime lab so that it can be dusted for fingerprints and blood samples."

"Okay. Let me know what you come up with," Marshall said, then asked a few more questions before ending the call.

A day had passed before Taylor called Marshall back to provide the location and time he planned to question Packard. Once Marshall jotted down the information, he went into the living room where Stacy and her parents were chatting while viewing baby photos of Lena. The moment he entered the room, a deafening silence erupted. They'd been acting funny with Marshall ever since the argument they'd had a few days ago. It was clear, at least in his mind, that the three of them were alienating him from their circle of trust.

"I wanted to tell you that they're bringing in the guy who owns the SUV for questioning. Taylor has agreed to allow me to watch and I wanted to know if you wanted to come with me, Stacy," Marshall asked her directly. Before Stacy could respond, Theodore spoke for her.

"There is no need to continue to upset my baby girl." Although Theodore's intentions may have been good, he came off as arrogant and rude.

"I want to go," Stacy answered. Marshall felt a bit vindicated. However, it was clear that Marshall and Theodore were both fighting for Stacy's loyalty and the tension between him and Theodore was still searching for the right moment to explode.

"I want to be there," Stacy continued.

"Then June and I are going as well," said Theodore as he rose to his feet, sucked in his belly and pulled his slacks up higher than they needed to be.

Arrogant prick, Marshall thought as he turned and walked out toward the garage to pull the car around.

Once they arrived at the police station, Taylor allowed Theodore, June, and Stacy to view the conversation with Packard in another room through a two-way glass. Taylor once again carefully assessed Marshall's state of mind.

"Are you okay?" he asked.

"Trust me. I'm fine." Marshall entered the interrogation room and sat down at the table with Taylor and Packard.

"Thank you for coming down, sir," Taylor began. He set a modest-sized storage box on the table.

"Please call me Packard," the man insisted.

"Okay," Taylor continued. "As you know, we found your SUV abandoned in a parking lot of a public housing complex. It's been stripped down. Can you tell me if there was any front end damage to the vehicle before it was stolen?"

"No," Packard replied. "There wasn't a ding or scratch on it."

"Here is what we found inside your truck." Taylor removed some tools from the storage box that had been sealed in plastic. "Do the initials 'L.P.' mean anything to you?"

Packard looked at the tools and a small smirk came over his face as if he knew something.

"Do you have any idea of whom they belong to?" Marshall quickly asked, sensing that Packard was withholding information.

"None whatsoever." Packard looked Marshall directly in the eyes.

Marshall pressed the issue. "Are you sure?"

"Positive, man. I have no idea who those tools belong to. I'm a businessman, trying to live the American dream," Packard answered with a bit of sarcasm in his voice.

"Now, on the day your truck was stolen, you were over on Prairie Street with an insurance adjuster looking into a property of yours that had caught on fire. Is that correct?" Taylor asked.

"Yeah, a building I owned burned up. The police tried to say it was arson, but after an investigation, they concluded that it was a gas line fire." Packard rubbed the tip of his nose a few times with an index finger and folded his arms across his chest.

"Wait a minute." Marshall's mind began racing. *Quentin was investigating that fire, but handed the case over to someone else when Quentin asked for family time to deal with everything that had happened with Lena.* Marshall finally recalled what Quentin had mentioned to him. "Were they sure it was a gas leak? Perhaps it really wasn't a leak. Perhaps the person who stole your car was a tenant. Did you have any upset tenants? Can we get a list of tenants who lived there?" Marshall asked, not wanting to leave any stone unturned.

"Look, man. I'm sorry about your kid, but like I said, the fire was ruled a gas leak. The building was old and needed work—too much work to make it livable. I didn't have any tenants living in it at the time of the fire. The building had been vacant for a while."

"Well, then, why was the gas on?" Taylor asked.

"I don't know. That's something you need to take up with the gas company. Squatters could've gotten in the place, for all I know. What is this?" Packard got defensive. "I come down here on good faith and now you guys want to grill me about something else. I don't have to take this crap." Packard stood up to leave.

"No. Please sit down," Taylor said. "You used to be a police officer. You know we're only trying to help you think of things that might trigger a memory for you. This investigation is not about the property."

"I'm trying to find the person who stole your car and ran down my daughter." Marshall tried to gain Packard's sympathy.

"I understand," Packard said, but Marshall didn't believe him. There was something about Packard that didn't sit well with him.

"Okay, look, I had been doing some work around the place. Trying to fix it up to see if I could rent at least one apartment," Packard started lying.

"Was there anyone helping you do the work?" Taylor asked, still searching for clues.

"No. It was just me." Packard continued to lie.

"What kind of work were you doing in there?" Marshall asked because he'd become extremely suspicious of Packard's story.

He often did work around the property he owned on Eighty-seventh Street and was interested in knowing what Packard could have done to spark a gas leak.

"I was pulling out some pipes," Packard said.

Marshall was leery. "By yourself?"

"Marshall, this wasn't about his property; it was about who stole Packard's car," Taylor reminded Marshall. "Did you have an alarm system on your car, Packard?"

"No."

"Really? Not even a factory alarm?" Marshall could tell that Taylor was setting Packard up for something Packard couldn't see.

"I had my mechanic uninstall it."

"Why would you do that, Packard?" Taylor asked.

"What are you driving at?" Packard suddenly jumped to his feet.

"Can you tell me the name of your mechanic, Packard?" Taylor asked.

"You know what. I'm done with you guys. The insurance company has already totaled the truck. I reported it stolen. Now you two are in here treating me like I'm a criminal. If I'm not under arrest or a suspect, then I'm leaving." Packard went to the door, but stopped before opening it. "Oh, and for your information, I don't recall the mechanic's name. I purchased that SUV used and the alarm kept going off for no reason. It was faulty wiring. So I took it in and had it removed. Good luck with your investigation. And if I get hauled in here again, I'm bringing my attorney with me." Packard left. Taylor and Marshall got up to join Stacy, June, and Theodore. But before they could enter the room, Theodore had flung the door open and stepped out into the hallway in an emotionally charged rage.

"Go bring him back!" he demanded. "That son-of-a-bitch knows something that he's not telling us."

"Sir," Taylor attempted to calm down the old man, "we can not detain him. He is not a suspect."

"But he knows something. He's lying about what he knows!" Theodore was yelling at the top of his voice and tried to get around Taylor to go get Packard himself. "I can smell a liar a mile away and that man is lying. He knew who those tools belong to; the look on his face said it all." Theodore continued his tirade.

"Daddy, you're not making this any easier." Stacy tried to calm him down.

"Somebody go and get him and bring him back here for more questioning." Theodore was pointing toward the ground where he was standing. "Let me interrogate him; I'll pull it out of him. I'll make him talk." He was tensed up and his voice was fading from all of his yelling.

"Why is no one listening to me, June? Tell them! I know what I'm talking about." Theodore demanded that he be heard.

"Of course you do," offered June as she rubbed his back and pulled him back inside the room to have a seat and calm down.

"I'm not an old fool!" he shouted. "Do you hear me, Marshall!" Theodore turned his anger toward Marshall and began a verbal assault. "You didn't push him hard enough, Soldier! You failed! You're a no-good failure!"

"Listen, you sick, twisted bastard! I've had just about enough of your criticism of me. Say one more word to me and I'll—" Marshall stopped abruptly. The last thing he wanted to do was issue a death threat in a police station.

"It's all your fault!" Theodore continued to run his mouth. He was about to say something else, but his hand suddenly closed and he couldn't open it back up. He clutched his chest and tried to speak, but he could only grunt. Theodore fell to his knees and rolled over to his back. He was gasping for air.

"Theodore!" June shrieked.

"Daddy! What's wrong? What's happening?!" Stacy screamed as she kneeled down by her father.

"You!" Taylor pointed to a uniformed officer who was coming down the hall toward them. "Call an ambulance. I believe this man is having a heart attack."

—17—
LUTHER

Luther got the housekeeping job at the Cook County Hospital just like he thought he would. In addition to his janitorial duties, sometimes he'd pitch in and help transport patients to get an X-ray or a CAT scan. Overall, Luther hated his job. Working around sick people wasn't easy and most of the time, it was unbearably depressing. The scent of sickness kept his stomach upset. There was always someone wailing due to the loss of a loved one. He swore every day that he'd contracted some type of unknown disease.

By December, five months had passed since the accident. Since Luther hadn't been caught, he felt as if the entire incident was safely behind him. His conscience wouldn't let him forget the accident and working around the sick and injured constantly reminded him of the life he'd taken. The only thing that made his life bearable and kept him from going completely mad with guilt was Carmen. Over the past few months, she'd become his inspiration and his reason for not giving up on life or himself. He loved her. He loved everything about her. The way she walked, the way she talked, and the way she encouraged him to succeed and strive for a better life. He loved her for caring about him. He loved her for wanting to be with him. He loved her because he could depend on her if things went sour.

"What do you want to do with your life, Luther?" she had

asked him one evening back in August when they were taking an evening stroll down Fifty-third Street.

"I don't know," he answered, "right now I have everything I want. I have a place to stay; I have a job; and I have you as my friend."

"Don't you want more than that?" Carmen hoped that Luther had loftier goals and bigger dreams.

"What? Like a house and a nice car? That would be nice, but I don't think I'd ever be able to afford those things. I'm really a simple kind of guy. It doesn't take much to make me happy," Luther explained as he held onto her hand as they strolled along.

"Luther, honey, being successful isn't rocket science. It's simple. You go to school and get your education so that you can land a better job or learn how you can start up a company of your own."

"A job is a job," Luther responded. "If it's a good-paying job that covers my basic needs, then I'm cool."

"That's it right there, Luther."

"What?"

"Luther, anyone can get a job. What you want to do is choose a career. Something you can do. Something that you know you will enjoy. Like me. I love teaching. The pay enables me to have a decent life and I have a reasonable amount of job security. If you could choose a career in a field, what would you like to do?"

Luther had never thought about it.

"You know, Carmen, I've always wanted to do social work. I would like to help people turn their life around, find a job—no, a career," Luther corrected himself. "I'd like to open up a safe house for abused women. A place where they'd feel safe. I'd have daycare for their children while they went to work, and I'd even build affordable housing for them so they wouldn't be so dependent on the men who beat them."

"Luther, it sounds as if you've got the beginnings of a plan. Why don't you start taking steps toward making that goal a reality?"

Luther downplayed his desire to work toward his dream. "What? Carmen, that's a silly dream I once had when I was a kid."

"Luther, that's what this country is all about. Making your dreams a reality. You may be the hope for a lot of other children out there who are going through what you went through. Imagine how they'd feel if they heard about this man named Luther Parker building a shelter that their mothers could come to." Luther was silent. He'd never thought about actually making a difference.

"What are you thinking about?" Carmen asked.

"Do you really think I could do something like that?" Carmen could see she'd opened up Luther's eyes to new possibilities.

"Luther, you can do anything that you set your mind to."

"But how?"

"Well, my daddy always said, 'The key to everything is education.' It's not too late, Luther. There is no cut-off age for going back to school."

"Will you help me?" Luther asked.

"If you make the commitment to finish what you start, I will help you in any way I can. Set a goal, Luther, and once you reach that goal, set another one, and so on and so forth."

"Then I guess that my first goal would be to get a degree." Luther laughed at the thought. "Me with a college degree."

"You know Malcolm X College is within walking distance of your job. It's a city college and it's affordable."

"Yeah, I know where it is," Luther said nervously.

"Then I suggest that you walk over there, pick up a fall course schedule, and do what you have to do to get yourself a degree."

Luther remained quiet as he thought to himself. He couldn't believe Carmen was actually pushing him to go back to school.

"Luther, you have absolutely nothing to lose and everything to gain. That includes me." Carmen gave him an extra incentive to put fire under his ass to make him move forward with his life.

— ● —

The year had quickly arrived at its end. To celebrate, Carmen and Luther decided to go to a comedy club on New Year's Eve. The evening's headline act was an up-and-coming comedian named Pork Chop. They got to the comedy club early. Luther wanted to ensure they got seats near the front of the stage. When the show began, the comic came onstage grooving to "Party People" by Nelly. Pork Chop began his opening monologue by cracking jokes on Luther.

"Damn, man. You're just like me. You don't miss a damn meal, do you?" Pork Chop glanced at Luther. "You're a big, collard-greens-and-pig-feet-eating brother, aren't you?" Luther and the audience laughed.

"Yeah, I know you are," Pork Chop continued, "I see that you brought your pig with you." Pork Chop pointed to Carmen and snorted. "Miss Piggy is in the house, yawl." The crowd burst into loud laughter. Carmen was stunned that the brunt of his joke was actually aimed at her and not Luther. However, she took the joke good-naturedly, even though she didn't consider herself to be fat by any measure. Sure, she'd picked up a little weight; she'd gone from a size eight to a ten.

"What are you laughing at, brother?" Pork Chop picked out another man in the crowd. "You look like a damn Billy Dee Williams wannabe." There was another huge outburst of laughter.

"I bet your ass is in here drinking a Colt 45, aren't you?" There was an even louder outburst of laughter. "Billy was the shit, though. Back in the seventies. Do you guys remember *Lady Sings the Blues*?" Pork Chop asked, "Billy had his pimp hat and shit on. He stuck his hand out to give Diana Ross some money and said all low and shit, 'Do you want my arm to fall off?'" Pork Chop imitated Billy's voice exactly and the crowd loved it. By the stroke of midnight, when everyone was singing and toasting in the New Year, Luther looked at Carmen. "Happy New Year, Carmen."

"Happy New Year to you, too, Luther." They clicked their champagne glasses, took a sip, and then hugged each other.

"Here's to another year filled with success and happiness," Carmen said.

"Without you in my life, Carmen, I'd be lost. Because of you, I'm able to dream and think bigger than I ever thought I could." Luther began professing his deep affection for Carmen.

"Do you really mean that, Luther?" she asked as she picked up her dry martini and took a sip.

"Yes, I do. I think I'm in love with you, Carmen." Carmen glanced at him for a long moment and then smiled. Although she wasn't ready to call her fascination with him "love," she did have to admit that she enjoyed watching him blossom. And if he continued to grow, then her fascination would most certainly develop into love.

"Here's to the promise of love," Carmen said, as she raised her glass to toast to the New Year and her ongoing friendship with Luther.

-18-
CARMEN

Carmen was true to her word. She helped Luther enroll at Malcolm X Community College. Luther took twelve full-credit hours and attended classes four nights a week and all day on Saturdays. On Sundays, he and Carmen spent their days at the Woodson Library on Ninety-fifty Street. Luther studied while Carmen graded papers and planned out her lessons. At the end of the first semester, Luther had a 3.6 grade-point average—something both he and Carmen were very proud of.

Carmen was proud of herself for convincing Luther that he should go back to school to pursue a degree. Their relationship had grown into what she considered strong and healthy. Although Luther was still rather rough in the intimacy department, he'd improved some. Luther didn't like to eat pussy and Carmen felt as if that was cruel and unusual punishment. However, she did take comfort in knowing that she didn't have to worry about Luther cheating. The man was like clockwork and extremely predictable. He frequently called to let her know his whereabouts and constantly told her that he loved her. Luther was proud to be her man and, she knew one day, he hoped to be her husband. Coaching Luther was easy for Carmen because he was willing and so determined to reach his goal. He didn't allow distractions to interfere with what he'd set his mind to do.

By spring, Luther had finished his second semester and was still holding that 3.6 grade-point average. Since Luther had been so focused and had worked so hard, Carmen thought he'd want to take a break for the summer.

"Are you kidding me?" he said one morning when they were having breakfast at the Pancake House in Hyde Park. "I'm on a high. I can't stop now. I'm going to register for the summer session and knock down another biology class, an English class, and a physiology class."

"Luther, baby, are you sure you can handle all of those classes? That's going to be a very heavy load."

"Carmen, I keep telling you, you have opened my eyes to a whole new world. I'm going to continue and I'm going to finish what I set out to do. I'm going to make you proud of me." Luther poured some sugar in his coffee.

"Luther, don't you realize I'm already proud of you?" Carmen said, as she cut her sausage into bite-size portions.

"I know, baby, but for the first time in my life, things are working. It's not all fucked up and twisted. I like being in control of my own future. I've never had this type of confidence before and I don't want to lose it." Luther paused in thought for a moment. "You know, I see people come in and out of that hospital every day. People who are lost, confused, abused, and have absolutely no place else to go. Every time I see them, I think about my mother. I think about making a difference. When I was studying the other night, I decided to put together a ten-year plan."

"A ten-year plan?" Carmen was amazed Luther was thinking so far in advance.

"Yes. I'm not getting any younger. By the time I'm forty, I want to have my bachelor's degree and I want to be working for the Illinois Department of Children and Family Services. I want to be in those board meetings with the legislators when they're working on the budget, child safety issues, and abuse issues. I want to go in there and tell them like it is." Carmen's heart swelled with pride. She could see his passion and determination.

"And don't forget children's education issues," Carmen reminded him.

"Of course. We can't forget that. But most importantly, by then, I want us to be married."

"Do you really want to marry me, Luther?" Carmen didn't take his proclamation too seriously.

"Like I tell you all the time, baby, success means nothing without someone you love to share it with." Luther smiled.

"Okay, Billy Dee. You'd better stop toying with my emotions." Carmen laughed, but allowed herself to get caught up in the fantasy of being married to Luther. "We will have a grand house," Carmen spoke aloud. "Maybe four bedrooms. One for us, one will be your office, and the remaining rooms will be for our two children."

"Whoa! No, no, no." Luther quickly brought Carmen's fantasy to a halt. "I don't want children. I don't want any kids of my own. It will just be you and me."

"What? How can you be all for helping children and not want any of your own?" Carmen was puzzled by Luther's logic.

"What's wrong with not wanting children?" Luther said, suddenly getting defensive.

"That's what people do when they get married, Luther. They raise a family." The word "family" hit Luther hard; it reminded him of the family he'd destroyed. It reminded him of the horrible secret he'd been hiding from Carmen. "Well, not us." He added unyieldingly, "I don't want children. I don't want a family."

"Luther, that sounds crazy and it doesn't make any sense." Carmen glared at him as if he'd transformed into a complete stranger.

"Well, that's the way it is with me." Luther gave his unwavering position on the matter. He hadn't thought about the hit-and-run accident for a long time. It had taken a while for him to get the images of Lena's bloody and mangled body out of his mind. He would feel guilty if he started his own family, knowing that he had taken another man's family away from him.

Carmen let the conversation go for now. There wasn't enough time to work through the issue with Luther. She would have to get to the bottom of his reasoning. If he married her, she fully planned on having some children, whether he liked it or not.

— —

Carmen was having a difficult day at work. Earlier in her day, she'd had to break up a fight in the hallway as well as deal with an angry parent over their child's failing grade. To top it off, the principal had informed her that she was getting three more students who'd transferred into the district. Carmen wanted to scream because her classroom was already overfilled.

She couldn't wait to get home and submerge her tired body into a hot tub of water. She was feeling cranky and crazy, as well as bloated; she was about to begin her cycle. When she finally arrived home, she went directly into the bathroom to run bath water but got grossed out when she saw a black ring of dirt around the tub.

"Goddamn you, Luther!" she hissed out loud. "How many damn times do I have to tell you to wash out my damn tub after you get out. You nasty motherfucker." She growled as she opened the door under the basin in search of her cleaning products.

"Luther, I'm so sick of your ass coming over here and leaving messes like this." She began trying to scrub the scum out of her bathtub. The job was taking more effort and energy than she wanted to put into it. "Augh!" Carmen griped, then became irritable and mad.

"That does it. Luther, I'm calling your ass up to come over here and clean up this damn mess." Carmen marched out of the bathroom and into the kitchen. As soon as she picked up the receiver, there was someone on the other end trying to reach her.

"Hello?" the voice said.

"Hello? Who is this?" Carmen asked, annoyed.

"This is the operator. I have a collect call for you from Nikki. Will you accept the charge?" asked the operator.

Frustrated, Carmen huffed, "Yes." There was a quick series of clicking sounds and then Nikki was on the line.

"Hey, big sister." Nikki was attempting to feel Carmen out. Carmen hadn't heard from her in weeks and was now wondering why she was calling her collect.

"Hey, Nikki. It's been a while since I've heard from you. Ever since you hooked up with that Packard dude, your ass has been like the fucking magician David Copperfield. I see you one minute and then you disappear the next. You must need something," Carmen said sarcastically.

"Why do you have to talk to me like that?" Nikki's temper quickly flared up.

"Talk to you like what? Everything I said was the God honest truth." Carmen wasn't about to apologize for her comments.

"You know what? I don't have to listen to you. I'll keep my ass right here in jail and die because my uppity-ass sister wasn't there for me when I really needed her," Nikki snapped.

"Jail? What in the hell are you doing in jail?" Nikki had finally gotten Carmen's attention.

"What do you care? It's not like you ever cared about me anyway. Not the way Daddy did." Nikki was trying to make Carmen feel guilty.

"Nikki, that's not true. I did everything that I could—"

Nikki interrupted her mid-sentence. "Yeah, right."

"If Daddy were here, he'd be down here right now raising holy hell about me being behind bars." Nikki's voice inflections were full of self-righteous attitude.

"Nikki, what are you in jail for?" Carmen felt a migraine forming in her temple.

"See, that's another thing. Daddy wouldn't be asking questions; he'd be down here seeing about posting bail and getting me out." Nikki had done it again. She'd made Carmen feel bad about the incident with their father that had happened so many years ago.

"Where are you?"

"I'm at the police station on Fifty-first Street and Wentworth. How long will it be before you get here?"

"Give me about thirty minutes." Carmen sighed.

"Bring five hundred dollars cash with you. That will get me out on bail," Nikki said and hung up the phone.

By 7:30 p.m., Carmen was at the police station posting Nikki's bail. "What did she get arrested for?" Carmen asked the desk sergeant. "Driving on an expired license," he replied.

"That's it? Five hundred dollars for that?" Carmen raised her voice at the man, who was not shaken by her sudden mood swing.

"We would have issued her a ticket and let her go, but she got belligerent with the officer. The officer was suspicious of her behavior. He thought she was driving under the influence of alcohol. When he got her out of the vehicle, he searched the car and found illegal drugs."

"Oh, God." Carmen placed her face in her hands.

"Have a seat, Miss." The sergeant pointed to a row of blue and white plastic seats. "They'll bring her out once she's been processed."

An hour later, Nikki was released from the lockup and strutted through the lobby like she owned the place. She was loud, defiant, and disrespectful.

"That's right!" she shouted. "You can't keep a sister like me down!" Nikki had transformed herself into something Carmen couldn't believe. She had on a short, black miniskirt that barely came down over her ass. She had on red, fishnet pantyhose, a low-cut blouse showing cleavage, and a wild assortment of hoop bracelets and earrings. She giggled as she approached Carmen in high-heeled shoes that she had a difficult time walking in.

"Hey, big sister!" Nikki opened her arms and hugged Carmen. Nikki smelled like a mixture of cheap perfume, sweat, and cigarette smoke. Carmen studied Nikki a bit more. Her eyeliner was smudged, her skin was pale, and she was noticeably thinner.

"I know. I look sexy like a motherfucker, don't I?" Nikki said, as she directed Carmen to follow her out the door. "Come on. I need you to take me back to my car before the police tow truck gets to it."

"You look different," Carmen said, not exactly sure of what to make of her sister as they walked across the parking lot to Carmen's car.

"Girl, you still pushing around town in this old-ass thing?" Nikki criticized.

"It gets me from point A to point B, and that's all I need."

"Yeah, yeah, yeah. Come on; hurry up. You have got to get me over to Fifty-fifth and Ashland. That's where I had to leave my car." Nikki was suddenly in a major rush.

"Wait a minute. We have some things we need to talk about." Carmen was not willing to allow Nikki to run her all over town without an explanation.

"Look, if this is about your money, when we get to my car, I'll give it you. But we've got to get over to Fifty-fifth and Ashland right now. Come on, girl, start this motherfucker up and let's roll." Nikki was clearly impatient and antsy.

"What's the big damn rush, Nikki?" Carmen was taking her sweet time.

"My goddamn car is sitting over there and I've got some valuable stuff in it. Now would you please start this raggedy motherfucker up and take me to where I need to go!" Nikki hollered at Carmen like a deranged woman. Carmen glared at her for a long moment as she tried to figure out what Nikki had gotten herself into. Drugs had to be involved; Nikki's behavior was completely blowing her mind.

"Fine. I'll take you, but we need to stay in touch a little better."

"Girl, please. Now that you're getting some dick on a regular basis, I don't even hear from your ass," Nikki said as she cranked down Carmen's car window. "Do you mind if I smoke?"

"Yes, I do mind." Carmen sped off down Fifty-first Street toward Ashland Avenue. Once they arrived, Carmen began looking for Nikki's Nissan Sentra but didn't see it.

"I don't see your car," Carmen said.

"That's it right there, the white Lexus."

Carmen's heart almost stopped with fear when she saw the expensive car. She told herself that Nikki was pulling her leg. But then Nikki pulled out some car keys and hit a button, causing the car's alarm system to chirp.

"Nikki, whose car is that?" Carmen asked as she parked directly behind the car.

"It's mine for right now. My man gave it to me. But I've got to get that motherfucker away from over here before the tow truck comes. I had to suck some serious dick in order to get the arresting officer to delay making the call for the tow truck."

"Suck some dick? Nikki. Baby. Slow down. Help me out here. What the hell is going on with you? Are you prostituting? Does that Packard dude have you walking the streets?"

"Girl, please, you're tripping. Calm your ass down. I sucked the motherfucker's dick so that I'd have enough time to come back and get my shit. Do you know how much Packard paid for that car? He'd put his foot all in my ass if I allowed the police to take that car."

"Nikki," Carmen interrupted, "the police told me about the drugs they found on you. Are you dating a drug dealer?

"Nikki, you're scaring me." Carmen took a few deep breaths to calm down her nerves.

"Look...don't worry, girl. I got everything under control." Nikki snapped her fingers. "I'm the magic lady. That's what Packard calls me."

"Nikki. I don't think Packard is good for you. I've never met the man, but—"

"Packard doesn't run me. I'm Nikki, baby. I'm in control. I come and go as I please and do whatever I want," Nikki boasted. "I got all of them bitches down at Big Daddy's mad because he treats me like a queen and treats them bitches like stank-ass whores. I can't help it if my shit is sweeter, tighter, and better than theirs. Shit. Even Frieda's ass has been tripping." The more Nikki talked, the angrier she grew. "Fuck all of them bitches!"

"Oh, hell no. Your ass needs help. That man has got you

strung out on drugs. You're coming home with me," Carmen said, and was about to pull off.

"I'm not high, bitch!" Nikki opened the car door to stop Carmen.

"If you're not high, then you've obviously had some type of mental breakdown. Either way, you need help," Carmen barked back at her sister.

"I don't need your help." Nikki eyes were wild and filled with damnation.

"Yes, you do. You had me bail you out of jail. What are you talking about?" Carmen was trying to talk some sense into her sister. Nikki suddenly burst out laughing, for no reason at all.

"Nikki. Please. Listen to me. You're unstable. You need to make a change in your life. How long do you think you'll be able to be a stripper?" Carmen asked.

"I'm an exotic dancer, thank you very much. And I can shake my ass until the day I die if I want to. I don't need you judging me." Nikki gave Carmen a nasty look.

"Nikki, I'm not judging you. I want you to think about what you want in life. I want you to consider—"

"What? Going back to school? Shit, what for when I can pull down as much as two thousand dollars in a night? On the weekends, I can pull down a little bit more. How long does it take you to make money like that?"

"Nikki, this lifestyle is not you and I know it isn't. Why are you doing this to yourself? Why won't you allow me to help you?"

"You've already helped me out, big sister. Thanks, but I've got to go now." Nikki stepped out of the car. "I'll catch you later." She shut the car door, shuffled up to the Lexus and got in. She started the car and took off. Carmen sat in her car and tried to manage her massive migraine while praying for Nikki at the same time.

-19-
MARSHALL

Marshall held a bouquet of flowers as he kneeled at the accident site where Lena had been run down. He'd just finished tapping a crucifix he'd picked up from the flower shop into the ground. The day was sunny and warm and the jogging path was filled with joggers and cyclists just as it was on the same day one year earlier. Marshall swept away a tear that was coursing down his cheek and whispered, "I miss you, baby girl. Daddy misses you so much." Marshall said a little prayer and then rose to his feet. He took a few deep breaths to calm his emotions before stepping away. As Marshall walked back to his car, he began to reflect and think about his once beautiful life filled with happiness and love. They were only ghostly memories now.

After Theodore was released from the hospital after the heart attack he'd suffered at the police station, Stacy and Marshall began to have serious problems. Stacy took some time off from work and traveled back to Florida with her parents to help run the business that Theodore had built. She stayed longer than necessary, which deeply upset Marshall. Upon Stacy's return, she was very cold, distant, and evasive. She threw herself back into her work so she wasn't forced to spend time with Marshall. Marshall didn't know exactly when they'd made the transition from a loving couple to total strangers, but that was now the reality of their marriage. They no longer had sex with each other and Stacy moved out of their bedroom. The ache of an unhealthy marriage was like an infected wound that had the stench of death emanating from it. If Marshall had to guess when Stacy decided to circle the wagons and protect her emotions, it would've been after Theodore's heart attack. Over the past year, she'd refused to focus on anything except her career. Marshall spent all of his spare time searching for the mysterious man who'd run down his baby in cold blood. As a result of their unwillingness to communicate with each other, Marshall and Stacy's marriage had come to a crippling halt. It had died and now it was merely waiting to be buried.

Marshall pulled his car into the driveway and noticed Stacy's car sitting there as well.

"Oh. This is a surprise," Marshall said aloud. He wasn't expecting to run into Stacy. He'd planned on driving over to the cemetery to see Lena and thought that perhaps Stacy would accompany him. Marshall parked his car and walked through the back yard toward the house. He entered the kitchen and saw Stacy gathering up several stacks of papers and placing them inside her briefcase.

"Hey," Marshall spoke softly.

"Hey," Stacy said without even looking at him. The tension was like steam in a pressure cooker.

"I know that you know what today is. I took some vacation time to visit the cemetery and place flowers near Lena's headstone. Would you like to come with me?" Marshall continued to speak softly.

"I have an appointment I have to keep, Marshall," Stacy said, as she placed a mug still filled with coffee in the sink. She still refused to look at Marshall and treated him as if his very presence annoyed her.

"Goddamn, Stacy! You mean to tell me you don't even have thirty minutes to visit with your daughter!" Marshall couldn't take it anymore and snapped at her.

"I've cried all that I can, Marshall. I can't be all emotional and take care of business this afternoon!" Stacy's words were as bitter as a subzero winter. She put her sunglasses on and turned to walk out the door.

"Stacy…" Marshall trailed behind her. "Stop. Why can't we talk about this?"

"There is nothing to talk about, Marshall." Stacy walked around to the driver's side of her car and got inside.

"Where are we, Stacy? What's happened to us? Why can't we get through this?" Marshall asked as she slammed her car door shut.

"I'm getting through it just fine, Marshall. You're the one who can't let it go. Maybe it's because you feel guilty. I don't know, but I certainly don't have the time or energy to deal with you right now." Stacy fired up the motor and backed out of the driveway. Marshall exhaled with aggravation as he watched her drive off down the street.

After Marshall had visited the cemetery, he came home to an empty house and decided to watch family videos he'd made of Lena over the years. He put in a tape of Lena when she was three years old. He and Stacy had taken Lena to a local neighborhood playground. It was summertime and Stacy was wearing a pair of white shorts, and an Old Navy T-shirt along with her favorite pair of thong sandals. Lena was wearing flat brown sandals, some mini blue jean shorts, and a white T-shirt decorated with a picture of Barney the dinosaur. Marshall was filming as

Lena explored the sandbox. She had a yellow plastic bucket and matching shovel with her. Lena's little feet rushed over to the sandbox where she squatted down and began the task of digging.

"Come here. Come here." Lena was speaking to Marshall and motioning with her fingers for him to join her in the sandbox.

"What did you find?" Marshall asked her. "You help," Lena said, and began placing sand in the bucket. Stacy began laughing.

"I guess she told you, baby," Stacy said to Marshall. "She wants to put you to work."

Marshall pressed fast forward on the remote. When he pressed play again, the screen showed Lena a couple of years later at the age of five. The video was during a warm Easter holiday.

"The Easter Bunny is coming," said Lena who believed in the Easter Bunny just as much as she did Santa Claus. She was thrilled to learn that a bunny rabbit would be bringing her gifts and Easter eggs. That particular Easter Sunday was rather warm so they did their filming outside along the side of the house. Marshall, not wanting to disappoint Lena, went out to a costume shop and rented a white Easter Bunny outfit. That year the Easter Bunny had brought Lena a pink Barbie bicycle that had training wheels and pink and white streamers in the handle-bars. Lena, who was also taking ballet lessons at the time, want-ed to wear her pink dancing skirt and white tights. She wanted her clothes to match her bike. Quentin, who had stopped by that day, was the person behind the camera. Stacy was helping Lena with her helmet, knee pads, and elbow pads.

"I got it, Mommy. I can do it by myself," Lena said.

"Where did you get that pretty bike from?" Quentin asked Lena.

"The Easter Bunny brought it for me. I think he left it in the house for me while I was sleeping," Lena said, in a high-pitched voice.

"Really now?" Quentin's voice was full of excitement. "Did he bring me a bike, too?"

"No, because you don't live here. You have to go home and check in the closet."

Quentin laughed. "The closet? Why the closet?"

"The Easter Bunny likes to hide everything in closets."

"Oh, does he?" Quentin chuckled with delight.

"The girl is too smart for her own good," chimed in Stacy, who had finally finished fiddling with all of Lena's padding.

"I'm going to start riding now," Lena said. "You have to follow me." No sooner had Lena begun pedaling, than Marshall stepped out in plain view wearing the giant, white Easter Bunny costume. Marshall kneeled down and opened up his arms for a big hug. Lena's eyes grew wide. She inhaled a big breath and held it for a moment before shouting, "It's the Easter Bunny! Get him before he hops away!" Lena pedaled as fast as she could and rammed into the Easter Bunny, knocking him down.

Marshall pressed *stop* on the videotape. He was in the middle of laughing and crying, somewhere between tears of joy and tears of sorrow. He got on his hands and knees, crawled over to the television screen, and touched it. He wished he could turn back the hands of time. He wished he could make his nightmare end.

Marshall was asleep on the sofa with the television on when Stacy returned home.

"Marshall, wake up." Stacy shook his shoulder. "Come on; wake up. I have something important I need to tell you." Marshall slowly came to life. He was happy to see Stacy had made it home safely.

"What's going on?"

"I have something important I need to tell you. Come into the kitchen. I've made some coffee."

"Coffee? What's going on? What's this about?" Marshall could sense immediately that something wasn't right.

"Just come in the kitchen." Marshall remained on the sofa for a moment and watched as Stacy went down the corridor and into the kitchen. He collected himself and then went in to see what was so important. Marshall sat down at the table while Stacy brought over cups of coffee.

"There is no easy way to say this, so I'm just going to say it."

"Wait a minute. What is this all about?" Marshall asked not wanting to deal with any drama at that particular moment.

"It's about us, Marshall. I think deep down inside you know what this is about."

Marshall's heart began racing. "Ah, no, Stacy, we can get some help. I don't want this. We can work though this. Just give me a chance."

"I don't feel for you anymore, Marshall. I'm not in love with you anymore. And it's not fair to either one of us to live in misery," Stacy explained.

"Stacy, listen, I'm still working on the case, okay? I haven't given up. I'm going to find out who did this. I've been talking to some private investigators. And I wanted to talk to you about it—"

"Marshall, stop. This is not about the investigation. I know you've been working on it. I know that you've been trying, but—" Stacy paused. "You and I are like two ships sailing on the ocean in a very bad storm. This storm has taken its toll on both of us. You want to sail right through the storm and continue on, hoping it will clear up. I don't. I need to sail around this storm and move on. I've filed for a divorce, Marshall."

"What do you mean you've filed for a divorce?" Marshall didn't want to believe what she'd told him. He didn't want to believe what he was hearing.

"I can't go on like this." "Whatever happened to those vows we took? For better or for worse, Stacy? What happened to them?"

"I don't know. I don't have the answer to that. All I know is, I want out."

"Stacy, I'm going to find the guy. You don't have to do this. I'm going to find the guy who did this to us and I'm going to hurt him. I'm going to make him pay. I'm going to make him suffer. I'm going to rip his fucking head off."

"Marshall, listen to what you're saying. You've changed. You're so damn obsessed with finding the guilty person. You're so filled with anger and rage and it has consumed you. I'm afraid of you."

"Afraid of me? Why are you afraid of me?" Marshall didn't understand.

"You pulled a gun on me, Marshall. You pulled it on my mother and my father." "That was last year!" Marshall barked in anger.

"I saw a different side of you, Marshall. I saw the vengeance and rage of retribution in your eyes. I thought I'd only see that one time, but I see it every day that you leave here, searching for the person responsible. I live in fear that you're going crazy and will shoot an innocent person. I live in fear of you getting so angry that you'll pull a gun on me again. You don't have time for our marriage. I come home late because I can't stand to hear you constantly talk about what has happened. I don't want you to talk to me because that's all you talk about. You have to move on, Marshall. Finding this person and hurting them is not going to bring Lena back. It is not going to change what has happened."

"Don't say that to me!" Marshall had a wild look in his eyes that made Stacy flinch with fear.

"No man ruins my life and gets away with it. Nobody is going to destroy my life." Marshall picked up the cup of coffee and threw it across the room, smashing it against the wall. "I'm going to kill that motherfucker when I find him!" Marshall's chest was heaving and he kept clenching his fists.

"You can have the house, Marshall. I don't want it. I'm moving back to Florida." Stacy began crying. "You're not the man I married anymore."

"You can't leave me. I'm not going to let you. I'll lock your ass up in this house before I let you leave me."

"Marshall, you shouldn't say stuff like that." Stacy's voice trembled.

"Okay." Marshall held up his hands and tried to reassure Stacy that he was calm. "I shouldn't have said that."

"Marshall, I emotionally removed myself from our marriage long ago. I'm just now getting the courage to tell you."

"We can see a therapist or a marriage counselor. Why don't we try to work this out? Why are you giving up?" Marshall didn't understand.

"I don't want our marriage anymore. I've had enough," Stacy said as she rose to her feet.

"Where are you going? We have to talk about this some more." Marshall heard a voice in his mind tell him to beat Stacy's ass so that she'd stay. "Stacy, don't do this to me. Please!"

"Bye, Marshall. I'll be in touch." Stacy walked toward the door and then out of the house. Marshall felt like a wounded animal that was too crippled to move, yet too strong to die.

—20—
LUTHER

Luther was speeding down Highway 53 in a rush to get back home from Woodfield Mall. He and Carmen had spent the entire day there shopping and enjoying each other's company. Luther raised his wrist a bit and checked the speedometer, which was holding steady at eighty miles per hour. He momentarily focused on Carmen, who was in the passenger seat. She had let the seat back to rest her weary eyes from the glare of the bright sunlight. He loved her more than he loved himself. In his mind, there was no doubt about it. Without her, he was nothing. She was his reason for living and he felt so blessed to have a woman like Carmen in his life. It was she who had saved him from simply existing without a purpose in life. He hated himself for not being forthcoming about what he'd done. He couldn't tell her out of fear she'd leave him or even worse, encourage him to turn himself in to the authorities. At this point, there was no way in hell he'd ever do that.

As he fought to hide the memories of running down Lena, other disturbing memories from his past began surfacing. Memories of his troubled youth invaded his thoughts without warning. They moved through him like the death choking every morsel of breath from his body. His mother, Sugar, entered his thoughts now. Sugar was bony, short-haired, a double-talking dope addict whose only purpose in life seemed to be getting high at any cost. He hated his mother. Luther closed his eyes for a brief moment and pushed the image of Sugar out of his mind, willing himself to not think about her. Especially not now, after he'd come so far and was doing so well, in spite of the shitty way she'd abandoned him.

Luther attempted to fight off yawning, but as he tried to suppress it, his mouth opened wide and he released a mellow roar. The sound of his yawning caught Carmen's attention. She let her hand search for the seat release, then brought the seat's back to an upright position.

"Do you want me to drive?" Carmen offered.

"No, I've got it."

"Where are we?" Carmen asked, stretching out her body. She took a sip from a soda she'd brought along with her from the mall.

"We passed North Avenue a minute ago." Just as Luther flashed his turn signal to switch lanes, he saw lights flashing in his rearview mirror.

"Oh, shit." Luther's heart began to race.

"What is it?" Carmen asked.

"A state trooper is pulling me over." Luther began to panic. Any run-in with law enforcement made him paranoid. The first image that formed in his mind was the hit-and-run accident. For an instant, he contemplated trying to outrun the officer.

"Well, pull over," Carmen said, as she opened up the glove compartment. "I have my insurance papers in here somewhere." She pulled out a small stack of papers that contained bank statements, junk mail, and other miscellaneous bills.

"Hmm, if anyone ever broke into this car, they wouldn't have any trouble finding out where you lived," Luther said. He was extremely anxious and couldn't decide what he wanted to do.

"I know. I've got to do better about keeping this thing cleaned out." Carmen heard the squad car's siren and looked up at the road for a moment. "Luther, stop playing around and pull over."

"Okay," Luther answered, breathing heavily with nervous anticipation. *Nothing is going to happen,* he told himself. *I was doing eighty in a fifty-five-mile-an-hour speed zone. That's the reason I'm being stopped.* Luther pulled over to the right shoulder and brought the car to a stop. He lifted himself up and reached into his back pocket for his driver's license.

"Okay, here it is," Carmen said. "Here is my proof of insurance." She handed the card to Luther, who was busy looking out of the rearview mirror at the tall, dark-skinned trooper approaching the car. Luther twisted around in his seat and looked up and over his left shoulder at the officer.

"Do you know why I pulled you over?" The officer's breath reeked of alcohol. The stench of it was very apparent. Luther glanced down at the trooper's name badge which read "M. Turner."

"No, sir, I don't," Luther answered politely.

"I clocked you doing eighty in a fifty-five," the officer slurred.

"Yes, sir." Luther was being careful not to tip the trooper any further over the edge than he already was.

"I need your driver's license and proof of insurance. I'm going to issue you a ci-ci-citation." Luther handed Marshall his information and Marshall walked back to his cruiser.

"Man, I think that trooper has been drinking," Luther told Carmen.

"Are you serious?" she said. "Isn't that against the law?"

"The last time I checked it was." Luther was very puzzled about the trooper.

"We should call in and report it." Carmen searched for her cellular phone.

"No," Luther said quickly, "I don't think we should."

"Why not? I mean drinking and driving is very dangerous. He could actually hurt someone."

"Carmen, I said no. I have my reasons," Luther said as he studied his rearview mirror. The trooper looked very familiar to him, but Luther couldn't remember where he'd seen him before. He was desperately searching his memory trying to recall where he'd seen the man's face.

"Luther," Carmen persisted.

"Shhhh!" he said. "I'm thinking." When Luther saw Marshall step back out of his car and approach them, he got a better look at the trooper's face.

"Look. I'm going to let you off with a warning this time," Marshall said. Luther looked up over his shoulder again and suddenly realized who the man was. It was the father of the little girl he'd run down. Luther's heart and mind began racing at a feverish pace. Never, in his wildest dreams, did he expect to come face-to-face with Marshall.

"You have a good driving record," Marshall explained. Luther could still smell the strong presence of alcohol. "Just be careful, okay?" Marshall handed Luther back his information and then returned to his police cruiser.

———

"Luther, we need to report him!" Carmen was now agitated. "Did you get a good look at his name or badge number?"

"Shut the hell up, Carmen!" Luther barked, glaring at her with daggers in his eyes. He wanted her to be quiet and stop talking.

"Excuse me?" Carmen was shocked by the look in his eyes and the tone of his voice. She'd never heard him use that tone with her.

"I'm not reporting him; all right?" Luther put the car in gear and eased back out into traffic, then sped off.

"Why not?" Carmen wanted a good explanation.

"He gave me a break, okay. I'd look like a real asshole if I turned him in," Luther said as he tried to quell a mild panic attack.

"Look at you. You're all sweaty. Are you okay? Maybe you should let me drive."

"Carmen! Just shut up. Please," Luther barked louder.

"You don't have to yell at me like that. I'm only trying to help. What the hell has gotten into you?" Carmen asked, turning around in her seat to look back at the state trooper, who had sat down on the ground near the guardrail and coiled his knees up to his chest.

"Luther, I think something is wrong with that officer. We should go back." Carmen was now concerned about the man's well-being.

"No. I'm not going back." Luther pressed down on the accelerator harder.

"Luther, slow down!" Carmen shouted. "And stop acting like a fugitive trying to avoid the law. Now why won't you go back and let me check on the man? You can get off of the expressway right here and loop back around."

"We don't have time for all that." Luther once again pressed the accelerator harder.

"Fine. We don't have to go back, but I am going to call in about it." Carmen removed her cell phone from her purse and phoned in her concerns about the trooper's well-being.

—21—
MARSHALL

Tired and miserable, Marshall pulled his cruiser into his driveway, put it in park, and turned off the motor. He reached up under his front seat and pulled out the bottle of rum and Coke he'd mixed and been drinking from. He twisted off the cap, puckered his lips and took several deep, hard gulps of the liquid. He growled with satisfaction and wiped his lips with the back of his hand.

"She fucking left me after all of these damn years," he spoke out loud to hear himself talk.

"You can have the house, Marshall," he mocked Stacy. "I don't want anything from you. I can make it on my own—well, fuck you, too, Stacy. I don't need you. I don't need anybody." An angry tear began to run down Marshall's cheek.

"I'm so sorry, Lena." The alcohol was speaking for Marshall now. "Daddy is so sorry. I'm a bad father. I'm a horrible father and I don't deserve to live," Marshall proclaimed as he took several more gulps of the alcohol. "I don't like coming home to an empty house." He pointed at his house. "Yeah, you motherfucker! I'm talking to you." He pointed at the house as if it were a person. "You keep torturing me with memories. Every damn room I go into has a memory. And you toss it up in my face every time I turn a corner. Well, let me tell you something, you bastard! Not today. Not this time. No, not anymore. You're not going to torture me anymore." Marshall removed his weapon from its holster. The Glock forty-caliber weapon would definitely make a big mess if he blew his brains out, but it would put him out of his misery. He took a few more gulps of the liquor and finished it off. He then placed the barrel of the weapon inside the cave of his mouth. He bit down on the steel, leaned his head back and closed his eyes. He placed his index finger around the trigger and paused when he heard another car pulling into his driveway behind him. He immediately assumed it was Stacy coming back home to him. He opened up the car door and stepped out but was disappointed when he saw it wasn't her. It was Quentin.

"Marshall!" Quentin called out to him. "What are you doing?"

Marshall brandished his weapon in a threatening manner. "Back up, Quentin!"

Quentin was unafraid of Marshall's display of aggression. "Boy, if you don't put that damn thing away—"

"I'm warning you, man! Get the hell away from me."

Suddenly, Quentin stopped in his tracks, realizing the dangerous situation he'd just wandered into.

"Marshall, brother dear, you don't want to hurt yourself or anyone else. You're upset, that's all. I can understand that. Why don't we go in the house and talk about this."

"No, that's the damn problem. The house is torturing me." Marshall turned toward the house and fired a round through the back door window.

"Marshall!" Quentin was firmer now. "You're going to hurt someone; put your weapon down, now!"

"No, man! Tell me why she left me! She threw away fifteen years just like that. Like she didn't give a damn."

Quentin cautiously approached Marshall.

"I know, brother dear. I know how much it must hurt, but we can talk about it. We can work through this."

Quentin moved even closer to his brother.

"She was my baby, man. Why did someone run over my baby? Lena!" Marshall looked up at the sky and called out to her. "Lena!"

Marshall began sobbing uncontrollably.

Quentin was finally directly in front of him.

"I do believe you've flipped out."

Marshall was silent for a long moment as he digested what Quentin had said.

"Let me have the weapon, Marshall." Quentin placed his hand on the weapon. "Just open your fingers and let it go," he spoke softly.

Marshall opened his hand and let Quentin take the weapon from him.

"Come on, man. Come on home with me. You don't have to stay here. It's too painful right now." Quentin cradled Marshall's head and held him tightly.

—22—
LUTHER

The two years it took to get his degree flew by quickly. Luther didn't feel so alone and isolated anymore. He felt like he was a productive member of society. He got a credit card and established good credit. He got his very first checking account and even saved up a little money for himself so he wouldn't have to live from paycheck to paycheck. He'd turned his life completely around. He'd gone from a man who had no ambition, direction, or motivation to a man who had set a goal and reached it. Everything in Luther's world was absolutely fabulous.

He stood in the bathroom mirror, with his face up close to the glass, debating whether to squeeze a pimple that had formed on the side of his nose. He studied it for a moment and then spooled a clump of tissue off the roll. He stretched his skin by pulling his upper lip down over his teeth and pushed hard against the pimple, causing it to erupt like a miniature volcano.

"Damn!" he hissed in pain as the core of the pimple coiled up. He pulled back a bit from the mirror and surveyed the red area on his face. *It doesn't look too bad*, he thought. He opened the medicine cabinet and pulled down a bottle of rubbing alcohol from the shelf. He dabbed some on the tissue and placed it up to the small crater that the pimple had left.

"Ouch," he said out loud as his face began to sting. At that moment, Carmen knocked on the bathroom door.

"Hurry up, Luther. I've got to get in there, too. Are you dressed yet?"

"Almost."

"Luther, it's already nine forty-five. You're going to miss your graduation if you don't hurry it up."

"Okay. I'll be out in a moment," he replied. He could hardly contain his excitement at the reality he was about to graduate from college with an associates degree. He opened the door and Carmen came rushing toward him with her navy blue dress unzipped.

"Can you zip me up, babe?" She turned her back to Luther who kissed her on the shoulder before he zipped up her dress. Carmen smiled at the touch of his soft lips.

"Don't you try to start anything now," she said as she moved away from him and made her way into the washroom.

"How do I look?" she asked, posing for him.

"You look good, babe," Luther replied as he inspected her.

"How do I look?"

"As handsome as ever. I am so proud of you, Luther."

"It's all because of you," Luther returned her compliment. "If you had not walked into my life, I'd still be lost."

"That is such a sweet thing to say." Carmen stepped closer and kissed him. "When we get back from the ceremonies this afternoon, we are really going to celebrate, okay?"

"Is that a promise?"

"You better believe it is."

When Luther returned to work, William, his boss, called him into his office. William offered Luther a seat at the conference table.

"Luther." William was very casual. Over the past two years, they'd developed more than a boss-and-employee relationship. Luther had done some service on William's car which William was grateful for.

"What's up, man?" asked Luther as he took a seat.

"Well, Mr. College Graduate. You just don't know how happy I am for you. It's hard to go back to school, but you did it, man."

"Yeah, it does feel good," Luther agreed.

"Well, look, I called you in here because I've gotten a promotion. I'll be the new director over the house staff, working with all of the new resident doctors."

"Wow, man, congratulations. When did you find out?" Luther asked.

"Actually, I found out last week but I wanted to talk with you about this job." William thumped his index finger down on the table. "I have to hire and train someone to supervise the housekeeping staff."

"Okay, so what does that have to do with me?"

"I don't want to hire anyone, Luther. I want to train you to do the job. Now that you have a degree, I can justify the promotion."

"What?" Luther hardly believed his ears.

"So what do you think? Are you interested?"

"Hell, yeah," Luther responded.

"Good." William smiled. "Give me a day or so to file the paperwork and schedule an interview with my boss. Oh, and, Luther, keep this to yourself. Our conversation stays in this room, all right?"

"Hey. My lips are sealed, man." He and William continued with their pleasantries for another few minutes and then Luther left William's office and returned to work.

— —

Later in the evening, Luther and Carmen were sitting on the beach at Fifty-seventh Street. Carmen had brought a blanket and Luther had brought an ice cooler with an assortment of wine coolers. They picked a spot on a grassy area adjacent to the beach where parents were letting their children run freely with little supervision. There was a mixture of loud squealing voices, traffic noise from Lake Shore Drive, and music from radios that others had brought with them. Somewhere in the background, Luther could hear the faint sounds of R. Kelly singing his hit song "Step, in the Name of Love."

"Look at that, baby," said Carmen, pointing at the horizon. "Look at how beautiful the horizon is." She was sitting Indian-style and wearing a pair of blue jean shorts along with a Rihanna T-shirt that read, *Disturbia*. Luther studied her thick, juicy, brown thighs he was fond of caressing.

"Yeah," Luther turned his attention to the horizon, "it is very pretty."

"Sometimes the horizon looks close enough to reach out and touch it." Carmen continued to admire the sun, which was now starting its descent below the horizon.

"Something amazing happened at work today," announced Luther.

"Really? What happened?"

"They want to promote me. Now that I've finished college, they want me to become the supervisor of the housekeeping staff."

"Baby, that's wonderful news." Carmen turned her head toward him. "You deserve it. As hard as you work around that place, dealing with all of the mess that goes on, it's about time they realize what a valuable asset you are."

"True," Luther responded, "but I'm not stopping there. I'm going to take the promotion and I'm also going to register at DePaul University. I want my bachelor's degree. That's next on my list, along with something else I've been thinking about."

"What do you have cooking up there in that head of yours?" asked Carmen as she opened up the cooler and grabbed a wine cooler.

"I've been thinking about us. Without you, I feel as if I'm nothing. And I don't want to risk losing you." Carmen felt her heart beating hard in her chest. She was convinced Luther could hear it. Over the past two years, she'd never brought up the issue of marriage, although it had run across her mind a few times. She didn't want to be the one to ask Luther to marry her. That would have seemed like she was giving him an ultimatum, something she didn't want to do.

"I don't have much to offer you right now, but I'm willing to work and build a life with you. I will do anything for you," he said.

"Uhm-hmm."

"Now that I have a degree and now that I'll be getting a new job and making more money, I thought…" Luther got in front of Carmen and kneeled down on one knee.

"Baby, let's get married."

"Yes," Carmen said with a smile. "I will marry you." Carmen flung her arms around him, knocking him off balance. He landed on his back and she began kissing him. "I've got so many wedding plans to make." She showered him with more kisses.

"Wait a minute; hold on now." Luther began pushing her off

of him. "I was thinking of something a little different than all of that fancy, expensive stuff. I've saved up a little bit of money and I thought we could make this simple."

"What do you mean, 'simple'?" Carmen began to pout a little.

"Why start off our life together in debt? Weddings cost a lot of money. The dress, the tuxedo, the cake, the photographer, all of that is going to cost big time. So what I wanted to do was go down to city hall, see a judge, get married, and then use the money I've saved up for a trip to Vegas." Luther smiled.

"Luther, you're kidding, right?" Carmen said with disappointment.

"No, I'm serious. We'll elope, baby. What's more romantic than running off and eloping?"

"A wedding, Luther. With people and flower girls and a church and wedding gifts and bridesmaids and—"

"Shhhh," Luther pressed his fingers to her lips, "we don't need all of those people in our business, baby. It will be just you and me. That's all I want." Luther then took Carmen's face into his hands and kissed her.

"Luther," Carmen tried to speak.

"That's what I want," he repeated softly.

"Okay. You win," she agreed reluctantly, allowing her dream of a large, fancy wedding to disappear.

Two months later, Luther and Carmen boarded an early flight from Chicago's Midway Airport bound for Las Vegas. They would be staying at the MGM Grand, on the strip. Although Carmen wasn't keen on the idea of eloping, she'd agreed to it but she was going to do it right. There was no way she was going to head down to city hall and see a judge for her marriage. She decided that it'd be much better to be married in Las Vegas. She was excited about getting married even though it wouldn't be the dream wedding she'd wanted since she was a little girl. They arrived in Las Vegas and took a cab to their hotel. They unpacked their suitcases, then decided to take a walk, look around, get something to eat and gamble a little.

Bright and early the following morning, Luther and Carmen got up and tossed on matching blue jean outfits. Carmen locked her arm in Luther's and they went over to the chapel for their wedding ceremony that was scheduled for ten o'clock. The chapel provided a witness and they stood before a judge. They were married and then returned to the hotel room where they consummated the marriage. It marked the first time that they'd made love without protection.

Later, while Carmen rested, Luther went to the casino to try his luck with the slot machines. He walked the floor, searching for a machine that looked as if it wanted to make him a winner. He settled for a dollar machine in the center of the noisy room. The moment Luther sat down, a waitress came up to him and set a drink down next to him.

"Hello, sir," she said pleasantly.

"Oh wow, free drinks? This is nice. What is it?" Luther asked.

"Gin and orange juice, sir, and it's compliments of the gentlemen standing over there." The waitress nodded her head to the right and then left. Luther looked in the direction she nodded to see who'd purchased the drink. Luther's eyes searched through the crowd and finally stopped at a tall, evil-looking man, wearing a hot-red suit with a matching red fedora. Even his trimmed goatee was shaped and pointed, like that of a wicked spirit. The man smiled wickedly and waved at Luther. Luther couldn't believe that he was staring directly at Packard. Luther's eyes bucked wide like he'd seen an apparition. Luther suddenly felt dizzy and had to sit the drink down. The last person in the world he needed to run into was Packard. Packard approached Luther, along with several of his goons. Packard was smiling and laughing slowly and deeply as if he'd been waiting for this moment all of his life.

"Well, well, well." Packard rubbed the corner of his lip with his thumb as if he were savoring the moment. "Luther!" he said with a sinister voice. "Boy, I've been looking for your ass for a long time." He placed his hand down on Luther's shoulders. "What's the matter, Luther? You look like you've seen a ghost or something."

"No. It's so good to see you, Packard." Luther tried to sound cordial. "Listen, I've got to run, man. My wife is waiting on me." Luther made a move to get up from the stool, but Packard forcefully pushed him back down. Luther, who was much more confident and had much more to lose, stood up in defiance of Packard.

"Luther!" Packard growled. "You getting bold now, boy!" Packard opened up his coat and showed Luther the pistol he was carrying. "Sit your ass down. We've got some unsettled business."

Luther tried to act like he had no idea what Packard was talking about. "What do you mean, Packard? What are you talking about? We don't have any unsettled business."

Packard laughed wickedly. "Ooo, I've been wishing for this day to come. I'll tell you what I'm talking about." Packard paused and studied Luther for a moment. He then sucked in a wisp of air through his nose. "So, tell me, Luther, what have you been doing with yourself for the past two years? How have you been surviving? How in the fuck did you make it all the way out here to Vegas?"

"I got married," Luther answered him.

"That's good, man," Packard said condescendingly. "Every man needs a good bitch. Is your bitch here, with you?"

"She's not a bitch, man, so don't call her that!"

"Ooo, she must have some good pussy because you've grown some fucking big-ass balls! I'll bet she even helped you get a job, too. Didn't she?"

"I'm working at the county hospital. I'm the supervisor over housekeeping."

"A supervisor!" Packard said with much more excitement than necessary.

"Yeah, and I went back to school and got my degree."

"Well, hush my mouth! Luther done jumped up and become a college-educated man! I might have to get me a taste of that pussy you're fucking and then put her ass out on the corner."

"You know what, fuck you, Packard!" Luther made a move to leave, but Packard quickly pulled out a razor and placed it at Luther's throat.

"Boy! I want to fuck you up so bad that my dick is hard! Sit the fuck down before I gut your bitch ass like a fish!" Luther met Packard's evil gaze with one of his own. Packard was slightly taller than Luther, much more muscular than Luther, and willing to prove that he could still knock Luther around like he did when he was a young boy.

"See there, Luther. Now everything between us is all tense with anger and hostility." Packard put away the razor and popped his collar. "So let me get to my point before I knock your bitch ass out." Packard leaned forward and spoke purposely in his ear. "I've had a hard-on for you, boy, for two years now. I know what you did, motherfucker! You committed vehicular homicide when you stole my ride. Hell, boy, you're considered a goddamn fugitive! I'm surprised they haven't profiled your ass on *America's Most Wanted*."

Luther suddenly felt the room spinning around. He didn't like having to face what he'd done. He didn't want to admit that he'd fucked up that badly.

"What's the matter, Luther?" Packard laughed. "You didn't think that shit was ever going to come back to haunt you. Did you? Your dumb ass has been in denial, haven't you?" Packard glared directly into his eyes and searched them for the truth. He was toying with Luther and was enjoying every moment of it.

"That's what I thought. What you do in the dark, mother-fucker, will come to light. Now, Luther, I could have turned your bitch ass over to the police two years ago, but there is the matter of my five-thousand dollars you stole from me. And you know that I can't let that shit go."

"Packard, I… I…" Luther couldn't finish his thought. Packard had him and would make him pay dearly for his mistake.

"Tsk, tsk, tsk, Luther. You've fucked up, as always! I've got you by the balls, boy! And it feels so damn good, knowing you owe me like this," Packard spoke through gritted teeth.

"Packard, if this is about the money, I'll pay you back. Just give me a little time, okay?"

"Luther. This has gone beyond money now. I've taken the shit personal. I'm going to ride you, Luther. I'm going to ride your ass until I ride you to your grave. Nobody—and I mean, nobody—steals my money. And that bitch of yours with that sweet, succulent, ball-inflating pussy, is going to give it up to me one way or another." Packard released another sinister laugh as he pulled out his cell phone.

"What's your phone number, boy?" Packard looked at him sideways.

Luther didn't answer Packard.

"Boys, make this punk bitch talk." Packard instructed his goons to harm Luther.

"Wait a minute now," Luther said nervously.

"Let me tell you how this shit is going to go down. I want you to steal drugs from the hospital. Several of my most loyal clients will be pleased to know that I have access to a variety of goodies."

"I can't do that, Packard. I don't even have access to medical supplies," Luther explained.

"Well, you'd better transform into Freddy Five Fingers, motherfucker, and find a way to access the shit. Because if you don't do it"—Packard paused and captured Luther's gaze— "I'm going to make a phone call to a Detective Taylor in Chicago. And I'm going to tell him that the tools he found in my SUV with the initials 'L.P.' stand for Luther Parker. I'll tell him where you used to work. Then all they'd have to do is get a hold of your employee records that have all of your personal information. Next, they'll send a squad car to pick you up and bring you in for fingerprinting. When they match the prints to the ones they lifted from the SUV, guess what? Bye-bye, Luther. Your ass will be going to jail. Then say, bye-bye, wife; bye-bye, job; and everything you've worked so hard for over the past two years. Now, Luther, what is your motherfucking phone number and address?"

-23-
CARMEN

Carmen's period was two weeks late so she went out to the pharmacy and purchased a home pregnancy test to confirm suspicions. When she got back into the house, she was delighted Luther hadn't yet made it home. They'd just gotten married and already he'd changed on her. He was suddenly more distant and irritable for no apparent reason. He was much more tense, irritable, and bad-tempered. She assumed the sudden change in behavior was job related and once he got fully acclimated to his new responsibilities, he'd turn back into the man she'd grown to love. Carmen went into the bathroom, slid the pink-and-white shower curtain all the way back, and sat on the side of the bathtub. She read the instructions carefully, being certain that she didn't miss a step. She took the test and waited for the results.

When the little plus sign began to form, Carmen shouted out with joy. She'd been longing for the day when the situation was right to have a baby and start a family. Now that she was married and both she and her husband were working, it was the perfect time, in her mind, to begin. Ever since she was a young girl, she'd wanted two children, a girl and a boy. She'd already given great thought to their names. Her son would be named Nicholas and her daughter Roslyn.

"Yes, yes, yes!" she squealed out loud with joy.

The realization that she was going to become a mother exhilarated her so much she changed her clothes and rushed out the door. She had to go to a mall. She had to look at things for the baby. Her thoughts were racing as she imagined all the things she and Luther would need to get. They would have to sell her one-bedroom condo and buy a house. She got into her car, cut down the side street, turned onto Fifty-fifth Street, and headed west toward Cicero Avenue. She was going out to Sears at Ford City Mall. They had a nice selection of baby furniture, clothes and accessories. Although it was too early to spend any serious money, she felt compelled to buy something for the baby: a bib, a blanket, a rattle, or maybe a book.

"I need to make an appointment with my doctor," she reminded herself as she drove. "I need to see about getting some maternity clothes. I need to start saving more money and do a budget plan." Carmen was calculating approximate costs of everything in her head. "I need to call my real estate agent so he we can put the condo on the market and start looking for a new one. Luther will have to throw a fresh coat of paint on all of the walls so everything looks neutral.

"I need to plan a special candlelight dinner so I can tell Luther the great news," she continued to talk out loud. *He's going to make a good father*, she thought. *He's patient, caring, loving and doesn't raise his voice too much, which is a good thing because children can be so frightened by the sound of a loud, threatening, male voice.*

When Carmen walked into Sears, she headed straight for the baby section. Everything she saw was cute and adorable to her. While looking at teething toys, she saw another woman who appeared to be in her early thirties and was in the late stages of her pregnancy. Her husband was pushing a shopping cart close behind her. They were looking at the baby strollers trying to decide which one they wanted. Carmen began fantasizing for a moment. In a few short months, she and Luther would be shopping together for their child. *My baby is going to be spoiled rotten*, she thought. *Just like Momma and Daddy spoiled Nikki and me*. Then her mind drifted for a moment when she thought about Nikki. She hadn't talked to her sister since she'd gotten jammed up and had to bail her out of jail. When Nikki took off and didn't pay her back the bail money, Carmen had caught up with Nikki at Big Daddy's.

"Nikki," she'd called out her name as she walked into the dressing room where all of the dancers changed outfits, "I need to have a word with you."

"What are you doing, coming down here to my job?" Nikki had asked, full of attitude.

"Bitch, you owe me five hundred dollars and I need my money," Carmen had snapped out on her sister.

"Newsflash for you, Carmen. If I truly had your money, I would've given it to you. I don't have it, okay?" Nikki had said, totally annoyed.

"No. Bitch, you said you were making tall-ass dollars up in here. Now I want my damn money."

"Carmen. I don't have it right now. What part of that don't you understand?" Nikki didn't seem to care that she'd put Carmen in a bind.

"Nikki, I really need my money. So you'd better stop bullshitting and give it to me," Carmen had demanded as more of a threat than a request.

"Look. Let me make this clear enough so that even your dumb ass can understand. I used you, Carmen, to get out of jail. You like rescuing people, so I let you rescue me. You like being the superwoman who comes in to save the day. You've missed your calling. You should be working for the Red Cross or some other disaster relief agency." Nikki had paused briefly. "I told you I had the money so that you would drive me back to the car before something happened to it. I don't have your money and I have no plans of giving it back to you."

"You are such a bitch, Nikki."

"Well. I've been called worse by better people," Nikki had responded defiantly.

"What happened to you? You don't care about anybody but yourself. How did you get this way?" Carmen had asked as Nikki put on a long, blonde wig.

"That's life, baby. You've got to look out for number one. Packard taught me that," Nikki had boasted proudly.

"Momma and Daddy are probably turning over in their graves at the way you turned out. You're a disgrace to the family. "

"What? Like your shit don't stank?" Nikki had pointed her finger in Carmen's face. "You're the one who sent Daddy to his grave, not me!" Nikki's words had cut Carmen to her core.

"You shouldn't have said that, Nikki." Carmen's heart had swelled with emotional rage.

"Well, it's the damn truth. I saw the autopsy report you tried to hide from me, Carmen. And I read it." Nikki had worked her neck.

"What?" Carmen had answered her with surprise.

"That's right; I said I saw it. The report said that had Daddy been able to get medical assistance, he would have lived. It's your fault he died, Carmen. All because you couldn't pick up a phone and dial nine-one-one. Daddy sat on that kitchen floor all night by himself, suffering and bleeding to death because your ass didn't know what to do. I had to go down there the next morning and find him like that. I was the one who called for help when it was too late. I was the one who cleaned up fucking blood stains. And ever since that day, nothing has been right in my life. You allowed my daddy to die! And because of that, Carmen, nothing in your life will ever go right. Something will always go wrong. No matter how hard you try to make things right by rescuing someone!"

"Nikki, I…" Carmen was in tears.

"You know what, Carmen. I consider Frieda to be more of a sister to me than you. So as far as I'm concerned, we don't ever have to see each other again." Nikki had turned her back on her sister and walked away. Nikki's words cut Carmen deeply. She couldn't defend herself against what Nikki had said; all of it was true.

"Do you feel better, now that you've gotten that off of your chest?" Carmen had asked.

"Get lost, Carmen," Nikki had said, as she exited the dressing room.

"I'll always be here for you, Nikki," Carmen had mustered up the courage to say between her tears.

Thinking about Nikki and her issues gave Carmen a migraine. She refocused her energy and thought about the baby that was growing inside of her and how she was going to break the exciting news to Luther.

When Carmen left work the following evening, she stopped at the store to pick up groceries for a romantic candlelight dinner. She planned to cook a dish called Chicken Alfredo Lasagna

Casserole. She pushed the cart through the store, picking up the ingredients she needed: lasagna noodles, four boneless, skinless chicken breast halves, carrots, onions, broccoli, alfredo sauce, ricotta cheese, parmesan cheese and mozzarella cheese. She was about to pick up a bottle of wine but quickly remembered she was pregnant and drinking wine wasn't a good idea.

Carmen greeted Luther at the door with hugs and kisses when he arrived home.

"Hey, baby." Carmen kissed him on his lips, cheek, and then his neck.

"What's in those bags you're carrying? Are they presents for me?" Carmen tried to take the bags from him but Luther quickly moved them out of her reach.

"No. These are some tools from my old apartment. I'll put them up," he said, nervously.

"Okay, baby," she said, sensing that something was slightly off with Luther. "After you do that, why don't you go wash up for dinner? I've got a special surprise for you tonight."

Carmen set Luther's plate on the table and then closed the blinds in the dining room so she could light the candles. Once she got everything set, she sat down and waited for Luther to come out of the washroom. She found it odd that he was taking much longer than usual.

"Luther, honey, are you okay in there?" Carmen called out to him.

"Yeah. I'll be out in a second." When Luther emerged, Carmen could tell that he was surprised by all of the effort she'd gone through preparing dinner.

"What's this all about?" Luther asked with an unmistakable edginess in his voice that Carmen picked up on right away. However, she decided to ignore it. She wasn't about to let his new attitude ruin her evening.

"Sit down and relax," she said.

Luther sat at the dinner table, feeling jittery. He didn't touch his food.

"What's wrong with you? Why aren't you eating? Did you eat already or something?" Carmen asked suspiciously.

Luther shoveled a heap of food into his mouth. "No. I'm fine."

"Luther, we have to be able to communicate. Without communication, we will run into problems. Now, baby, if something is bothering you, tell me so we can work it out."

"Carmen, I said, I'm okay. Nothing is wrong." Luther raised his voice at her and she didn't like it. "I'm sorry. I didn't mean to yell at you. I'm under a lot of pressure at work," Luther lied. "I'm having some trouble adjusting to my new responsibilities, that's all."

"I understand. If I can do anything to help, let me know and I'll be there for you, baby."

"Thank you for offering, but I have to work through this on my own."

"Well. I have some good news, baby," Carmen said, scooting her seat back and walking over to the china cabinet. She opened up one of the drawers and pulled out a small gift box.

"I have a surprise in here for you." Carmen giggled as she walked over to Luther, who scooted his seat back and motioned for her to sit on his lap. Carmen complied and handed him the box.

"You shouldn't have, baby. I don't need any presents. I have you and that's all that matters to me."

"Go ahead, open it." Carmen was anxious. Luther opened

the box and saw a Winnie the Pooh and Tigger Too book with a note stuck to it that read, *Daddy, will you please read to me?*

Luther was not amused. "What in the hell is this?"

"We're going to be parents." Carmen smiled at him. "I'm pregnant, baby." Carmen hugged him.

Luther snatched her arms from around his neck and stood up, abruptly knocking over the chair. He looked at her like a madman. Carmen didn't know what to make of his sudden change in behavior.

"How did this happen?"

"What do you mean, 'how did this happen'? You know how it happened." Carmen now raised her voice in anger; this was not the response she had expected.

"Vegas," Luther hissed. "You purposely got pregnant in Vegas, didn't you?"

"No, Luther, it wasn't on purpose; it just happened. What are you so angry about? We're married. It's okay; that's what married people do."

"I told you from jump street that I didn't want any damn kids."

"Excuse me!" Carmen was pissed off now. "And you knew that I wanted to have children."

"You knew I didn't want to have children and you purposely got pregnant and I won't take my words back!"

"I didn't get pregnant by myself and you knew that I wasn't taking anything. What is it with you and kids? Why don't you want to have any?"

"Carmen, I—" Luther was interrupted by his cell phone. He looked at the caller ID and saw that it was Packard. "Shit!"

"Who in the hell is that?" Carmen demanded answers.

"That's some business I have to handle," Luther said as he

answered the phone, rushing to pick up the bags he'd walked in with.

"Who is that, Luther?" Carmen demanded to know since Luther was acting strangely.

"Shhh!" Luther looked at her with murderous eyes. "Yeah. I'll be right there," Luther said and hung up the phone. He looked at Carmen as he moved toward the door.

"Get an abortion, Carmen. I'll pay for it," Luther said as he opened the front door.

"What did you just say to me?" Carmen asked for clarification.

"You heard me, Carmen. Get an abortion."

"Fuck you, Luther! Go to hell, you bastard. I don't believe you said that to me. I don't believe that you told me to kill our baby."

"Carmen, this is not a good time for us to have a kid! End of conversation!"

"Why?"

"I have my reasons, Carmen, and you really don't want to know what they are." Luther walked out the door.

—24—
LUTHER

Luther wished that he could tell Carmen about the jam he was in with Packard, but that would mean telling her his horrible secret. He didn't want to break her heart and felt that keeping his dark secret away from her would protect it. To bring a child into a situation like the one he was in would most certainly end up in disaster. He'd make everything up to her somehow, someway, but right now, Packard had him between a rock and a hard place. And until he figured a way to get him off his back, that was the way things had to be.

Luther was doing exactly what Packard wanted him to do. Luther had obtained and used a master key to sneak into the medical storage area and steal needles and prescription drugs. But that wasn't enough for Packard. He started giving Luther a list of pills his customers wanted like amphetamines known as uppers. Every time Luther saw Packard, the variety and quantity would increase. When Packard called Luther, he had to answer his phone no matter what time of the day or night.

"If I call you and you don't answer the phone, I'm turning your motherfucking ass in. I'm not even going to hesitate. So you'd better stay in an area where you get damn good reception. If my dope comes up short, or if you fuck up my order, I'm turning your ass in. And when I'm ready for your wife to come suck my dick, she'd better suck on it like her life depends on it."

"Packard, please. Can't I just pay you the money back?" Luther asked once again.

"If you ask me that shit again, Luther, not only will I beat your motherfucking ass, I'm going to drive you to the police station my damn self. And if you ever think about running away or trying to turn me in, I'm going to have your ass taken out. Are we clear?"

"Yeah, man."

When Luther exited the building, he walked across the street to where Packard was waiting with his henchmen. Luther handed the bags to one of the men sitting in the back seat.

"So tell me, Luther," Packard asked, "Do you ever think about what you did? I mean, doesn't that bother you? Doesn't it eat away at your conscience?"

"I don't want to talk about that, Packard," Luther said softly.

"We'll talk about whatever I want to, Luther. I know you. I helped to raise you, boy! I know you're afraid to fuck up. You don't like being the cause of something going wrong or the person that is blamed. You feel too guilty. You can thank your mother for making you feel that way. So now tell me. How do you feel about killing someone?" Luther's jaws grew tight because he didn't want to relive what he'd done.

"I don't think about it."

Packard laughed and then reached for a package and handed it to Luther.

"That's what I thought. Here." Packard handed him the package. "I took the liberty of keeping all of the newspaper articles that were written about the murder. Read them. The next time I see you, I want you to tell me how you feel." Packard laughed and then took off.

Luther continued to steal for Packard for months. He was stealing so much that hospital administrators asked the Cook

County Sheriff's Department to investigate. It frightened the hell out of Luther because it meant it was now going to be difficult, if not impossible, to continue stealing for Packard. He had to stop, or else he'd be caught, and imprisoned.

—◦—

Angry with how his life was currently going, Luther took out a lot of his frustration on Carmen, who had completely ignored his demand to get an abortion. Luther did everything he possibly could to make her do want he wanted and refused to be involved in any aspect of the pregnancy. He didn't go shopping or to the doctor with her, and refused to sign up for Lamaze class. As she got further along with her pregnancy, he criticized and belittled her. Carmen had finally had enough of Luther's antagonistic ways and decided that if her marriage was going to work, she needed to rescue it.

"Luther," Carmen said to him one evening while they were watching sitcoms, "we need to get some help. I want us to see a marriage counselor."

"I'm not going to see a marriage counselor, Carmen. I don't need any help."

"Luther, things between us are bad and I think we need to get some help."

"No. Maybe you should get some help. You're the one who has caused all of the stress in the marriage." Luther pointed his finger in her face.

"Luther, the first thing we need to do is stop pointing fingers and blaming each other and find out what it's going to take to get us back to happy. What would make you happy, Luther?"

"Putting that damn baby up for adoption. We don't need it. We could go on with our lives and it would be just the two of us. You need to focus on me and my needs and not some baby's needs."

Carmen couldn't believe the words that were coming out of Luther's mouth. She was trying to figure out at what point his alternate personality had been born. What signs did she miss? Why wasn't he happy to be having a baby? She wondered what horrible incident had taken place in his life that she didn't know about.

"Is there something you need to tell me, Luther? Has something happened?" Carmen was trying to get to the root of his aggression.

"Like I said, I only want you to take care of me and my needs. There is not enough room in my heart for a baby."

"Luther, I think you need to see a specialist," Carmen said, and then left the room.

＊ ＊

As the months continued, Luther realized that Carmen had no intentions of terminating the pregnancy. And by the beginning of the New Year, she gave birth to their son and named him Nicholas. A day after his son was born, Luther learned that the Cook County Sheriff's Department had focused its criminal investigation on the hospital's housekeeping staff. Luther knew it would not take them long to figure out he was the man they were searching for. So he beat them to the punch and resigned from his job.

Packard was furious that his free pipeline to prescription drugs was now severed. But instead of turning Luther in like he'd promised, he forced Luther to work for him indefinitely.

It was 7 p.m. and heavy snow had been falling for about an hour. Luther and Carmen were driving on the highway heading home from a suburban grocery store that they'd gone to before the snowstorm hit. Carmen turned around in her seat to make sure Nicholas, who had drifted off to sleep, was securely strapped into his car seat. Once she was confident that Nicholas was safe, she focused her attention on Luther and all of the bullshit he'd been putting her through. She'd found out that Luther was selling drugs and she wasn't happy about it.

"After all of the hard work you've done going back to school and getting a degree, I can't believe you want to blow it on something ignorant like being a damn drug dealer."

"You don't understand, Carmen. It's not like that."

"Well then, make me understand, Luther. What is it all about? I've been trying to understand you ever since we got married."

"I can't tell you, okay? I just can't."

Carmen folded her arms with disgust.

"Luther, I have really had it with you. I can't go down this road with you. I can do bad by myself."

"You can't leave me, Carmen. I need a little more time to figure things out."

"Figure what things out, Luther? You've been saying that shit for months and it has worn thin with me." Carmen paused for a moment, waiting for his explanation. "Fuck it. You're going to have to find a place of your own. You can do whatever it is you want to do. Just don't come around to see me and the baby at all."

Carmen's words connected directly to Luther's heart. Her words hurt him. The last thing that he wanted to do was lose her. All he wanted was for her to understand he was dealing with something he couldn't tell her about. The fact that he couldn't tell her made him edgy and he pressed the accelerator and picked up speed as he sped up an incline. The car fishtailed a little, but Luther quickly gained control over it.

"Slow down, Luther, you're driving too fast in this snowstorm," Carmen snapped.

"You don't tell me what to do!" Luther shouted back and sped up even more.

"Luther! Slow down! The road is slick out here!"

Luther ignored her and went even faster down the other side of the incline.

"Luther!"

"I got this! I'm tired of people telling me what to do all of the damn time," Luther growled at Carmen and pinned the accelerator to the floor of the car.

"Luther! There are police lights ahead."

Carmen pointed out of the window to the flashing lights of a squad car. Luther ignored her and refused to slow down. He zoomed past the state trooper and tried to switch lanes but quickly lost control of the car. The car spun around like a spinning top. Carmen braced her arm against the dashboard and screamed. Luther pressed hard against the brakes and kept turning the steering wheel, attempting to gain control, but he couldn't. The car ran off the road and onto a frozen lake. The car spun around at a dizzying pace until it came to a complete halt about fifty yards from the shoreline. It was eerily silent and calm for a brief moment. Once she realized that she was alive, Carmen glanced over at Luther with murderous eyes before unloading on him.

"What the fuck is wrong with you!"

"Shhhh!" Luther held his hand up. He needed her to be quiet.

He tried to turn the car around and drive back to shore but the ice wasn't strong enough to hold the weight of the car. In an instant, the horrific roar of ice splitting a thousand ways began singing its gruesome melody.

"I've got to get out of here. This ice isn't going to hold the car! I'm going to make a run for it!" Luther panicked and thought only of his own survival. He immediately unlocked the door, exited the car and ran as quickly as he could on the slick ice toward the shoreline.

"Luther!" Carmen called after him. He was crazy, but never, in her wildest dreams, did she think he'd leave her and the baby in such a life-or-death situation.

"Luther, get your ass back here and help me!" she called to him again, but Luther had disappeared into the driving snow-storm. Carmen quickly unlocked her seatbelt, turned around, got on her knees, and began to free Nicholas.

"Oh, God; oh, God!" Carmen yelled in terror as she fumbled with her son's seatbelt. The moment Carmen freed Nicholas from his car seat, she heard a thunderous snap, followed by a violent jerk of the car. She twisted her body, glanced over her left shoulder, and saw that the nose of the car was about to drop below the surface. She immediately rolled down the window before turning back around and snatching Nicholas up in her arms. Her hasty movements caused the ice to groan even louder.

-25-
MARSHALL

Marshall was on duty when the heavy snowstorm hit. Weather forecasters were predicting eight to ten inches. Marshall had pulled over and turned on his squad car lights in an effort to slow motorists driving down a slick incline. He was waiting for a snowplow to clear the roadway. As he waited, he spotted a car pass him at an alarming rate of speed. Before Marshall could even put his squad car back in gear, the driver lost control of the vehicle and drove straight into a nearby lake. Marshall immediately radioed in the location of the accident and requested emergency personnel. He then drove his squad car to the accident site and got out. He opened the trunk, grabbed some emergency blankets, and rushed to the shore. He saw a man rushing toward him in a hurry to get off of the thin ice. Marshall quickly rushed over to help the man. Several motorists who were passing by also pulled over to help.

"Were you the only one in the car?!" Marshall shouted into Luther's ear as he tossed a blanket around him.

"No. My wife is still out there," Luther said, as another motorist tossed a second blanket around him.

"Damn!" Marshall said, "What's her name?"

"Carmen."

"You." Marshall pointed to another motorist who rushed over

with a flashlight to help. "You make sure the fire department comes to this spot."

"Yes, sir," said the motorist.

"And shine the beam of the light out onto the dark lake so I will know where the shore is," Marshall said as he prepared to walk out onto the thin ice.

"Okay," the man said.

Marshall removed his gun belt and rushed off into the darkness, calling out to Carmen.

"I'm over here; help me, please! The car is sinking fast!" Carmen shrieked. When Marshall reached Carmen, she was desperately trying to get out the car through the passenger window but was having difficulty because she had an infant in her arms. Marshall knew that every second counted. The moment the car began taking on water, it would sink rapidly and take Carmen and her baby with it.

"Give me the baby." Marshall reached out and took the child from Carmen so that she could escape more easily. Every maneuver Carmen made to get out caused the ice to crack and split some more. The sound was unsettling.

Once Carmen was out, Marshall said, "Let's go now!"

He held on tightly to her son and they both began walking as briskly as they could on the slick and unsteady ice. Marshall heard a thunderous snap followed by the sound of the car sinking into the frozen lake.

"Keep moving!" Marshall urged Carmen to get ahead of him. "Don't look back!" Marshall yelled. Carmen had just about made it to the shoreline when the ice buckled beneath her feet and sucked her down. Marshall immediately stopped moving because he couldn't see where she'd fallen through. He heard a chorus of voices screaming and shouting, "Pull her out!" Through the blinding snow Marshall could see the silhouettes of motorists and rescue workers who'd arrived on the scene frantically working to pull Carmen from the icy water.

"I'm over here!" Marshall shrieked. "Shine the light over here so I can see!" Within an instant there were lights shining on him. He saw that if he'd taken another four or five steps, he would've plunged into the icy water with the baby. Marshall took a few steps to the left and was unnerved by the moaning of the ice.

"Hurry! Run for it!" he heard one of the rescue workers shout. Marshall was able to take two steps before the ice caved in and swallowed him and Nicholas.

Marshall's heart was thudding against his chest so hard and fast he feared it would burst from the electricity of adrenaline pumping through it. He held Nicholas close to his chest and kicked his legs ferociously in the icy water. Marshall kept kicking with all his might. He finally split the surface, and took a big breath of air before he rolled onto his back. He released the baby's nose and heard Nicholas cough before he began crying.

With his last bit of breath, Marshall shouted, "Over here!"

He couldn't hear his own voice because his ears were filled with water. Out of the corner of his eye, all he could see was a series of bright white lights shining his way.

"Over here!" he shouted out again as he shivered and twitched uncontrollably. Hypothermia would take over in a matter of moments if he and Nicolas didn't get out of the water.

The icy water felt like a million ice picks jabbing him all at once. His legs began stiffening up and he felt as if he was going to go back under. Both his arms and legs felt like a sack of bricks, but he clutched Nicholas tightly, refusing to let him go. Marshall used only the strength in his legs to keep them afloat until help arrived. The last thing he wanted was to give up and sink into a dark watery tomb. At that moment, Marshall needed the miracle of an angel or some other type of divine intervention.

"Lena!" He screamed out his daughter's name. "Help me!" At that very instant, Marshall felt hands pulling Nicholas away from him. Then he felt someone pulling him up and out of the water onto a small lifeboat. The last thing Marshall saw before he passed out was a fireman giving him the thumbs-up sign.

—26—
LUTHER

"Luther, you have got to be the unluckiest bastard in the world," Packard said to Luther as they sat in Packard's white Lexus outside of Big Daddy's Exotic Dance Club. One month had passed since Luther had run off the road during the snowstorm.

"There is a bad voodoo root on you; like the one that was on your mother. Unexplainable shit happened to her all of the time. Bad luck. She always had bad fucking luck. She was a damn jinx, to be honest. Because of her, I almost did twenty-five years; that's why I had to drop that bitch. I don't need people like her, or you, around me. So, Luther, I'm going to have mercy on you and let you go. All I want you to do is disappear like you did before. Don't come around me or come into my club. If I ever see your face again, even by accident, I'm going to shoot to kill."

"Just like that?" Luther snapped his fingers. "No apology for stressing me out or for making me fuck up the good life that I had?" Luther was sounding off and losing his mind.

"None of your fucked-up decisions are my fault, boy." Packard spoke with emptiness in his voice. "I'm not the reason everything has gone wrong in your life. You need to ask your mama about that. You and her share a common bond that's rather bizarre."

"Leave my mother out of this, Packard!" Luther snarled.

"Fine. We don't have to bring her into this, but, Luther, you've got some bad karma. You took the life of that state trooper's daughter and he turned around and risked his own life to save your son. That's some freaky shit! That state trooper has been searching high and low for you and doesn't even realize that you were right in front of his face on more than one occasion. You've got some unnatural shit looming over your head and I don't want to be near you when it comes booming down. Now, get the hell out of my car before I kill you," Packard spoke through gritted teeth.

Luther got out of Packard's car but still had a few things he needed to get off his chest.

"You've fucked up my life, Packard, and I don't appreciate that shit!" Luther felt himself teetering on the edge of madness. Luther felt as if his mind was on overload and that he was on the brink of a major meltdown. "I should fuck you up, Packard!" Luther shouted as he threw a punch at Packard. Luther missed.

"Oh, you think I'm bullshitting with you? You think I'm soft!" Packard quickly got out of the car with his loaded revolver. Luther got scared and immediately turned and sprinted away as fast as he could. Packard fired several shots, missing Luther but hitting several trees.

"What are you running for? There is no need to get scared now!" Packard shouted.

Luther didn't stop running until he was several blocks away.

"Stupid, stupid, stupid." Luther beat himself up over foolishly trying to hit Packard. He calmed himself down as best as he could and then continued on his way. Luther stopped at a nearby flower shop and purchased a dozen red roses for Carmen. He wanted to make everything up to her. He wanted things to get back to the way they were. He wanted to be with her and only her. She was the love of his life and he'd broken her heart, but he could fix her bruised emotions. Now that Packard was out of his life, he wanted to continue with their plans. Luther wanted to get to know his son and learn how to be a father. Carmen could teach him how and he was now in a better position.

When Luther returned home from his meeting with Packard, there were two large suitcases at the front door.

"Carmen," Luther called out her name, but got no answer. He heard Nicholas begin to cry so he walked toward the bedroom where he found Carmen changing Nicholas's Pamper. Luther stood and watched without saying a word. When Carmen was done, she snuggled up next to Nicholas and began to breast-feed him.

Ever since the accident a month ago, Carmen had become disillusioned with Luther and their relationship. She had kicked him out of the bedroom and refused to do anything for him. She only communicated with him when it was absolutely necessary, and even then, she only spoke to him as she was walking away.

"I bought you some flowers," Luther said, hoping she'd open up. "They're red roses." Luther set them on the bed.

"Uhm… I was thinking we could take us a mini-vacation someplace. You know, once I got a job and everything. A real job, I mean. I'm not selling drugs anymore. I've stopped. I'm never going to get involved with that stuff again, baby. I promise. I'm going to find a new job and go back to school and do all of the things we'd planned to do," Luther said with sincerity in his heart and his voice.

Carmen refused to acknowledge what he was saying. He was starting to sound like a CD that kept skipping on the same lyrics.

"Carmen, I know I've messed up but, I promise, from now

on, everything will be just fine. Everything will be like it was. I'll stop being so evil to you. I'll stop treating my son so poorly."

"Luther," Carmen finally broke her silence, "I've packed your shit. Now get out. I don't care where the fuck you go. I just want you out of the house and out of my life!"

"Baby, why?"

"Luther, you abandoned me and Nicholas on a frozen lake! You acted as if you couldn't have cared less if we lived or died. Plus, you're a motherfucking drug dealer and that's unacceptable!" Carmen's heart was blazing with hatred and contempt for Luther.

"No, no, no, that's not true," Luther said, rushing his words. "Of course, I cared. I—"

"Luther. Stop lying. You never even wanted our son. You never wanted children. It's okay. I'm going to make it, just like the millions of other single moms out there."

"Look, baby, I was wrong for what I did. It was an accident and accidents happen all the time. You and Nicholas are the loves of my life and I'm going to make this up to you. I can't live without you. Don't you know that?" Luther tried to caress Carmen but she immediately swatted his hand away.

"Luther." Carmen glared at him with utter disgust. She couldn't stand him and the sight of him repulsed her. "If you don't leave, I will call the police and have you escorted out of my condo. Your name isn't on the mortgage; nor will it ever be."

"Carmen, don't say that! We can work through this." Luther began whining.

"Get out!" Carmen barked at him. "You can go straight to hell for all I care!"

"Carmen, be careful of what you say to me!" Luther was now suddenly angry with her.

"Get your whining, bitch ass out of my motherfucking house,

Luther!" Carmen didn't hold back. "Your shit is packed and at the front door!"

Carmen's words plunged into Luther's heart with the precision of a Samurai's sword. She stared angrily into his eyes so that he understood she meant every word she'd said. Carmen turned her back on him, then fixed her clothing because Nicholas had finished with his feeding.

"Get out!" she howled again. "Nicholas and I don't want you!"

Luther was stunned, dazed, hurt, and emotionally tattered. He left the room, trying to puzzle together a way to make up. He wanted and needed Carmen. He couldn't go back to being homeless. He couldn't return to wandering the streets like a vagrant. There was no one he could turn to. He had no family or friends he could lean on at a time like this. He didn't have a job and he had a limited amount of money in the bank. Without the love and support of Carmen, Luther had absolutely nothing.

He wandered into the dining room and sat at the table, rapidly going out of his mind. He sat and talked to himself. When he got tired, he got up and paced the floor. He was under a tremendous amount of duress and his mind jumped wildly from one thought to another. His mind was beginning to split and crack into mental uncertainty. Finally, something happened; he had a revelation.

"That's it. That's what she wants," he said aloud. "I'm going to give her what she wants. She wants me to suffer."

Luther reentered the bedroom where Carmen was resting with Nicholas. He had lighter fluid from the barbecue grill and began squirting the liquid on the walls and the furniture in the room.

The strong odor of the accelerant caused Carmen to spring up quickly. She saw Luther standing at the foot of the bed about to strike a match.

"I know what you want, Carmen." Luther's body was twitching and jerking as if he were having some type of convulsion.

"Luther, what are you doing?"

"You want to see me suffer, don't you? You want to see me in pain. That's why you want me to go to hell." Luther struck the match. "Well, I can't go to hell by myself. I want you and Nicholas to come with me." Luther then tossed the match against the wall; it quickly ignited. Carmen's eyes were wide with horror. She gasped in disbelief at the fire raging before her eyes. She panicked as a wave of red flames and black smoke rolled up the wall and blanketed the bedroom ceiling. The toxins from the wall paint were burning her eyes.

"You want to see me suffer!" Luther was shouting. "Watch!" He stuck his arm in the middle of the flame, and screamed as it charred his skin. Luther pulled his arm out of the flames. "Is that enough?" Luther was crying. "Don't you know I love you, woman!" The black smoke was quickly choking all of the oxygen out of the room. Carmen's eyes burned like sticks of wood in a camp fire. Nicholas began wailing at the top of his lungs. Carmen grabbed Nicholas, and tumbled down to the floor where she began coughing violently. The fire was now raging, and made a hideous sound as it began consuming everything in its path. She grabbed a pillow off of the bed, and removed the pillowcase to cover Nicholas's nose and mouth. She scooped Nicholas up in one arm crawled on her knees over to the bedroom window, and pushed it open. She needed to act swiftly; the sudden burst of oxygen would give added energy to the flames. At the instant she realized what she needed to do, she began feeling dizzy, disoriented, and weak. She heard Luther cry out.

"Have I suffered enough yet?" he howled, "I will die for you, Carmen." Luther had gone mad.

Carmen summoned the strength she needed and leaped out of the window with Nicholas clutched in her arms. She fell a short distance down the side of her building, and into the snow-covered bushes below. She stood up, and hobbled away from the building, coughing and hacking up black soot from her lungs.

"Nicholas, are you okay?" Carmen pulled him away from her, and checked him over for burn marks. His screams were loud, and Carmen hugged him tightly to keep him warm. A moment later, she saw Luther fall and land safely in the bushes. Then everything seemed to move in slow motion. She rushed away from the building as a fire engine was coming to a halt.

-27-
CARMEN

It took time for Carmen to get Luther out of her system. After everything that had gone wrong, she'd gotten depressed and found it difficult to want to move forward on the days that immediately followed the fire. At the recommendation of a coworker, Carmen joined a local church where she found a loving spiritual family who helped guide and support her through her darkest days.

From time to time, Carmen became emotional about the way her relationship with Luther had ended. Not even in her wildest dreams did she ever think that Luther would snap on her the way he'd done two and a half years ago. Once authorities had arrived to extinguish the fire, Carmen had immediately explained how Luther had lost control and started the blaze with lighter fluid. She was thankful that the fire was contained to her unit, and no other part of the building was damaged. She and Nicholas escaped with only minor scrapes and bruises. Luther was treated for the burns he'd sustained and was then charged with arson. After being found guilty, he was sentenced to four years behind bars. Following Luther's conviction, Carmen saw a lawyer who helped to petition the court and dissolve her marriage.

Carmen contacted her insurance company which responded quickly. She was provided with money, shelter, and other necessities she needed until her condo was suitable for living. Once she was able to return home, she put her condo up for sale. She wanted to move forward and create a good life for her and Nicholas and put her relationship with Luther behind her. She'd always wanted to raise a family in a home, so she purchased a modest-sized bungalow in Oak Park, Illinois. She was able to find a job as a sixth-grade teacher at a local elementary school. Carmen loved living in the Village of Oak Park. She loved its cultural diversity, the local shops as well as the family- oriented community events. She knew that this would be an excellent place to raise Nicholas.

On a hot, July afternoon, Carmen was attending an event called "A Day in the Village." It was held in a local park and organized by volunteers so that members of the community could meet their neighbors and local business owners, as well as learn about their wonderful township.

Carmen and Nicholas, who now was almost three years old, had been walking around shopping, making friends, and eating corn on the cob. Carmen had met several of her upcoming sixth-grade students and their families. Carmen and Nicholas were now making their way over to the music stage to listen to a local band entertain the crowd by singing Chicago-style blues music. After they listened and danced with each other, Carmen walked Nicholas to a nearby playground. She took a seat on a bench and watched as he quickly made a new friend who was about his age. Soon the children began laughing and chasing each other. Then a happy-go-lucky, black Labrador retriever wandered up to her, wagging its tail and nudging her arm, hoping she'd pet him.

"I'm so sorry. It's okay; he won't bite." The dog's owner was rushing over. "I'm so sorry." He was putting the leash back on the dog. "I shouldn't have him out here without his leash on."

Carmen never looked up; she focused on the dog.

"Lovie never runs off like that. I don't know what got into him."

Carmen began rubbing the dog behind his ears. Lovie was so grateful for the attention, he attempted to lick Carmen's face. Carmen was tickled by his efforts to reach her cheek.

"Lovie, sit!" The man yanked the dog's leash and Lovie obediently sat down.

"It's okay." Carmen giggled. "No harm done."

"I'm Marshall. I'm one of the volunteer organizers of the celebration." Marshall extended his hand. Carmen rose to her feet, met his gaze and shook his hand.

Carmen greeted him with a smile. "I'm Carmen."

Marshall looked at her curiously for a long moment.

She felt a bit self-conscious. "What?"

"Have we met before?"

"No, I don't think so."

Carmen focused her attention back on Nicholas, who was still running around laughing.

"You look so familiar to me."

Carmen thought perhaps they had met at some school function. "Are you a school teacher?"

Marshall chuckled. "No. I'm not a teacher."

"Did you ever live in Hyde Park?" Carmen asked, wondering if she'd crossed his path during one of her many evening walks when she lived in that community.

Marshall smiled and then laughed.

"No, I've never lived there, although it's a great community."

Carmen was now looking at Marshall curiously. "You do look familiar to me, now that you mention it."

"See there. Now we've got to figure out how we know each other," Marshall said, scratching the back of his neck.

"You're not an exotic dancer named Shotgun, are you?"

Marshall split open with laughter at that one. "Oh, God no!"

"Good." Carmen laughed along with him. "So what do you do, besides volunteer in the community?"

"I'm a police officer. A state trooper, to be exact."

Carmen immediately stopped smiling and covered her heart with her hand.

"Are you okay?" Marshall asked, noticing a sudden change.

Carmen sat back down. "I know who you are."

"Did I give you a ticket?" Marshall asked, hoping she wasn't an upset motorist.

"No," Carmen assured him as she once again glanced at Nicholas. "Nicholas! Put that sand down."

She watched as Nicholas tossed the sand in the air above his head and then stood still as it came showering down on him.

"It looks like you're going to be washing sand out of his hair tonight," Marshall said.

"Yeah, I know." Carmen redirected her attention back to Marshall. "Marshall, I owe you."

He was puzzled. "Owe me what?"

"About three years ago, you risked your life to save me and Nicholas when our car skidded off the highway and onto a frozen lake."

Marshall's eyes suddenly lit up. "That's where I know you from," he said, popping his fingers. "How are you? I'm so glad that everything turned out okay."

"Well, not everything. My marriage didn't survive the accident," Carmen said lightheartedly.

"I'm sorry to hear that." Marshall glanced back at Nicholas. "He's gotten much bigger since the last time I saw him."

"Oh, yeah. He seems to grow overnight. Every time I turn around, he needs new shoes or a new OshKosh jean outfit."

"Well, he looks very happy." Lovie rose to his feet and barked. "That means that Lovie is ready to continue walking."

"Relax, Lovie," Carmen spoke directly to him.

Lovie glanced at her curiously and then sat back down.

"So, Marshall, do you think that Nicholas and I could buy you a cup of coffee sometime? It's the least we could do for saving both of our lives."

"There is no need for you to do that—"

"No, please. Let me buy you a cup of coffee or tea, take you out to lunch, or something. It means a lot to me to be able to say thank you in some small way."

Marshall paused for a long moment because he felt a little strange. It had been a long time since he'd allowed himself to enjoy the company of a woman. Quentin had been prodding him for some time to move forward with his life and learn how to fall in love again.

"Okay. I live over on Forest Avenue. I'd have to take Lovie back home first."

"Really?" Carmen chuckled. "I live on Forest Avenue, too. I purchased a home there recently."

"Did you purchase a bungalow?"

"Yes. How did you know?"

"Your house is a few doors down from me. Wow. What a small world."

"Very small," Carmen agreed.

"Why don't we do this? I'll take Lovie home and then come back up here to meet you and Nicholas. Then we could walk over to the Starbucks booth at the festival. Is that okay with you?"

"That sounds like a plan," said Carmen as she once again glanced at Nicholas, who'd picked up some more sand. "Let me go pull him out of the sandbox. I'll see you back here in about twenty minutes?"

"Yes, that will work," Marshall agreed as he tugged on Lovie's leash and headed home.

-28-
MARSHALL

Over the years, Marshall had dated sporadically, but none of the relationships had ever flourished to the point of becoming serious. Marshall missed being in a committed relationship and looked forward to the day he'd be able to fall in love and perhaps settle down and start a new family. However, that was easier said than done. The mature, career-oriented ladies he'd been dating were done with having children.

"It's hard as hell being out there, man," he told Quentin when he'd stopped by the house the following afternoon after he'd had coffee with Carmen. Marshall had fired up the barbecue grill and was grilling fish. "The ladies I've met are in their early forties with solid careers and aren't looking to have kids."

Quentin slouched down in a seat and placed his feet up on a small table. "Maybe you need to look at a younger woman. Get you some of that young and energetic stuff."

"Man, please! I don't want to date a twenty-one-year-old. I'm not trying to be anyone's sugar daddy."

Quentin and Marshall burst out laughing.

"Marshall, you make it sound as if you're an old man. You're only forty-two. A young piece of ass may be just what you need. I know that if I were in your shoes, I'd have them coming and going." Quentin smiled at the thought.

"Yeah, right." Marshall disagreed with him. "What do I do when I go meet her parents and her father and I are the same damn age? I'd feel like a male version of Stella. I can see the book title now: *How Marshall Got His Cradle Robbing On.*" Both men laughed.

"Well, it's not uncommon, you know. Men our age have always dated younger women," Quentin reminded Marshall.

"Quentin, I want what you have."

"What's that?"

"A relationship that can weather a storm. Like you and Dawn. You guys have had your share of ups and downs, but you've always managed to stick together and tough it out. I thought I had that with Stacy, but I didn't. It hurt like hell when she left me and moved back to Florida. I'm still tripping out on the fact that I needed to see a therapist after she left me."

"Marshall, you needed help. You'd gone through a lot and that was a difficult time in your life. You got through all that and I don't ever want to see you that distraught and hurt again. Now I'm telling you, brother, a tender, young piece of ass would straighten you out," Quentin said with absolute certainty. "You need to get out more and get to know more people."

"What, am I supposed to go out and get tattooed up, put on a pair of sagging pants and walk into the club holding my dick?" Marshall demonstrated how silly he'd look.

"Okay, you've made your point. You should let Dawn hook you up with one of her girlfriends."

"Naw. That's okay. I don't need someone playing matchmaker for me," Marshall said as he stepped inside the house for a moment. He returned with a small radio and plugged it in. The voice of Timberland singing "Apologize" filled the air. Marshall went over to the grill and checked the fish. He almost tripped over a sledgehammer that was resting against the side of the house. He'd planned to use it to break up a section of concrete that a tree root had cracked. He made a mental note to himself to place it back in the garage where it belonged.

"Dawn and I have made plans to go on a three-day Steppers' dance cruise and I was wondering if you'd keep your nephew for me. The boy is a senior in high school now and thinks he knows everything. I don't want him making me a grandfather before my time," Quentin said.

"No problem. When do you want to drop him off? I haven't spent time with my nephew in a while."

"We don't leave for another three weeks. You really should learn how to step. It's a lot of fun."

"I need a partner for that, don't I?" Marshall asked.

"No, not really. There are more than enough women who will be happy to dance with you. All you have to do is take a class and learn the—-"

"Hello there, neighbor." Carmen waved to Marshall from the sidewalk.

"Oh hey, Carmen," Marshall greeted her. Quentin turned around in his seat to see what woman had come up to the fence.

"She's a cutie," Quentin whispered. "Who is she and how come you haven't said anything about her?"

"It's not like that."

"Is she single?" Quentin asked.

"Yes."

"Then it's like that, man!"

"So this is your home?" Carmen said as she looked around at Marshall's property.

"Yeah, this is home," Marshall said.

"That fish you're grilling smells good. The scent of it is wafting all the way down the block. Are you a master chef also?" Carmen teased.

"Invite her into the backyard, fool." Quentin was whispering instructions to his brother.

"Shut up." Marshall tried to silence his brother. "Where are you headed?"

"I'm headed down to the hardware store to pick up a pipe wrench. There is a pipe leaking under my sink and I need to fix it," Carmen responded.

"She needs a plumber to fix her pipes." Quentin began snickering. "You need to go lay some pipe, partner."

"Do you know what to do?" Marshall asked.

"No. Not really," Carmen replied.

"Excuse me. My name is Quentin. I'm this knucklehead's brother. Why don't you come on in for a minute?"

"Oh no. I couldn't. I was walking past and happened to see Marshall. I hate to be the type of person who walks past and doesn't speak," Carmen explained.

"Don't be silly. Come on in." Quentin got up and walked toward the gate. "Marshall will be more than happy to help you. He's really good at that sort of stuff. He owns a rental property and is constantly having to fix broken pipes and patch holes in the wall."

"Carmen, you'll have to forgive my meddling brother," Marshall said as he walked toward the fence. "How is your little man?"

"He's fine. He's got his arms wrapped around my legs right now." Carmen reached down to pick up Nicholas.

"Why don't you come up and have a seat with us. We're just shooting the breeze," Quentin offered.

"Really guys, I should go." Carmen tried to excuse herself.

"Are you sure?" Quentin asked.

"I'm positive."

"I can drop by in about an hour," Marshall said. "In the meantime, put a bucket under the leaking pipe so that you don't get water damage."

"I've already done that." Carmen smiled at Marshall. "I'll see you in a little while, okay?" Carmen said, and then continued on her way.

"Okay, fool. Who is she and how come you haven't told me about her?" Quentin began grilling Marshall.

"There is nothing to tell." Marshall looked almost insulted by the ridiculous question.

"Nothing to tell? Aw, come on, man. That woman came down here because she wanted to see you. It was written all over her face. Obviously, at some point, you made one hell of an impression on her."

"Quentin, I met her yesterday at the community festival." Marshall paused. "Actually, we'd met before then."

"And?" Quentin was awaiting further details.

"She's the woman I saved from the lake a few years back."

"Really..." Disbelief filled Quentin's voice.

"Yes, really. She purchased a home a few doors down. She's divorced now and raising her son on her own. That's about all that I know." Marshall walked over to his cooler and removed a soda before sitting back down.

"Do you find her attractive?" Quentin asked.

"She's pretty."

"Would you fuck her if you got the chance?" Quentin boldly asked.

Marshall paused in thought, and then laughed. "You know I would."

"Then take your ass down there, fix her pipes, and get to know her. I'm willing to bet you a million bucks that she's dying to get to know you better."

"Do you really think so?" Marshall was now considering Quentin's suggestion.

"Dude. Trust me. I've overheard enough conversations that Dawn has had with her single girlfriends to know that Carmen has more than a casual interest in you. Get your head out of your ass, Marshall, and start living," Quentin said as he rose to his feet. "I'm going to head on out so that you can put on your tool belt and help that woman out."

"It's not going to take me that long to fix a leaking pipe. You don't have to leave."

"Oh, I have a feeling that you're going to be at her house longer than you think. Don't forget to feed Lovie before you head down there," Quentin said as he got into his car and headed home.

*

A short while later, Marshall grabbed his tool belt and his plumbing equipment and walked down to Carmen's house. When he arrived, Carmen was glad to see him and escorted him into the kitchen and showed him the pipe. As Marshall inspected it, he immediately saw that the pipe had cracked and needed to be replaced.

"This is going to take a little longer than I thought," Marshall explained.

"What's wrong?" Carmen asked.

"The pipe is cracked, but I can take care of it. Don't worry," Marshall said. He spent the remainder of the afternoon finishing up the repair job. When he was done, Carmen invited him to sit on her deck and enjoy a glass of lemonade with her.

"Now, that tastes good," Marshall said as he placed the ice-filled glass up to his forehead.

'I'm glad you like it," Carmen said, as she sipped her drink. "I love summer nights like this. They're so peaceful and relaxing."

"Yes, they are," Marshall agreed, as a gentle breeze blew past.

"I still can't believe that I'm actually sitting here with the man who saved my life." Carmen's voice was filled with gratefulness.

Marshall smiled and took another sip of his drink.

"So what do you like to do for fun, Marshall?"

"Oh, I like traveling. Since my divorce, I've taken several trips." Marshall glanced over at Carmen.

"Where have you been? I'd love to travel more but I have to find the time." Carmen tucked her legs beneath herself and focused on Marshall.

"I've been to Costa Rica, Belize, the West Indies, and I've taken an Alaskan cruise." Carmen saw how Marshall's face lit up when he talked about his vacations.

"Wow! What was your favorite of those trips?" Carmen asked.

"I'd have to say the Alaskan cruise."

"Really?" Carmen's voice filled with disbelief. "Why? I would've thought the trip to Belize would be at the top of your list."

"Well, the Alaskan cruise was different and, believe it or not, it is really beautiful up there. The mountains are so peaceful. While there, I did a lot of soul searching and—" Marshall paused. "Let's say I was able to finally accept a lot of things that didn't go the way that I'd planned."

"Did you have a spiritual experience or something?" Carmen wanted to know more.

"Yeah. I guess you could say it was something like that."

"Well, what else do you like to do?" Carmen asked, because she really wanted to get to know him.

"Well, I do volunteer work for the village. I cycle, although not as much as I used to. I like to swim and read books as well. I'm a pretty flexible person. I can do just about anything and enjoy it. What about you? What do you like to do?"

"That's a good question," Carmen said, as she readjusted her position in her chair. "Like you, I love to travel, although I haven't had the money to do much of that since I purchased this house."

"Oh, I can understand that. A house will suck a bank account dry," Marshall joked.

"I like taking evening walks, going to concerts and—" Carmen laughed. "I've been thinking about taking a dance class to learn how to step, which would be something totally new for me. I have two left feet."

Marshall laughed.

"What? You don't think I'd do well at it?" Carmen asked defensively.

"No, it's not that. My brother and his wife have become serious Steppers. They enter dance contests and are even going on a steppers' cruise in a few weeks. He and his wife, Dawn, have been trying to get me to take classes for the longest. Like you, I have two left feet."

"Then you and I would make perfect dance partners." Carmen laughed.

"Oh no. I'm not taking a dance class," Marshall said as he took another sip of his drink.

"Why not? It would be fun. Besides, I'd feel more comfortable if I took the class with someone who was just as bad as me."

Marshall felt as if Carmen were issuing him a challenge. "Now wait a minute. You don't even know me that well and already you're calling me a bad dancer."

"Well, do you want to prove me wrong? You said that you were a pretty flexible person and could have fun doing just about anything. The community center offers classes on Friday evenings."

Carmen flirted with Marshall as she offered up the information. Marshall was silent for a long moment.

"What the hell! You only live once, right?" Marshall said.

"Exactly," Carmen agreed. "I can leave the details about the class in your mailbox. I'll pick the information up after my summer school class gets dismissed."

Marshall laughed again. "I can't believe that I'm agreeing to this, but okay, I'll do it."

"Great. I'm sure we'll have a lot of fun," Carmen said, as she stood up and offered to take Marshall's glass.

"Can I get another glass of that before I go?" Marshall asked.

"Absolutely," Carmen said. As she walked back inside the house, Marshall turned so that he could get a peek at her ass.

"Uhm," he uttered to himself as he imagined what her ass would feel like in his hands.

~29~
CARMEN

Carmen had most certainly grown as a person over the years and she prided herself on her ability to learn and grow from her experiences. She refused to allow the mistakes and misfortunes of her time with Luther to deter her learning how to love again, or to at least reach a place in her life where she was happy. Now that she was in her mid-thirties, she was more determined than ever to find love, peace and joy. She'd also learned that she couldn't help individuals like Luther or her sister, Nikki, especially if they didn't want her assistance. That was one of the most difficult flaws in her personality that she had to correct. She'd kept in touch with Nikki just to let her know that if rubber hit the road and she needed a change, she'd know where to find her. Otherwise, she wasn't going to continue wasting her time and energy trying to put her on a better path.

She and Marshall took the steppers' classes and enjoyed them tremendously. Once they got the basic moves, they learned how to incorporate the spins, the twirls, and the stylish footwork that made bop-style couples' dance so fun, exciting, and energetic. At the conclusion of the course, they decided to sign up for the advanced steppers' class and learned how to truly create provocative, sensual, and creative dance moves. They soon learned that stepping was more than just couples dancing. It was sensual and often erotic, how a man and woman could express themselves to each other.

Marshall and Carmen both admitted to each other that they hadn't had so much fun in years. Through dance, they experienced a sense of freedom and excitement that they'd lost somewhere along the road of life.

Over time, Marshall and Carmen became better acquainted and began dating. They discussed their previous marriages, the events that went wrong, and emotional scars that were still healing. Carmen talked about her sister and their rift because of how her father died.

"A burglar got into our house one night," Carmen explained one fall evening when she was visiting Marshall. Carmen was positioned with her head resting on Marshall's chest. "Both my father and I heard the person enter the house and came out of our bedrooms at the same time. My father told me to stay as he grabbed a baseball bat and walked down the stairs and into the kitchen. The moment he flipped on the light switch, I heard a gunshot and then the sound of his body thudding against the floor. I wanted to rush to him but I froze up. I freaked out. I couldn't move. I called out to him a few times, but I got so choked up that I couldn't speak anymore. I literally stood frozen with fear all night long. It wasn't until the following morning, when my sister woke up, that the police and an ambulance were called. My father died that night, but he wouldn't have had I had the courage to do something." Carmen smeared away tears running down her cheeks.

"It's never easy dealing with situations like that," Marshall explained. "When a person has to deal with a traumatic situation, it's not uncommon to freeze with fear," Marshall said as he stroked her hair and caressed her back. He felt his heart intertwine with hers and, at that moment, he knew that he'd always want his chest to be the pillow that she cried on.

Having Marshall in her life lifted Carmen's spirits and gave her renewed hope for finding happiness. Over the next several months, she and Marshall grew very close to each other. They spent time going to museums, jazz concerts, and stage plays. They read books and discussed them. Marshall took the time to get to know Nicholas and Carmen loved the way they interacted. Marshall was so patient, loving, and caring with her son. He took time out of his schedule to take Nicholas to swim class at the community center. He got along well with Nicholas, who enjoyed being with Marshall. Marshall never raised his voice in anger at her son or placed a hand on him. That went a long way with Carmen because she wanted a man who'd accept her and her son. She didn't want a man who'd abuse or mistreat her baby.

It was now New Year's Eve, and Carmen was standing in front of the bathroom mirror putting the finishing touches on her makeup. She was in a rush because she'd just returned from getting Nicholas situated with her babysitter. She was looking forward to bringing in the New Year with Marshall, his brother, Quentin, and his wife, Dawn. They'd planned on attending a party at the Hyatt in downtown Chicago. Just as she was slipping on her high-heeled shoes, she heard her doorbell ring. She went to open the door and saw Marshall wearing a tailored, black, Bill Blass tux with a perfectly matched silver shirt, tie, and cuff links.

"Damn, you look good," Carmen said to him as she stepped into his embrace and kissed him.

"And you look hot," Marshall said as his hands slid down and caressed her ass.

"Damn. You do that so well. And you're wearing that Michael Jordan cologne that turns me on."

Carmen gave him a saucy smile as she turned and walked away from him. Marshall was like no other lover Carmen had ever had before. He was able to bring out a sensual side of her that she didn't even know existed. After making love to Marshall, there was no way that she could deny that he was slowly turning her out.

As Carmen sashayed away, Marshall was in awe at how beautiful she looked in her black dress. It had a generous split on the left leg that ran up dangerously high on her muscular thigh. He allowed his eyes to float up and down her brown leg that was accessorized with a gold ankle bracelet. Her open-heeled shoes were made of the same fabric as the dress. She pivoted and turned her back to him. The back of the dress showed a lot of skin. Two straps crisscrossed and ran across her shoulder blades. Another strap came around and clasped at the center of her back. There was a U-shaped scoop that ran hazardously low on her hips. She pivoted once again and highlighted the front of the dress. All of her neck and chest was exposed because of a deep, V-shaped scoop.

"So how do I look, officer?" Carmen said, batting her eyes playfully at Marshall.

"Baby, the way you look in that dress. Shit! You are going to do more damage than a nuclear bomb."

Carmen laughed. She was tickled by his comment.

"Oh, really." Carmen rested her hand on her tummy as she continued to laugh.

"Yes, really." Marshall cracked his knuckles. "I'm going to have to fight the hounds off you tonight."

"Well, I'm confident you're a man who knows how to protect

a lady." Carmen walked back over to Marshall. She put her arms around his neck and looked into his eyes. Marshall slid his hands around her waist and locked his fingers. He moved closer to Carmen and kissed her passionately. The moment their lips met, Carmen felt little twinges of excitement in the bottom of her stomach.

"Damn. You're making me wet just by kissing," Carmen said, as she pulled away from his succulent lips and smeared away the red lipstick that she'd left.

"If we don't get out of here, you're going to end up with your head in a pillow and your ass in the air," Marshall said with absolute certainty.

Carmen could see his desire for her in his eyes and it turned her on.

"You are such a sensual man." Carmen felt her desire for him increasing with each passing moment.

"Let's stay in," Marshall said as he pulled her back into him.

"Don't play with me," Carmen said, feeling herself tingling with nervous sexual energy. "You are taking me out tonight, mister man. I spent all day yesterday getting a manicure, pedicure and my hair done." Carmen stepped away from him, showed Marshall her fingernails and directed him to look at her toenail polish.

"See, there, that's a foul," Marshall said. "You know how I am about feet." A wide grin spread across Carmen's face.

"If you're a good boy, I'll let your rub them down for me tonight in our hotel room," Carmen said, as she went to the closet and grabbed her coat and gloves.

When they arrived at the hotel, it was filled with guests wearing party favors and making their way to the ballroom. Marshall and Carmen maneuvered through the crowd and entered the ballroom. Once inside, they located Quentin and Dawn, who'd arrived earlier, dressed and ready to do some serious Stepping.

"Hey, girl," Carmen greeted Dawn when she saw her. The two of them had become good friends over the course of her relationship with Marshall.

"Oh no, you ain't cutting up like that." Dawn was looking at Carmen with envy.

"Wow!" said Quentin. "You look great!" And he gave Carmen a quick hug.

Quentin glanced over at Carmen. "Marshall, you're handling that, right?" He wanted to make sure that his brother was fucking Carmen well.

"You know I am," Marshall boasted.

"Alright, now. You know the Powell men don't slough when it comes to getting that ass," Quentin bragged.

"How many drinks have you had?" Marshall laughed.

"Don't worry about it. I'm not driving. Dawn and I have a room and, at the stroke of midnight, I'm going to have her legs in the air."

Quentin and Marshall laughed.

"Quentin, behave yourself. Everyone doesn't have to know our business," Dawn lovingly scolded her husband.

"Happy New Year to you, man," Marshall said as he sat down.

"Hey, same to you," Quentin said as everyone else sat down.

Dawn continued to compliment Carmen. "Girl, that dress is hot!"

"This is the most revealing dress I've ever worn," Carmen explained. "If my sister could see me now, she'd freak the hell out. Marshall makes me feel so—" Carmen searched her mind for the right words. "He makes feel free and alive. He's exactly what I need at this point and time of my life." Carmen reached over and held onto his hand.

"Oh. That's so special." Dawn was happy for them.

"Come on, babe. Let's go dance," Marshall said and led Carmen out to the dance floor.

Marshall, Carmen, Quentin, and Dawn enjoyed the evening's festivities. Then, at about twenty minutes before midnight, Quentin and Dawn decided to leave.

"I have to go get on my job. I'll talk to you later," Quentin said jokingly as he and Dawn headed out to their hotel room.

Carmen and Marshall decided to stay and bring in the New Year, slow dancing with each other.

"Thirty seconds left until the New Year!" announced the master of ceremonies.

"Ten, nine, eight," he said, "seven, six, five, four, three, two, one."

"Happy New Year!" the crowd shouted out as "Auld Lang Syne" began playing. A large balloon dropped, filled with black and silver balloons and party streamers. Marshall took his attention off of the floating balloons and put it back on Carmen, who was also looking up at them. Marshall took Carmen's face into his hands. She'd been waiting for this moment. When he kissed her, electricity tickled every inch of her body.

MARSHALL

Marshall wanted to do something extra on their six-month anniversary. He decided that a romantic spa weekend would be the perfect way to celebrate their blossoming love as well as further strengthen their relationship. He worked with Dawn, who helped him locate the ideal get-away spot.

"Okay. I spoke with two of my girlfriends who both told me about a place in the Wisconsin Dells."

Marshall was on his cell phone with Dawn. He'd just arrived home from work and was about to enter the house.

"Both of my girlfriends swear that Sundara is the perfect place for you to take Carmen. When I looked the place up on the Internet, I knew that it would be wonderful for you guys. Shit, if the truth were to be told, I need to slap Quentin's ass and have him take me to this place as well."

"I want it to be a real experience. You know me, Dawn. When I do something, I want it to be right." Marshall removed his shoes as he entered the house. He then opened up the basement door and allowed Lovie to run out into the yard to take care of his business.

"I know how you are. Just listen to this description of the place. Sundara was conceived as a place of wellness, where lives would be transformed one person at a time. Wellness would be defined as a balance of four cornerstones—spiritual, emotional, mental, and physical. A sanctuary where guests would leave with more than they came. Now doesn't that sound like the perfect place to relax and enjoy each other's company?"

"Yes, it does," Marshall admitted. "Send me the link to their website and I'll take care of making the arrangements."

"Okay, I'm sending it now. Oh, when you return I want to know all about it. Well, not the sex part, but about the spa itself." Dawn laughed.

"You are so crazy. I'll be sure to bring you a full report." Marshall glanced back into the yard and saw Lovie sniffing around the base of the tree. He and Dawn spoke a little longer before finally ending their conversation.

Once Marshall got settled for the evening, he logged onto his computer and retrieved Dawn's e-mail with the website information. He reserved a villa designed for tranquility and privacy. The villa came with a master spa suite with a canopied king featherbed and private bath sanctuary separated by a glass partition that took on the appearance of a rainfall. The villa also had a soaring, three-way fireplace linking the entrance, living space, and gourmet kitchen. It included an entertainment console with TV, VCR and DVD. Marshall didn't spare any expense as he carefully studied the spa menu. He reserved time for a couples' thirty-minute soak in a chromatherapy bath, followed by a Marma Massage. He reserved time for them to both have a manicure and pedicure, as well as dinner by candlelight.

Once he made the reservation, he informed Carmen so she could make babysitting arrangements for Nicholas.

Two weeks later, Marshall and Carmen were on the highway heading toward their destination. Carmen had plugged her iPod into the adapter and selected one of her favorite Robin Thicke songs, "2 the Sky."

"I love Robin Thicke," Carmen declared as she sang along. Ever since Marshall had told her about his plans for a hot weekend, she hadn't been able to stop thinking about it. She placed her hand on Marshall's thigh, then leaned over and kissed him on the cheek.

"What are you doing to me?" she asked, feeling her yearning for him mounting.

"Everything that you want me to do," he answered, as he briefly glanced at her.

"You know that you're fucking with my head, right? I mean, I've never been so sexually open and turned on as I am with you." Carmen exhaled as she began sweeping her hand up and down his thigh.

"That's because you're getting some grown-ass man loving. There is a difference. I plan on bringing out the freak in you." Marshall spoke with supreme confidence regarding his ability to satisfy her.

"Damn! I can't wait for you to take me to new levels of exquisite pleasure." Carmen sighed as she caressed his manhood. "I love the way your dick feels as it grows in my hand. That shit excites the fuck out of me."

"It excites the fuck out of me, too." Marshall laughed as he flexed his manhood and made it jump.

"Ohhh, I have never in my life liked to suck a dick until I met you. It's like the minute I see your dick, I want to put my mouth all over it." Carmen allowed herself to be swept away by her desire. She unzipped Marshall's pants, reached inside, and pulled out his Pride.

"Don't take it out unless you plan on handling business." Marshall spread his thighs a little wider.

"Damn. Your dick looks so good to me. It's so chocolate and silky to the touch. The head of it—damn. I want to put my mouth on it," Carmen admitted as she stroked and squeezed his Pride. "Can you handle it, if I suck it while you drive?"

"Go on and get it, baby," Marshall said as she moistened the head of his cock with her saliva. She circled her sweet tongue around the head of his dick and then opened her mouth wider and put his dick at the back of her throat. She suctioned her lips around his Pride and slowly pulled him back out of her mouth.

"Ohhh, shit," Marshall cooed. "Stroke it." He gave her additional instructions.

"Um-hmmm," Carmen muttered as she squeezed and continued to suck. She circled her tongue around the head, savoring the taste of his sweet nectar. "Your ass is horny."

"You're going to make me pull over at a rest stop and fuck you, if you keep this up." Marshall combed his fingers through her hair.

"Ohhh," Carmen cooed. She was deliciously delighted by Marshall's threat. "If it was dark outside, I'd let you bend me over one of the picnic tables and put my ass in the air." She laughed as she began placing sweet, luscious kisses on his dick. She loved how strong and how tall his cock was. Just the thought of him being inside of her, rubbing the head of his log against her pussy walls, made her ache for him.

"God, I can't wait to get there so I can fuck you!" Carmen screamed as she repositioned herself in her seat. She closed her eyes for a moment, as an image of his glistening body ravishing her demanded her attention.

"Unzip your blue jeans," Marshall ordered.

"Damn, baby, you're going to play with my pussy while you drive?" Carmen asked, pleasantly excited.

"You know that you want to feel my fingers rubbing your walls." Marshall was eager to feel her soft, moist folds. Carmen loosened her pants, reclined the seat back, and parted her thighs for him. Marshall moistened his fingers with his saliva and began rubbing the outer folds of her pussy.

"It's a damn shame how wet I get when you touch me," Carmen cried out with pleasure. "Oh, the way you handle me sends sensual chills throughout my body."

Marshall skillfully glided two fingers inside of her juicy Honey Pot. The moment his fingers penetrated, her pussy walls immediately gripped his fingers and showered them with her juices. Marshall moved his fingers in small, circular motions on the left wall of her vagina.

"Ohhh, you make me melt when you do that." Carmen clasped her legs closed as an intense contraction ballooned up. "Oh shit! Damn! Oh, stop!" Carmen tried to push his fingers out of her, but Marshall fought back.

"What are you doing?" he scolded her as he continued to play with her while focusing on the highway at the same time.

"Marshall, baby, please stop." Carmen grabbed his wrist. Marshall managed to brush his fingertips across her clit a few times before she was able to pull his fingers out of her. Marshall gazed at his silky and glistening fingers for a brief moment before sticking them in his mouth to enjoy the taste of her fruit.

"I swear. You are turning my ass out," Carmen confessed as she curled up and waited until a tidal wave of ecstasy subsided. "Every time you touch me, my body goes crazy. I don't under-stand it. I have never been this orgasmic," Carmen conceded as she tried to compose herself. Once the waves of passion had subsided, she looked at Marshall lovingly.

"I'm a dangerous motherfucker. I told you not to come over

here unless you were ready to handle business," Marshall reminded her.

"You wait until we get to our room. I'm going to fuck your
ass up."

"Bring it on, baby." Marshall was eager to travel to paradise
with her.

"You think I'm bullshitting," Carmen stated as she fastened
her pants. "I'm going to murder your dick when we get there."

"I know you're not bullshitting, baby." Marshall slapped her on
the thigh a few times as he exited the highway to get more gas.

As soon as they checked into their villa, Carmen immediately
kicked off her shoes and relaxed on the bed.

"Oh, this bed feels so heavenly." She exhaled as she sank into
the mattress. "My God, Marshall, this place is so beautiful."

"Yes it is," he agreed as he inspected the accommodations to
make sure he'd gotten exactly what he'd ordered. Marshall and
Carmen went about the business of settling in and freshening
up. They took a shower together, and scrubbed each other's
body before finishing up. Then Marshall put on soft music that
he'd brought with him and asked Carmen to get into the bed
and lie on her stomach.

"What are you about to do?" Carmen asked, feeling excited
and very nervous at the same time.

"I want you to relax. I want to do something special for you.
I want to slowly caress and explore your body. I want to find all
of the secret hot spots that I haven't discovered yet," Marshall
said as he poured some massage oil into a small dish.

Excited about the treat she was about to receive, Carmen
positioned herself on the bed, like Marshall had requested, and
relaxed. As Marshall caressed her legs and feet, he began speaking
softly.

"I love the way your feet talk to me," he whispered. "Your toes curl up into tight fists when I grab your ankles, and spread your legs open, while my hard glistening dick is hitting your special spot. Whenever I see your feet talk to me like that, the urge to put your toes in my mouth is overwhelming. I enjoy sucking on your toes while my dick is deep inside of you." Marshall began caressing the back of her thighs. "You have the sexiest thighs I've ever seen. Whenever I think about your thighs, I always picture my face buried between them. I love sweeping the tip of my tongue up and down your inner thigh. I love the feel of your thighs against my cheeks and ears when I'm licking your overflowing nectar."

"Ohhh, I like it when you do that, baby." Just the thought of Marshall in action was making her juices flow.

"And your ass. Your ass is so sexy and full of attitude. Whenever you walk by me, I want to give it a light slap—like this." Marshall whacked Carmen's ass.

"Yes, baby! Slap my ass! Damn, that shit feels so good to me." Carmen arched her ass up so that Marshall could slap it again. Instead of giving her what she wanted, Marshall decided to give her a different type of sensation. He spread her ass cheeks apart and circled his tongue around her asshole.

"Oh shit! Oh God!" Carmen cried in a fit of ecstasy as her body began to tremble, twitch, and shudder uncontrollably. Carmen automatically raised her ass up. Marshall inserted three fingers inside of her and rhythmically pressed the pads of his fingertips against her pubic bone. Carmen exhaled loudly and repeated Marshall's name over and over again as the ringed muscles of her pussy clutched his fingers with orgasmic pleasure. He enjoyed watching the pulsating undulations of her ass, back, and hips as she fucked his fingers until she was thoroughly satisfied. Marshall began caressing her spine and placing soft kisses on her back.

"You've got my entire body tingling with electricity," Carmen whimpered as she tried to contain her tears of pleasure. "I've never felt like this before in my life. I can't believe that I've waited this long to be loved and pampered like this."

"I'll treat you like this for a lifetime, if you let me," Marshall whispered in her ear.

"Yes, baby. I want you to pamper me like this all the time," Carmen cooed.

"Turn over, baby," Marshall whispered.

"You've got my body so relaxed, I can hardly move," Carmen uttered as she willed herself to turn over and rest on her back.

"Lay still," Marshall spoke purposely in her ear. He had a surprise for her. He'd gone out and purchased several peacock feathers. Once he retrieved them, he began tickling her nipples with the feathers until they became erect.

"You're giving my skin goose bumps," Carmen's voice quivered with shuddering pleasure.

Marshall positioned himself over her breasts and exhaled his warm breath on them. He then took one into his warm mouth and sucked on it gently.

"Harder. Suck on it harder," Carmen insisted as she cradled the back of his head. "Ohhh," Carmen echoed as a delicious swell of bliss ravished her body. Carmen pushed down on the top of Marshall's head. "Kiss my stomach." Her entire body had come alive. "Yes. That feels so good to me."

Marshall continued kissing her stomach and then moved down to her luscious pussy that was waiting on him. He slurped up some of her juices with the moist tip of his tongue and savored the taste of her for a moment.

"You have some delicious pussy," he said as he pulled back her vagina lips and rotated his tongue around her love bead.

"Oh, God!" Carmen cried as her body responded immediately to the sensation. Marshall once again slid two fingers inside of her folds and massaged her pussy walls while simultaneously flicking his tongue up and down on her clit.

"Oh, God, you're going to make me cum, baby," Carmen warned him.

"Cum for me then. Give me my shit!" Marshall demanded as he continued to simulate her.

Carmen snapped her thighs shut and locked them tightly around Marshall's neck as she came with thunderous pleasure. She wailed so loudly with satisfaction that she didn't recognize the sound of her own voice.

"Marshall!" Carmen curled up and began crying into the pillow. Marshall cuddled with her and held her for a long moment.

"I'm so glad that you've come into my life," he whispered in her ear. "I never thought I'd ever fall in love again until you came along."

"Do you really mean that?" Carmen asked.

"Yes. I love you." Carmen turned to face him. With both of their heads resting on the same pillow, she gazed into his almond eyes and caressed his face.

"I love you, too," she admitted. "Our relationship feels so good and so right. I know that I'll always be safe with you."

"Yes, you will," Marshall said. Carmen kissed him passionately and then gently eased him over until he was resting on his back. She positioned herself on top of him. She savored the feeling of her nipples against the hair on his chest. She eased her way down his body until his dick was at her mouth. She held it in one hand and raised his balls up with the other. The moment she began toying with his silky and shaved sac, his legs opened wider.

"You like that, baby?" Carmen asked.

"Yes."

Carmen decided to reciprocate and share some of the same pleasures that Marshall had given her. She gently eased his legs high in the air and licked his anus.

"Oh damn!" Marshall howled with exquisite pleasure as Carmen's tongue made tiny circles around his ass.

Carmen licked him from his asshole to the tip of his dick. She opened her mouth wide and placed his shaft deep inside of her mouth. She sucked on him until some of his juices oozed out.

"I love your dick so much that I want to swallow your cum," Carmen said as she sucked hard.

"You want to swallow me, baby?" Marshall asked. He wanted to hear her say that shit again.

"Yes, I want to swallow all of your load," Carmen repeated as she rose up and straddled him.

She positioned herself above him, spread her legs, and teased her clit with the head of his cock. She then carefully lowered onto his manhood. She let out a gasp as his massive cock filled her up. Even after having his fingers inside of her, it still felt like a stretch to take all of Marshall inside of her.

She slowly began gliding herself up along the length of his Pride, from top to bottom. She savored every moment and every inch of him. Marshall's hands were caressing her breasts and teasing her nipples, sending sparks of pleasure throughout her body. She began to move quicker as the urge to fuck him to death consumed her. She placed her hands on his shoulders and held him down. She rose up until just the head of his dick was past her vagina lips. She rode his dick faster. She enjoyed being the jockey of this thoroughbred stallion. She felt him growing and getting harder inside of her.

"Oh, baby, this dick feels so good to me," she cried as she gazed into his eyes. "This dick is so fucking good to me," she repeated.

"This dick has never been ridden the way you ride it," Marshall admitted as he thrust his hips and plunged himself deep inside of her. "Damn. You have a juicy, motherfucking pussy!"

Marshall's words tickled Carmen's ears with such delight that her pussy clutched his dick so hard she thought for sure she'd choke it to death. The pleasure she felt was so overwhelming that she wanted to get off his dick, but he wouldn't allow her.

"Don't you move off of this dick!" he told her as he guided her movements. He circled his hips, causing his thoroughbred to touch every wall of her paradise.

Carmen sat upright and began riding him once again. She toyed with her clit as she rode. She'd never felt her love bead so swollen and she couldn't keep the tidal gates back much longer. Finally, Carmen gushed all over him. The orgasmic pleasure that swept over her made her entire body weak with euphoric pleasure.

"Keep going. Don't stop. Please, baby, keep moving!" Marshall begged. Carmen could feel Marshall's massive cock throbbing inside of her.

"Are you going to cum for me, baby?" Carmen asked as she kept pounding down on his dick. She could feel his balls slapping her ass so she reached behind her and fondled him.

"Ohhh! That's it, baby!" Marshall moaned. "Come get it, baby. Put it in your mouth." Carmen immediately got off of this thoroughbred and put him in her mouth. She sucked and stroked him until she felt his hot seed stream out and flood the cave of her mouth.

—31—
LUTHER

Luther was being released and he was overjoyed to have his freedom back. Despite the fact that Carmen had divorced him, never contacted him, and never came to see him, Luther still loved and wanted to be with her. He wanted to pick up where they'd left off and win her heart back. Setting the house on fire and asking her to come to hell with him was a major mistake, he now realized. He'd reduced his inexcusable actions to mere accidents, like everything else that had gone wrong in his life.

When Luther got out of jail, he discovered Carmen had brought what was left of his belongings in a box to the jailhouse for him to take upon his release. That was his only indication she'd even bothered to come near him. He twisted that reality in his mind and told himself if she cared enough to give him back his belongings, then there was still hope for the two of them. He could save their marriage and they could be a team again. He wanted to move back in with her. He wanted her to rescue him like she'd done before. He would be a better person this time. He would try extra hard to make their life together work. *I will tell her everything*, he thought. *I'll tell her about the accident, the little girl, the state trooper, Packard, everything. Once I tell her what I was dealing with at the time, she'll understand.* That is what Luther believed and that is what drove him to find Carmen.

After his release, the first stop was Carmen's condo. He quickly discovered she no longer lived there. He went to Bret Harte Elementary School to see if he could catch her at work. He was told she hadn't worked there for years. Luther took a big risk and went to Big Daddy's Exotic Dance Club to track down Carmen's sister, Nikki. By showing his face there, he'd run the risk of running into Packard and being shot on sight. However, it was a risk he was willing to take. When he arrived at Big Daddy's, Nikki was nowhere to be found. With no place to go and no one to turn to, the reality of his situation hit him hard. Luther tried to hang on to his mental stability, but he couldn't. His mind cracked.

Luther wandered the streets of Chicago— disturbed, penniless, and homeless. He was now shabby, with thick, untamed hair, dirty-looking skin, and layers of clothes that were filthy with dirt and grime from lying in the gutter. He drifted into downtown Chicago and hung out around the train stations, begging for money and hoping that chance would allow him to see his beloved Carmen. When he couldn't find any sign of her, Luther fell deep in despair. He started talking to himself out loud, which caused people to cross the street when they saw him. Luther even got to the point where he began having arguments with his reflection.

"I didn't do it. I told you that already!" he barked at the reflection of himself in a restaurant window at Michigan Avenue and Adams Street. He yelled at patrons who brushed him off as some homeless lunatic who was disturbing their meal. Luther walked away from the window, but his reflection followed him. "What? You want a piece of me? Huh? I'll whip your ass!" Luther threatened himself. "I told you already, man, you're not listening. I did not kill that little girl! I wasn't there!" Luther yelled as he continued walking down the street and arguing with himself.

"What do you mean? What about my son? My son loves me. He knows that I didn't mean to leave him in the sinking car. Don't ask me about that anymore." Luther pointed to himself and then stopped walking. He stood on the sidewalk and postured as if someone were threatening him. "If you ask me another goddamn question, I'm going to kill you! Now leave me the fuck alone."

It was now winter and the bitter-cold February wind bit through the layers of his grossly soiled clothing. It was one of the coldest nights Chicago had experienced in some time. It was fourteen degrees below zero, but with the wind chill, it was about thirty below. Luther could no longer feel his toes and he tucked his fingers inside of his armpits to keep them warm. The howling wind froze everything in its path, forcing everyone to remain indoors where it was warm. Luther's breathing had become short and labored and he felt as if his tragic existence was about to come to an end. He reached the front porch steps of his old abandoned and burned-out apartment building. He made his way up the steps and inside the front hallway. He stumbled down the steps of his old basement apartment and sat on the floor, resting his head against the wall. He shivered violently as a gust of wind blew in from somewhere and spun around his body like an angry twister. He closed his eyes and welcomed the thought of freezing to death.

When Luther opened his eyes, he was in a different place. He was no longer curled up against the wall of his basement apartment. His eyes darted wildly from right to left. He was lying on his side on a bathroom floor. He sat up and looked around. Broken chunks of wood and tile were scattered all over the floor and he could hear the wind howling like a wolf through an open window. He noticed that someone had started a fire with wood from the wall. The person had grabbed a steel garbage can from the alley and used it to contain the fire. In the shadow of the red flame, he saw someone emerge and move toward him. His heart began racing with fear and uncertainty.

"You had better get on over here if you want to stay warm." It was a woman and the pitch in her voice seemed familiar to him. He'd heard that voice somewhere before.

"And grab another piece of wood to throw on the fire," said the woman.

Luther stood up, grabbed some more wood from the floor, and walked toward the flame. He tossed the wood into the fire and then sat down on the floor and gawked at the woman before him. He couldn't believe who he was looking at. After all of the years that had passed, he'd finally come face to face with his drug-addicted mother, Sugar.

"I saw you when you sat down."

Luther didn't say a word; he glared at her, unable to speak. He wasn't sure if she even realized who he was.

"It's too cold to be outside, Luther. You know that, don't you?"

Luther nodded his head at his frail mother. Her eyes were set deep in their sockets and she coughed a lot. It was the same sick cough he'd heard when he worked at the hospital. He called it the "cough of death." Sugar shivered uncontrollably.

"Do you have anything on you?" She sniffled. "You know. Something for my nerves."

Luther swung his head from side to side, indicating he didn't. He couldn't believe she was asking him for drugs. She hadn't changed one bit. The memories of the countless times he had to pull needles out of her arm came rushing back.

"You ain't got no cigarette or nothing, man?" She stood up and warmed her hands against the heat of the fire. "I'm in bad shape! I need something for my damn nerves! Do you want me to suck you off real good? I'll do a good job, I promise." She glared at Luther through the flames with pleading eyes. Luther's sympathy for her quickly became as cold as the weather outside.

"Luther, baby, I'm sorry. I didn't mean that, okay? I'm sorry. Forgive Mama. She is so sorry for saying that," Sugar pleaded. "Life has been hard for me, you know," explained Sugar, who tossed another piece of wood inside the barrel. "I've got one foot in the grave and the other foot is on the edge. The only thing of value I have left in this world is the blood in my veins, and I'm not so sure that's worth much."

Luther was confused. He didn't know if he should be happy or angry.

"Don't look at me like that! I'm still your mother. No matter how bad off I am, I'm the one who gave birth to you." Sugar trembled violently and started coughing and couldn't stop. When she finally did quiet her cough, she stuck her fingers down her collar and pulled up a shoestring necklace with a small heart-shaped locket. She removed the necklace and opened the locket. "Here."

She extended her bony arm to him. Luther took the locket, which has his baby picture in it, from her hand. The picture looked like his son, Nicholas. Luther closed it and then asked her a question he'd always wanted to know.

"Why?" he asked. "Why did you leave me in the store that day?"

"So you want to know the truth, huh?" Sugar whispered as she tried to keep warm.

"Yes."

"Well, ain't no sense in telling part of the truth, so I'm going tell it all. It's not pretty, so I hope you got the stomach for what I'm about to tell you."

Sugar had yet another violent coughing attack. She spat and Luther noticed her saliva was filled with blood.

Luther suddenly felt concern for her. "Are you okay?"

"I'm fine," she barked. "I wish that death would come on in and get it over with. Death wants to torture me," said Sugar as she eased herself back down onto the floor. "I think dragging you in here took most of my strength." She looked exhausted.

Luther moved closer to the fire. "When the sun comes up, I'll get you to the hospital."

"You were always a good boy, Luther."

Sugar wrapped her arms around herself in an effort to comfort her trembling body. A long moment of silence hung in the air as Luther waited for her to begin her explanation.

She took a deep breath and slowly exhaled.

"I did love you, Luther," Sugar whispered. "I loved you enough to know that if I didn't get you away from me, I was going to kill you. And I didn't want to kill you. I never wanted to kill nobody, for that matter."

Luther was puzzled by her comment. "Kill me? Why would you have killed me?"

"So that you wouldn't have to know the truth of what I'd done." Sugar wiped tears from her cheek with trembling hands. "I killed somebody. I'm a murderer."

Luther was silent. He didn't see that one coming.

"It happened years ago, but it was an accident."

Luther's heart skipped a beat. She was starting to sound just like him.

Luther asked for clarification. "What do you mean, it was an accident?"

Sugar began coughing again. "I'm tired, Luther. I am so tired of carrying around my guilt. I thought that, by getting high, I'd forget all about it, but I can't. Guilt has been slowly eating away at my soul." Sugar was silent for another long moment.

"I've never told anyone about this. The only other person in the world who knows about it is Packard. Years ago, when I was prostituting myself for Packard, he pulled me off the street one night and asked me to take a ride with him. One of his informants had given him the home address of a rival drug dealer. We were going out there to rob him. Packard had learned that the dude kept his money in a sack that was in the kitchen under a loose floorboard. Packard wanted to break in, find the money, and get out. It was a real simple job because the dude was out of town and the informant had disabled the alarm system. So we drove out to the house in the middle of the night and found the place. Packard parked the car, gave me a gun, and said to use it if there were any surprises, like a dog. He said he was going to be on the lookout, in case anyone came home unexpectedly. I went around to the back and broke a window to get in. Once I was in, I started looking all over for the loose floorboard. The next thing I know, someone switches on the light. Without even thinking, I pointed the gun and shot a man who was holding a baseball bat. I heard the voice of a girl call out 'Daddy.' I didn't mean to squeeze the trigger; I was just so damned scared. I can still see his eyes. He looked like he was so surprised I shot him." Sugar was crying now. "I ran out of the house and jumped into the car with Packard. It wasn't until we'd driven away that we figured out the address of the house

I'd broken into was three-six-three Main Street and not three-nine-three. The number above the front door had fallen and turned the six into a nine. I would later find out that I'd killed a single father who had two daughters. His name was Anthony and his daughters were Nikki and Carmen."

"No!" Luther howled. "You take that back." He sprang to his feet. "Tell me that's not true!"

"Luther, it's the truth. I swear to God, it's the truth!" Sugar shouted back at him as best as she could.

"You killed my wife's father!" Luther was in hysterics. His mind was having trouble accepting what he'd heard.

"Luther, I swear. It was an accident. Accidents happen."

"No! No! No!" Luther dropped to his knees, placed his face in his hands, and screamed.

"I'm sorry, Luther," said Sugar, with pain in her voice. "I didn't know. How was I supposed to know?" Sugar began coughing again.

"I didn't know that you married one of that man's daughters. I had no idea."

"You ruined their lives. Everything fell apart for them after their father was murdered. Carmen used to cry every time she thought about how she'd lost her father," Luther recalled.

"Well, what's done is done. I can't do nothing about it now. I've been carrying that guilt around for years and it's been eating away at my soul. I'm tired of carrying that burden."

"That's what Packard meant when he said that I had bad karma." It was all making sense to Luther now as he sat back down and processed everything Sugar had told him.

When he awoke the following afternoon, he sat upright and looked over at Sugar, who was sitting with her head slumped.

"Mama?" Luther called to her but she didn't answer. "Mama, wake up."

Still there was no answer from her. Luther scooted over to her, and the moment he touched her frozen hand, he realized she was gone.

"You rest, Mama," said Luther peacefully. "You don't have to live with guilt on your shoulders anymore. I'm going to find my wife and tell her she doesn't have to feel guilty anymore, either. It was an accident, like you said, and accidents happen."

Luther left his apartment building, walked to a nearby pay phone, and dialed 9-1-1. He informed the operator of where the police would find a Jane Doe, so his mother could be laid to rest.

The first thing Luther wanted to do was find Packard and make him pay. If Packard could hold a crime above his head and ruin his life, then so could he. Packard wouldn't be hard to find. At some point, he'd come by his club. So that's where Luther went and waited until he saw Packard pull up one day before the club opened.

"Packard," Luther called to him as he rushed across the street to catch him before he went inside. "Packard, I need to talk to you."

Packard didn't recognize Luther in his shabby grubs and thought he was some homeless nut case wanting money. Luther caught him as he was stepping inside.

"Sugar is gone!" said Luther, which got Packard's attention.

"Who the fuck are you?" Packard asked.

"Don't you recognize me?" Luther paused for a moment. "I'm Luther."

"What do you want, Luther? And when the fuck did you get out of jail?" Packard was suspicious of him.

"I want to talk to you about something very important."

"Boy. You are some funky concern! Damn. You need to wash your ass!"

Luther didn't care what Packard thought about his body odor. He only wanted to get even with him in some way.

"I'll give your funky-smelling ass five seconds, but you have to sit at another table, away from me."

Packard led him inside of the club. They sat down at one of the tables in front of the stage.

"Nikki!" Packard hollered.

A naked woman came out of the back room with a silver platter of cocaine with horizontal lines. She sat down on Packard's lap.

Packard asked. "Do you want some?"

"No." Luther glanced over at Carmen's sister. He wanted to ask her about Carmen's whereabouts, but figured that she probably didn't know since she and Carmen were estranged from each other. Nikki didn't even come to the hospital when Carmen and Luther had their baby.

"Good. That means more for me. Nikki, baby, go over to the bar; mix me up something."

"Okay, Big Daddy. Hey, Luther." Nikki looked at Luther with eyes asking a number of questions that Luther didn't feel like answering at the moment. Nikki held onto her questions and moved over to the bar, within earshot of Packard and Luther.

"I came here to talk about Anthony Baker. I know all about

how he got killed." Nikki, hearing her father's name, dropped the bottle of gin she was pouring for Packard.

"You'd better not break another damn bottle, Nikki, or I'm going to put my foot in your motherfucking ass!" Packard turned around in his seat and launched daggers at her with his eyes as he barked.

"I know all about it, Packard. Sugar told me. She told me how you gave her the gun and how she broke into the wrong house for you."

"So fucking what, Luther? That shit happened twenty years ago and now the only witness is dead."

Luther hadn't thought his plan out very well. He had planned to hold that over Packard's head, but now he realized he couldn't.

"You thought you were going to blackmail me, didn't you, Luther?" Packard laughed at him. "Boy, people don't fuck with me. I fuck with people." Packard leaned back in his seat and reached for his gun. "Let me guess. You feel you need to get even with me because of all of the crap that has gone wrong in your life, right? You want old Packard to pay."

Luther, suddenly fearing for his own safety, sprang to his feet and rushed out the door. He heard Packard's haunting and evil laugh as he made his hasty exit.

A few days later, Luther returned to the club hoping to catch Nikki so he could ask about Carmen's whereabouts. However, every time he saw her exit the club, she was either with Packard or hastily ducking into the back seat of a sedan that immediately sped away.

—32—
CARMEN

Carmen was in love and there was nothing she could do about it. She and Marshall had now been officially dating for a year and things couldn't have been better. It was the way that Marshall treated her, and the way he treated Nicholas. It was the way he took care of her and the way he made love to her.

"Oh, God!" she shouted out loud as she stood in the kitchen preparing a meal. She'd reach a point where she was happy with life and she couldn't deny the way she felt. As she opened up the refrigerator, she heard her cell phone ringing. She dashed into the living room and picked up the phone.

"Hello?" Carmen answered.

"Hey, babe. Do you want me to pick up something to eat?" Marshall asked.

"No. I'll have dinner ready when you get here. You're putting it down so well that you got a sister in the kitchen cooking," Carmen joked.

"Now that's what I'm talking about."

"Speaking of talking…There is something very important that we have to discuss when you get here."

"Really. Is it serious?"

"Yeah, it's pretty serious, but if you're the man that I know you are, you'll feel the exact same way I do."

"Okay." Marshall paused for a long moment.

"Don't try to figure out what it is. Just come on by. Nicholas and I are waiting on you."

"Okay. I'll see you in a bit. I'm almost there," Marshall said before he ended the call.

Carmen had prepared lasagna with asparagus and garlic bread. By the time Marshall rang her doorbell, she was placing food on her dinette table for the three of them.

"Mmmm, smells good, babe," Marshall said as he came in the door.

"Hey, Marshall." Nicholas came running toward the front door, carrying action figures in both hands.

"Hey, Nicholas," Marshall said as he stooped down to pick him up. "Have you washed your hands for dinner yet, fella?"

"Nope."

"Then let's go take care of that," Marshall said as he carried him into the bathroom. Once he and Nicholas were done freshening up, they went and sat down at the dinner table.

"So, what do we need to talk about?" Marshall asked.

"I want you to eat first," said Carmen, as she sat down. After dinner, Carmen offered him some dessert.

"It's Jell-O with fruit chilled on the inside of it," said Carmen. "It's real good," Carmen tempted him unnecessarily.

"Okay, you've talked me into it." Carmen put some Jell-O in a cup and then walked over to Marshall and sat on his lap. She scooped up a spoonful and fed it to him.

"Baby?" Carmen said.

"Hmmm," answered Marshall.

"You said that we could always talk about anything, right?"

"Yes, babe, *anything*. It doesn't matter what. Just lay it on me."

"Okay." Carmen set the cup down and then straddled Marshall so she could look into his eyes. "Are you ready?"

Marshall smiled. "I'm ready."

"I'm pregnant."

Carmen studied his every expression. It took a slight second for it to register fully to Marshall.

"For real?" Marshall had undeniable excitement in his eyes and voice. Carmen exhaled, relieved that his reaction was the one she'd hoped for.

"Yes, baby, I'm for real," she said excitedly.

"Hot damn!" Marshall squeezed her with all his might. "Ooh, I'm sorry, I don't want to squeeze the baby too hard. You should be resting. You shouldn't be cooking for me. I should be cooking for you. When are we due?"

"What did you say?" asked Carmen.

"I said, when are we due?"

"That's what I thought you said," Carmen responded. "I don't know. I still have to go to the doctor so that can be determined."

"Okay, I'm going with you. Let me know when you want to go. There is so much we have to do. We have to sign up for Lamaze class, get some prenatal care, and I have got to build a nursery."

Carmen could see Marshall's mind was racing with things that he wanted to get done.

"Oh, and the most important thing…"

Carmen was full of joy. "What's that, baby?"

"We have to shop for a wedding ring so that we can get married. I'm not into that baby-daddy mess." Carmen's emotions took over and she hugged Marshall tightly.

"I take it that means you'll marry me?" Marshall asked.

"I don't know; you may not be my type." Carmen giggled.

"What's so funny?" Nicholas walked over to Marshall and Carmen. Marshall rubbed Nicholas's head. "We're going to be a family."

Carmen was at Marshall's house, borrowing his car. She was headed to her old Hyde Park community to visit her hairstylist. She had to drive Marshall's car because hers needed servicing, and Marshall was taking care of it for her.

"Here, toss this in the glove compartment." Marshall handed her a community newspaper. She looked at the address label that said "Resident" and simply listed Marshall's address.

"Why are you keeping this?"

"I need the paper for Lovie when I pick him up from the veterinarian this afternoon," Marshall explained.

"Oh, okay. Well, call me when you and Nicholas get to the repair shop and let me know how much I'm going to be in for."

"Now you know that you don't have to worry about that," Marshall said as he kissed her.

"I know, baby. But I'm the type of woman who likes to pay her own bills." She fired up Marshall's car and blew the horn as she pulled away.

Parking in Hyde Park was difficult; there were limited spaces. As a result, Carmen had to park a block away from the salon. As soon as she got out of the car, a homeless man spoke to her. She refused to acknowledge the crazy-looking man and began walking away from him at a brisk pace.

"You don't have to run from me," the homeless man said. "Come back. Why won't you talk to me?"

As soon as Carmen entered the salon, Mary, her hairstylist, greeted her.

"Hey, Carmen."

Carmen approached Mary. "Girl, some crazy homeless man was following me."

"What?" Mary was surprised that someone would follow her.

"Yeah, girl. The man looked crazy as hell." At that moment,

the homeless man knocked on the door and tried to gain entrance. Carmen turned.

She was a bit alarmed. "That's him, girl. That's the fool that was following me."

"Girl, he's crazy. That fool comes around here begging for money and talking to himself all of the time. He is a certified nut case," Mary said. "Get away from the door before I call the police!" Mary shouted at the man.

"I need to use your bathroom," he said.

"There are no public restrooms in here!" Mary shouted back across the salon.

The homeless man glared at Carmen for a long moment before he turned and left.

"What was that about? Why was he looking at you like that, I wonder?" Mary said.

"Shit, girl, I don't know. People are crazy nowadays," Carmen replied as she took a seat in Mary's chair.

Carmen left the hair salon, feeling and looking like a million bucks. She couldn't wait to see if Marshall liked her new hairstyle. As she walked back to the car, she noticed that the window had been smashed.

"What the hell?!" Carmen hollered. When she arrived at the car, she saw a bloodstained brick sitting on the driver's seat. She immediately phoned Marshall to let him know what had happened.

By the time Marshall got there, Carmen had already called the Chicago police who were taking a property damage report. Marshall got out of the car, hustled over to Carmen and embraced her.

"I dropped Nicholas off with Quentin. Are you okay, baby?" he asked.

"Yeah, I'm fine," Carmen said. "I'm a bit confused as to why someone would smash a window and not take anything."

"Well, ma'am," said the officer, "sometimes these homeless crackpots do random crimes for no reason at all."

"Baby, what happened?" Marshall asked.

"When I parked here, there was this homeless guy who followed me to the shop."

"Followed you? Why would someone follow you?"

"He was probably some low-life purse snatcher, sir," said the beat officer. "He wasn't too bright. He left bloodstains on the brick that he used to smash out the window. I had one of the lab boys come down and take it in for fingerprints and DNA tests. Chances are he has a record, and if he does, we'll issue a warrant for his arrest."

Marshall turned to the officer. "Say, is Detective Mike Taylor still around?"

"Yeah, Detective Taylor is a good friend of mine. In fact, I saw him down at the station no more than ten minutes ago. Do you know him?" asked the beat officer.

"Yeah, I know him. Carmen, why don't you take your car and head on home. I'll drive my car back. I want to stop and talk to Detective Taylor for a minute to see if he can speed up the testing process for me."

"I think that I'm going to head on back to your place," Carmen said. "Do you want anything in particular for dinner?" Carmen asked, not willing to allow the little wrinkle to destroy her day.

"You don't have to cook. I'll pick up some Chinese food on my way in. I won't be long."

"Okay," Carmen said and then left.

-33-
LUTHER

Luther now knew why he wasn't able to find Carmen. She'd moved to Oak Park. He found out when he'd smashed out the car window and took the *Village* newsletter with her address on it. Luther had also taken several dollars' worth of change out of the coin tray. He paid his fare, hopped on a bus, and then a train to Oak Park. When he arrived, he asked someone to point him in the direction of the street where Carmen lived. As he walked toward her house, his mind began to tell him that she'd welcome him back into her life with open arms. *She looked at me funny at the beauty shop because she didn't recognize me, that's all*, his twisted reasoning told him.

When he got to the address and saw the stately home sitting on a corner lot, Luther's heart began to sore. He quickly envisioned himself living in the bungalow. He saw himself mowing the lawn and trimming the hedges. He saw himself with Carmen barbecuing in the back yard and making love all over the house. His delusional and twisted mind was telling him that Carmen needed and wanted him in her life and the only thing that he had to do was show up, make love to her, apologize to her, and tell her everything. *She will understand. I know that she will*, he thought. Luther entered the back yard gate and walked up to the back door. He wasn't thinking logically. He put his hand on the doorknob and tried to turn it, but it was locked. He looked down at the doorknob and saw blood on it. He looked at his hand and noticed his sliced-open skin for the first time. He was so preoccupied with his thoughts that he hadn't realized he'd cut himself. He didn't care, though. He had to get inside. Carmen would have bandages for him. He could take care of himself on the inside. He tried to force the back door open, but it wouldn't budge. Luther looked for another way to gain entrance, but when he didn't see one, he looked around for something he could use to smash the door. As he searched, he saw a sledgehammer resting against the side of the house.

"Perfect. Just what I need," Luther uttered. He picked it up and swung it mightily against the door. It took a total of seven hits before the door finally gave way. Before entering the house, Luther surveyed his surroundings to make sure that the loud banging didn't alarm any of the neighbors. Confident that no one had noticed him, Luther entered the house. He stepped inside the kitchen and closed the door as best as he could.

"I'm home," he spoke aloud. "I'm finally home."

-34-
MARSHALL

Inside the police station, Marshall ran into Detective Taylor as he was exiting the washroom.

"Detective Taylor, you're just the man I want to see," Marshall said.

"Hey, Marshall." Detective Taylor smiled and they shook hands. "How have you been, my friend?"

"I've been good. Life is being good to me again. I'm about to get remarried and have another baby."

"Really?" Detective Taylor was genuinely happy for Marshall.

"Yes. It's taken me a long time to put my life back in order, but better late than never, right?" Marshall joked.

"I wish I had more news for you about Lena's investigation, but I'm afraid the trail has been cold for some time now."

"I know. Let's not go down that road right now," Marshall said.

"Okay. So what brings you by?" asked Taylor.

"Someone broke into my car this afternoon and the lab tech brought in some evidence for DNA and finger testing. I wanted to see if you could talk to the boys down at the lab and have them take a look at it right away."

"Well, the DNA test has to be sent out. But the fingerprints can be lifted and I can do an initial check against the database files for you."

"If you do that, I'll owe you big time."

"Don't worry about it. It's the least I can do," Taylor said. "Come on; follow me."

Detective Taylor found the lab work for Marshall and asked him to sit tight. Forty-five minutes later, Taylor returned and told Marshall to follow him into another room.

"I've got something interesting here, Marshall," Detective Taylor said as he sat down at a computer that had images for fingerprints on the screen.

"Last month, we got a Jane Doe phone call. When we found the body, the woman had a locket in her hand. We lifted the fingerprints off the locket, but we didn't do anything with them because the medical examiner's report came back and said that she'd died of a massive stroke. So that meant no foul play involved and we closed the case."

"Okay, I'm with you so far," Marshall said.

"Hang on, man, it gets weird. The fingerprints on the brick match the fingerprints on Jane Doe's locket. Whoever this guy is knew who Jane Doe was and was around when she checked out."

"Well, run a more extensive search on the prints and see what you come up with," Marshall said.

"That's what the computer over there is doing. Come on; it should be just about finished." The two men walked to the other computer terminal, which was finishing its search. The screen began displaying information indicating that it had matched the information that Detective Taylor had input. Horror came over Marshall's face when he saw the results.

"Oh, my God!" said Detective Taylor. The computer was flashing the words "EXACT MATCH" to the fingerprints lifted off the tools found in the car that had struck and killed Marshall's daughter, Lena. At that very moment, Taylor's cell phone rang.

"Yeah, this is Taylor. What? You're bullshitting me. What interrogation room is she in? Okay, I'll be right there."

"You have to go now?" Marshall asked, feeling his emotions swell up. He couldn't believe that the same guy who had killed his daughter had smashed out his car window.

"Marshall, come with me. Something very interesting has happened. We may have stumbled upon a very big break in your daughter's case," Taylor explained.

Marshall and Taylor walked down to an interrogation room where Detective Downs was in the middle of another investigation involving illegal activity at Big Daddy's Exotic Dance Club. Detective Downs brought Marshall and Detective Taylor up to speed on his investigation.

"You're not going to fucking believe this," he said. "But do you remember that guy Packard we brought in for questioning about his stolen SUV and the hit-and-run accident?"

"Yeah, I remember Packard very well," Taylor said. He and Marshall were both waiting with bated breath for more information.

"He's now saying that he knows the perpetrator who stole his car and killed the young girl."

"Why is he confessing this now?" Marshall asked, feeling himself getting angry.

"We've got the son-of-a-bitch on narcotics charges and a connection to a murder that dates back twenty years. He is trying to cut a deal to save his ass!"

"How did all of this come about?" Marshall was still trying to piece everything together.

"Come down here with me to the other interrogation room." Marshall and Detective Taylor followed Detective Downs to another room. They saw a young woman sobbing. "Nikki, this is Trooper Marshall and Detective Taylor," announced Detective Downs. "I want you to tell them what you've told me."

"I want my sister," Nikki cried uncontrollably. "You said that someone would help me contact her. I need my sister. Oh, God. I've been such a fool."

"And we're going to do that," said Detective Downs, "but I need you to tell me again what you know."

"My sister's homeless ex-husband, Luther, came into the club a few weeks back, talking about some woman named Sugar who had died in an abandoned building on Prairie Street.

"I guess the woman who died was his mother or something. Luther said that he knew about this murder that Packard was involved in twenty years ago. It was the murder of Anthony Baker, my father." Marshall's heart damn near stopped.

"I'd been sleeping with the son-of-a-bitch who murdered my father and didn't even know. I blamed everything on my sister, Carmen. I made her feel guilty about his death and I was wrong for that." Nikki fell apart again.

"Come on; let's step outside. I'll tell you the rest," said Detective Downs. The men stepped outside of the room.

"After girlfriend learns of what Packard has done, she decides that she's going to make Packard pay. So she calls me up and tells me that she'll provide me with whatever information I need, as long as I make sure he's convicted. So we put a special ops team on it for a couple of weeks and, with her help, got enough on Packard to put him away for a long time. But now he is trying to cut a deal by saying he'll give up a name in the case of your daughter's hit-and-run driver," said Detective Downs.

"We don't need the full name," said Detective Taylor, "we've already got it. It's Luther. Luther Parker."

"My woman's ex-husband," Marshall uttered with disgust.

~36~
LUTHER

Luther got upset when he entered the house and discovered photos of Marshall and Carmen. He became irate and smashed the frames and ripped the pictures. He walked throughout the house on an emotional rampage. His mind had flipped out. He couldn't comprehend what was going on. He didn't understand why Carmen wanted to be with Marshall, of all men. Then it came to him. *It was because he saved her life that day when he lost control of the car.* He told to himself, *I can't let him have her.*

"I will not let you have her!" Luther shouted at a photograph of Marshall and his daughter, Lena, on a nearby end table. "I had her first! She belongs to me! Not you! Me!" As Luther continued his rampage throughout the house, he ran across Marshall's Glock pistol—the one with scope and laser. He took the revolver and went upstairs and sat down on the living room sofa and waited.

❦

Carmen didn't go directly back to Marshall's house; she wanted to run a few errands while Nicholas was with Dawn and Quentin. When she returned to Marshall's house, she parked out front and came in through the front door.

Luther watched Carmen as she entered. He waited for her to set down her belongings and notice him. She pulled her shoes off by the heels and took off her coat. When Carmen looked up, she saw the homeless man who had been following her sitting on Marshall's sofa. Carmen gasped with fear. Her eyes grew wide and her pulse rate shot up. She was about to turn and run out the door but she panicked. Although her mind told her to move, her body wouldn't listen.

"What's the matter, baby? You don't recognize your husband?" Carmen was finally about to move and run out the door.

"I wouldn't do that if I were you," Luther said, pointing the gun at her. "If you move another inch, I'll shoot," he warned. "You didn't call me; you didn't come to see me; and you didn't write me. I was rotting in that jail cell and you couldn't have cared less. I burned myself to a fucking crisp to prove my love for you!"

Carmen willed herself to speak, her voice trembling. "Luther, you need to put the gun down."

"I don't have to do shit except stay black and die! But it's okay now. We can work this out," Luther said. "I'm here to explain everything to you. You know, set things straight so that you and I can get on with our lives. I know who killed your father," Luther said, thinking that it would make Carmen happy.

"I don't want you, Luther." Tension was running through Carmen's body. Her shoulders were tight and remained near her ears. Her neck was stiff and her palms were sweating.

"Didn't you hear what I said? I know who killed your father."

"I don't care. I want you to leave," Carmen said, hoping that Luther would do as she asked.

"Don't say that! You have no idea of what I've been through! Don't say that! Don't make me hurt you!" Luther growled, finally going over the edge and falling into complete insanity.

–37–
MARSHALL

The missing pieces of the puzzle had come together for Marshall, and the truth of the events made his stomach turn sour. Packard admitted he'd burned down his own building in order to get the insurance money, which rendered Luther homeless. Luther, seeking revenge, had stolen Packard's car. While drinking and driving in the stolen car, he'd lost control and killed Marshall's daughter. He then fled the crime scene, ditched the car, and went on to live his life. At some point, Luther had met Carmen and had started a new life while Marshall's life with Stacy crumbled. Then, through chance, Luther's and Marshall's paths crossed and Marshall risked his own life to save the lives of Carmen and Nicholas.

Marshall recalled what Carmen had told him. Luther's mind had snapped and he set their home on fire when she told him that she wanted a divorce after he'd left her and Nicholas to die on the frozen lake. Then investigators failed to connect Luther to his daughter's investigation when he was arrested and convicted of arson.

Marshall left the police station with his mind in a fog. The reality of what he'd learned was twisted and sick.

"Marshall!" Detective Taylor had followed him outside to check on him.

"Look, do you want me to drive you home or something? Are you okay? You don't look so good."

"I need some time to think. I feel like I've been shot with a double-barrel shotgun," Marshall said as he got into his car.

"We're issuing a warrant for Luther's arrest. We'll find him and bring him in. The police have already begun searching the Hyde Park neighborhood for him," Taylor said. "I'm going to call Quentin and tell him that he should catch up with you. That was some pretty heavy shit you learned. I don't want you going loco on me. Call me if you need anything, my friend." Taylor shook Marshall's hand and patted him on the shoulder a few times.

"Thanks," Marshall spoke softly and then drove off. He took his time getting home. He couldn't stop thinking. His thoughts told him that perhaps this was all some sort of sick game that Carmen and Luther were playing on him, but he knew that wasn't true.

The old emotional wound involving Lena's death had been sliced open once again. Marshall was angry that he hadn't put all of this together sooner. He was angry that there was no way that he could have prevented any of it from happening.

"This is some bizarre shit. Mercy," Marshall uttered as he continued to digest all of the facts.

It took thirty minutes for Marshall to drive back home. When he arrived, he pulled into the driveway and got out of the car. He noticed some mail in the back seat of the car covered with glass from the shattered window. His mind quickly began thinking. He put together more pieces of the bizarre puzzle. He stared at the mail for a moment. Then it hit him.

Luther was looking for her address! He must have seen her getting out of the car and taken the mail to get her current address. Marshall sprinted across the backyard to his door and saw that it had been smashed open with the sledgehammer he'd left outside.

"Oh no!" Marshall's heart began racing wildly.

He quickly ran out to his police cruiser. He opened the trunk, and grabbed his bulletproof vest and another revolver that was in a locked gun case. Just as he was opening the gun case, he heard Carmen scream. With his nerves on edge and his weapon drawn and loaded, he cautiously ran to the rear door of the house.

"Don't come any closer!" he heard Carmen shriek. He could tell that they were screams of terror. Without thinking about his own safety, he rushed into the kitchen, down the hall, and into the living room with his arms extended, eager to make Luther his target.

"Put the goddamn gun down, Luther!" Marshall commanded him as he stepped directly in front of Luther's line of fire. Marshall was protecting not only Carmen but their unborn child. Marshall looked Luther directly in the eyes, which were wild and blazing with fury.

"Luther, put the gun down!" Marshall commanded again.

"You can't have her!" Luther barked. "She's mine. I had her first! She doesn't understand. I'm trying to make her understand!" Luther pointed the laser beam at Marshall's chest.

"Luther, if you don't put the gun down, I'm going to shoot you dead." Marshall's nerves were vibrating with anticipation. He was trying to allow his training to guide him instead of revenge. Taking a man's life is never easy, but in this instance, Marshall was a hair trigger away from committing homicide.

"She loves me, not you! She's just confused right now!" Luther called to Carmen. "Carmen! Carmen! Get over here." Luther wanted her by his side.

"Luther," Marshall narrowed his vision, "this is the last time I'm going to tell you, put the damned gun down!" Luther met Marshall's gaze once again. The two men's eyes were locked on each other, both of them unyielding and unwilling to give up their position. Luther felt his mind completely melt down. He felt numb, and suddenly nothing in the world mattered anymore.

Marshall saw something change in Luther's eyes. He took aim at Luther's shoulder and discharged his revolver. The impact dislodged the weapon Luther had and knocked him flat on his back.

Marshall rushed over, kicked Luther's gun out of the way and hovered over him. Marshall immediately began fighting with himself.

"An eye for an eye and a tooth for a tooth, you son-of-a-bitch!" Marshall was about to finish the job. He had every right to. Luther had broken into his home and threatened his family. This would be viewed as a clear case of self-defense. Marshall's philosophy of what was right and what was wrong was being put to the test.

As Marshall looked into Luther's eyes, they began to look distant and hollow. Luther's hand was covering his bloody wound. His body was twitching violently. Luther was going comatose, but that didn't seem like a suitable enough punishment. Marshall's breathing became heavy as he thought about that day years ago when Luther ran down his baby and kept on going. Then, somewhere, in the back of his own mind, Marshall heard his inner voice. It was a pearl of wisdom he'd heard long ago.

"*Mercy!*" his inner voice said. "*Mercy! Show him mercy, Marshall.*" Marshall heard what it said but he didn't want to listen.

At that moment, Quentin walked into the room.

"Marshall, don't do it." He heard Quentin's pleading voice. "You've got a new family on the way. Don't throw that new life away. You don't want to traumatize Carmen by letting her see you kill someone." Marshall had tears of anger and rage. He wanted to squeeze the trigger and put a bullet between Luther's eyes.

Marshall called to his brother. "Quentin! Is that you?"

"Yes, Marshall. I'm here for you," Quentin responded.

"I've got to do this, man. You know that this is justifiable homicide." Marshall squeezed a little harder on the trigger.

"Marshall. My dear brother, listen to what you're saying." Quentin paused for a moment as he assessed the volatility of the moment. "Marshall, I'm going to get on my knees." Quentin slowly lowered himself. "I'm going to pray for you."

"Have mercy, Jesus," Carmen whispered as she knelt down beside Quentin to pray with him.

"Oh Heavenly Father," Quentin quaked with nervous adrenaline, "I come to You at a very desperate time. I come to You asking that you to deliver my brother Marshall from the dark evil that has taken over his mind. I ask that You ease the burden on his heart and soul. I ask that You help him find peace instead of vengeance. I ask for Your loving hand at this critical time to help guide him away from the seduction of selling his soul to the pawn shop of hell for the false promises of revenge." Quentin paused. "Please, God, I love my brother."

There was a long moment of silence. Neither Quentin nor Carmen moved; they remained in the praying position. Finally, Marshall spoke.

"Quentin. Come get me…before I squeeze this trigger again."

ABOUT THE AUTHOR

National bestselling author and award-winning author Earl Sewell has written ten novels including *The Good Got to Suffer with the Bad*, *Through Thick and Thin*, *The Flip Side of Money*, *When Push Comes to Shove*, *Keysha's Drama*, *If I Were Your Boyfriend*, *Lesson Learned*, *Love Lies and Scandal*, *Have Mercy* and his debut title *Taken For Granted*, which was originally self-published through his own publishing company, Katie Books. His work has also appeared in four separate anthologies including *On the Line*, *Whispers Between the Sheets*, *Sistergirls.com* and *Afterhours: A Collection of Erotic Writing by Black Men*. He has written numerous romantic short stories for *Black Romance* magazine and has been featured in *Black Issues Book Review* and *Upscale* magazine. Recently the African American Arts Alliance presented Sewell an Excellence Award for outstanding achievement in literature for his novel *The Flip Side of Money*. He is also the founder of a travel agency, Earl Sewell's Travel Network, www.earlsewells travelnetwork.com. In addition Earl is a lifelong athlete who has completed several marathons and triathlons. Earl lives in South Holland, Illinois with his family. To learn more about Earl Sewell, visit his websites at www.earlsewell.com, www.aabookclubs.ning.com and www.myspace.com/earlsewell

READING GUIDE QUESTIONS FOR "HAVE MERCY"

1) Marshall could've justifiably murdered Luther and gotten away with it. After chasing Luther for so long and finally apprehending him, why do you think Marshall hesitated?

2) Luther is without a doubt a very complicated character who is living with an enormous amount of guilt, and an equal amount of emotional problems. Throughout the story Luther was trying to find peace and harmony. Why do you think it was so hard for Luther to find happiness?

3) Marshall loved the comfortable life he'd built for himself and his family. Losing it was the most horrific thing that could've ever happened to him. If you were put in Marshall's position, how would you have dealt with emotional and psychological difficulties that Marshall was forced to contend with?

4) A major turning point occurred when Luther left Carmen and Nicholas on a frozen lake to die. Why do you think Luther felt completely at ease with abandoning Carmen and their baby?

5) Carmen was a complex character who always wanted the best for those who were closest to her. Do you feel that she was naïve or gullible for wanting to help those who only wanted to use her? Why or why not?

6) Every relationship has a deal breaker. Some people will not put up with cheating and others will not put up with lying or

financial irresponsibility. With that in mind, in your opinion, why do you think Marshall's marriage failed?

7) Why do you think Nikki allowed herself to be seduced by the seedy underworld that Packard was a part of?

8) If Luther had turned himself in for his crime and gone to jail, do you think he would've been rehabilitated while imprisoned? Why or why not?

9) At the end of the book, Marshall decides to have mercy and allow Luther to live. Marshall and Carmen also eventually have another child and move forward with their lives. However, there is still the issue of Marshall accepting and raising Luther's son, Nicholas. If you were Marshall, would you be able to love Nicholas as your own son? Why or why not?

10) If had a chance to give each of the major characters in this book a pearl of wisdom, what would you tell them?